FILTHY RICH

By
Richard Hood

MAPLE
PUBLISHERS

Filthy Rich

Author: Richard Hood

ISBN 978-1-83538-476-3 (Paperback)
    978-1-83538-477-0 (E-Book)

Cover Design and Book Layout by:
    White Magic Studios
    www.whitemagicstudios.co.uk

Published by:
    Maple Publishers
    Fairbourne Drive, Atterbury,
    Milton Keynes,
    MK10 9RG, UK
    www.maplepublishers.com

A CIP catalogue record for this title is available from the British Library.

*For my darling wife Jo and
wonderful son Jonathan.*

CONTENTS

Chapter One

As Oliver gradually regained consciousness, the cacophony of sounds and sensations enveloping him slowly began to resolve into a semblance of coherence. The steady, rhythmic beeping of medical equipment filled the sterile air, its soft tone a constant reminder of life tethered to machines. It echoed through the room, occasionally accompanied by the shuffle of rubber-soled shoes and the low murmur of voices that hovered just outside his field of comprehension. A fluorescent overhead light burned harsh and bright, piercing through the dense fog clouding his mind, forcing him to squint as his eyes fluttered open.

His senses began to align, though the process was slow and arduous, as if his mind was waking up from a long and treacherous slumber. The fog lifted in increments, like the delicate retreat of morning mist under the first rays of dawn, revealing fragments of the world around him. The muffled voices that once seemed so far away became sharper, clearer, their cadence imbued with a blend of urgency and reassurance. They ebbed and flowed like waves on a distant shore, inching closer, pulling him back from the abyss of unconsciousness. Somewhere, deep within the tangled recesses of his mind, he felt a tether pulling him back to reality, as if these voices were beacons guiding him through the haze.

Disoriented, Oliver struggled to make sense of his surroundings. His limbs felt sluggish, heavy as though weighted down by an unseen force, and his thoughts were clouded, fragmented, like the shattered remnants of a forgotten dream. As he shifted slightly, a faint rustling of sheets met his ears, the sensation of the cool hospital linens brushing against his skin providing the first real, tangible connection to his physical state. Slowly, he began to orient himself, though his body resisted with each movement, sore and unfamiliar.

A shadow leaned over him, and after a moment of blurred vision, the figure came into focus. The face, though still slightly distorted through the lingering fog of his perception, was lined with concern, their eyes searching his for any sign of awareness. "Can you hear me, Oliver?" the voice cut through the ambient noise with a gentle but insistent clarity, as though it were a lifeline being cast to him from across a great divide.

Oliver tried to speak, but his throat felt like sandpaper, dry and scratchy, and his tongue rested uselessly in his mouth, heavy and uncooperative. He fought to gather the strength to respond, to say anything at all, but all he managed was a faint nod—a feeble but undeniable acknowledgment of his reawakening.

"How is his pulse?" another voice, this one slightly more distant but no less pressing, broke through the stillness that had briefly settled over the room.

"It's weak, but steady," came the reply, calm yet suffused with a subtle undercurrent of professional concern. The speaker's words were softened with empathy, offering Oliver a small sliver of comfort amidst the overwhelming disorientation.

Though the words reached him, their meaning seemed to hover at the edge of his consciousness, eluding full comprehension like fleeting fragments of a half-remembered dream. Oliver's mind fought to claw its way toward clarity, but something—an invisible barrier—stood in the way, preventing his thoughts from fully coalescing. His memory felt like a jigsaw puzzle with crucial pieces missing, leaving gaping holes where knowledge and understanding should have been.

Frustration simmered beneath the surface as he grappled with the nebulous edges of his consciousness, his thoughts disjointed, elusive. Yet through the confusion and mental haze, one thing remained clear: he was on the verge of something. A realisation. A truth hidden behind the veil of his mind. He was teetering on the precipice of understanding, tantalisingly close to unravelling the mystery that had enshrouded him since the moment his eyes had fluttered open.

Chapter Two

Oliver's assistant Jenny sat by Oliver's bedside, her fingers nervously fiddling with the edge of the blanket as she watched the rise and fall of his chest. The soft hum of medical machinery provided a background to the silence between them, though her mind was far from quiet. It had only been twelve hours since the heart attack—a terrifying moment that now played on a loop in her head, refusing to let her rest.

She could still vividly recall the sound that had set everything into motion—a loud crash, followed by an unsettling stillness. Her heart had jumped to her throat as she rushed into his office, only to find Oliver lying on the floor, unconscious, his skin pale and clammy. The shock had paralysed her for a moment, her brain struggling to process what she was seeing. But as the weight of the situation sank in, her instincts took over.

Her hands had trembled uncontrollably as she dialled emergency services, her voice quivering as she described the scene. The operator's calm voice was like an anchor in the storm, guiding her through the initial steps of assessing his condition. She had checked his breathing first shallow and uneven. Then, with shaking fingers, she searched for his pulse, her panic rising as it seemed to evade her grasp. Finally, she found it—faint and irregular, but there.

"Okay, he's breathing, but it's weak," Jenny had stammered into the phone, her voice breaking with fear. The operator reassured her, telling her to stay calm, to keep talking to Oliver, even if he couldn't respond. Help was coming, they promised. She just needed to hold on.

The memory still haunted her, and now, sitting here in the private hospital room, she could scarcely believe he was awake. His breathing had stabilised, and though his complexion was still pale, the worst was over. The doctors had assured her he would recover, but the fragile state he was in filled her with dread. She had never seen him so vulnerable.

When Oliver finally stirred, his eyelids fluttering as consciousness returned, Jenny's heart leapt in her chest. Her eyes, glassy with unshed tears, widened with relief. She leaned forward; her voice shaky with emotion.

"Oh, Oliver, I was so afraid," she whispered, struggling to keep her composure. "I thought I'd lost you."

Oliver's lips twitched into a weak smile, though the effort seemed to exhaust him. His voice was hoarse, barely above a whisper. "It's okay, Jenny. You saved me," he rasped, his words slow and laboured. He gazed at her; his eyes filled with gratitude. "I'm forever in your debt. How can I repay you?"

Jenny let out a soft, nervous laugh, her tears breaking free as she wiped at her eyes. Despite the gravity of the situation, a flicker of humour found its way through her worry. "Well, a pay rise would be nice," she said, forcing a small smile to lighten the mood.

Oliver attempted to laugh but winced in pain, his hand instinctively moving to his chest, where the tightness still lingered. Jenny instantly bolted upright, reaching for his arm as her eyes widened in alarm.

"I'm so sorry," she gasped, her voice tinged with panic. "I didn't mean to make you laugh—are you okay? I didn't mean to hurt you."

Oliver waved her concern away with a faint, dismissive gesture, though he was clearly still in discomfort. "It's fine, Jenny," he murmured, his voice strained but sincere. "I'm just glad we can still find some humour in all of this." He looked at her, his expression softening. "But seriously, I do owe you. You saved my life."

Jenny's smile faded, replaced by a look of steely determination. She met his gaze, her brow furrowed as she leaned in closer, her voice filled with quiet resolve. "First things first, Oliver," she said firmly. "You need to get better. And you have to promise me that you'll listen to your doctors." Her tone left no room for argument, her concern now overshadowed by the fierce protectiveness she felt.

Oliver's gaze softened as he saw the worry etched in her features. He gave a small nod, the pain momentarily forgotten as he looked at his assistant—his friend—who had not left his side since that terrifying moment. "I will," he promised quietly. "I'll do whatever they say."

Jenny exhaled slowly, some of the tension easing from her shoulders. "Good," she said softly, though the intensity in her voice remained. "Because we can't have a repeat of this, Oliver. You scared the life out of me."

Oliver's weak smile returned, and though he was still fragile, there was a glimmer of reassurance in his eyes. "I'll try not to," he said, his voice barely a whisper.

⊷⊱❖⊰⊶

Chapter Three

Jenny spent most of the day with Oliver, meticulously taking notes on the most important clients she needed to contact. She sat by his bedside, her notepad filled with scribbles, diagrams, and highlighted names. Oliver, though physically worn, still had a sharp mind, guiding her through the intricacies of the accounts and deals they had worked so hard to build.

"You'll want to prioritise Shaw first," Oliver muttered, his voice gravelly from the medication. "He's the key to expanding our reach on the East Coast."

Jenny nodded, jotting down more details. "Got it. Shaw first," she repeated aloud, making sure the name was underlined. She stole a glance at Oliver, his face pale and lined with the strain of his illness. But even bedridden, his presence was commanding, his will unwavering.

Throughout the day, doctors and nurses drifted in and out, checking Oliver's vitals, adjusting his IV, and administering medication. Every intrusion, though brief, gnawed at Oliver's patience.

"Do they really need to come in every fifteen minutes?" Oliver grumbled as a nurse adjusted his pillows. "I'm not a child. I can manage."

Jenny offered a small smile, attempting to diffuse his irritation. "They're just doing their job, Oliver. You want to get out of here as quickly as possible, don't you?"

Oliver snorted but didn't argue. "If they'd just leave me be, I'd be out of here already," he muttered under his breath. Despite his frustration, it was clear to Jenny that the medical staff wasn't taking any chances with his condition.

As the hours dragged on, the weight of the day began to settle heavily on Jenny's shoulders. Her hand cramped from constant notetaking, and her eyes burned from staring at pages filled with tiny text. The steady hum of machines in Oliver's room, coupled with the clinical smell of antiseptic, only added to her growing fatigue.

By the time the clock approached 4 p.m., she felt a palpable sense of relief when the head nurse entered, clipboard in hand, her demeanour brisk but not unkind.

"Jenny," the nurse said with a slight smile, "It's time for you to take a break. You've been here all day. Mr. Wright needs his rest, and you do too."

Jenny opened her mouth to protest but stopped when she saw Oliver's tired eyes. He might not say it out loud, but he needed the space. Besides, she still had her own mountain of work waiting for her back at the office.

"Alright, alright," Jenny said, packing up her notes, her energy running on the fumes of determination. She stood and approached Oliver's bedside, giving him a warm, reassuring smile. "I'll be back first thing tomorrow. You just rest up, okay?"

Oliver gave a half-hearted wave, though there was a flicker of gratitude in his eyes. "Don't work too hard," he said gruffly, softening his usual authoritative tone for just a moment.

Jenny let out a faint laugh. "You know I will."

As she made her way out of the room, the weight of the day seemed to cling to her like a heavy cloak. The fluorescent lights of the hospital hallways cast long shadows, and her footsteps echoed softly. She rubbed her temples, willing the headache that had been forming to disappear. Even though she was exhausted, there was still a fire in her — a drive to make everything they had worked for succeed.

By the time she reached the exit, the cool evening air hit her face, providing a momentary sense of refreshment. She stood still for a moment, inhaling deeply, grounding herself. The office still awaited her, and while the day had been long, her commitment to their shared goals had not waned. With a final glance at the hospital behind her, Jenny straightened her shoulders and started toward her car, mentally preparing herself for the tasks ahead.

Chapter Four

Dr. Scott stood solemnly at the end of Oliver's bed, his usually calm and composed demeanour now overshadowed by a palpable tension. His white coat, usually crisp, appeared slightly wrinkled from the long hours of a demanding shift. In his hand, he clutched Oliver's medical file, the pages marked with notes, test results, and a diagnosis that he dreaded having to deliver. The beeping of machines and the sterile smell of the hospital hung in the air, only adding to the weight of the moment.

Oliver lay beneath the thin hospital sheets, his body rigid as his mind raced with anxiety. His heart, though stable now, still seemed to pound with the remnants of fear. The quiet of the room was deafening, and every second that passed felt like a countdown to something he wasn't sure he was prepared for. He watched as Dr. Scott, his long-time physician and friend, flipped through the file, the man's brow furrowed in deep concentration.

When Dr. Scott finally looked up, their eyes met, and Oliver knew immediately that the news wasn't going to be good. Dr. Scott sighed heavily, a sign of the burden he carried. "Well, Oliver," he began, his voice steady but filled with concern, "we've been friends for several years now, and I've always believed in being straightforward with you."

Oliver swallowed hard, his throat suddenly dry. He could feel the tension building in his chest, a gnawing sensation of impending dread. Mustering what little courage he had left, he pushed himself up slightly, gripping the sides of the bed for support. "Just tell me, Scott. I can take it," Oliver said, though his voice wavered, betraying his anxiety.

Dr. Scott took a deep breath before continuing, his words measured and deliberate. "You've been very lucky," he said, his expression still grave, though there was a flicker of relief in his eyes.

"Lucky?" Oliver snapped, the word tasting bitter on his tongue. His frustration, long bottled up, now began to spill over. "I don't feel lucky at all, Scott. I'm lying here in a hospital bed, my chest still aching, and you're telling me I'm *lucky*?"

Dr. Scott didn't flinch at the outburst. He had expected it, even understood it. His gaze remained steady, his voice calm but firm. "In terms of your health, Oliver, yes, you've been lucky. You've experienced a mild cardiac infarction."

"Mild?" Oliver repeated, incredulous. He could feel his pulse quickening again. "This doesn't feel mild. My heart just… it failed, didn't it? I thought I was dying!" His voice rose, the memories of the sudden pain, the breathlessness, the panic still fresh in his mind. He had never felt more vulnerable.

Dr. Scott nodded solemnly, understanding the fear behind Oliver's words. "If it hadn't been mild, Oliver," he replied bluntly, "you wouldn't be here right now. You might not have made it to the hospital at all."

The gravity of those words sank in slowly, like a stone dropping into the pit of Oliver's stomach. He felt a sudden wave of nausea as reality began to settle in. He was alive, but only just. He stared up at the ceiling, blinking rapidly, trying to hold onto something—anything—that felt real.

"What now?" he asked quietly, his voice barely above a whisper. The question hung in the air, fragile, like he wasn't entirely sure he wanted the answer.

Dr. Scott's expression softened as he approached the bed, his voice adopting a gentler tone, one he reserved for the truly difficult moments. "Now, you take it easy, Oliver. You've pushed your body hard for years, and this is its way of telling you it can't take any more."

He paused, letting his words sink in before continuing. "No more high living. You'll need to cut out the fatty foods, stop drinking, and start exercising—regularly this time. And I'm advising you to take a few months off work."

Oliver scoffed, the bitterness creeping back into his tone. "So, what you're saying is I should just stop living altogether? Quit everything I enjoy?" He felt the weight of resignation creeping in, pulling him down. The life he had worked so hard for seemed to be slipping through his fingers, one indulgence at a time.

Dr. Scott remained quiet for a moment, allowing the frustration to settle. Then, with a tone of quiet firmness, he spoke again. "If you want to avoid another event—one that might not be so mild next time—then yes, Oliver. You need to make these changes. This is your chance. I don't want to be standing over you again in worse circumstances." His words, though harsh, carried the weight of someone who cared deeply.

Oliver sighed, his head sinking back into the pillow. The exhaustion, both mental and physical, was overwhelming. He felt as though the ground had shifted beneath him, and now, he was left to navigate a world that no longer felt familiar. The silence stretched between them, the beeping of the machines the only sound.

"I don't know if I can do this," Oliver finally admitted, his voice small, vulnerable. He turned his head to look at Dr. Scott, the facade of toughness he had tried to maintain now crumbling.

Dr. Scott placed a hand on his shoulder, his grip firm yet reassuring. "You can, Oliver. And I'll be with you every step of the way. But this… this is something only you can decide. Your life is in your hands now."

Oliver closed his eyes, the weight of those words sinking deep. He didn't respond immediately, too overwhelmed to think of a reply. He just lay there, grappling with the reality that his life had irrevocably changed—and that the choices he made next could very well determine whether he would survive to see another day.

Chapter Five

After Dr. Scott left, Oliver sat up in his bed, the weight of the news settling heavily upon him. He had spent countless hours pouring his heart and soul into his work, striving to be the best in his field. And now, when success had finally come knocking at his door, it was accompanied by the stark realisation that he might have to give it all up.

He leaned back in his hospital bed thinking about his framed certificates and awards that lined his office walls. What good were they now? The thought of abandoning everything he had worked for felt like a betrayal—of himself, of his dreams, of the relentless dedication he'd invested. His hands clenched into fists on his lap, and his jaw tightened. The bitterness was almost unbearable, a sharp, hollow ache in his chest. How could he walk away from something he'd built with every ounce of his being?

The room was silent, save for the occasional distant hum of the building's HVAC system. As the evening crept on, exhaustion seeped into his bones. His body, worn down by sleepless nights and stress, began to betray him, and despite his determination to figure it all out, Oliver found himself drifting into a fitful sleep.

When he awoke, the room was bathed in the dim glow of late evening, the pale light casting long shadows across the floor. For a moment, Oliver was disoriented, unsure how much time had passed. His eyes fluttered open, adjusting to the soft light, and then they landed on Jenny, his faithful assistant. She was sitting in the chair beside his bed, fast asleep, her head resting against the back of the chair, her face serene.

A pang of guilt hit him. Jenny had been with him through thick and thin, managing his schedule, fielding phone calls, and dealing with crises that popped up daily. She had never complained, never asked for more recognition. And yet, in all these years, how much did he really know about her? He knew she liked her coffee black, that she was fiercely organised, and that she had a sharp eye for detail. But beyond that? He realised, with a sinking feeling, that he knew next to nothing about her personal life, her dreams, her struggles.

How could he have been so blind?

Oliver exhaled softly; his gaze still fixed on Jenny. His pursuit of success had cost him more than sleepless nights and missed vacations. It had cost him meaningful relationships, chances to connect with the people around him. How many birthdays had he forgotten? How many times had he pushed people away because he was too focused on his career?

He rubbed his temples, the dull ache of regret settling in. Dr. Scott's words came back to him, gnawing at the edges of his mind. Was there a way out of this? Could he still find balance, or was it too late?

As if sensing his thoughts, Jenny stirred, blinking awake. She sat up, brushing a stray strand of hair from her face, her eyes bleary. "I must have dozed off," she said softly, stifling a yawn. "I didn't mean to—"

"No," Oliver interrupted, his voice rough from sleep. "I should be the one apologizing. I didn't realise how late it was, or that you were still here."

Jenny smiled weakly. "I just wanted to make sure you were okay. It seemed like you had a lot on your mind after Dr. Scott left."

Oliver hesitated, the vulnerability of the moment catching him off guard. He had always been so careful to keep his walls up, to stay composed and focused. But now, sitting here in the quiet of his hospital room the reality of his situation pressed down on him, heavy and inescapable.

"Yeah," he murmured, staring down at his hands. "I do."

For a moment, there was silence, broken only by the soft ticking of the clock on the wall. Jenny shifted in her seat, her expression turning serious. "You don't have to go through this alone, Oliver. Whatever decision you have to make, we're all here for you. I'm here for you."

Her words took him by surprise, and for the first time in a long while, Oliver felt something close to comfort. It was as if a small crack had opened in the wall he had built around himself, allowing just a sliver of light to filter through. He hadn't realised how much he had needed to hear that—needed to know that someone was in his corner.

"Thank you, Jenny," he said quietly, the weight of his exhaustion evident in his voice. "I appreciate that more than you know."

Jenny nodded, standing up from her chair. "Get some rest, okay? We'll figure this out tomorrow."

As she walked out of the room, Oliver leaned back in his bed, staring up at the ceiling. His mind was still clouded with doubt, the path forward uncertain, but there was something different now—a small flicker of hope. Maybe, just maybe, he hadn't lost everything yet.

Chapter Six

Over the next few days, Oliver and his assistant, Jenny, were fully immersed in the process of packing up his office and apartment in Canary Wharf. The mood was bittersweet, as he prepared to leave a life he'd built for years. Oliver had made a few trips to Shoreham-by-Sea in search of a new home. The coastal town where he and his father spent happy times sailing seemed like the perfect place to start fresh, but the right house hadn't presented itself yet. Each visit left him feeling both eager and anxious, knowing he would soon need to settle somewhere new.

Meanwhile, Jenny proved to be indispensable. She had meticulously cancelled his most pressing appointments, cleared his calendar for the next three months, and sorted through important correspondence. Her organisational skills were nothing short of brilliant, and Oliver was deeply appreciative. She would continue to manage the remaining administrative tasks in his absence, and they had agreed to keep in close contact to ensure the transition went smoothly.

As the day wore on, and the early autumn evening began to darken outside, Jenny had just about finished packing everything but the essential documents that needed immediate attention. Oliver sat at his desk, staring at the dim light streaming through the large windows, lost in thought about what lay ahead. The soft knock on his office door stirred him from his reverie.

"Come in, Jenny," he called out, already knowing it was her.

Jenny stepped into the room, carrying a faint smile. "I'm about to leave for the day," she said, glancing at the time. It was nearly 7 p.m., and the office had taken on that quiet, after-hours stillness.

"More like evening," Oliver observed, returning her smile but with a trace of fatigue in his voice.

Jenny laughed lightly. "True enough," she said. "But I wanted to make sure you were set for the weekend. Is there anything else you need?"

"You've been an absolute lifesaver. I can't thank you enough," Oliver said sincerely, leaning back in his chair.

Jenny brushed it off modestly. "Just doing my job. I only hope you really do take the time to rest. Knowing you, you'd be back at your desk first thing tomorrow morning if you could."

Oliver smiled, though the truth in her words wasn't lost on him. "You know me too well."

As Jenny gathered her things, she paused at the door and held up a small stack of papers. "Before I forget, there are a few final documents that need your signature. I can always send them over on Monday if you're too tired to deal with them now."

Oliver sighed, eyeing the stack. "It never ends, does it?" he muttered under his breath, though with a playful glint in his eye.

"I could leave them here for you to review later," Jenny offered, already sensing his reluctance.

But Oliver waved her suggestion off. "No, let's get it over with. The sooner I sign, the sooner you can enjoy a well-earned weekend."

Jenny handed him the papers, waiting patiently as Oliver scrawled his signature on each one without even bothering to read them. He trusted her implicitly; she knew his preferences and had already briefed him on the details earlier.

"There, all done," he said, handing them back with a relieved sigh.

"Thanks, Oliver," Jenny said, tucking the documents safely away. "Be sure to get some rest, and I'll touch base with you on Monday to go over anything else."

"You too. Have a great weekend," Oliver replied, standing to see her out.

"You as well," she said, offering one last smile before disappearing down the hall.

As the door closed behind her, Oliver found himself alone in the quiet office. The reality of his situation settled in. He looked around at the now-bare walls and empty bookshelves. The place that had been his professional home for years was just about ready to be left behind. He sat down again, the weight of his decisions and the uncertainty of the future finally sinking in.

For now, though, all he could do was rest and wait for whatever came next.

Chapter Seven

The empty space where Oliver's office and his life once took place in his penthouse apartment left him with a hollow feeling, a void that echoed louder with every passing second. The pristine, white walls, once vibrant with life and energy, now stood bare and soulless, devoid of the framed accolades and cherished photographs that had proudly chronicled his remarkable rise. Those walls had once been a canvas, reflecting the milestones of his journey, from a fledgling entrepreneur hustling in cramped coffee shops to the titan of a business empire. Each frame had told a story—of triumphs, of setbacks, of relentless determination. Now, they were packed away, their absence amplifying the eerie stillness of a space that had once been buzzing with life and ambition.

The large desk, where countless deals had been sealed, where plans had been sketched out on long nights fuelled by coffee and adrenaline, now sat empty, its polished surface untouched. The chair, which once felt like a throne as he commanded meetings and drove negotiations, now seemed like a relic of a life left behind. He had poured not only his wealth but his very soul into the office— his sanctuary. It had been more than just a workplace; it was the heartbeat of his ambition, a physical manifestation of everything he had worked for. In the quiet of the now-empty room, the faint hum of the city below felt distant, detached from the fast-paced world he had once thrived in.

Yet, as Oliver stood there, taking in the hollow scene, there was an undeniable ache in his chest that wasn't just the remnants of his recent health scare. It was the emotional weight of reflection. He had always prided himself on being a man with few regrets. But in the stillness of the night, one regret gnawed at him, casting a long, unshakable shadow over his thoughts. The choices he had made in the pursuit of success had carried heavy consequences, ones he couldn't undo. The relationships that had frayed, the moments he had missed, the years he had sacrificed—these haunted him now more than ever. The heart attack, which his doctor claimed had been a stroke of luck to survive, had been a wake-up call. It had brought his relentless pace to an abrupt and sobering halt, forcing him to confront not just his mortality a reminder of his father's death and the life he had built and the cost it had exacted on him.

For the first time, he was truly staring at a clean slate, not the kind he had sought after in business, but a personal one. A chance to rebuild not just his career but his life. The opportunity was rare, almost like a whisper from fate, and Oliver knew he couldn't afford to squander it. The time to recalibrate had arrived.

Shoreham had come to him in the weeks after his recovery, like a beacon of possibility. The coastal town, far removed from the high-stakes, cutthroat environment he was used to, seemed to beckon with its promise of simplicity and solace. He imagined the gentle lapping of waves against the shore, the tang of salty air, and the calming rhythm of the ocean—a far cry from the chaos and deadlines that had once defined him. There, he envisioned a place where he could shed the heavy armour of ambition, even if only for a while. Shoreham wasn't just a new setting—it was a symbol of redemption, a place to reclaim parts of himself he had long neglected.

Oliver enjoyed himself strolling along the beach, his thoughts no longer consumed by profit margins or mergers but instead focused on finding peace. He could already feel the catharsis of the ocean breeze, washing over him, clearing away the debris of his former life. There was something poetic about starting again by the sea, where the tides could sweep away the past and leave room for something new. For the first time in years, Oliver was ready to embrace that stillness, that quiet, and let it guide him toward a new sense of purpose. He was determined to not only rebuild but to rediscover the man he wanted to become, with Shoreham as the backdrop to his second chance at life.

Chapter Eight

The phone on Oliver's night table rang, cutting through the stillness of the room. It was 8:30 a.m. on a Friday, and the early sunlight filtered in through the curtains, casting a soft glow on the furniture. Glancing at the illuminated screen of the caller ID, Oliver's pulse quickened when he saw the familiar number from the hospital. His stomach knotted, a nervous anticipation rising in his chest. For days, he had been bracing himself for this call, waiting for the results of his latest blood test.

"Hello," Oliver greeted, his voice betraying a slight tremor.

"Hello, Mr. Wright. This is Mary from the hospital. Is it a good time to talk?" came the gentle, yet professional voice from the other end of the line.

"Yes, it's fine," Oliver said, swallowing hard as he tried to maintain a calm exterior, despite the tension building inside.

There was a moment of suspenseful silence before Mary spoke again. "Well, I have your results." The pause that followed felt like an eternity, each second stretching longer in Oliver's anxious mind. "We are pleased with the results. All levels are normal. The doctor will be in touch to arrange an appointment in the next three months."

Oliver let out a deep, audible exhale, the weight of his worry evaporating in an instant. Relief washed over him like a wave, softening his tense muscles. "Thank you so much, Mary. That's such a relief."

"You're welcome, Mr. Wright. Take care and have a wonderful day," Mary responded warmly before the line clicked off.

For a moment, Oliver sat still, letting the good news settle over him like a comforting blanket. He reached for the small orange bottle of pills resting on his night table—a daily reminder of the fragile balance of his health. His doctor had been explicit: in the event of sudden symptoms like cold sweats or irregular heartbeat, he was to place one pill under his tongue and call for immediate medical assistance. The thought of those instructions had weighed heavily on him, but now, staring at the untouched bottle, he was filled with gratitude that today wasn't the day he would need them. With a deep breath, he carefully placed the bottle back hoping he wouldn't need to use them.

The cool air brushed against his bare skin as he pushed the covers aside and swung his legs over the edge of the bed. He stretched for a moment, loosening the tension in his back, and then padded across the room to the master bathroom. The steam from the shower soon filled the space, and the warm water cascading over him felt therapeutic, easing both his mind and body.

After finishing his shower, Oliver dried off and dressed in comfortable, casual attire—jeans, a soft white t-shirt, and his favourite leather loafers. As he packed his overnight bag, he carefully checked the items he had listed earlier in the week: his laptop for any work that couldn't wait, important documents, a novel to keep him company during the quiet evenings, and his trusty navy-blue sweater for the cooler nights on deck.

Before heading out, he took a final glance around his bedroom, ensuring that nothing essential had been left behind. Satisfied, he grabbed his car keys from the hook by the door and stepped outside. The crisp morning air filled his lungs as he locked the door behind him, a gentle breeze brushing past him. The sunlight bathed the driveway in a soft glow, and for the first time in a long while, Oliver felt like the future was something to look forward to.

Sliding into the driver's seat of his car, the engine purred to life with a smooth hum. As he drove through the familiar streets of his neighbourhood, he felt a growing sense of anticipation. The relief from the hospital news still buoyed his spirits, but more than that, he was ready for the weekend—ready for the salty air, the quiet isolation of the sea, and the freedom that only the ocean could provide.

Chapter Nine

The drive out of London was long, with the traffic heavy as though everyone had the same idea: to escape the city for the weekend, heading south in search of sunshine and fresh air. Cars crawled along in clusters, the sound of engines humming in the warm afternoon air.

Once he finally hit the M23, the drive became smoother. The open road stretched out ahead of him, bordered by green fields and the occasional farm, with the distant shimmer of the South Downs on the horizon. The heavy pulse of London's traffic faded to a distant memory, replaced by the quieter hum of countryside roads. He made good progress now, arriving in Brighton just before 1 PM, the coastal town welcoming him with the scent of saltwater in the air and the distant cries of seagulls. He glanced at the clock and smiled, relieved to have the rest of the day to settle in.

At the Grand Hotel, Oliver checked into the best suite available, one that offered an unobstructed view of the seafront. The hotel itself was steeped in history, its grand facade speaking of Victorian opulence. Inside, the suite was equally impressive: spacious and elegantly furnished, with rich fabrics and polished wood accents. Large bay windows framed a panoramic view of the beach and pier, bathed in sunlight that spilled generously into the room, warming the plush armchairs and gleaming surfaces. He stepped toward the windows, breathing in deeply as the cool sea breeze drifted through, carrying with it the briny scent of the ocean mixed with the faintest hint of distant street food stalls.

Below, the seafront buzzed with activity. Families ambled along the promenade, ice cream cones in hand, while cyclists whizzed past, and groups of friends lounged on the pebbled beach. Brighton seemed alive with the kind of energy that only a sun-soaked weekend could bring. Oliver watched for a moment, absorbing the scene. Though it was central and teeming with life, his suite offered a tranquil escape, a perfect contrast to the busy town below.

Feeling a pleasant hunger building, he decided it was time to explore and indulge in some local cuisine. After unpacking, he headed downstairs, where the front desk greeted him warmly. The receptionist, a lovely young woman with stunning deep blue eyes and a welcoming smile, recommended a popular seafood restaurant tucked away in The Lanes—a quaint and historic part of Brighton known for its narrow alleyways and eclectic mix of shops and eateries. Her directions were detailed, and her enthusiasm for the place left Oliver eager to taste what the seaside town had to offer.

The streets of Brighton were as vibrant as ever, with an eclectic mix of street performers, weekend markets, and the chatter of locals and tourists alike. It had been a few years since Oliver's last visit, and he was reminded why Brighton was often affectionately dubbed 'London by the sea'. The town blended the charm of a coastal retreat with the bustling energy of a metropolitan hub, a balance that appealed to him.

He wandered through The Lanes, passing colourful storefronts and artisan boutiques, the atmosphere lively but intimate. When he arrived at the restaurant, it was just as busy as the receptionist had promised, with patrons spilling out onto the street. The tantalising smell of grilled fish and garlic butter wafted through the air, drawing him in.

Once inside, he was shown to a corner table, nestled away from the main crowd but with a perfect view of the lively dining room. The restaurant had a rustic, nautical theme—wooden beams overhead, lantern-style lights casting a warm glow, and walls adorned with maritime memorabilia. The low murmur of conversation and the clinking of glasses created a relaxed yet vibrant ambiance. Oliver ordered a large glass of chilled Chardonnay and began perusing the menu, which was brimming with fresh seafood options—from succulent prawns to tender scallops and rich, buttery lobster.

Sipping his wine, Oliver took a moment to savour the blend of flavours, the crispness of the Chardonnay complementing the salty tang in the air. The restaurant buzzed with laughter and lively conversation, and for the first time in a while, Oliver felt truly at ease. Brighton, with its mix of coastal charm and urban vibrancy, seemed to offer the kind of lifestyle he had been craving—something slower than London but still full of life and culture.

Chapter Ten

On the way back to London, Oliver felt a renewed sense of excitement and relief. Shoreham, he realised, might just be the place where he could finally get the rest and recuperation his doctor had strongly emphasised was critical for his recovery. After a recent heart problem, Oliver had been prescribed medication that was working, but his doctor was clear: he needed a few months off from work to fully recover. This break, though necessary, came with its own set of challenges. His career had always been central to his identity, and the thought of stepping away from it, even temporarily, weighed heavily on him. Yet, the idea of sailing again brought a flicker of hope. Sailing had always been therapeutic for Oliver—a space where the pressures of daily life seemed to melt away, leaving only the soothing rhythm of the waves.

As he sped through the countryside, Oliver watched the scenery blur by, his thoughts drifting to the peaceful days that awaited him in Shoreham. He imagined mornings spent sipping coffee while watching boats bob gently in the harbour. The sound of seagulls, the fresh, salty tang of the sea air, and the peacefulness of the small town filled him with a sense of calm. He looked forward to wandering through the narrow, cobbled streets, exploring charming boutiques and cafes, and browsing through the bustling local market, where vendors sold fresh produce and artisanal goods. The prospect of engaging with friendly locals and perhaps making a few new acquaintances gave him something to look forward to.

The thought of reconnecting with his old passion for sailing brought an involuntary smile to his face. It had been years since he last set sail, but the idea of feeling the wind in his hair and the sun on his face while gliding across the water was deeply appealing. He remembered the unique sense of freedom and clarity that came with sailing—how the world seemed to simplify when he was out on the open water. For Oliver, sailing was never just a hobby; it was a form of meditation, a way to reconnect with himself and find balance amid life's chaos.

Still, despite these warm feelings, Oliver couldn't entirely shake his worries. His work had always been a significant part of his identity, and the thought of stepping away filled him with unease. What would his colleagues think? How would his projects continue without him? Would he be seen as weak for needing this time off? These thoughts swirled in his mind, but he knew deep down that the break was necessary. His health had to come first, and pushing himself too hard would only lead to further complications. The doctor had made it clear: continuing at his current pace was not sustainable if he wanted to make a full recovery.

As he mulled over these thoughts, Oliver reassured himself that a few months in Shoreham, with its calming coastal charm and the possibility of rekindling his joy in sailing, might be exactly what he needed to restore his strength. This break would be a chance not only to heal physically but also to reflect and reconnect with the simpler pleasures in life—pleasures he had long neglected. Embracing the excitement, Oliver allowed himself to believe that this new chapter could be filled with hope and renewal.

In the weeks leading up to the move, Oliver found himself thinking about Shoreham more and more. His evenings were spent researching the town, its history, and the activities he could immerse himself in once he settled in. He even began connecting with local sailing enthusiasts through online forums, hoping to foster some friendships before his arrival. The idea of a slower, more deliberate pace of life began to replace the anxiety he had initially felt about stepping away from work.

The day of the move arrived, and as Oliver packed the last of his belongings, he felt a mixture of excitement and nervousness. The cottage by the sea awaited, along with the promise of peaceful days and the gentle embrace of the ocean. Driving toward the coast, Oliver felt ready—ready not just for a break but for a realignment, a chance to rediscover balance in his life.

When he arrived in Shoreham, the crisp sea breeze greeted him, and he felt an immediate sense of calm. The cottage was charming, with a small garden leading down to the water's edge, and large windows that offered stunning views of the harbour. Unpacking, Oliver was filled with contentment. This move marked the beginning of a much-needed chapter of healing and restoration.

Soon, his days fell into a pleasant routine. He would start his mornings with coffee by the water, followed by slow strolls through the town. He quickly became a familiar face at the market, where the vendors greeted him warmly. Afternoons were often spent on *Filthy Rich*, as he reacquainted himself with the joys of sailing, navigating the coastline and savouring the freedom it brought.

Evenings became a time of quiet reflection. Sitting by the window with a book or watching the sunset, Oliver found a peace he hadn't felt in years. The sound of the waves became a comforting lullaby, and he slept better than he had in a long time. The stress and worry that once consumed him seemed to melt away, replaced by a sense of contentment and well-being.

As weeks turned into months, Oliver's health improved. He felt stronger, more energetic, and most importantly, happier. His time away from work gave him a new perspective—he realised that while his career was important, it wasn't the only thing that defined him. The simple pleasures of life—sailing, nature, and human connection—were just as essential.

Chapter Eleven

He walked down from the station, heading for the town centre. It was a Saturday, and the sun was shining, casting a warm glow over the cobbled streets and pastel-coloured houses. A steady throng of people seemed to be heading in the same direction, so Oliver, with no clue where anything was, followed them, feeling like a small fish in a very small pond.

The salty tang of the sea breeze hit his senses, mingling with the scent of fish and chips that wafted from a nearby shop. He took in the sights and had to admit he was quite taken by the buildings. The old church in the middle of the town was interesting, its ancient stone walls standing as a testament to centuries gone by. He imagined the generations of townsfolk who had walked these same paths, feeling a brief connection to the town's history. It was picturesque in a way that almost felt surreal, like walking into a postcard or an old English film set.

As he ventured further into the centre of the town, the sound of chatter grew louder. There was a street market on, with vendors selling their wares. Colourful stalls lined the square, offering everything from local produce to homemade crafts. The lively scene was a stark contrast to his initial impression, but it didn't quite make up for the sense of isolation he felt compared to London's vibrant streets. The market stalls, though charming, lacked the diversity and scale of London's bustling markets. There were no exotic foods, no sounds of different languages mingling in the air. Instead, it was all very quaint, almost too quaint for his liking.

Oliver's walk began to come to a standstill due to the crowd of people squeezing into the tight lanes. The marketgoers were engrossed in their leisurely browsing, chatting with vendors, and enjoying the sunny day, oblivious to his growing frustration. He could hear snippets of conversation, people talking about their plans for the evening or catching up on local gossip, but none of it interested him. Getting frustrated, he looked for a way out. Seeing a gap in the crowd, he took his chance, swiftly moving into the space where it was less crowded. He sighed in relief as he broke free from the throng, finally able to move at his own pace.

Now that he wasn't boxed in by the crowd, Oliver noticed the details of the town that he had initially overlooked. The small, independent shops that lined the streets each had a unique charm. Handwritten signs in the windows advertised 'freshly baked scones' or 'locally sourced honey', and the cafés had an inviting, homely feel. The kind of places where you could sit for hours with a book or chat with the friendly owners. He found himself appreciating the slow pace of life here, where people seemed to know each other by name, where time wasn't dictated by the relentless ticking of the city clock.

He walked further, coming to a road crossing that took him to the riverside. On the left of the bridge was a new building, contrasting sharply with the historic architecture surrounding it. The modern structure hinted at a town trying to blend the old with the new, an endeavour that intrigued him. It suggested a community looking towards the future while still honouring its past. The river itself was serene, its calm waters reflecting the pale blue sky, and for a moment, Oliver felt a pang of peace. The scene was beautiful, he couldn't deny that.

As he leaned against the railing of the bridge, watching a boat gently bob along the water, Oliver felt a quiet sense of possibility. Maybe Shoreham wasn't quite as lifeless as he'd thought. It was certainly different from London—slower, quieter, more intimate—but perhaps that wasn't such a bad thing. Maybe, just maybe, this little seaside town had more to offer than he had initially given it credit for.

Chapter Twelve

After lunch, which featured perfectly roasted turbot served with seasonal green vegetables nestled on a bed of creamy mashed potatoes, drizzled with a delicate saffron-infused cream sauce, Oliver felt deeply satisfied. The subtle flavours of the fish, complemented by the richness of the mashed potatoes and the aromatic hints of saffron, left him in a reflective mood as he leisurely made his way back to his hotel. The lively streets buzzed with energy as he strolled past an eclectic mix of boutique shops, quaint cafés, and vibrant street performers showcasing their talents. The city's urban hum was a fitting backdrop to his contemplative walk.

Upon reaching his room, Oliver promptly made a series of calls to check on his yacht, ensuring everything was progressing smoothly. He confirmed that the vessel was en route and that the moorings at Sussex Yacht Club were secured without issue. A quick conversation with Ben, the bosun, reminded him to meet early on Saturday morning to finalize the mooring arrangements. With all his plans in place, a sense of ease washed over him.

As the afternoon wore on, Oliver decided to visit Shoreham. He hailed a taxi, watching the scenery shift from city bustle to the quieter charm of the coastal town. Arriving in Shoreham, he wandered the quaint streets, noting the local architecture and the warm, welcoming vibe. By the time he reached East Street, the sun was setting, casting soft amber and pink hues across the sky. The entire street was bathed in the golden glow of the evening sun, making it feel almost magical. Cafés and restaurants lined the streets, their outdoor tables filled with people soaking in the last rays of sunlight. After considering his options, Oliver chose to dine at the Tap House, enticed by its quiet and inviting atmosphere.

The meal was simple but satisfying, a light reprieve after his decadent lunch. Afterward, he took a brief walk to his new club, eager for a nightcap. However, upon arrival, he was surprised to find the place unusually quiet for a Saturday night. The lack of energy left him feeling a bit deflated, and after nursing one drink in the nearly empty room, he decided to move on.

He made his way to Shoreham's railway station to find a taxi, feeling content but seeking a livelier end to his evening. The short ride back to the Grand Hotel passed quickly, and by the time he arrived, it was only 9:30 PM. Despite the late hour, Oliver didn't feel ready for bed. The allure of the hotel bar, with its low, warm lighting and soft hum of conversation, beckoned. He ordered a drink, joined in casual conversation with fellow guests, and enjoyed a few light hearted exchanges and shared laughter. The easy camaraderie of the bar patrons was a perfect way to wind down after his day.

As the evening wore on, Oliver felt a sense of fulfilment, his day balanced between exploration and relaxation. Finally, he retired to his room, the pleasant buzz of the evening still lingering, ready to rest and prepare for the busy weekend ahead.

⸻◈⸻

Chapter Thirteen

On a crisp Saturday morning, Oliver finished his hearty breakfast of eggs, bacon, and toast, washing it down with a final sip of rich, black coffee. He glanced at the clock and realised it was time to head out. Grabbing his jacket, he made his way to the yacht club, where Ben, his long-time friend and sailing companion, was waiting. Today was a big day—Steve, the experienced skipper, was bringing Oliver's prized yacht, *Filthy Rich*, to its new home. The yacht had been sailing overnight from London, and Oliver was eager to see it safely moored in the estuary's harbour.

The sky was slightly overcast, and the air carried the distinct tang of saltwater, with a strong westerly wind sweeping through the marina—perfect conditions for sailing. As Oliver arrived at the dock, he spotted Ben, a tall and lean man with a rugged look, the type that only years of battling wind, rain, and the open sea could give. His face, weathered from countless days spent on the water, broke into a knowing smile as Oliver approached. Together, they gazed out over the estuary, waiting for *Filthy Rich* to appear on the horizon.

Steve, at the helm of *Filthy Rich*, received his final instructions from the harbour master via radio, carefully navigating the narrow mouth of the river estuary. The yacht sliced through the water smoothly, riding the wind as if it were born for these conditions. Steve, calm and collected, had been steering through challenging conditions all day, but now, as the yacht neared its new mooring, the hardest part was behind him.

Oliver's anticipation grew as he and Ben spotted *Filthy Rich* making her way upriver. "There she is!" Oliver exclaimed. Steve, standing tall at the wheel, waved energetically as the yacht neared the dock. The gleaming white vessel seemed to glide effortlessly through the water, its sleek hull cutting through the waves, and within minutes, it was securely moored at its new berth.

"Great job, Steve," Oliver said as he shook the skipper's hand firmly. "You made excellent time."

Steve, his face still carrying a grin from the smooth sail, replied, "Couldn't have asked for better weather. It was a dream to sail."

Oliver turned to Ben, whose eyes were already scanning the horizon, ever the watchful sailor. "Thanks for your help today, Ben. Everything looks great."

Ben gave a brief nod, his voice gruff but sincere. "Always happy to help. She's a fine vessel, Oliver. You've got yourself a beauty here."

Pleased with the outcome, Oliver decided a celebration was in order. "Steve, what do you say we head to the restaurant dinner is on me. You and the crew have earned it."

Steve's eyes lit up at the suggestion. "Sounds perfect."

As they made their way to a nearby seafood restaurant, Ben stayed behind, attending to his duties at the marina. He moved from boat to boat, ensuring everything was in place, his presence as steady and reliable as ever. The yacht club was buzzing with activity, sailors preparing their vessels for the weekend's sailing under the brisk wind, while gulls called overhead, carried by the strong gusts.

At the restaurant, they settled into a table overlooking the marina, the smell of fresh seafood filling the air. Oliver and Steve discussed the next steps for *Filthy Rich* over a meal of grilled fish, shellfish, and a crisp white wine to toast the successful voyage. "We should take her out for a proper sail tomorrow," Oliver suggested as he speared a piece of fish with his fork. "Test her out in these waters now that she's settled here."

Steve nodded. "I like that idea. The forecast looks good—clear skies, steady wind. Should be a great sail."

The conversation flowed easily as they talked about future trips, races, and how they could push *Filthy Rich* to her limits. As the evening sun began to break through the clouds, casting a warm golden glow over the marina, Oliver felt a deep sense of satisfaction. His yacht was safe, the voyage had gone smoothly, and the future was full of possibilities.

Raising his glass, he smiled at Steve and the crew. "To *Filthy Rich* and many more adventures ahead."

The glasses clinked in unison as they toasted the success of the day. Outside, the strong westerly wind continued to blow, promising more exhilarating sails on the horizon, and Oliver couldn't help but look forward to the many voyages yet to come.

Chapter Fourteen

Sunday morning, Oliver sat up in bed, his head still a bit foggy after the previous night's celebrations with the crew. They had spent the evening marking the successful relocation of *Filthy Rich* to her new mooring. The night had been filled with laughter, clinking glasses, and the shared camaraderie of sailors who had completed a job well done. But now, in the quiet of his hotel room, the revelry of the evening felt distant. He glanced at the clock and noticed the time—late. With no time for breakfast, he hurriedly settled his bill at the front desk, casting a final glance at the quaint hotel lobby before stepping outside.

The morning air was brisk, a gentle breeze carrying the salty tang of the nearby sea. Oliver inhaled deeply, the cool air helping to clear the remnants of sleep and alcohol from his head. He crossed the small parking lot, his shoes crunching lightly on the gravel, and climbed into his car. The soft purr of the engine cut through the stillness of the Sunday morning as he set off toward the M23, the open road ahead of him.

Surprisingly, the traffic was light for a Monday morning, and the drive toward London was smooth. As he passed familiar landmarks, his mind wandered back over the last few days. The feeling of the sea beneath him, the thrill of the wind in his hair, the laughter of the crew—they were fleeting moments now, vivid but fading as reality crept back in. His chest tightened slightly as he thought of the bittersweet end to the trip. For all its joy, there was an undertone of finality.

Soon, the towering skyline of London appeared on the horizon, the city standing proud and imposing as it always did. The glass and steel giants glistened in the morning light, their cold beauty offering little comfort as Oliver made his way through the familiar streets toward his apartment. Pulling into the underground garage, he turned off the engine and sat for a moment, listening to the silence that followed. He felt the familiar weight of weariness settle on his shoulders as he finally stepped out of the car and made his way upstairs.

The apartment was exactly as he had left it: immaculate, modern, and entirely lifeless. The large windows that usually let in streams of natural light now framed a grey cityscape, their glass cold to the touch as he ran his fingers along the edge. Despite its beauty, the space felt hollow, more a showroom than a home. He hadn't been home much lately, and it showed. The space had a kind of sterile, untouched quality, as if time itself had paused in his absence.

As he stood there, lost in thought, his phone buzzed from the countertop. It was a reminder to take his medication—another task that had become part of his daily rhythm, a reminder of the fragility that now governed his life. He made his way to the kitchen, opened the cupboard, and pulled out the orange bottle of pills. The faint rattle of tablets against plastic echoed in the quiet room as he swallowed them with a sip of water.

Leaning against the counter, Oliver glanced out at the city once more. The streets below were starting to come to life, small dots of people going about their Sunday routines, unaware of the invisible wall separating him from their world. There was a time when he had been part of it—when the pulse of the city had mirrored his own— but now, standing here, he felt detached, as if the life unfolding before him belonged to someone else.

His phone buzzed again, this time with a message. It was a calendar reminder: dinner with Jenny. The final step in wrapping up the last loose ends of his life before stepping back. The paperwork needed signing, and Jenny had graciously agreed to take over in his absence. She was more than capable, and he trusted her implicitly, but there was still something unsettling about handing over control of everything he had built.

He exhaled slowly, feeling a mix of anticipation and anxiety tighten in his chest. The enforced break was necessary—he knew that. His doctors had been firm on the matter. But what lay ahead was unknown, an empty canvas that both excited and terrified him. He hoped that the time away would bring him the clarity he desperately sought, but there was no denying that the thought of stepping away left him with a profound sense of loss.

As Oliver prepared to leave for dinner, he caught a glimpse of himself in the hallway mirror. He hardly recognised the man staring back at him—tired, weathered, and no longer the confident figure he once was. This dinner with Jenny wasn't just the closing of a chapter. It was the turning of a page into the unknown. He only hoped that whatever came next would offer the peace and direction that had eluded him for so long.

❖

Chapter Fifteen

Caroline stood in front of the mirror, carefully applying her lipstick, the final touch to her polished look. Her long, honey-brown hair shimmered as it cascaded over her shoulders. She stepped back to admire her reflection, turning slightly to check how the sleek fabric of her little black dress hugged her figure. It still fit perfectly, accentuating the curves she had worked hard to maintain over the years. She wasn't the same wide-eyed girl who had married David, but the years had been kind to her, and she felt confident— something that seemed to be slipping away from her husband.

David. Her thoughts drifted back to the man she'd once been so madly in love with. In their twenties, he was energetic, spontaneous, always making her laugh. They had built a life together, shared dreams, and raised a daughter, Emily, who was now had her own life. But somewhere along the line, things had shifted. David had become distant, more focused on work and his endless excuses of being too tired. His hair was thinning faster than either of them had expected, and the extra weight he'd put on had made him even more sluggish.

"Is this it?" she whispered to her reflection, unsure if she meant her marriage or the night ahead.

Her phone buzzed on the vanity, interrupting her thoughts. It was a message from Lisa: *"Ready for tonight? We're going to have a blast!"*

Caroline smiled, grateful for the distraction. She typed back quickly: *"Absolutely! Can't wait. See you soon!"*

As she placed her phone down, David shuffled into the bedroom. He wore the same tired expression he had been sporting for months now. His eyes lingered on her outfit for a brief moment.

"You look nice," he said, though his voice was devoid of any real emotion.

"Thanks, David," Caroline replied, her cheerfulness slightly forced. She picked up her clutch and moved toward the door, feeling the awkwardness thicken between them. "It's just the girls tonight. Same old Sussex Yacht Club thing."

David gave a slow nod and sank down on the bed, reaching for the remote. He clicked on the TV without even looking at her. "Have fun," he mumbled, already half-focused on the screen.

Caroline paused, her hand resting on the door handle. Something tugged at her, a mix of frustration and sadness. They couldn't keep going on like this. She walked over to the bed and sat beside him, folding her hands in her lap.

"David, are you okay? You've seemed... off lately," she ventured.

He sighed, a heavy sound that seemed to carry the weight of years. "I don't know, Caroline. Work is just... draining. And I'm not young anymore. I feel it in my bones, you know?"

She placed a hand gently on his knee, trying to find the right words. "I get that, but it feels like we're not even trying anymore. You know, with each other. We're not the same, sure, but we can't just let things slide." She hesitated, searching his face for a sign, any sign, that he still cared as much as she did. "Maybe we could plan a weekend away? Just the two of us. No distractions, just... us."

David finally turned to look at her. His eyes softened, and for the first time in what felt like forever, there was something behind them, something real. "Maybe we should. I've been a lousy husband lately, haven't I?"

Caroline smiled gently. "It's not just you. We've both been letting things slip. But we can fix it, can't we?"

"Yeah," David said, his voice quiet but sincere. "We can try."

She kissed him softly on the cheek, feeling a sliver of hope in the pit of her stomach. "Okay, I'll be home by midnight. We'll talk more, alright?"

"Alright," David replied, squeezing her hand before she stood up.

Caroline walked out, her heels clicking softly against the wooden floor, and headed to her car. As she drove through the crisp evening air, her heart was lighter than it had been in weeks. Maybe tonight would be the start of something new, she thought. Maybe they could find their way back to each other.

At the Sussex Yacht Club, the party was in full swing. The warm glow of the hanging lights reflected off the polished mahogany bar and the gleaming yachts docked outside. Laughter and chatter filled the space, along with the familiar hum of music that always invited people to the dance floor.

"Caroline!" Lisa called out as she spotted her from across the room, waving enthusiastically. Caroline made her way to their usual table, where her friends greeted her with excited hugs.

"You look incredible," Lisa said, admiring Caroline's outfit. "Seriously, if I didn't know you better, I'd think you were about to catch the eye of every guy here."

Caroline laughed, but there was a flicker of something behind her smile—an unease she couldn't quite shake off. "Thanks. I needed a good night out."

Lisa's eyes narrowed slightly. "Everything alright at home?"

Caroline took a deep breath and nodded, swirling the cocktail Lisa had handed her. "It's... complicated. David and I aren't exactly in sync these days, but I think we're finally talking about it. So, maybe there's hope."

Lisa squeezed her hand. "I'm glad you're talking. You deserve to be happy, Caroline."

For a moment, Caroline just let Lisa's words sink in. She did deserve to be happy. And tonight, she would be. As the music picked up, Lisa pulled her onto the dance floor, and soon they were dancing, laughing, and letting the rhythm take them away from all the worries of the outside world.

Hours later, when the evening had wound down, Caroline walked home. The streets were quiet, and she found herself thinking of David. Maybe they could rekindle what they once had. The thought filled her with cautious optimism.

When she walked through the door, David was waiting on the couch, the TV off, a book in his lap. He looked up, smiling softly.

"How was it?" he asked.

"It was fun," Caroline said, sitting down next to him. "But I kept thinking about you."

David's arm came around her, pulling her close. "I've been thinking about us, too."

And for the first time in a long time, Caroline felt like they were both finally on the same page. They sat in silence, but this time, it was a comfortable one, full of the unspoken promise that they would try again.

Chapter Sixteen

Caroline had kept a secret from David, one she wasn't sure she'd ever reveal—that night, she had danced with Oliver. The stranger had only recently arrived in Shoreham, yet he already commanded attention with his confident air. Tall, with strikingly good looks, Oliver had walked into the club wearing light blue jeans, a crisp white shirt, and polished brown shoes. Conversations paused as eyes drifted toward him. Caroline and her group of friends couldn't help but notice.

As Oliver scanned the room, his gaze found hers, lingering just a little too long to be casual. Caroline felt her heart skip a beat before she shyly looked away, her friends giggling beside her. His knowing smile deepened as he raised his glass in acknowledgment. Then, without a word, he strolled toward the balcony, disappearing into the night. Caroline, despite herself, couldn't stop wondering about him.

"Go on, Caroline," one of her friends nudged her. "Find out who he is. He obviously noticed you."

"I don't know," Caroline hesitated. "It seems too bold."

Her friends, relentless, eventually convinced her. With her pulse quickening, she slipped outside into the cool evening air. They're stood Oliver, his silhouette framed by the gentle light of the river. He appeared lost in thought, until he sensed her presence.

"Hello," she ventured, her voice soft but steady.

He turned, and the moment their eyes met again, a smile played on his lips. "Hello," he responded warmly.

"Caroline," she introduced herself. "I hope I'm not intruding, but I haven't seen you around. Are you new to Shoreham?"

Oliver nodded. "I am. Arrived just a few weeks ago, actually. I joined the club hoping to settle here, but I've yet to find a place to call home."

Caroline's business instincts kicked in. "Well, you're in luck. I work for the best estate agency in town. If you're still looking, I could show you a few properties."

"I like a woman who knows what she wants," he replied, a teasing glint in his eye. "But I have one condition."

"Oh? And what's that?"

"You dance with me," he said, the words less a question and more a playful challenge.

Caroline's lips curved into a smile as she glanced toward the dance floor. "Shall we?"

Without another word, Oliver extended his hand. She took it, her heart racing as they walked back inside. Her friends were wide-eyed with amusement as they watched the two glide onto the dance floor. For a few moments, time seemed to stop, and under the glow of the dim club lights, it felt as if Caroline and Oliver were the only two people in the room.

⊶⊷◆⊶⊷

Chapter Seventeen

The sun shone brightly as Oliver made his way to his appointment with Caroline. They had agreed to meet at the newly constructed luxury apartments early in the morning, and Oliver felt a spring in his step as he reminisced about their first meeting. Initially, the idea of relocating from bustling London to a sleepy seaside town had felt daunting, but he quickly found that life here was far from boring.

Caroline arrived in her sleek BMW convertible, the sunlight glinting off its polished surface. She pulled up in front of the exclusive apartment complex, which had been garnering attention for its modern design and prime location. Oliver had expressed interest in the penthouse, and Caroline was thrilled—after all, a commission on a property valued at over £1.5 million would be quite the windfall.

Oliver, a little past 9 a.m., approached the property, where Caroline stood waiting, her presence luminous in a flowing yellow summer dress that danced in the breeze. Her blue wedge shoes clicked softly against the pavement, adding a playful contrast to her otherwise sophisticated appearance. As Oliver drew near, his sharp blue two-piece suit emphasized his polished demeanour, the black slip-on square-toed shoes complementing his look with understated elegance. When he reached Caroline, they exchanged a formal handshake—quite the contrast to the intimate dance they had shared just a few nights earlier, where his arms had been wrapped tightly around her.

"Good morning," Oliver greeted her, his voice steady but with a hint of warmth.

Caroline smiled; her eyes sparkling. "Yes, it's a very good morning," she replied, her tone carrying a playful lilt.

Reaching into her designer handbag, she retrieved a set of gleaming keys, gesturing for Oliver to follow her inside. They stepped through the front entrance into a grand, open hallway, the scent of fresh paint and new beginnings lingering in the air. Caroline immediately slipped into her professional mode, highlighting the apartment's luxurious features: the private elevator that opened directly into the penthouse, underground parking for residents, and even a mooring for those who enjoyed the seaside life in style.

Oliver, however, found himself more distracted by Caroline's presence than by the apartment's details. He feigned interest as she continued her tour, his gaze occasionally drifting back to her animated gestures and warm smile.

"Yes, I'll take it," he said suddenly, his decision catching Caroline by surprise.

She blinked, her sales pitch faltering. "Already? You're sure?"

"Yes, I'm sure," he responded with a confidence that made her heart skip a beat. "I'll transfer the funds this afternoon."

Caroline's face lit up with genuine delight, her surprise giving way to a wave of satisfaction. "Well, that's wonderful!" she said, her mind already calculating the substantial commission coming her way.

"Shall we celebrate with a glass of champagne?" Oliver suggested smoothly, his eyes glinting with a playful challenge.

Caroline hesitated for a second. "It's a bit early for champagne, but... why not?" she replied with a grin, intrigued by the unexpected turn of the day.

"Perfect. How about we meet at the club in thirty minutes?" Oliver proposed, his charm undeniable.

She agreed, still marvelling at how decisively he had acted. As they parted ways, Caroline felt a ripple of excitement she hadn't anticipated.

When Caroline arrived at the exclusive club thirty minutes later, Oliver was already seated at a table, a bottle of champagne chilling in an elegant ice bucket beside him. The ambience of the club was warm, its soft lighting and gentle hum of conversation adding a layer of intimacy to the moment. She spotted Oliver and made her way toward him, her heart skipping a beat as their eyes met.

"To new beginnings," Oliver said, raising his glass when she sat down.

"To new beginnings," Caroline echoed, clinking her glass with his.

The champagne sparkled in their glasses, the effervescence reflecting the unspoken energy between them. Their conversation quickly moved beyond the apartment, flowing into more personal territory. Oliver spoke of his life in London, the fast-paced corporate environment he had grown tired of, and his desire for a quieter existence. Caroline, in turn, found herself opening up about her strained marriage to David, the growing emotional distance between them, and the dreams she had once held but now felt slipping away.

"And are you finding what you're looking for here?" Caroline asked, her voice soft, her eyes meeting his.

Oliver paused for a moment, then replied, "I think I might be." His gaze lingered on her, the weight of his words heavy with implication.

Caroline felt a blush rise to her cheeks, her pulse quickening. She hadn't expected this—this undeniable connection with Oliver. But here it was, a palpable chemistry that seemed to grow stronger with every shared glance, every word spoken between them.

As the morning stretched into the afternoon, time seemed to slip away unnoticed. They sipped champagne, exchanging stories and laughter, their connection deepening. By the time they left the club, it was clear to that this wasn't just a professional interaction—it was the beginning of something far more profound.

They strolled along the waterfront, the conversation now entirely personal. The breeze carried the scent of the sea as Oliver talked about his escape from the chaos of London and his desire for peace, while Caroline shared the difficulties of her marriage and her longing for change.

As they stopped by a bench overlooking the river, Oliver turned to Caroline, his expression serious yet tender. "It's brave to admit when something isn't working," he said softly. "And even braver to seek what makes you truly happy."

Caroline felt her heart flutter. "It's not easy," she admitted, her voice barely above a whisper. "But sometimes you meet someone who makes you realise what you've been missing."

Oliver's eyes locked onto hers, the intensity of his gaze sending a shiver down her spine. "Caroline," he began, his voice thick with emotion, "I feel like I've known you forever. There's something about you… something I can't explain."

Caroline's breath caught in her throat. She had never felt so seen, so understood. "I feel it too, Oliver," she whispered. "But I don't know what to do about it."

Oliver reached for her hand, his touch both gentle and electric. "Let's not rush," he said softly. "Let's take this one step at a time and see where it leads."

Caroline nodded; her heart full of anticipation. Together, they sat watching the boats drift by on the river, knowing that whatever this was between them, it was only the beginning of something far more meaningful than they had expected.

Chapter Eighteen

Oliver's transition from the bustling streets of London to the tranquil shores of Shoreham-by-Sea marked a profound shift in his life—one that rippled through his every thought and action. Once deeply embedded in the high-octane world of finance, he had thrived on the adrenaline rush of closing deals, navigating intense negotiations, and savouring the sweet satisfaction of outpacing the competition. It had been his life's rhythm, his identity, until a sudden, devastating heart attack forced him to confront a truth he had long avoided: he was not invincible.

The heart attack, a sharp and merciless reminder of his mortality, shook him to his core. Lying in the sterile, too-bright hospital room, Oliver had felt the world slow down, his life's frenetic pace suddenly at odds with the quiet beeping of the machines monitoring his heart. His consultant's stern words echoed in his mind, *"You need to slow down, Oliver. Or next time, there won't be a warning."* It wasn't advice—it was a stark ultimatum.

Reluctantly, and with a mixture of apprehension and defiance, Oliver made the decision to leave behind the relentless stress of city life. He couldn't completely abandon London—his penthouse on the Isle of Dogs still held too much sentimental value, a reminder of his former self. But he knew deep down that staying would be a risk he could no longer afford. And so, Shoreham-by-Sea, with its quieter, slower rhythm, beckoned.

The first time Oliver stood on the balcony of his new penthouse overlooking the Adur River, a sense of calm washed over him that he hadn't felt in years. The shimmering waters reflected the vast, open sky, stretching into a horizon where the sea met the clouds in a soft, almost ethereal embrace. It was nothing like the view from his London apartment—no jagged skyline or distant roar of traffic. Here, the air was cleaner, the sky seemed wider, and the endless calls of seagulls replaced the constant hum of the town.

The real estate agent, a vivacious woman with sun-kissed hair and a knowing smile, had been pleasantly surprised when Oliver decided to purchase the penthouse on the spot, without hesitation. He'd would transfer the money in the morning, and she, ever the opportunist, accepted an invitation to tour his yacht a few weeks later. Now, as she lounged lazily on its deck, sipping a glass of chilled wine, Oliver couldn't help but smile at the change in his life. There was a lightness to it all—he was no longer tethered to his phone, his inbox, or his clients' never-ending demands.

Each morning, Oliver would rise early, drawn to the promise of dawn. He took his coffee black and strong, just as he always had, but now, instead of gulping it down between meetings, he lingered on the balcony. The sunrise was a daily spectacle—one he never tired of. The sky would slowly transform, blushing shades of pink, gold, and lavender, as the sun crept up from the horizon. The gentle breeze off the coast, carrying the briny scent of the sea, would tug at his robe, reminding him he was free from the suffocating grip of city life.

In the afternoons, he strolled leisurely along the promenade. At first, his steps had been quick and purposeful, his mind still wired for efficiency and speed, but over time, he learned to slow down. He would stop to admire the children playing on the beach, their carefree laughter mingling with the sound of waves lapping against the shore. He even started chatting with local shop owners, some of whom were intrigued by the mysterious city man who had suddenly appeared in their sleepy town. His neighbours, too, became familiar faces—people who appreciated the simple joys of life, and who welcomed him with warmth that he hadn't expected.

It was during one such quiet afternoon that Oliver discovered a small art gallery tucked away behind a café. Inside, the walls were adorned with landscapes of the sea and sky, painted in vibrant oils and watercolours. For reasons he couldn't fully explain, he felt drawn to the idea of creating something like that himself. So, he bought a set of paints, brushes, and canvases, and began to experiment in his spare time. Painting became a new outlet—one that allowed him to capture the beauty around him and express a part of himself he hadn't known existed.

In those quiet moments, brush in hand, as he recreated the swirling blues of the sea or the fiery oranges of the sunset, Oliver felt truly at peace. The urgency, the stress, and the constant hum of anxiety that had followed him for years now seemed distant, like an echo from a past life. Shoreham-by-Sea had given him something that money and success in the city never could—a sense of belonging, of contentment.

As the seasons passed, he found that his heart, once fragile and overworked, had begun to heal—not just physically, but emotionally too. He had built a new rhythm, one filled with simplicity and grace. In the stillness of Shoreham's quiet nights, as the moonlight danced on the water and the distant sound of waves lulled him to sleep, Oliver knew with certainty that he had finally found his sanctuary.

It wasn't just the view, or the slower pace, or even the warm company of his newfound friends—it was the realisation that in letting go of his old life, he had discovered something far more precious. Time. Time to live, to breathe, to love, and to appreciate the fleeting beauty of each moment. And as he stood at the edge of the sea, gazing out at the horizon, he felt no desire to return to the life he once knew. Here, on the shores of Shoreham-by-Sea, Oliver had truly found himself.

Chapter Ninteen

Oliver waited in his new penthouse apartment, glancing at the clock on his phone. It was now a little after 10 a.m. on a Tuesday morning, and the sun poured through the expansive windows overlooking the Adur River. The space gleamed in the natural light, casting reflections off the polished wooden floors and illuminating the minimal furniture he currently had in place—a few sleek, modern pieces he'd chosen when he first moved in. The room was serene, quiet, yet filled with a subtle anticipation. He was eager to see what Lisa Armstrong, the interior designer Caroline had recommended, had to offer.

His phone buzzed, pulling him from his thoughts. A message popped up: "Sorry to keep you waiting, but traffic is getting worse."

Oliver chuckled softly to himself as he typed back, "No worries at all, Lisa. Living in London, I'm used to waiting around."

He set the phone aside and wandered toward the window, admiring the view of the river below. He loved how the light danced across the water, sparkling in a way that always seemed to calm his nerves. The Adur had been one of the reasons he fell in love with the apartment in the first place.

Just as he was lost in the rhythm of the river, the doorbell rang. He took a deep breath and strode over, opening the door to let Lisa in.

"Good morning, Oliver," she greeted him with a warm smile.

"Good morning, Lisa," Oliver replied, stepping aside to let her in. She was exactly as he remembered—tall, poised, and effortlessly elegant in a tan two-piece suit that complemented her confident air.

Her short, cropped black hair framed her face perfectly, drawing attention to her striking blue eyes.

As Lisa entered, her gaze swept across the apartment. "This place has great potential," she said, her voice filled with a hint of admiration. "The light in here is incredible."

"That's one of the things I love most about it," Oliver responded, guiding her towards the spacious living area. "I'm really looking forward to hearing your ideas."

"Well, you're in luck," Lisa said with a grin, setting down her leather portfolio on the sleek glass coffee table. She began to pull out her design materials—sketches, fabric swatches, and detailed kitchen plans. "I've been here a couple of times already with Caroline when they were first built, and I've had a lot of time to think about how to make the most of the space. Let's dive right in, shall we?"

Oliver watched as she laid out her plans, admiring the thoughtfulness and attention to detail in each sketch. The colour palettes were warm yet sophisticated, with tones that would enhance the natural light in the apartment. The kitchen design caught his eye.

"These are amazing," he said, feeling genuinely enthused as he leaned closer to one of the drawings. "I really love the kitchen layout. It's clean but functional, and I can see myself enjoying cooking in there."

"That's exactly what I wanted to hear," Lisa responded, pleased. "Caroline mentioned you enjoy cooking, so I made sure to design a space that's both stylish and practical. The materials I chose are durable, but they won't sacrifice that modern, polished look."

Oliver nodded, his mind already racing with thoughts of hosting dinners and experimenting with new recipes in the upgraded space. "It's perfect. I'm sold on the kitchen already."

Lisa smiled, pulling out another set of plans. "Great! Now, let's move on to the living area. Given the fantastic view of the river, I thought about incorporating some design elements that wouldn't obstruct that. Maybe floor-to-ceiling shelving along this wall," she gestured, "to add storage without blocking the windows. What do you think?"

Oliver tilted his head thoughtfully. "I like that idea. It keeps the space open but gives me somewhere to store my books and maybe display a few things."

"Exactly," Lisa said. "It would frame the windows rather than compete with them. I also thought we could add some comfortable seating, maybe a sectional in a soft, neutral tone to keep the focus on the view."

They spent the next hour working through every room of the penthouse. Lisa's expertise was evident as she explained each design choice, considering not only the aesthetics but also how Oliver would use the space in his day-to-day life. Her ideas for the bedroom were cosy yet minimal, and she had a particularly clever plan for maximising the storage in the entryway without making it feel cramped.

"Wow," Oliver said, glancing over the final sketches spread out before them. "This is really coming together. I love your vision for the place."

"I'm glad to hear that," Lisa replied, smiling as she packed up her materials. "I think it's going to turn out beautifully. I'll coordinate with the contractors and start ordering some of the key pieces. We can begin work within the next couple of weeks."

"Perfect," Oliver said, walking her to the door. "I can't wait to see it all come together. Thank you so much for your time today, Lisa."

"My pleasure," Lisa said warmly, pausing before she stepped out into the hallway. "I'll keep you updated on the progress, and if you ever want to make any tweaks, don't hesitate to let me know."

"I will. Have a great day, Lisa."

"You too, Oliver," she replied with a friendly nod before heading off down the corridor.

Oliver closed the door behind her and stood in the quiet of the apartment, feeling a surge of excitement. For the first time since he'd moved in, the space felt like it was on the verge of becoming a real home.

Chapter Twenty

Lisa sat behind the wheel, her thoughts swirling as she navigated the busy streets. The conversation with Caroline only deepened her unease. She had always known Caroline to be impulsive, diving headfirst into excitement when life became too mundane. But Oliver—there was something off about him. Sure, he was smooth, charismatic, and exuded an air of mystery, but that's precisely what unsettled Lisa.

As her white Porsche cruised through the town, her mind wandered back to the penthouse. The way Oliver's eyes lingered on her for just a bit too long, or how he seemed overly interested in the smallest details about her life—questions that seemed casual but felt loaded with intention. And the way Caroline had been with him, completely enamoured, ignoring every subtle red flag Lisa tried to raise.

Her phone buzzed again, pulling her from her thoughts. She glanced at the screen and saw it was David this time. She hesitated before answering, knowing the conversation could quickly get heavy.

"David, hi," she greeted cautiously, turning onto a quieter street.

"Lisa, I need to talk to you," his voice was strained, tired. "It's about Caroline."

Lisa's grip tightened on the steering wheel. "What's going on? Did something happen?"

David sighed deeply, the weight of months of tension evident in his voice. "I don't know what to do anymore. We've been distant for so long, and now, it feels like I've already lost her."

"David..." Lisa began, searching for the right words. She didn't want to choose sides, but her heart ached for him. He had always been good to Caroline, and though their relationship had its struggles, Lisa had never doubted his love for her friend. "I've been worried about Oliver too. I don't know what it is, but something feels... off."

"You feel it too?" David sounded relieved, as though he had finally found someone who understood his unease. "I've been trying to give Caroline space, to let her figure things out.

Lisa nodded, glancing out the window at the setting sun. "She says she's just having fun, but I think it's more than that for her. She's using him as an escape, and with everything going on between you two, it's making it easy for her to get swept up."

David was quiet for a moment, and when he spoke again, his voice was softer, more vulnerable. "Do you think I still have a chance? Or is it too late?"

Lisa's heart sank. She hated being in this position—caught between two people she cared about. "I don't know, David. But if you love her, you need to fight for her. Talk to her, really talk."

"I'm trying," he said, sounding defeated. "But it feels like she's already made up her mind."

They spoke a little longer, Lisa offering as much comfort as she could before ending the call. The knot in her stomach tightened further as she thought about how complicated things had become.

Later that night, as Lisa sat in her apartment, she opened her laptop to review her sketches. But her thoughts kept drifting back to Caroline, Oliver, and David. The uneasy feeling refused to leave her. She contemplated reaching out to Caroline again, maybe trying to convince her to slow things down. But she knew her friend too well. Caroline was stubborn—once she had her mind set on something, it was hard to sway her.

Suddenly, a new message popped up on her phone. It was from Oliver.

Oliver Hope you got home safely. I've been thinking about your designs. They're impressive, really. Would love to discuss some ideas with you soon, maybe over dinner?

Lisa stared at the message, her fingers hovering over the screen. There it was again—Oliver's charm, wrapped in casual professionalism. She didn't trust him, and now he was trying to pull her in too.

With a deep breath, she typed out a polite response.

Lisa Thanks, Oliver. I'll be in touch when I have some time to go over the designs in more detail.

She hit send, then tossed the phone aside, feeling the weight of the situation pressing down on her even more. Something told her this wasn't just about business anymore. Oliver had a plan, and she had a sinking feeling that it involved more than just Caroline.

Chapter Twenty One

Caroline knew Lisa was right, but after years of a stale marriage, she couldn't see how she and David could survive another year the way things were. Oliver was a breath of fresh air, just the thing she needed—something to remind her that life could be different.

"Caroline, you have to talk to David," Lisa said firmly, her voice laced with concern. "You can't keep living like this. You're only going to hurt yourself, and him."

Caroline sighed, her eyes fixed on the swirling red wine in her glass. She took a sip, feeling the warmth of the alcohol wash over her. "I know, Lisa. But it's so hard. David and I... we've grown so distant. It's like we're just roommates now. We don't even fight anymore—we just exist."

Lisa leaned forward, her expression softening with empathy. "I get that. But it won't change unless you do something. You need to make a choice, one way or another. Either you fight for your marriage, or you admit it's over."

Caroline swallowed, the weight of the decision crushing her chest. "But what if I fight and it still doesn't work? What if it's too late? What if I don't even want to fight anymore?" Her voice was barely above a whisper.

Lisa hesitated. "That's something only you can answer," she said softly. "But pretending everything is fine when it's not... it's only going to get worse."

That evening, Caroline stood in the kitchen, pouring herself another glass of wine as she prepared dinner. The smell of garlic and onions filled the room, but all she could think about was how suffocating everything felt. David was in the living room, where he always was—his face glued to the TV. She glanced at him through the kitchen door. He looked so distant, so disconnected from her life.

"Is dinner almost ready?" David called out, his eyes never leaving the screen.

Caroline closed her eyes for a moment, steadying herself before answering. "Yeah, just a few more minutes." Her voice was devoid of energy, a flat echo of the enthusiasm she once had when speaking to him.

As she stirred the pasta, her mind wandered to Oliver—his smile, his laugh, the way he made her feel seen. She felt a pang of guilt but quickly pushed it aside. With him, she felt alive. With David, she felt like a ghost.

When dinner was ready, Caroline set the table, barely acknowledging David as he sat down. "Dinner's ready," she muttered.

David muted the TV and walked over to the table. "Thanks," he said, his voice equally drained, as if politeness was all that was left between them.

They ate in silence. The only sounds in the room were the occasional clink of forks on plates and the soft rustling of Caroline's book, which she had picked up midway through dinner, more out of habit than interest.

"How was your day?" David asked suddenly, his tone flat but the attempt notable.

"Fine," Caroline responded without looking up. She turned a page. "Yours?"

"Same as always," he replied, the words carrying a sense of resignation.

After dinner, as David returned to the living room, Caroline began cleaning up. The dishes clattered in the sink, but her mind was far away, wandering back to Oliver. She knew it wasn't fair to David—or to herself—but every time she was around Oliver, it felt like she could breathe again. He was exciting, vibrant, attentive—all the things David used to be but no longer was.

At 9 p.m., like clockwork, David rose from the couch. "Goodnight," he said softly, pausing at the base of the stairs as if waiting for some kind of acknowledgment.

"Goodnight," Caroline mumbled, not lifting her head from her book.

David sighed, the weight of their unspoken tension lingering in the air as he disappeared upstairs.

Caroline finished her wine, her heart heavy. She knew something had to change, but the thought of confronting David—of unravelling the tangled mess of their lives—was terrifying. She poured herself another glass, sinking back into her chair, staring at the pages of her book but not really reading.

She thought about Oliver again, and for a fleeting moment, she allowed herself to imagine what life would be like with him—free from the weight of this marriage, from the dull ache of routine.

But guilt gnawed at her. David wasn't a bad man; he didn't deserve this. Yet every time she thought about trying to fix things, she felt exhausted before she even began. It was easier to stay in the fog, to let things continue as they were, even if it meant slowly eroding what was left of her.

Lisa's words echoed in her mind: *You must talk to him.*

Caroline closed her eyes, trying to imagine that conversation, but it felt impossible. She wasn't sure she had the strength for it. She wasn't sure if she wanted to.

The room was quiet, except for the soft hum of the refrigerator. The house felt too big, too empty. Caroline glanced at the clock. It was nearing 10 p.m. David would be asleep by now.

She took a deep breath, stood up, and poured the rest of the wine down the sink.

Chapter Twenty Two

The sun dipped lower on the horizon, casting a golden hue over the glistening waters as Oliver Wright stood tall at the helm of his 2025 Fountaine Pajot 24-meter Catamaran yacht, the sleek and opulent '"Filthy Rich'" The vessel cut smoothly through the shimmering waves, its polished white hull reflecting the sun's glow like a beacon of luxury and adventure. Sea spray rose with each crest, catching the light as it danced around Oliver, tousling his sun-kissed hair. He inhaled deeply, savouring the salty air that clung to his skin and the familiar tug of the wind filling the sails. There was something about being at the helm of his yacht that gave him an unshakable sense of mastery, as if the world bent to his will beneath the endless blue sky.

Beside him, Caroline Davidson leaned against the railing, her auburn hair catching the light in fiery hues that contrasted against the deep blues of the ocean. She closed her eyes briefly, the cool breeze brushing against her sun-warmed cheeks, and let the sound of the waves mingle with the quiet excitement she felt. Her gaze soon found the distant shoreline, the shores of Sussex bathed in the warm glow of late afternoon.

"This is incredible, Oliver," she murmured, her voice a soft melody rising above the rhythmic hum of the sea and wind. "I never imagined sailing could be so exhilarating."

Oliver turned to her, his sharp eyes taking in the sight of her relaxed, wind-kissed form. A smile curved at the corners of his lips, confident and playful. "It's just the beginning, Caroline," he replied, his tone rich with promise. "Wait until you see what else I have in store for us."

Caroline laughed, a sound that blended with the wind, her eyes sparkling with a mixture of curiosity and amusement. "I have a feeling it's going to be quite the adventure with you," she teased, a mischievous glint in her gaze as she held his eye.

As the yacht approached the busy marina of the Sussex Yacht Club, the atmosphere shifted. The peaceful solitude of open water was gradually replaced by the lively bustle of the harbour. Sailboats of every size bobbed on the gentle waves, their sleek masts slicing through the sky like spires. Dockhands hurried back and forth, securing vessels, while sailors gathered in clusters along the docks, their voices rising in laughter and animated conversation. The air was tinged with the smell of salt, freshly grilled seafood, and the faintest whiff of engine oil.

Oliver's attention shifted smoothly to the task at hand. With a deftness that came from years of practice, he guided '"Filthy Rich'" into her designated berth. His hands moved expertly across the controls, the yacht responding to his command with precision as he manoeuvred her alongside the dock. The engine's hum softened to a whisper as he secured the ropes, bringing the journey to a graceful end.

"Another successful voyage," Caroline said softly, brushing a hand lightly along his arm as they stepped onto the dock.

Oliver gave a satisfied nod, his gaze sweeping over the marina as the setting sun cast long shadows over the water. "Indeed," he murmured, though his mind was already moving ahead to the next adventure, the next horizon waiting to be conquered.

They made their way toward the Sussex Yacht Club's grand entrance, the sounds of lively conversation and music growing louder with each step. The club itself, a stately building adorned with nautical flags and ivy-covered terraces, bustled with activity. As they walked, familiar faces turned toward them, offering nods and smiles of greeting. Inside, sailors swapped stories of daring races and far-flung voyages, their glasses raised in lively toasts. The mouth-watering aroma of seafood grilled over open flames filled the air, mixing with the sound of clinking glasses and the festive chatter of the evening's guests.

They were soon joined by James Harrington, Oliver's longtime friend and fellow yachtsman. Dressed in his usual breezy linen attire and donning a worn straw hat, James greeted them with his signature wide grin. "Another grand entrance, Wright," he quipped, clapping Oliver on the back with a hearty laugh. "You never disappoint."

"Only the best for my friends," Oliver replied, laughing as his eyes drifted toward the veranda where a live band was setting up. The soft strains of jazz music floated through the warm air. "Shall we celebrate?"

At a table reserved with the perfect view of the marina, the trio settled in as a waiter appeared with a bottle of chilled champagne. The crystal glasses sparkled under the amber glow of the yacht club's lanterns. As the bottle was uncorked with a satisfying pop, Oliver raised his glass, his gaze locking with Caroline's across the table. The flickering light of candles danced between them, casting a soft glow on their faces.

"To new adventures and the open sea," he said, his voice low and filled with excitement.

Caroline's smile was radiant as she raised her glass in return. "To new adventures," she echoed, the clink of their glasses a promise that lingered in the air.

As the night unfolded, laughter, stories, and music filled the air. Oliver regaled the table with tales of daring expeditions, recounting encounters with treacherous storms and remote islands with a flair that had everyone hanging on his every word. Caroline's eyes never left him, her admiration growing with each tale he told, each glimpse into the life of the man she found herself irresistibly drawn to.

As the evening wore on and the band's tempo slowed, Oliver rose from his seat and extended his hand toward Caroline. His eyes softened as he spoke. "May I have this dance?"

Caroline's breath caught for just a moment before she smiled and took his hand. "I'd love to," she said, standing to join him.

Under the starlit sky, surrounded by the twinkling lights of the marina and the soft strains of a romantic melody, they swayed together. The world seemed to fall away, leaving only the two of them, moving in sync, lost in the magic of the moment. The gentle rhythm of the waves lapping against the docks mirrored the slow sway of their dance, creating a harmony that felt as natural as the tides themselves.

As the song drew to a close, Oliver leaned in, his voice a soft whisper in her ear. "This is just the beginning, Caroline. There's so much more I want to share with you."

Caroline looked up at him, her heart full and her eyes alight with the same sense of wonder. "I can't wait to see what the future holds, Oliver," she whispered back.

In that moment, with the ocean stretching endlessly before them and the world at their feet, they both knew that their journey together had only just begun—an adventure that would take them to new horizons, one exhilarating sail at a time.

Chapter Twenty Three

As they strolled along the waterfront promenade, the lights from the yacht club danced on the ripples of the river, casting a serene glow on their path. Oliver's arm around Caroline provided a comforting warmth against the evening chill, his touch sending shivers of anticipation down her spine. She nestled closer to him, the scent of his cologne—a subtle blend of cedarwood and spice—mingling with the salty tang of the sea air. It was an intoxicating mix that made her feel both safe and exhilarated, as though she were on the precipice of something new and thrilling.

"Looks like the whole town decided to come out tonight," Oliver mused with a smile, his voice low and smooth, a pleasant contrast to the bustling energy around them.

Caroline laughed, her eyes twinkling as she glanced around at the crowded promenade. "It's definitely lively," she said, her tone playful. "But I don't mind. It feels like the perfect way to start the weekend."

Oliver nodded in agreement, pulling her slightly closer as they wove through the throngs of people enjoying the Friday night ambience. The clinking of glasses, the murmur of conversations, and the distant strains of live music from a nearby bar added to the lively atmosphere. Caroline felt a rush of excitement coursing through her veins, fuelled not only by the wine from their earlier dinner but also by Oliver's magnetic presence. Everything about him—from his easy confidence to the way he looked at her with that mischievous glint in his eyes—made her heart race.

"Did you enjoy dinner?" Oliver asked, his thumb gently brushing against her arm, the subtle touch sending another wave of warmth through her.

"I did," she replied, her voice softening as she met his gaze. "Everything was perfect. The food, the view...and the company."

Oliver's lips curved into a smile, his eyes never leaving hers. "I'm glad. I wanted tonight to be special."

As they approached Oliver's apartment building, a sleek, modern structure with glass panels that reflected the twinkling town lights, Caroline couldn't help but admire the elegant architecture and the sweeping views of the waterfront. It was a testament to his success and sophistication, a world away from the modest surroundings she was accustomed to in company. Yet, despite the opulence surrounding him, Oliver remained down-to-earth and charming, his genuine smile putting her at ease in a way she hadn't expected.

The elevator doors opened, and they stepped out into a private hallway leading to his apartment. Inside, the warm confines of Oliver's home welcomed them like a comforting embrace. The soft glow of ambient lighting cast a romantic aura, accentuating the tasteful decor and luxurious furnishings. Caroline felt a sense of wonderment as she took in her surroundings, marvelling at the impeccable attention to detail—the carefully chosen art pieces, the plush rugs that felt like clouds underfoot, the sleek furniture that spoke of understated elegance. It was all so perfectly *him*.

"Lisa has amazing taste," she remarked, her voice tinged with admiration as she wandered further into the living room, her fingers lightly grazing the surface of a polished coffee table.

Oliver followed her with a glass of wine in hand, watching her with a warm smile. "I can't thank you enough for recommending your friend. Lisa has done a great job," he admitted, handing her the glass. "I do like things to feel...balanced. Comfortable, yet refined."

Caroline accepted the glass, taking a sip as she settled onto the plush couch. "Well, you've definitely achieved that."

As they settled in, Oliver prepared a nightcap, his skilled hands expertly crafting cocktails with effortless grace. The clink of ice cubes against crystal glasses filled the air, mingling with their laughter and whispered conversations. Caroline felt herself falling under Oliver's spell, drawn to him like a moth to a flame. Every glance, every brush of his hand against hers, seemed to heighten the electric connection between them.

As he handed her the drink, their fingers briefly touched, and Caroline felt a flutter in her chest. "Thank you," she whispered, her eyes searching his face, trying to read the emotions that flickered in his gaze.

He sat beside her, close enough that she could feel the warmth radiating from his body, but not too close—always leaving her wanting just a little more. "To a perfect evening," he said softly, raising his glass. His eyes lingered on hers, filled with unspoken promises.

Caroline clinked her glass against his, the soft sound echoing in the intimate space around them. "To more perfect evenings," she replied, her voice a little breathless.

Outside, the starlit skyline shimmered in the distance, but inside, the world had shrunk to just the two of them, wrapped in the warmth of the moment. Caroline found herself leaning in, drawn by the invisible pull between them, eager to explore the depths of this connection.

Chapter Twenty Four

Oliver's footsteps echoed softly against the polished marble floors as he made his way to the kitchen, the sleek lines and modern design of the apartment providing a stark contrast to the timeless elegance of the riverside view. Outside, Caroline lingered on the balcony, her eyes following the meandering river below as it reflected the twinkling lights of the town. The wind was gentle but carried with it the coolness of the approaching evening. She took a deep breath, feeling a sense of calm, something she had been missing for so long. This place, with its understated luxury and peaceful view, felt transformed from the property she once showed as a real estate agent. Now, it felt like a retreat—a sanctuary.

Oliver emerged from the apartment moments later, carrying two generous glasses of Chardonnay. The golden hue of the wine caught the last rays of the setting sun, casting a soft, amber light across the balcony. He handed a glass to Caroline, his eyes lingering on her as she turned to face him, her silhouette framed by the deepening twilight. "For you," he said with a smile, his voice low and warm.

"Thank you," Caroline replied, returning the smile. She took a sip of the wine, savouring its crispness as it glided down her throat. The quiet between them was comfortable, punctuated only by the distant hum of the city below and the occasional clink of their glasses.

"The air's getting cooler," Oliver observed after a moment, glancing at the fading horizon. "Why don't we move inside? It's more comfortable."

Caroline nodded, and they both retreated into the inviting embrace of the apartment's sitting room. Inside, the space was a reflection of Oliver's eclectic tastes, where modern elegance met an exotic flair. Intricately patterned Moroccan rugs spread across the floor, while rich, colourful throws were draped over the furniture. The soft glow of flickering candles illuminated the room, casting playful shadows on the walls, creating an atmosphere that was intimate and inviting.

Chapter Twenty Five

Caroline's breath quickened as Oliver's hand glided along the smooth fabric of her white silk blouse, tracing the outline of each button with tantalising slowness. Each button seemed to hold its own promise, a promise of the unveiling to come. Her heart raced with anticipation as Oliver's fingers deftly undid the first button, then the next, until the blouse parted, revealing the delicate lace of the bra she had indulged in from Victoria's Secret. It was a deliberate choice—one she hadn't made lightly—now revealed in the intimate glow of the dimly lit room, its intricate details a whisper of what lay beneath.

Her skin tingled with a mixture of nerves and excitement as Oliver's practised hands worked their magic, undoing the clasp of her bra with a fluid motion. With a soft sigh, the tension released, and the fabric slipped away, allowing her ample breasts to spill forth, freed from the confines of the strained bra. They swayed gently, the soft curves of flesh catching the dim light in the room, a mesmerising sight that held Oliver's gaze captive. He paused for a moment, drinking her in, the contrast of her pale skin against the darker tones of the room creating an image of vulnerability wrapped in desire.

Caroline's cheeks flushed with a mixture of embarrassment and arousal as she stood before him, her chest rising and falling with each breath, her body laid bare and vulnerable yet tingling with a newfound sense of liberation. Her nipples, hardened by both the cool air and the electric charge between them, stood proudly. In that moment, as their eyes met, she felt a surge of desire course through her veins, igniting a fire that threatened to consume them both in its passionate embrace.

Oliver leaned in, his breath warm against her neck as he whispered, "You are absolutely beautiful." His voice was husky, laced with the kind of awe that made her feel seen, not just for her body but for the unspoken connection they shared. His words sent a shiver down her spine, and she felt a growing need to be closer to him, to feel his touch and the heat of his body against hers. Her hands reached out instinctively, brushing the rough fabric of his shirt, eager to feel the strength of him beneath.

With a gentle but insistent tug, Oliver pulled her towards the plush sofa, guiding her to sit down. The Moroccan-inspired patterns and vibrant colours of the throws contrasted beautifully with her pale skin, creating a scene of intimate contrast and allure. The intricate reds, golds, and deep blues seemed to highlight her every curve as if the room itself conspired to amplify the moment. Oliver knelt in front of her, his hands tracing the curves of her thighs before sliding upwards, fingers dancing along the waistband of her skirt.

Caroline's anticipation grew as Oliver's hands slowly, almost teasingly, inched her skirt up, exposing more of her legs. His touch was electric, sending waves of pleasure through her with each gentle caress. She could feel the heat building between them, the air thick with unspoken desires and the promise of what was to come. The tension between them was palpable, an invisible thread pulling them closer, making her acutely aware of every inch of her body and its growing yearning for his touch.

As Oliver's hands reached the hem of her skirt, he paused for a moment, looking up at her with a smouldering intensity that made her heart skip a beat. "May I?" he asked, his voice a low, sensual rumble that sent another thrill of excitement coursing through her. His eyes locked onto hers, seeking permission not just for the physical act, but for the vulnerability it implied.

Caroline nodded, her breath hitching in her throat as she whispered, "Yes, please." The words barely escaped her lips, yet they hung heavy in the air between them, carrying the weight of everything she desired in that moment.

With a swift, fluid motion, Oliver lifted her skirt, exposing the delicate lace of her matching panties. The soft material clung to her hips, highlighting her curves, and the sight of her, so vulnerable and inviting, stirred something primal within him. He leaned in, pressing a soft kiss to the inside of her thigh, his lips brushing against her skin with a tenderness that belied the hunger in his eyes. The contrast of his gentle touch against the fire that smouldered within him made her head spin.

Caroline's hands, trembling with both desire and anticipation, found their way to Oliver's hair, her fingers threading through the soft strands as she pulled him closer, her body arching towards him in silent plea. The anticipation was almost too much to bear, each second stretching into eternity as she waited for his next move. The weight of his presence between her legs, the scent of his cologne mixing with the heat rising from her body, was intoxicating.

Oliver didn't disappoint. His hands slid up her thighs, gently parting them as he moved closer, his lips trailing kisses along the way. The sensation was exquisite, each touch sending ripples of pleasure through her, igniting a fire that burned hotter with every passing moment. Each kiss was slow, deliberate, as though he was savouring the taste of her, drawing out her pleasure with the kind of patience that only deepened her desire.

As Oliver's lips finally met the sensitive skin just above the waistband of her panties, Caroline let out a soft moan, her body trembling with desire. She could feel the heat of his breath against her most intimate area, the anticipation of what was to come driving her wild with need. Her hips lifted slightly, an unspoken plea for more, for him to bridge the aching gap between them.

Oliver looked up at her, his eyes dark with passion, his pupils dilated in the dim light. "You are incredible," he murmured, his voice thick with desire. "I want to make you feel amazing." His words were more than just an affirmation—they were a promise, a vow to explore every inch of her with a tenderness that belied the burning passion in his gaze.

Caroline's heart swelled at his words, her body aching for his touch. "Please, Oliver," she whispered, her voice barely more than a breath. "I need you." There was no hesitation, no doubt in her voice. She wanted him, all of him, now.

With a growl of hunger, Oliver complied, his hands and lips exploring her body with a skill and tenderness that left her breathless. Each touch, each kiss, was a symphony of sensation, building towards a crescendo of pleasure that promised to be unlike anything she had ever experienced. His touch was at once gentle and demanding, teasing and relentless, pulling her deeper into the spiral of desire that consumed them both.

In that moment, as their bodies moved together in perfect harmony, Caroline knew that this was just the beginning of something extraordinary. The connection between them was electric, a powerful force that drew them together and ignited a passion that burned brighter than anything she had ever known. And as they lost themselves in the heat of the moment, she felt a sense of liberation and fulfilment that she had long thought lost forever. A flame that had been dormant now roared to life, consuming them in a dance of raw, unfiltered desire.

Chapter Twenty Six

As Oliver's lips trailed down Caroline's neck, each soft, deliberate kiss ignited a slow-burning fire beneath her skin. A shiver of anticipation surged through her, the feeling both intoxicating and unsettling, tinged with the shadow of guilt that crept at the edges of her thoughts. The room was heavy with unspoken words, thick with the conflicting pull of desire and the burdens they both carried. Responsibilities, obligations, the outside world—none of that held any sway here, not in this fleeting cocoon of stolen moments.

Her fingertips danced lightly across the planes of Oliver's back, tracing the curve of his spine with a touch so soft it was almost a whisper. She marvelled at the warmth of his skin, at the way his muscles tensed and relaxed beneath her hands as if responding to her every touch. It felt real, vivid, and alive—a stark contrast to the monotonous rhythm of her daily life, where passion seemed a distant memory, buried beneath layers of obligation and expectation.

The world around them seemed to dissolve, melting into a blur of muted colours and distant sounds, leaving only the heady heat of their bodies intertwined. Time lost its meaning in the tangle of limbs and soft murmurs, replaced by a primal, urgent rhythm that pulsed between them. Every caress, every breathless sigh, felt like an unspoken promise, a vow that this moment, however fleeting, was real.

Yet, beneath the rush of sensation, a quiet voice in the back of Caroline's mind persisted, a nagging whisper that refused to be silenced. It reminded her of the lives waiting outside this room, of the consequences they couldn't escape forever. The thought was like a shadow, casting doubt on the fragile sanctuary they'd built. But as Oliver's hands roamed over her body, drawing soft gasps from her lips, the voice was drowned out by the intoxicating rhythm of their connection.

For now, this was all that mattered—the heat of his breath on her skin, the way their bodies moved in sync, as though they had been made for each other. In this suspended moment, nothing else existed. No future, no past. Just the raw, unbridled desire that tethered them together, if only for a fleeting night.

And as Caroline sank deeper into the intensity of the embrace, she let herself believe, just for a moment, that perhaps they could stay here, lost in each other, and forget the rest of the world—if only until dawn.

Chapter Twenty Seven

Oliver moved closer to Caroline, his eyes reflecting a mixture of desire and concern, a storm of emotions swirling beneath his calm exterior. The dim light from the room flickered across his face, highlighting the tension that hung in the air between them. His hand, warm and steady, reached up to gently cup her cheek, his thumb brushing against her skin with the tenderness of someone deeply conflicted. "Caroline," he whispered, his voice barely audible but heavy with meaning, "I know this isn't easy, but what we have is real. We can't keep denying it. Not anymore."

Caroline's heart raced as she met his gaze, her breath catching in her throat. She could feel the intensity of his emotions pouring into her, both thrilling and terrifying her in equal measure. Her thoughts were a tangled mess, torn between the undeniable passion that simmered between them and the guilt gnawing relentlessly at her conscience. The room seemed to close in on her as she struggled to find her voice, to make sense of the maelstrom within her. "I just... I never thought I'd find myself in this situation," she admitted, her words faltering, the uncertainty in her voice mirroring the chaos in her mind.

"I understand," Oliver replied, his tone soft but resolute, as if trying to convince both of them that this was the right path. His thumb traced gentle circles on her cheek, the soothing motion at odds with the intensity of the moment. "But sometimes life surprises us," he continued, his voice steady but laden with emotion. "And maybe... maybe this is our chance to finally be happy. To stop pretending we're okay with living half-lives."

Caroline's eyes fluttered closed for a brief moment, overwhelmed by the sincerity in his words and the comfort she found in his touch. A part of her wanted to surrender to the feeling, to let go of everything else and allow herself to be consumed by the moment. But reality, as always, crept back in, cold and unforgiving. "But what about David?" she asked, her voice trembling as the weight of her marriage—the promises, the memories, the years of shared life—pressed down on her like an anchor. The thought of her husband, so unaware of what was happening, filled her with a deep, aching guilt.

Oliver's expression shifted, a flicker of pain crossing his features. He sighed, the sound heavy and full of regret, as if he too was battling his own demons. "I don't have all the answers, Caroline," he admitted, his voice soft but firm, his gaze never leaving hers. "I wish I did. But what I do know is that we can't keep living in limbo like this. It's tearing us apart. We deserve to be happy, don't we?"

Caroline swallowed hard; her chest tight with emotion. His words made sense—more sense than she wanted to admit—but the path ahead was shrouded in uncertainty. Could she really tear apart her marriage for this? Could she trust that what she felt with Oliver was enough to risk everything? "I just don't know if I'm strong enough to do this," she confessed, her voice barely above a whisper, as if saying it aloud would make the truth all too real.

Oliver leaned in, his breath warm against her skin as he pressed his lips to her forehead in a gesture so tender it made her heart ache. His arms wrapped around her, pulling her into the safety of his embrace. "You don't have to do it alone," he murmured into her hair, his voice low and reassuring. "I'll be here. Every step of the way. Whatever happens, we'll face it together."

They stood there, wrapped in each other's arms, the quiet hum of the room filling the space around them. The scent of his cologne mingled with the faint traces of perfume that still lingered on her skin, the sensory memories stirring feelings of both longing and trepidation. In that moment, time seemed to stretch out, the world reduced to just the two of them—two souls caught between desire and duty, love and loyalty.

As they held each other, the sound of their quiet breaths syncing with the rhythm of their hearts, Caroline couldn't help but wonder. Could this really be the beginning of something new? Or was it merely the start of a painful unravelling? The answer lay somewhere ahead, shrouded in the haze of an uncertain future.

Chapter Twenty Eight

As Oliver approached the yacht club, the briny scent of the ocean mingled with the evening breeze, pulling him out of his thoughts, if only for a moment. His mind raced with a mix of guilt and determination. He knew what had to be done, but the weight of it settled heavily in his chest. Caroline didn't deserve this, not after everything they'd been through together. Yet, there was no denying the truth anymore: it wasn't working. He had to end things with her, though the feeling that he was somehow betraying her gnawed at him.

He paused at the entrance, the polished wooden door gleaming under the soft glow of the chandeliers inside. A deep breath didn't calm his nerves, but it steadied his resolve. Pushing the door open, he stepped inside, immediately scanning the room. His eyes landed on Caroline, sitting alone at a table near the window, her face softly illuminated by the fading evening light. She wore the same hopeful expression she always had when she saw him, and it twisted the knife in Oliver's chest just a little deeper.

Her smile widened as he approached, lighting up her face with an innocence that made what he had to do so much harder. "Oliver, darling," she greeted, her voice bright but tinged with something fragile, "I'm so glad you could make it." She reached out to take his hand as he sat down, her touch warm and familiar.

Oliver forced a smile, masking the inner conflict raging within him. "Of course, Caroline," he said smoothly, though his heart wasn't in it. "How could I resist an invitation from such a charming lady?" His words felt hollow, and he hated himself for it.

Caroline's eyes sparkled for a moment, but Oliver caught a glimmer of something else there—something deeper, more vulnerable, as if she sensed the undercurrent of tension beneath his calm demeanour. "I ordered us some drinks," she said softly, gesturing toward the two glasses on the table. "I hope that's alright."

"Of course," he replied, taking the seat across from her. He cleared his throat, trying to find the right words, though none came easily. His hands fidgeted on the table, his mind replaying everything he had rehearsed in front of the mirror that morning. Finally, he spoke. "Caroline, there's something we need to talk about."

Caroline's smile faltered, and her fingers tensed around the glass. She leaned forward slightly, concern clouding her features. "Is everything alright, Oliver? You look a bit pale." Her voice was soft, as if afraid the wrong words might break the fragile balance between them.

Oliver forced a light chuckle, waving off her concern, though inwardly, he felt the weight of her gaze. "I'm fine, Caroline. It's just..." He hesitated, then looked away toward the ocean view behind her. "I think we need to take a step back from this... whatever it is we have."

Caroline's brow furrowed, and her expression shifted from concern to confusion, then quickly to hurt. "What do you mean, Oliver?" she asked, her voice wavering slightly. "I thought everything was going so well between us."

Oliver sighed, running a hand through his hair, his throat tightening. He hated this—hated seeing the pain he was causing her, but there was no turning back. "It's not that I don't enjoy spending time with you, Caroline. I do, but... I'm not sure I'm ready for something serious right now. Especially with everything going on with my health." The words hung in the air, heavy and uncomfortable.

Caroline's eyes widened slightly, tears welling up as the truth sank in. She looked down, her fingers trembling as she clutched the edge of the table. "I understand," she whispered, her voice fragile, barely holding itself together. "I guess... I guess I just got carried away." She blinked rapidly, her eyes glistening. "I'm sorry if I made you uncomfortable, Oliver."

Oliver's heart ached at the sight of her fighting back tears. He reached across the table, taking her hand gently in his. "You didn't make me uncomfortable, Caroline. You've been nothing but wonderful to me, and I care about you. I really do." His voice was earnest, though it couldn't soften the blow of what he had to say next. "But I think it's best if we both take some time. Time to figure things out, for ourselves."

Caroline nodded slowly, wiping at her cheeks with the back of her hand. She tried to smile, but it didn't reach her eyes. "I suppose you're right," she said, her voice trembling. "I just... I'll miss you, Oliver."

His grip tightened on her hand as a pang of regret surged through him. "I'll miss you too," he admitted, his voice low. "But this isn't goodbye forever. Who knows what the future holds?" He gave her a small, sad smile, but the words felt distant, empty even as he said them.

The two of them sat in a heavy silence, the energy between them slowly ebbing away. The yacht club's warm, ambient chatter faded into the background as they each retreated into their own thoughts. Caroline stared blankly out the window, the sky now deepening into dusk.

Neither noticed the figure lurking outside, hidden in the shadows just beyond the patio. David, Caroline's estranged husband, stood rigid, his posture coiled with barely contained rage. His sharp eyes, filled with bitterness, followed every movement inside.

Oliver had been hard to track down, but David had done it. And now, watching them together, seeing the way Oliver held her hand, it was all David could do to stop himself from storming in. His fists clenched at his sides, knuckles white from the force. He had lost Caroline long ago, but that didn't matter. He wasn't going to let anyone else have her. Not without making them pay.

From the shadows, David's eyes narrowed as his mind turned dark with twisted thoughts of revenge.

❖

Chapter Twenty Nine

Deborah was running a small flower shop on East Street, nestled between a bakery and a second-hand bookstore. It was a cosy, sunlit space, filled with the scent of fresh blooms and earth. On most days, she found peace in arranging delicate bouquets and chatting with the regulars who came in for their weekly orders. But today was different. The shop bustled with customers placing last-minute orders for an upcoming event, and one of her assistants had called in sick, leaving Deborah short-handed and overwhelmed. The phone rang incessantly, floral arrangements lay half-finished on the counter, and every surface seemed to be cluttered with vases, ribbons, and tools.

She hadn't had a break since the early morning rush, and as the afternoon dragged on, her legs ached from standing. The knot of tension in her back tightened with each passing hour, and her fingers were stiff from tying bows and trimming stems. Sweat formed at her temples, and though she tried to remain calm, her exhaustion was apparent in every hurried movement. She felt frazzled, juggling too many tasks at once, and the stress was starting to show.

The gentle chime of the bell above the door signalled another customer. Deborah looked up from her work, her heart sinking at the thought of yet another order to fill. But her breath caught when she saw who had entered. The man was striking—tall, with hair that curled just above his collar, dressed smartly in a tailored coat. His sharp features and confident stride made him stand out from the usual crowd of regulars.

Mortification hit her instantly. Of all days for a man like *him* to walk in! She looked down at herself and cringed. Her long, light brown hair, normally tied back neatly, had escaped its bun, falling messily around her face. Dirt smudged her apron, and her hands were dusted with pollen and bits of greenery. She raised a hand, attempting to smooth her dishevelled hair, but only succeeded in making it worse. Her cheeks flushed as she realised how bedraggled she must look to someone like him.

The handsome stranger walked further into the shop, his eyes scanning the displays of vibrant roses, lilies, and tulips. He moved with a casual ease, occasionally glancing her way as if taking in the whole scene.

Before she could compose herself, she made a quick decision to escape into the back of the shop. She fled to the cramped staff room, leaving her assistant Sally standing at the counter with wide eyes. The room was barely big enough for one person, crammed with boxes of supplies, an old mop leaning against the wall, and a small, crooked mirror hanging by the door. Deborah's reflection stared back at her, the image of a tired, overworked woman in desperate need of a break.

She grabbed a comb from the shelf and ran it through her tangled hair, wincing as she hit a snag. Her apron was wrinkled, but she did her best to smooth it out, wiping away the worst of the dirt with the back of her hand. A quick dab of powder to her shiny nose was all she could manage, her fingers trembling slightly as she tried to pull herself together. With one last glance in the mirror, she took a deep breath. Not perfect, but it would have to do. *Forty-something,* she thought to herself, with a wry smile. *Not bad for a forty-something woman.*

Steeling herself for whatever the handsome stranger might need, Deborah pushed open the door and stepped back into the shop. The scent of flowers hit her first, sweet and earthy, mixed with the distant hum of conversation. The shop felt alive again, buzzing with customers, but her attention was solely on Oliver. Despite the chaos, she was determined to make a good impression, even if the day hadn't gone as smoothly as she'd hoped.

Chapter Thirty

When Deborah returned to the front of the shop, she looked around, hoping to spot the stranger who had captured her attention. But to her disappointment, he was nowhere in sight. Her brows furrowed in mild confusion as she scanned the room, still half-expecting to see him tucked away in a corner or lingering near the entrance. He seemed to have disappeared as suddenly as he had arrived.

"Where did he go?" Deborah asked Sally, the shop's assistant, her voice tinged with curiosity and a little disappointment. Sally, still looking somewhat flustered from the interaction, glanced up from the counter where she was rearranging the till.

"Oh, he bought a big bunch of flowers—roses, I think—and left just a minute ago," Sally replied, shaking her head slightly as if she was trying to make sense of the abrupt encounter herself.

Deborah sighed softly, turning back toward her workstation, her thoughts drifting as she absently straightened a vase. Her pulse, which had quickened at the sight of the man, now returned to its usual, steady rhythm. She hadn't expected much from the brief interaction, but there had been something about him—a quiet, intriguing aura—that had sparked a flicker of hope in her. It wasn't often someone caught her attention like that anymore.

Ever since her divorce, Deborah had thrown herself into running the shop. The floral business had become her lifeline, filling her days with activity and routine. But lately, there was a gnawing sense of something missing. She hadn't been on a date in some time, and while she wasn't actively searching for love, the idea of meeting someone new occasionally tugged at her mind. There was a void that the shop couldn't fill—an ache for companionship, for the warmth of being desired, even if just for a fleeting moment.

As she picked up a half-finished bouquet for a regular customer, Deborah allowed herself to daydream. She imagined what it might be like to dress up for an evening out, her hair done, her lipstick carefully applied things she hadn't bothered with in far too long. Maybe she'd go somewhere with soft lighting, where the atmosphere hummed with quiet conversations and laughter. A place where she could feel like a woman again, not just the hardworking florist everyone relied on. The stranger, with his alluring eyes and easy smile, had reminded her of that yearning.

She wasn't searching for a new husband or anything serious, just something light—a few dates, some fun, a spark of attraction. It had been so long since she'd experienced the thrill of being pursued, of feeling that rush of anticipation before seeing someone again. Her last relationship had left her wary, guarded, but surely there was room for a little excitement in her life.

Still, the thought of putting herself out there again felt both exciting and terrifying. What if she had forgotten how to flirt, how to navigate those early stages of romance? Would she even know what to say if the opportunity arose? As much as she longed for connection, the fear of rejection—or worse, indifference—loomed large.

But as she finished arranging the bouquet, tying it neatly with a ribbon, Deborah smiled to herself. Perhaps today's fleeting encounter with the handsome stranger was a sign—a small reminder that life could still surprise her. Even if nothing came of it, the mere possibility had stirred something inside her. For the first time in a long while, she felt the faintest glimmer of hope.

Chapter Thirty One

Over the next few days, Deborah kept one eye on the front door of her flower shop, hoping to see the mysterious stranger again. She imagined his confident stride as he walked in, perhaps purchasing a bouquet of daisies or sunflowers, maybe even sparking up a conversation that would lead to something more. But each day ended the same: no sign of him. To distract herself from the lingering anticipation, Deborah threw herself into her work. She spent hours arranging roses, lilies, and hydrangeas with meticulous care, ensuring every petal was perfectly placed. The rhythmic tasks of trimming stems and misting the delicate flowers soothed her restless mind.

Outside the shop, she kept busy too. She met up with friends for coffee at the quaint café down the street, often bringing along a fresh bouquet as a gift. Her friends listened with interest when she recounted the brief yet intriguing encounter, their eyes lighting up with curiosity. They offered words of support, knowing she had been through a rough divorce the previous year, and encouraged her to stay open to new possibilities. "Maybe he's just waiting for the right moment," one of her friends said with a wink. "Or maybe he's shy," another chimed in.

Despite their words, the emptiness lingered in her heart, but Deborah pushed it aside. Life had taught her to find solace in the small things—the beauty in a perfectly arranged bouquet, the warmth of a good conversation with friends, and the quiet moments spent alone in her small two-bedroom house near the railway station.

One chilly evening, as the sun dipped below the horizon and the streetlights began to glow, Deborah locked up her shop and walked home through the crisp autumn air. Her footsteps crunched against the fallen leaves scattered across the pavement. By the time she reached her front door, the sky had turned a soft shade of violet, and the air was thick with the scent of woodsmoke from nearby chimneys.

Benson, her tabby cat, greeted her with a soft meow, weaving through her legs as she stepped inside. "Well, at least I have you to come home to," Deborah murmured, smiling as she bent down to scratch behind his ears. She shrugged off her coat, kicked off her shoes, and padded into the living room. The house was quiet, but it felt like a sanctuary—familiar and safe.

After a quick change into a pair of warm slippers, Deborah headed into the kitchen, where Benson was already circling her feet impatiently, his tail flicking with anticipation. "Alright, alright," she laughed, opening a can of his favourite tuna-flavoured cat food. As he ate, she set about making her own dinner: a simple but satisfying pasta dish with fresh vegetables and a spicy chili tomato sauce. The comforting aromas of garlic and basil soon filled the kitchen, warming the chilly air.

Once she'd finished her meal, Deborah washed the dishes with a sense of calm, the hot water running over her hands as she thought back on the day. No stranger. No grand moment of serendipity. But she told herself that was okay. Life had a way of unfolding in its own time.

With the dishes done, she poured herself a glass of crisp white wine and made her way to the front room, where her favourite armchair awaited. Sinking into its plush cushions, she switched on the TV, intending to catch up on the evening news. But after a few minutes, the grim headlines and bleak stories were too much, and she turned it off. Instead, she decided to treat herself to a bit of self-care.

Heading to the bathroom, she turned on the taps and began running a hot bath. As the water filled the tub, she lit a lavender-scented candle and placed it on the windowsill, its soft glow casting a warm, flickering light around the room. She dimmed the overhead lights and let the steam rise around her, creating a peaceful atmosphere.

Once the bath was ready, Deborah sank into the hot water, letting out a long sigh as the heat worked its way into her muscles, easing away the tension she'd been carrying all day. She closed her eyes, letting her mind drift as the lavender scent filled the room. In this moment, the world outside faded away, and for a while, it was just her, the warmth of the water, and the soft crackle of the candle's flame.

After a long soak, Deborah stepped out of the bath feeling lighter, both in body and spirit. She wrapped herself in a plush towel and dried off, then changed into her softest pyjamas, the fabric warm against her skin. Crawling into bed, she picked up the novel she'd been reading—a romance that swept her away into a world of possibility and second chances. Benson curled up at her feet, his purring like a soft lullaby, and for the first time in what felt like ages, Deborah felt truly content.

As she drifted toward sleep, her thoughts turned briefly to the stranger. Would she ever see him again? She didn't know, but for now, it didn't matter. Life was good, and that was enough.

Chapter Thirty Two

Over the next few weeks, Deborah continued her daily routine, working diligently at her quaint flower shop, tending to customers and managing inventory. Each day felt familiar, almost too predictable, but she found comfort in it. Her customers often commented on the warm, inviting atmosphere she cultivated in her shop, filled with curated pieces of handmade garden tools, hand tied flowers and the occasional large clay flowerpots. She always greeted them with a gentle smile, and despite the slight monotony, there was satisfaction in seeing the regulars who brought life to her little space.

Each evening, she returned home where Benson, her affectionate, tabby cat, waited for her at the door, tail flicking lazily. Benson had become her steadfast companion, providing a quiet solace in moments when the silence felt a little too heavy. After feeding him and preparing a simple dinner for herself, Deborah would often settle down with a book or listen to soft music, winding down from the day. Occasionally, she went out with her friends— usually Carol and a few others—sharing laughs and memories over coffee or dinner, trying to move on with her life as it was. She wasn't unhappy—far from it—but there was an undeniable sense that there had to be more to life. The days blurred together, and despite her contentment, Deborah couldn't shake the feeling that something vital was missing.

One sunny afternoon, as the golden light streamed through the shop's large windows, she was arranging a new display of fresh cut flowers. The chime above the door rang, and in walked Carol, bringing a burst of energy that jolted Deborah out of her introspection. Carol, always the social butterfly, with her bright smile and effortlessly chic style, bounced in with an air of excitement.

"Guess what?!" Carol exclaimed, her eyes sparkling. "The yacht club is hosting an event this weekend, and it's going to be fabulous! Spanish theme—think tapas, sangria, live flamenco music, the works! I can bring a guest, and you, my dear, are coming with me." Her words tumbled out in a rush of enthusiasm.

Deborah hesitated for a moment, but then the idea of breaking out of her usual routine started to appeal to her. It had been a while since she'd had a proper night out, dancing and meeting new people. The thought of being immersed in the lively atmosphere Carol described felt like a breath of fresh air. She could almost hear the rhythmic claps of flamenco and taste the rich flavours of Spanish cuisine. With a smile, Deborah nodded. "I could use a night like that," she admitted, a flicker of excitement stirring inside her.

As the week passed, the upcoming event loomed in her mind, giving her something to look forward to. The monotony of her days seemed to lift, and she found herself daydreaming of swirling dresses, clicking heels, and vibrant music. The idea of mingling with new people, of dancing and laughing without a care in the world, felt like something she had been missing without even realising it.

Finally, the day of the event arrived. After a long day at the shop, Deborah returned home, greeted as always by Benson, who wove between her legs, meowing for dinner. She fed him, then decided to indulge herself in some much-needed self-care. She took a long, relaxing bath, letting the warmth of the water ease the tension that had built up in her muscles over the week. She closed her eyes, inhaling the soft scent of lavender from the bath salts, feeling the worries of the day melt away.

Afterward, with a glass of wine in hand, she stood in front of her closet, contemplating what to wear. Just then, her phone buzzed

Carol, of course, full of excitement. "What are you going to wear tonight?!" she asked, her voice bubbling through the phone.

They laughed and chatted like two teenagers getting ready for prom, discussing outfits, makeup, and hairstyles. Deborah finally settled on a flowing red dress that hugged her in all the right places, perfect for the evening's Spanish theme. It was bold, a bit outside of her usual comfort zone, but it made her feel confident, ready to embrace the night ahead.

❦

Chapter Thirty Three

Oliver heard the lively music as he walked into the yacht club's members' bar. He had spent the day in London visiting his consultant for a monthly check-up following his heart attack, and now he felt the need for a drink before heading home. The bar was abuzz with energy, a stark contrast to the sterile calm of the doctor's office. Conversations overlapped, glasses clinked, and bursts of laughter punctuated the steady hum of voices. The smell of freshly polished wood and a hint of citrus cleaner mixed with the subtle aroma of cologne and perfume, adding to the club's upscale atmosphere.

His consultant was pleased with his progress but had cautioned him about his lifestyle. "You can have a drink or two," the doctor had said, "but don't overdo it." With those words in mind, Oliver approached the bar and ordered a large glass of Chardonnay. He could already imagine the cool, crisp taste of the wine, a small indulgence after the long day. "Doctor's orders," he said to Aimee, the bar steward, who gave him a puzzled look as she handed him his drink. She had started working there only recently and was still getting to know the regulars. Clearly, she didn't know what he was on about, but she smiled politely, nonetheless, her blonde hair catching the dim light as she moved away to serve another customer.

"It's a bit lively tonight," he remarked to one of the regulars propping up the bar. The man, Jack, an older gentleman with silver hair and a deep tan, looked up from his pint and nodded. He had the air of someone who had spent much of his life by the sea.

"Yeah, it's a club night. Spanish theme, I think," Jack replied, glancing toward the source of the music. "They've brought in a band for it."

Curious, Oliver took his glass and walked over to the doorway that led into the main room. He popped his head in just as the music swelled again, the sharp, percussive strums of a flamenco guitar accompanied by the tapping of castanets. The dance floor was quickly filling up with dancers, their movements synchronized to the rhythmic beats of flamenco and salsa. Couples twirled and dipped, their colourful dresses spinning with the music. Some wore red and black, traditional collars of Spanish dance, while others were simply dressed for a night of fun. The vibrant decor, with its red and yellow streamers, lanterns, and garlands of fake flowers, added to the festive atmosphere, making the room feel like a slice of Spain. The warm glow of the lanterns contrasted with the blue twilight just visible through the large windows overlooking the marina.

Taking a sip of his wine, Oliver allowed himself to relax. The consultant's words echoed in his mind, a gentle reminder of his mortality and the need for balance. His hand unconsciously brushed against his chest, the faintest reminder from his heart attack, a silent testament to his close brush with death. He gazed out over the lively scene, the carefree joy of the dancers seemingly a world away from the worries that had weighed on him earlier.

The music shifted tempo, the flamenco giving way to a sultry salsa, and the room buzzed with excitement as more people joined in. A group of women nearby raised their glasses in a toast, laughing, while a couple by the window shared a quiet conversation, their hands intertwined.

He turned back to the bar, where Jack was still nursing his pint. The bar's energy was infectious, the music and laughter mingling in the air. Oliver smiled to himself, feeling a sense of belonging here, among friends and familiar faces. This was his community, and even with the ups and downs of life, nights like these reminded him that there was still so much to enjoy.

As the evening wore on, Oliver found himself lingering, savouring not just the wine but the lively atmosphere. The club was alive with possibility, and for the first time in a while, he felt content.

Chapter Thirty Four

Oliver drained his glass, the clink of it touching the marble bar echoing faintly in the dimly lit lounge. He glanced at the bar steward, offering a small nod. "Goodnight," he said, his voice steady yet tinged with weariness from the long day, as he pushed himself up from the barstool. The evening was winding down, and the faint hum of conversation mixed with the soft strains of music playing overhead. He adjusted his jacket, slipping his phone into his hand as he turned towards the exit, the cool air from the open door beckoning him outside.

Just as he reached for the door handle, his phone buzzed in his palm, the vibrations jarring him out of his thoughts. He paused, curiosity getting the better of him, and glanced down at the screen. Without realising it, he stepped forward at the same moment someone was exiting the lounge. They collided with an awkward thud, and Oliver's phone slipped from his grip, flying before clattering to the floor.

"I am so sorry," he immediately apologised, bending down to retrieve the phone, which was still buzzing insistently on the polished wood floor. His voice was filled with genuine concern as he reached for it. "I wasn't looking where I was going. These damn things will be the death of me," he added with a rueful smile, straightening up as he finally looked at the person he had nearly knocked over.

The woman, a petite figure with a soft, kind face, let out a light laugh. "It's okay," she said, her tone forgiving as she brushed off the moment. "We're all guilty of looking at our phones these days. I'm just as bad," she added, her voice a little softer now. Her eyes flicked up to meet his, and then something shifted in her expression.

Recognition dawned on her features, and she suddenly seemed a bit flustered. She glanced down at her feet, tucking a loose strand of hair behind her ear with a nervous gesture.

Oliver's phone buzzed again in his hand, reminding him of the message still waiting. She noticed it too and tilted her head slightly. "Shouldn't you get that?" she asked, her voice carrying a hint of curiosity.

He looked down at the phone, then back at her. "No, it's fine," he said, pressing the red button to silence the notification. "I'll call back later." His gaze lingered on her for a moment before he continued, "I don't think I've seen you here before."

The woman smiled, her nerves seeming to settle a bit. "I'm here with a member of the club—Carol. She invited me for the club night," she explained, gesturing vaguely towards the bustling lounge behind her, where members were mingling and enjoying the ambience.

"And how's the night going? The music sounds wonderful," Oliver said, his tone warm and inviting, as if easing into the rhythm of the conversation.

She nodded, her smile widening. "Yes, it's been great. The music is really good, and the crowd is lively," she agreed, glancing over her shoulder towards the dance floor where the sound of laughter and music blended together.

They exchanged pleasantries for a few moments, the conversation flowing easily despite the brief awkward start. There was something comfortable in the way they spoke, as though they were old acquaintances rather than two people who had just met. Just as the conversation was hitting its stride, a familiar voice cut through the music. Carol, Deborah's friend, swooped in with a playful sway to her step, her cheeks flushed from dancing.

"Debs!" Carol called out, her excitement bubbling over as she reached for her friend's arm. "You must come back in! This is my favourite song, and I need to dance!" she exclaimed, pulling her towards the crowded dance floor.

Deborah shot Oliver an apologetic smile, though there was a hint of something more in her eyes. "Well, it was nice bumping into you," she said with a soft laugh.

Oliver returned the smile, a quiet warmth in his expression. "It would be nice if we could bump into each other again," he said, his words laced with a quiet hope.

Before Deborah could reply, Carol whisked her away, her laughter mixing with the music as they disappeared into the crowd. Oliver stood there for a moment, his gaze lingering on the spot where they'd been. He slipped his phone back into his pocket and turned towards the door once more. "I hope so too," he murmured to himself, stepping out into the cool night air.

Chapter Thirty Five

Monday morning arrived all too quickly for Deborah, who was still basking in the afterglow of a fabulous weekend. The excitement of the previous days seemed to evaporate as she faced the familiar reality of her daily routine. The grey sky mirrored her reluctance, heavy clouds looming as the rain began to pour, drenching the streets and transforming the world outside her window into a dreary spectacle. The rhythmic sound of rain against the glass only deepened her reluctance to leave the warm sanctuary of her home. However, Deborah knew the day couldn't wait. Sighing, she grabbed her umbrella and headed out early, aware that she needed to place the weekly order for her flower shop before the busyness of the day swept her away.

The streets were slick and glistening, reflecting the muted lights of storefronts that had only just begun to open. The air was damp and cool, the kind of weather that often kept people indoors. Yet, as Deborah walked, the rhythmic patter of raindrops against her umbrella provided an unexpected sense of calm. It was as if, despite the grey surroundings, she had found a small pocket of peace amidst the chaos of the world. She embraced the moment, appreciating the quiet before her hectic schedule began.

The week ahead promised to be a busy one, and Monday wasted no time proving it. As soon as Deborah arrived at the flower shop, the familiar bell above the door chimed repeatedly, signaling a steady stream of customers. The shop was bustling with activity as people came in to place orders for all sorts of occasions. A wedding was coming up that weekend, a 60th anniversary celebration needed an elaborate display, and there were multiple birthday arrangements to prepare. The flurry of orders and the constant hum of conversation kept her hands busy and her mind focused. Yet, despite the whirlwind of activity, Deborah found herself distracted by thoughts of one person Oliver, the tall, handsome man who had made quite an impression on her over the weekend.

Her mind drifted back to that Saturday, a stark contrast to the grey, rain-soaked Monday. The shop had been just as busy then, with the doorbell chiming incessantly as customers came and went. Among the crowd, Oliver had entered, immediately catching her eye. Deborah remembered the moment clearly—he had lingered near the doorway, scanning the vibrant displays of flowers, while she attended to an elderly woman searching for the perfect gift for her niece's 18th birthday. Deborah had taken her time with the woman, helping her select a delicate arrangement of pastel roses, all while feeling Oliver's presence in the background.

Once the shop had finally emptied, Oliver had approached the counter. "I thought they would never leave," he had said with a teasing smile, a trace of nervousness in his voice. Deborah had laughed, the sound easing the tension between them.

"It has been a busy day," she had replied. "But it's nice to see you again."

Without hesitation, Oliver had asked if she would join him for a drink later. Her heart had skipped a beat, and she had accepted with a smile. The rest of the day had been filled with anticipation, leading to what had become an unforgettable weekend.

Chapter Thirty Six

Deborah arrived at the yacht club just before 6 o'clock, her heart beating with a mix of excitement and nerves. The late afternoon air carried the faint scent of saltwater and fresh blooms from nearby gardens. As she made her way to the balcony, she spotted Oliver standing near a small table, where a bottle of Champagne sat chilling in an ice bucket. His casual yet elegant stance against the backdrop of the glowing horizon made her smile.

The sun was low, casting a soft golden light that danced on the surface of the water. The tide was high, and the gentle waves lapped rhythmically against the docks, creating a soothing melody. Sailboats bobbed lightly in the distance, their sails fluttering like white butterflies in the fading light. Deborah could already tell it was going to be a perfect evening.

"Hi, you look fantastic. I love your outfit," Oliver said warmly as he saw her approaching. His eyes sparkled, clearly pleased with what he saw. Deborah had chosen a flowing summer dress that moved with the breeze, a blend of soft blues and greens that mirrored the colours of the sea.

"I took the liberty of ordering us some champagne. I hope you don't mind," he added with a smile, gesturing to the bottle.

"No, it's perfect," Deborah replied, her heart lifting as she leaned in to give him a quick peck on the cheek. His skin was warm, and his presence immediately put her at ease.

They settled into their seats, the corner table offering a perfect view of the river. Deborah gazed out at the horizon, mesmerised by the serene beauty before her. The sun dipped lower, its golden rays slowly turning to shades of amber and pink. The light breeze carried with it the faint sounds of distant laughter and clinking glasses from other boats docked nearby, blending harmoniously with the soft murmur of the water.

"It's so beautiful here," Deborah said, her voice full of wonder. She glanced at Oliver, whose relaxed expression mirrored her contentment. He poured the champagne, and they clinked glasses, the soft bubbles of the drink perfectly matching the lightness in the air.

They talked easily, their conversation flowing as smoothly as the champagne. Oliver recounted stories of his travels and adventures, each tale revealing more layers of his charm and worldliness. Deborah found herself captivated by his wit and warmth, laughing at his anecdotes and sharing a few of her own. Their laughter mixed with the gentle lapping of the water, adding to the magic of the evening.

As the sun finally sank below the horizon, the temperature began to drop, and a light chill crept into the air. Without hesitation, Oliver stood up, removing his jacket and draping it over Deborah's shoulders. The gesture, simple yet thoughtful, filled her with a warmth she hadn't felt in a long time.

"Why, thank you. You're such a gentleman," she said, smiling up at him. His arm settled around her shoulders as they began the short walk back to her home, their steps in sync. The streets were quiet, lit by the soft glow of streetlamps, and the distant sound of the river still lingered in the background.

Deborah's mind raced as they walked. She couldn't help but wonder about the unspoken expectations. Should she invite him in? Was it too soon? The questions swirled, but just as quickly, they dissolved when Oliver spoke.

"I had a lovely time tonight," he said, his voice sincere as they reached her doorstep. He leaned in, kissing her gently on the cheek, the warmth of his touch lingering. "I hope to see you again soon. Good night."

Relief and gratitude washed over Deborah. His respectful parting reassured her, easing any doubts she had. "Thank you, Oliver. Good night," she replied, her heart lighter as she watched him walk away into the night.

Once inside, Deborah closed the door behind her and quickly made her way to the living room. She grabbed her phone, eager to share the details of the night with Carol, who had demanded a full report no matter how late it was. She pressed the green button, her excitement bubbling over as soon as Carol picked up.

"Tell me everything!" Carol's voice crackled with curiosity on the other end.

Deborah grinned, sparing no detail as she recounted the entire evening—Oliver's charm, the stunning sunset, the champagne, and their effortless conversation. Carol listened intently, gasping and laughing at all the right moments.

"Oh my gosh, that sounds amazing! When's the next date?" Carol asked, her excitement matching Deborah's.

"I don't know, but I hope it's soon. He's such a fantastic man, and there's so much more I want to learn about him.

"You lucky girl! You deserve this. It sounds like the start of something really special."

Deborah smiled, feeling a warmth spread through her. "I really hope so."

After they said their goodnights, Deborah hung up and sat back, letting the calm of the evening wash over her. She couldn't stop thinking about Oliver and the promise of what might come. Her heart fluttered with anticipation as she reflected on the night, a contented smile playing on her lips.

⁕

Chapter Thirty Seven

The sunlight streamed through Deborah's bedroom window early the next morning, casting a soft, golden glow across the room. The warmth of the sun blended with the cosiness of her bed, offering a serene start to the day. After a long, heartfelt late-night chat with her good friend Carol, Deborah woke feeling as though a significant weight had been lifted from her shoulders.

She padded softly into the kitchen, where she made herself a light breakfast of cereal, orange juice, and coffee. As she sat at her small, sun-dappled kitchen table, she reflected on the day ahead. Her shop awaited, as did a myriad of tasks and customer demands. Yet, despite the busy day looming, Deborah felt calmer than she had in weeks, buoyed by the thought of the approaching getaway. As if reading her mind, her phone buzzed with a message from Carol. The message was thoughtful, asking how Deborah felt about their conversation and hoping she had made the right decision. Carol signed off with a friendly reminder to keep her updated, ending the message with a cheerful "kiss kiss."

Deborah smiled at her phone before typing out a reply. She assured Carol she was feeling positive about her choice and thanked her for being such a steadfast friend. Deborah promised to keep her in the loop as the weekend approached. After finishing her breakfast, she moved on with her morning routine, taking a quick shower before getting dressed and heading out the door, ready to embrace the challenges of her day at the shop.

The week that followed was a rollercoaster of emotions and energy. The weather seemed to mirror her mood, as the skies remained mostly dull and rainy, casting a dreary shadow over her daily commute. The persistent drizzle dampened her spirits, and at times, made the excitement for her weekend getaway with Oliver feel distant and uncertain. She found herself staring out of the shop window at the rain, wondering if the weather would improve in time for their trip.

By mid-week, however, a spark of hope rekindled her enthusiasm. She met Oliver for coffee at a busy café near her shop, where his infectious excitement about their first weekend away together lifted her mood. He spoke eagerly about the plans they'd made, and Deborah couldn't help but get caught up in his energy. It had been so long since she'd allowed herself the luxury of a break, to relax and unwind away from the pressures of work and everyday life. Over steaming cups of coffee, they laughed and shared stories, and Deborah's excitement for the weekend started to grow.

As the weekend neared, Deborah focused on preparing for her absence. She meticulously planned out the details for her shop and ensured everything would run smoothly in her absence. Sally, one of her most reliable shop assistants, had agreed to check in on Benson, Deborah's beloved and somewhat spoiled cat. She gave Sally a spare key and ran through Benson's daily routine, including his feeding schedule and preferred playtime activities, making sure her pet would be well taken care of while she was away.

Saturday morning arrived faster than expected, and Deborah woke up early, the soft hum of excitement now replaced with a flurry of nervous energy. She stared at her open suitcase, contemplating what to pack. Practicality warred with indecision, and in the end, she chose to pack nearly everything from her wardrobe, just to be safe. She didn't want to leave anything to chance, especially since she wasn't quite sure what the weather would be like. Just as she was about to zip up her suitcase, she called Carol for some last-minute packing advice. They laughed about her overpacking tendencies, and by the end of the call, Deborah felt more reassured.

As she hung up the phone, Deborah promised Carol she would share every detail of the weekend getaway once she returned. With her suitcase finally packed, the shop arrangements made, and Benson's care sorted, Deborah found herself standing in her living room, taking a deep breath. A mix of excitement and nervousness swirled within her, but she was ready. The much-anticipated trip with Oliver was just hours away, and Deborah allowed herself to feel the thrill of what was to come. The promise of adventure, relaxation, and maybe even a deepening connection with Oliver awaited.

Chapter Thirty Eight

Deborah's date with Oliver was both intriguing and unforgettable, a blend of opulence and intimacy that left a lasting impression. Oliver had invited her to his luxurious penthouse, a space that seemed to mirror his sophisticated taste. From the moment they stepped inside, Deborah was captivated by the sweeping panoramic view of the town, made even more striking by the floor-to-ceiling windows that framed it. The city lights twinkled like stars, creating a mesmerising backdrop. The ambience was just as carefully curated, with soft jazz tunes floating in the air and the warm, flickering glow of candlelight casting a soft, romantic light across the room.

Oliver had spared no effort in making the evening special. He had taken to the kitchen himself, preparing a meal that was as extravagant as it was delicious. The centrepiece was a freshly prepared lobster, bathed in a rich, creamy saffron sauce that complemented its sweetness perfectly. Alongside this indulgent dish, he served tender broccoli stems, and a silky mash made from a blend of potato and celeriac, each bite melting in her mouth. The enticing aroma filled the room, and Deborah could feel her mouth watering even before she tasted the first forkful. As they ate, she couldn't help but admire his culinary talent; Oliver was not only a gracious host but also an excellent cook, seamlessly combining his skills with engaging conversation and sharp wit. His effortless charm made her laugh, and the evening felt like it was out of a dream.

Yet, despite the romantic setting and her growing attraction to Oliver, Deborah found herself holding back. The scars of past heartbreaks had made her cautious, and though the chemistry between them was undeniable, she hesitated to let her guard down completely. There was a palpable tension within her, an inner struggle between her desire to be vulnerable and her instinct to protect herself. The temptation to succumb to the moment was strong, especially as the evening unfolded so beautifully, but she couldn't bring herself to fully embrace it. Still, they shared a magical time, their connection deepening through laughter and heartfelt conversation.

As the night ended, Deborah decided it was time to leave. Ever the gentleman, Oliver insisted on calling her a taxi, ensuring her safe passage home. Sitting in the back of the cab, Deborah couldn't help but reflect on the evening. They had parted on warm, friendly terms, yet she couldn't shake the nagging fear that her reluctance might eventually drive Oliver away. She knew she needed to open more, to allow their relationship to develop naturally, but taking that next step felt daunting.

The next morning, Oliver sent her a message with an enticing proposal: a weekend getaway on his yacht, cruising the serene waters of Poole. He described it vividly, painting a picture of romantic sunsets and tranquil days. It was a tempting offer, one that promised even more intimate time together, but Deborah hesitated. She asked for time to think it over, promising to give him her decision by Monday.

As the weekend passed, Deborah wrestled with her conflicting emotions. The idea of spending a weekend with Oliver thrilled her, but it also made her anxious. Could she really let go of her fears and embrace this new chapter with him?

Chapter Thirty Nine

Carol arrived at Deborah's early Sunday afternoon; a bottle of Chardonnay tucked under her arm. She had been invited for lunch, but the real purpose of her visit was to lend an ear and offer advice about Oliver. Deborah had been dating him for only a few months, and now he had invited her away for a weekend on his yacht. It sounded like the dream scenario, but Deborah needed reassurance. Their relationship was still in its early, fragile stages, and the idea of going away together felt overwhelming to her.

When Deborah opened the door, she looked as elegant as ever in a white silk blouse, tailored black slacks, and matching black pumps. Her composure and style belied the nervousness she had confided over the phone. After a quick embrace and a kiss on the cheek, Carol smiled warmly. "Hi, lovely. It's so good to see you! Now, spill the details—I'm dying to know everything," she said playfully, not even waiting to step inside.

Deborah chuckled and led her friend through the house. "Come on, let's sit outside in the garden," she suggested, her voice trying to mask the tension she felt. Carol followed her through the small living room and out onto the patio, where the afternoon sun bathed the garden in golden light. Deborah's backyard was a sanctuary, brimming with flowers, herbs, and potted plants. The fragrant scent of jasmine and lavender floated through the air, a contrast to the whirlwind of emotions Deborah was battling. Carol always admired Deborah's green thumb—she could make anything flourish, while Carol's plants barely lasted a season.

Deborah soon returned with a tray of food—an assortment of cheese, fruits, and artisanal bread. The display looked effortlessly elegant, much like Deborah herself. Carol poured them each a glass of Chardonnay as Deborah arranged the spread on the table between them.

"So, what's going on?" Carol asked, her curiosity piqued. "I mean, come on—if a handsome, wealthy guy invited me away for a weekend on his yacht, I'd be floating on cloud nine. What's the problem?"

Deborah sighed deeply, her shoulders sagging as she sat beside Carol on the bench. "You know me," she began, her voice a little shaky. "I'm just… I don't know. It's been a long time since I've, you know, gotten close to someone." Her hands fidgeted in her lap, and her eyes filled with unshed tears.

Carol immediately reached out, resting her hand on Deborah's. "I know the divorce was tough, but you've got to stop holding yourself back. You're a gorgeous woman in the prime of your life, and you deserve this. Unlike me," she added with a self-deprecating laugh, "you've got plenty of time to enjoy it. So, what's stopping you?"

Deborah smiled faintly through her tears, grateful for her friend's candour. "It just feels… too soon. What if I'm making a mistake? What if I'm not ready for this, and it all goes wrong?" Her voice grew quieter with each sentence.

Carol gave her a reassuring squeeze. "Deb, there's no perfect moment to take a risk. You've got to jump in, even if it's scary. Oliver sounds like a great guy, and clearly, he cares about you. So, what if it doesn't work out? You're strong. You'll survive."

Deborah nodded slowly, absorbing Carol's words. "You're right," she said, taking a deep breath. "I can't keep letting fear control me. I'll never know unless I try."

"That's the spirit!" Carol raised her glass in a celebratory toast. "Here's to taking chances!"

"To taking chances," Deborah echoed, clinking her glass against Carol's. They sipped their wine, the taste of optimism and courage lingering longer than the Chardonnay itself.

Chapter Forty

Deborah was excited. She had a date with Oliver on his yacht. It was something she had been looking forward to for weeks. Oliver had promised her that he would take her out when the conditions were just right and today was that perfect day. The plan was to sail along the coast, heading towards Poole's famous Sandbanks, a place that held the reputation of being one of the most expensive and exclusive residential areas in the world. Known for its opulent homes and celebrity residents, it was a place Deborah had only ever heard of and dreamed of seeing up close. And now, thanks to Oliver, that dream was about to become a reality.

They had agreed to meet early on Saturday morning at the yacht club. Not one to leave anything to chance, Deborah had spent the previous evening meticulously packing for the trip. "Pack light," Oliver had told her, but what did that even mean for a day on a luxury yacht? Three suitcases and a holdall seemed reasonable, she reasoned, especially when you had no idea what the day might bring. After all, there were so many possibilities to consider: a sunbathing session on the deck, a light swim, a sunset dinner, and who knew what else! She smiled at her reflection in the mirror, feeling a surge of anticipation. She was prepared for every scenario.

Arriving at the yacht club, Deborah was greeted by the sight of a tranquil marina bathed in the soft, golden hues of sunrise. The water shimmered gently, and the rhythmic sound of the waves brushing against the docks filled the air with a calming melody. Oliver was already at the dock, standing tall and busy with the final touches on the yacht. He looked up, catching sight of her, and his face instantly lit up.

"Good morning, Deborah!" he called out with a grin, his voice filled with genuine excitement. "Are you ready for an unforgettable weekend?"

Deborah returned the smile, a flutter of excitement rising in her chest. "Absolutely!" she replied, her eyes sparkling. "I can't wait to see Sandbanks from the water. This is going to be amazing."

Oliver stepped forward and took her bags, chuckling softly when he saw the number of them. "I see you packed light," he teased, his tone playful but warm.

She laughed, a little self-conscious. "I like to be prepared for anything."

He shook his head, still smiling. "Don't worry. The yacht can handle it. Let me stow these away for you."

As Oliver disappeared below deck to put away her luggage, Deborah took a moment to admire the yacht. It was breathtaking. The sleek lines of the boat, the polished wood gleaming in the morning light, and the sheer elegance of its design were enough to take her breath away. This wasn't just a boat; it was a floating palace. The sun deck was perfect for lounging, the cabin below spacious and luxurious, with every amenity imaginable. Deborah could already imagine the memories they would make on this trip.

Once everything was in place, they set off. The yacht glided smoothly through the water, leaving the marina behind as the world opened before them. Deborah stood at the bow, her hair catching in the gentle breeze, her heart swelling with excitement. The early morning light danced on the surface of the water, and for the first time in a long while, Deborah felt a pure sense of freedom. The kind that comes with new experiences and uncharted adventures.

Oliver joined her at the bow, standing close but not too close, as if sensing her need to soak in the moment. "I thought you'd like this," he said quietly, his voice low against the wind. "It's one of my favourite routes."

"It's perfect," she murmured, turning her head to meet his gaze. "I had no idea it would feel this incredible."

The hours passed in a blissful blur. They sailed along the coastline, passing through quaint coastal towns and lush, rugged landscapes. Every so often, Oliver would point out landmarks or tell her fascinating stories about the area's history and culture. Deborah found herself enthralled, not just by the beauty of the surroundings, but by Oliver himself. There was something about his passion for sailing and his deep knowledge of the coast that made him even more attractive. She hadn't expected that.

When they finally approached Sandbanks, Deborah's breath caught in her throat. The sprawling mansions, each more extravagant than the last, lined the coast like something out of a movie. Their perfectly manicured lawns and private docks spoke of a level of wealth she could barely comprehend.

"Wow," she whispered. "People really live like this?"

Oliver laughed softly. "It's a different world, isn't it? You get used to it after a while, but the first time… well, it leaves an impression."

Deborah couldn't tear her eyes away from the view. "It's surreal. I can't even imagine living here."

"Neither can I, honestly. I prefer being out here, on the water. This is where I feel at home," Oliver admitted, his tone turning more introspective. "Sandbanks is beautiful, but it's not real freedom."

They anchored the yacht in a secluded cove, the kind that felt hidden from the world. Deborah stretched out on a plush sun lounger as Oliver set up lunch. The smell of fresh seafood and warm bread filled the air, mingling with the salty breeze. As they ate, their conversation flowed easily, from childhood memories to future dreams. Deborah found herself laughing more than she had in a long time, her guard slowly crumbling with each passing hour.

"You know," Oliver said as they sat in a comfortable silence, watching the waves lap against the yacht. "I don't think I've enjoyed a day like this in years. You make it… different. Special."

Deborah's heart skipped a beat. There was something in the way he looked at her that made her pulse quicken, but she forced herself to stay composed. "I could say the same about you."

As the sun began to sink lower in the sky, casting the world in a soft golden glow, they reluctantly turned the yacht back toward the marina. The sunset painted the sky in brilliant shades of pink, orange, and lavender, its reflection shimmering on the water's surface. It was the perfect end to a perfect day.

As they neared the marina, Deborah couldn't help but feel that something had shifted between them. What had started as an exciting day trip had turned into something far deeper—a connection that neither of them had expected, but both of them were eager to explore.

Chapter Forty One

The moonlight, a soft, celestial glow, filtered through the porthole into Oliver's stateroom, casting silvery threads that intertwined with the room's shadowy corners. Deborah lay sprawled, her naked form an ethereal vision on the queen-sized bed, the pristine Egyptian cotton sheets clinging to her like a second skin. A subtle blend of her delicate perfume—floral, sweet, and intoxicating—wafted through the air, mingling with the faint, briny scent of the sea that slipped through the slightly cracked porthole. The gentle hum of the ship's engines was a distant whisper beneath the rhythmic lapping of waves against the hull.

Oliver paused at the threshold, holding two glasses of chilled Chardonnay. His eyes immediately found Deborah's form, the moonlight highlighting her curves in tantalising contrast against the darkened room. The light traced a path along her figure, making her skin glisten as if kissed by the stars themselves. His lips curled into a smile, admiring the way her body seemed to glow in the pale light.

"Looks like you're not as tired as you thought," Oliver mused, his voice low and teasing, a hint of desire playing at the edges.

Deborah's eyes, dark with playful intent, met his gaze. She shifted slightly, her tousled hair framing her face like a halo as she stretched languidly, her body arching in a way that sent a shiver of anticipation through him. "I've caught a second wind," she purred, her voice velvety smooth, filled with mischief. With a teasing grin, she patted the bed beside her, beckoning him closer. "Join me."

The moonlight continued its dance on her skin, each movement revealing new facets of her form, igniting a desire within Oliver that made his pulse quicken. He placed the wine glasses on the sleek mahogany nightstand, the soft clink of glass against wood barely registering as he focused entirely on her. With deliberate ease, he approached the bed, his lean, muscular frame moving with the grace of a panther stalking its prey.

Deborah's hand reached out as he lay beside her, her fingers immediately finding his chest, her touch feather-light yet electrifying. She trailed her fingertips over his smooth, tanned skin, feeling the warmth of his body beneath her touch, her fingers tracing the hard lines of his muscles. His chest rose and fell rhythmically, betraying his calm exterior as he inhaled deeply. The moonlight played on his features, sharpening the angles of his face—his strong jawline, the intensity of his gaze, the slight parting of his lips.

Oliver's breath hitched as her hand travelled lower, her fingers exploring the tautness of his abdomen, each touch sending a ripple of pleasure through him. His body was a testament to years of discipline and hard work, sculpted by countless hours of effort, and Deborah's admiration was evident in every languid stroke of her hand.

The air between them thickened with the unspoken anticipation of what was to come, the world outside the stateroom slipping away, leaving only the two of them suspended in the intimate cocoon of the night. The waves, ever-present, provided a soothing rhythm—a steady heartbeat that mirrored the growing urgency in their movements.

Oliver's hand responded, his fingers trailing delicately over her skin, tracing the gentle curve of her hip, the soft swell of her waist, before finding the small of her back. He pulled her closer, their bodies aligning with a natural, undeniable magnetism, his lips brushing against the curve of her neck, tasting the salt of the sea on her skin. The connection between them deepened, each caress, each whispered breath a promise of the night that lay ahead, where the moon, the sea, and the pulse of their hearts would be the only witnesses to their embrace.

⌖

Chapter Forty Two

The journey home from Poole was far quicker than Deborah wanted. She stood behind Oliver as he expertly guided his yacht through the choppy sea, her arms wrapped around his waist. Resting her head on his back, she felt the wind and the smell of the salty sea air transfix her. She had never experienced anything like it before; it was exhilarating.

The gentle rocking of the yacht, the cool spray of the sea misting her skin—it was a sensory overload in the best possible way. The rolling of the deck, a rhythmic sensation under their feet, drew them closer. The world around them faded, leaving only the sea and sky as their companions. Oliver smiled, glancing over his shoulder at her, but the noise of the wind made it difficult to hear what he was saying.

Deborah leaned forward, brushing her lips against his ear, her breath warm against the cool sea breeze. "What did you say?" she asked, the vibration of her voice soft against his skin.

He turned his head slightly, his lips meeting hers in a quick, tender kiss. "We'll be at the yacht club within an hour," he repeated, his voice barely audible above the wind and crashing waves.

Deborah tightened her grip around his waist, unwilling to let this moment slip away so soon. "I wish we could stay out here longer," she murmured, her words nearly lost in the roar of the elements.

Oliver's laugh was soft but carried a note of understanding. He loved the sea as much as she did, perhaps even more. "Do you think we could sail forever?" he asked, his tone teasing but laced with curiosity.

She laughed along with him, the sound light and free, carried away by the wind. "Why not? Just you, me, and the open sea. No deadlines, no responsibilities. Just… this."

He glanced back at her, catching her gaze, his eyes reflecting the deep blue of the water below. "It's tempting," he admitted, "but I think we'd miss solid ground eventually."

"Maybe," she conceded with a soft smile, "but right now, I feel like I could sail with you to the ends of the earth."

Oliver's hand found hers, squeezing it gently, his thumb brushing over her knuckles. "We'll have more trips, Deborah. This is just the beginning."

Her heart fluttered at his words, a warmth spreading through her that had nothing to do with the sun overhead. She gazed at him, feeling a sense of contentment wash over her. "I like the sound of that," she whispered, her voice filled with quiet promise.

They fell into a comfortable silence, their bodies swaying in harmony with the yacht as it cut through the waves. The sea around them was a symphony of sound, the wind whistling through the sails, the water lapping against the twin hulls. Each moment seemed to stretch out, suspended in time, a perfect bubble of serenity she wished would never burst.

As they sailed closer to the shore, the outlines of the distant yacht club slowly coming into view, Deborah sighed softly, her thoughts drifting. "Do you think things will change when we get back?" she asked, her voice tinged with uncertainty.

Oliver glanced at her; his brow furrowed slightly. "What do you mean?"

She hesitated, biting her lower lip before answering. "I mean… everything feels so simple out here. It's just us, and the sea, and nothing else matters. But back on land, there are expectations, routines… responsibilities."

Oliver was quiet for a moment, then he turned to her fully, his expression serious but tender. "Things don't have to change. What we have here—we can bring it back with us. It's not the sea that makes this special, Deborah. It's you and me."

Her chest tightened with emotion, and she nodded, blinking away the sudden moisture in her eyes. "You're right. I just don't want to lose this feeling."

"You won't," Oliver promised, his voice steady and sure. "We'll make sure of it."

She smiled again, her fears easing with his words. The shore was closer now, the sails starting to lower as Oliver prepared to dock. But for a little while longer, as the wind tugged at her hair and the sea whispered beneath them, it was just them—boundless and free, with the promise of more adventures waiting just beyond the horizon.

Chapter Forty Three

As they reached the yacht club, Deborah's heart felt heavy with a mix of emotions. The weekend had been wonderful, almost too perfect, yet the nagging uncertainty about their relationship lingered in her mind. She cast a sidelong glance at Oliver as he expertly manoeuvred the yacht toward the dock. He looked as calm and composed as ever, but Deborah knew that behind those cool, blue eyes lay a mystery she still hadn't unravelled. Sometimes he was warm, pulling her close and making her feel like the centre of his world. Other times, a quiet distance grew between them, leaving her wondering where she truly stood.

Oliver, ever the gentleman, extended his hand as she stepped off the yacht. His touch was firm, but his eyes gave little away. They walked together toward the members' lounge, his hand lingering at the small of her back in a familiar gesture that somehow felt both intimate and distant at once. Deborah knew he would need time to secure the yacht, so she excused herself, making her way to a plush chair in the lounge where she could wait in comfort.

As soon as she sat down, she pulled out her phone, remembering the promise she'd made to Carol to call once the weekend was over. With a deep breath, she dialled her friend's number, hoping the conversation might help her untangle the mix of emotions swirling inside her.

"Hey, Carol! I just got back from the yacht club," Deborah began, her voice a bit more tentative than she had intended.

"Finally! I've been dying to hear all the details. Spill!" Carol's voice crackled through the phone, bright and eager as always.

Deborah smiled, though her heart was heavy. "It was a fantastic weekend," she started, her words laced with a tinge of confusion. "Oliver was charming and considerate, but then, I don't know... There were these moments when he felt so distant. It's like one minute we're completely in sync, and the next, he's a million miles away. I can't figure him out, Carol."

"Maybe he's just taking things slow," Carol offered, her tone thoughtful. "You know how some people can be, they need time to fully open up, especially if they've been hurt before."

"Maybe," Deborah agreed, though the uncertainty still gnawed at her. She wanted to believe that it was just a matter of time, that eventually Oliver would let her in completely. But something inside her was warning her not to get too attached just yet.

As she chatted with Carol, her eyes drifted across the room. That's when she saw Oliver re-enter the lounge, scanning the crowd until his gaze landed on her. There was that smile again, the one that always made her heart skip a beat. He noticed her empty glass and quietly made his way to the bar, ordering them both another round of drinks.

"Anyway, I have to go," Deborah said, feeling her heart flutter as she watched Oliver approach with two glasses of wine. "We'll catch up soon."

"Alright, take care, and remember, don't overthink it too much. Talk soon!" Carol said before hanging up.

Deborah tucked her phone away just as Oliver reached her, handing her a glass of wine with that disarming smile of his.

"Cheers," he said softly, his voice like velvet as he raised his glass. "Thanks for a wonderful weekend."

Deborah returned his smile, lifting her glass to meet his. "No, thank *you* for being such great company. Here's to our next voyage, wherever that may be."

They clinked glasses, the sound delicate and intimate, much like the tension between them. She sipped her wine, savouring the moment but still wondering if she'd ever fully understand the man sitting across from her. After they finished their drinks, the evening ended, and they called for a taxi.

The ride home was quiet, but it was a comfortable silence, the kind where no words were needed. Deborah stared out the window, the soft hum of the taxi engine and the occasional streetlight flickering by adding to the quiet intimacy of the night. Oliver sat close beside her, his presence steady, yet there was a sense of something unspoken between them.

When the taxi pulled up to her house, Oliver insisted on walking her to the door. His hand found the small of her back once more, and they stood there in the moonlight for a moment longer than necessary.

"Goodnight, Deborah," Oliver whispered, his lips brushing the edge of her ear as they embraced.

"Goodnight, Oliver," she replied softly, her voice barely above a whisper. There was so much she wanted to say, but the words stayed locked inside her heart. She watched him walk back to the taxi, feeling both closer to him and more distant than ever before.

Once inside, Deborah was greeted by the familiar sight of Benson, her grey tabby cat, eagerly waiting at the door. He immediately rubbed his face against her legs, his purring a warm welcome home.

"Hello, handsome," she cooed, scooping him up in her arms. "Miss me?"

Benson meowed in response, clearly thrilled to have her back. She carried him into the kitchen, pulling out his favourite treats from the cupboard. As he crunched happily on the snacks, Deborah let out a deep sigh, the weight of the weekend finally catching up to her.

Too tired to unpack, she made her way to the bathroom, filling the tub with warm, lavender-scented water. The bath was a balm to her weary body, and as she soaked, the tension began to melt away. But even in the quiet, her mind kept drifting back to Oliver—his touch, his smile, the way he could make her feel both seen and unseen all at once.

After her bath, she slipped into her favourite pyjamas and crawled into bed, pulling the soft covers around her. As soon as her head hit the pillow, the exhaustion took over, and she fell into a deep sleep, her dreams filled with images of the sea, the yacht, and Oliver's enigmatic smile.

In the quiet of the night, beneath the stars outside her window, Deborah's heart held on to the hope that perhaps, in time, she would finally understand the man who had so effortlessly captured her imagination.

Oliver grew ever more disappointed with Deborah. At first, her affection had been endearing—a sign of how much she cared—but now it felt suffocating. She had become too clingy, her constant need for reassurance weighing heavily on him. The incessant texts, the voice notes laced with longing, and the need for immediate replies set alarm bells ringing in his head. Love should feel like a partnership, not a duty. He looked at his phone again—more messages. His stomach tightened with frustration. This wasn't working. He had to end things.

Deborah sat in her dimly lit kitchen, a glass of wine clutched tightly in her hand. The candle on the table flickered as she stared at her phone, her mind racing. Why wasn't Oliver replying? Had she done something wrong? She had thought they were moving too slow—wasn't it time to take the next step? She wanted more than stolen kisses and half-hearted plans. She wanted commitment. A future. Her friends told her to slow down, to let things unfold naturally, but they didn't understand. She and Oliver had something special, something rare. It wasn't just love; it was friendship, a deep connection that couldn't be denied.

Oliver just needed to see it.

Her phone buzzed, jolting her from her thoughts. She snatched it up, her heart pounding when she saw his name on the screen. Finally, he had replied. Relief surged through her as she opened the message, expecting warmth, maybe even an apology for his silence.

But the words on the screen didn't match what she had hoped for.

"I'm sorry, Deborah. This isn't working. I think it's best we go our separate ways."

The room seemed to tilt around her as the words sank in. No. This couldn't be happening. They weren't over. They couldn't be. He just needed more time, more convincing. He was scared, that was all. He didn't understand yet, but he would. She would show him. She would make him see that.

Chapter Forty Four

Sophia Reed, a bright young woman with a keen intellect and a kind heart, had always yearned for more than the superficial banter that seemed to dominate her interactions with the young men she met. She wasn't interested in fleeting conversations about football or the latest video game craze; she longed for depth, for meaningful exchanges that could fuel her curiosity and ignite her passion for life. Beneath her outward poise, there was a hidden vulnerability—an unspoken fear that she might never find someone who truly understood her, someone with whom she could share her deepest desires, her wildest dreams, and her darkest fears. The young men she had encountered thus far, with their carefree attitudes and immaturity, left her feeling isolated, her intellectual and emotional needs unmet.

It was a warm, sun-soaked afternoon when Oliver Wright stepped into her world. Sophia had been working at the quaint little wine shop on the corner of her hometown, a job she had taken over the summer break from university. The shop, with its shelves lined with carefully curated bottles, always felt like a sanctuary to her. She enjoyed the quiet rhythm of her work, the meticulous organisation of the wine displays, and the occasional conversations with customers who appreciated the finer things in life. As she rearranged a display near the front window, she noticed him—a distinguished man, probably in his early forties with salt-and-pepper hair that gave him an air of sophistication. He moved with the kind of grace that spoke of confidence, but not arrogance.

Oliver was standing in front of the French red wines, deep in thought, his brow slightly furrowed as he examined a bottle of Chateauneuf-du-Pape. There was something about the way he carried himself that piqued Sophia's interest. He didn't seem like the typical customer; there was a quiet, assured presence about him, a sense of calm that drew her in.

"Hello, can I be of some assistance?" she asked, her voice soft yet confident, the kind of tone that invited conversation without being intrusive.

Oliver looked up, and when his eyes met hers, Sophia felt an unexpected jolt of connection. His warm smile reached his eyes, softening the sharp lines of his face. His gaze lingered on her for a moment, and in that brief pause, Sophia felt something stir within her—a flicker of curiosity, perhaps even attraction.

"Why yes, if you would be so kind," he replied, his voice rich and smooth, like the wines he was considering. "I'm hosting a small dinner party, and I want to impress my guests. I'd like to pick something special, but I could use some guidance."

Sophia's heart quickened slightly. Here was a man who wasn't trying to impress her with bravado or charm, but who was genuinely seeking her expertise. It was refreshing, and in that moment, she felt a spark of excitement, a sense that this interaction might be different from the countless others she had experienced.

"Chateauneuf-du-Pape is an excellent choice," she began, "but if you're open to suggestions, I can recommend a few other wines that might pair well with different courses you're planning."

Oliver nodded, clearly intrigued. "Please do. I must admit, while I enjoy wine, my knowledge is somewhat... limited."

Sophia smiled at his candour, appreciating his willingness to admit what he didn't know. It was a trait she found increasingly rare—especially in men. As she guided him through the wine selection, pointing out the subtle differences in flavour profiles and suggesting pairings based on the courses he described, she couldn't help but notice how attentively he listened. He wasn't just nodding along to be polite; he was engaged, asking thoughtful questions and showing a genuine interest in learning from her. His presence was calming, his energy steady and reassuring, and it felt like they were having a real conversation, a true exchange of ideas.

When they reached the end of their discussion and Oliver had made his selections, he turned to her with a look of sincere gratitude. "You've been incredibly helpful, Sophia," he said, using her name as if savouring it. "I feel much more confident about my choices now. Thank you."

Sophia's chest warmed with a sense of pride. "I'm glad I could help. I hope your dinner party is a great success."

As Oliver made his way to the door, he paused, turning back to give her one last, lingering smile. "I have a feeling it will be, thanks to you."

Sophia stood there, watching him leave, her heart beating a little faster than usual. The sound of the door closing behind him left a strange, almost electric silence in the shop. She couldn't shake the feeling that something significant had just happened. Maybe it was his quiet confidence, or the way he genuinely valued her input, but Sophia found herself intrigued by this man—this mature, sophisticated stranger who seemed to embody everything she had been searching for.

For the first time in a long while, a sense of hope flickered within her. Could Oliver be the one she had been longing for? It was too soon to tell, of course, but as Sophia continued with her day, she couldn't help but let her mind wander back to the warmth of his smile, the depth in his eyes, and the tantalising possibility that her search for a meaningful connection might finally be over.

Chapter Forty Five

Oliver's dinner party was a resounding success. The wines chosen by Sophia complemented the menu perfectly, impressing his guests not only with their quality but also with his apparent expertise in selecting them. His living room, elegantly decorated with modern art and soft candlelight, provided the ideal setting for the evening, enhancing the ambience of refinement. The dinner began with an entrée of seared scallops wrapped in crispy bacon and accompanied by a rich black pudding, which added depth to the delicate seafood. The starter was paired with a chilled Sauvignon Blanc, a bright, citrusy choice that Sophia had assured would cleanse the palate without overpowering the flavours.

The main course followed: roasted turbot, its skin perfectly crispy, served atop a bed of creamy mashed potatoes infused with a touch of truffle oil, complemented by green beans sautéed in butter and garlic. A saffron sauce, delicately fragrant, was drizzled around the dish, adding a splash of vibrant colour and luxurious flavour. The Chardonnay, recommended by Sophia, was an excellent match for the dish, its buttery texture and subtle oak notes enhancing the richness of the turbot and the creaminess of the potatoes. Each sip seemed to elevate the dining experience, enhancing the flavours and adding a touch of elegance to the evening.

For dessert, individual apple pies arrived at the table, their golden, flaky crusts releasing the sweet aroma of cinnamon and nutmeg as they were cut open. Served alongside was a scoop of rich vanilla ice cream, slowly melting into the warm pie, creating a delightful contrast of hot and cold. A sweet, late-harvest Riesling, also suggested by Sophia, rounded off the meal, its honeyed notes perfectly complementing the tartness of the apples.

Oliver's guests, influential figures who could help him secure a position on the board of his next acquisition—a small but significant microchip company based in California—were thoroughly impressed. They praised his culinary skills, admiring not only the presentation and flavours but also his impeccable taste in wine, which subtly showcased his sophistication and attention to detail. His carefully curated choices sent a message: Oliver was a man who understood the finer things in life, who paid attention to every detail, whether in business or pleasure.

The following morning, Oliver felt a lingering sense of satisfaction and a growing gratitude toward Sophia. The thought of her expertise and warm demeanour lingered in his mind as he made his way to the wine shop. As he pushed open the door, the small bell above it rang softly, its sound blending with the gentle hum of the town waking up. The shop, with its warm, earthy tones and shelves lined with bottles of wine from around the world, felt inviting and calm.

Sophia looked up from behind the counter, her brown eyes lighting up as she saw Oliver framed by the mid-morning sunlight streaming through the doorway. A soft smile spread across her face as she shielded her eyes from the bright rays, watching as Oliver approached with his usual combination of charm and confidence.

"Hello, Sophia," Oliver greeted her warmly, his voice carrying a note of genuine appreciation. "I just wanted to say a big thank you for your help with the wine choices. They were a great success, and I couldn't have done it without your expertise."

Sophia smiled, a rush of pride and happiness filling her chest. "I'm so glad to hear that, Oliver. It was my pleasure to help. I knew you'd pull off something wonderful."

Oliver shifted slightly, his expression softening as he continued, "I hope you don't mind, but I brought you a small gift as a token of my appreciation." He handed her a beautifully wrapped gift box with a crimson ribbon tied neatly on top.

Sophia's eyes widened in surprise, her heart skipping a beat at the unexpected gesture. "Oh, you shouldn't have, Oliver. This is so kind of you!" she exclaimed, genuinely touched.

"Just a little something to show my gratitude," Oliver replied, his smile sincere. "You made a real difference, and I wanted to thank you properly."

Sophia, feeling a warmth spread through her, carefully untied the ribbon and opened the box. Inside, nestled in soft tissue paper, was a set of hand-painted wine glasses, their delicate craftsmanship evident in the fine details of the intricate designs. She traced the edge of one glass with her fingertip, marvelling at its beauty.

"These are stunning, Oliver," she said softly, her voice filled with appreciation. "Thank you so much."

"It's the least I could do," he replied, his tone warm. "You have a real talent, Sophia. I'm sure you'll go far in whatever you pursue."

Sophia glanced up at him, her eyes meeting his with a mix of gratitude and curiosity. There was a sense of connection between them, something unspoken yet palpable. As they stood there, exchanging smiles and small talk, Sophia couldn't help but wonder if this simple gesture was the beginning of something more. For the first time in a long while, she felt a flutter of possibility, a sense that perhaps life had more in store for her than she had anticipated.

Chapter Forty Six

Oliver had become a familiar face at the Glug wine shop, and with every visit, he grew more appreciative of the expertise Sophia consistently provided. Her extensive knowledge of wines, coupled with her knack for pinpointing exactly the right bottle, never ceased to amaze him—especially when it came to hosting business dinners that could make or break his potential deals. Thanks to her impeccable recommendations, his gatherings had become a hallmark of sophistication, often leaving his guests raving about both the wine and the company.

One late afternoon, the familiar chime of the small brass bell above the shop door announced Oliver's arrival. The shop was bathed in the golden glow of the setting sun, casting long shadows over the polished wooden shelves. Sophia, in the back, was busy overseeing a new delivery, checking off bottles with meticulous care. Hearing the bell, she called out over the sound of rustling boxes, "I'll be out in just a moment!"

Oliver, in no particular rush, took his time, meandering down the rows of wine racks. He enjoyed these moments—there was something about the shop's charming atmosphere and the subtle smell of aged oak barrels that made him feel at ease. His fingers traced the cool glass of a Bordeaux bottle as his thoughts wandered to the upcoming dinner party he was planning.

When Sophia finally emerged from the back room, her eyes immediately landed on Oliver standing by the red wine section, a spot he frequented often. Today, however, there was something different about the scene. Perhaps it was the way the light hit his face, or maybe it was his relaxed demeanour—dressed casually in faded blue jeans, a crisp white open-neck shirt, and light brown loafers. Either way, he looked particularly dashing, and Sophia found herself momentarily taken aback.

"Sorry to keep you waiting," she said, her voice warm and friendly, though tinged with a hint of nervousness she couldn't quite place.

Oliver turned to her, a playful grin spreading across his face. "No need to apologise. I'm not in any rush, but I did want to talk to you about something."

Sophia's heart skipped a beat, her curiosity piqued. She composed herself, tucking a strand of hair behind her ear. "Of course," she replied, trying to sound casual. "Is there a specific wine you're looking for, or do you need another recommendation?"

Oliver chuckled softly and placed the bottle he'd been examining back on the shelf. He turned toward her, his expression serious yet kind. "Actually, it's not about wine this time," he said, meeting her gaze. "I've been meaning to thank you for all your help these past few weeks. Your suggestions have been nothing short of fantastic. They've made my dinner parties quite the success, and for that, I owe you."

Sophia blushed slightly at the compliment, though she tried to remain composed. "I'm glad to have been of help," she replied, her voice steady but laced with curiosity about where this conversation was heading.

Oliver hesitated for a moment, then smiled, a glimmer of nervous excitement flashing in his eyes. "I was wondering if you might like to join me for dinner this Friday evening. You know, as a thank you… for everything."

Sophia's heart raced. The formality of their professional exchanges suddenly felt lighter, more personal. She had always enjoyed their interactions, but this invitation was unexpected.

Still, there was something undeniably appealing about the idea of spending time with him outside of the shop.

"I'd love to, Oliver," she said, her voice warm with sincerity. "Dinner on Friday sounds perfect."

Oliver's face broke into a broad, genuine smile, the kind that reached his eyes and made him look even more handsome. "Fantastic! I can text you the details if you give me your number."

Sophia smiled, her heart still fluttering from the surprise of it all. She quickly jotted her number down on a small notepad she kept behind the counter, handing it to him. "Seven sounds perfect."

As Oliver tucked the note into his pocket and waved goodbye, Sophia watched him leave, the bell above the door tinkling softly in his wake. She couldn't shake the sense that this dinner wasn't just about wine or gratitude—it felt like the beginning of something far more meaningful. The excitement of the evening to come buzzed in her chest, and for the first time in a long while, she allowed herself to daydream.

⁕

Chapter Forty Seven

Sophia was already daydreaming about their first date as Oliver left the shop. She could vividly picture the intimate dinner: a small, cosy restaurant tucked away on a quiet street, the tables dressed in crisp white linens, and the room bathed in the warm, golden glow of soft candlelight. The clinking of glasses and soft murmur of conversation would blend with their laughter, creating a bubble of happiness around them. She imagined the way Oliver would lean in to speak, his eyes crinkling at the corners with a smile, and how they would lose track of time, wrapped up in each other's stories and shared glances.

Meanwhile, Oliver's mind was elsewhere, consumed by thoughts of his upcoming business trip. His phone buzzed in his hand, a reminder of the countless emails and meetings that awaited him. Despite his doctor's stern warnings about overworking, he couldn't seem to pull away; his work had been his anchor since childhood, something steady and reliable in a world that often felt unpredictable. He had grown up around business meetings and contracts, learning the ropes from his father as soon as he could tie his own shoes. Now, work was not just a responsibility, it was his identity.

His next stop was London—a city that held as many memories for him as it did opportunities. As he tapped his phone to call his housekeeper, there was a flicker of something in his chest, a familiar blend of anticipation and nostalgia. He instructed her to prepare his penthouse apartment, every detail already clear in his mind. It needed to be pristine—polished surfaces, fresh linens, and the fridge stocked with his favourite imported delicacies. Everything had to be perfect, ready for his arrival after what would surely be a gruelling string of meetings. London was familiar to him, not just because of the high-powered negotiations and deals he'd closed there, but because of the memories woven into its streets. As he hung up, a small smile tugged at his lips. Though the trip was all business, a part of him was looking forward to walking the old streets again, even if just for a moment between meetings.

Chapter Forty Eight

The week had crawled at a snail's pace for Sophia, every hour stretching painfully long as anticipation for her Friday evening date with Oliver consumed her thoughts. She tried to keep busy at work, but each task felt mundane, her mind constantly wandering back to the moment she would finally see him. When Thursday arrived, the excitement became unbearable. She had arranged to go clothes shopping with Sylvia, eager to find the perfect outfit, though she hadn't mentioned who the date was with.

Sophia knew Sylvia was thrilled that she was finally making an effort to meet someone again. Ever since Sophia's last relationship ended, she had avoided dating, immersing herself in work and home. But there was something different about Oliver, something that had brought a spark back to her life.

Rushing home, she grabbed a quick snack—a leftover sandwich from lunch—and quickly changed into something comfortable for shopping. She didn't want to waste time; she needed Sylvia's fashion advice, and she wanted it now.

By the time she reached the clock tower in Brighton's town centre, it was exactly 7 PM. She saw Sylvia waiting under the tall structure, her red scarf unmistakable among the evening crowd. The sky had begun to darken, casting a soft glow over the busy town square. Sophia caught her breath as she approached, her excitement growing with each step.

"Sophia!" Sylvia called, her face lighting up as she spotted her friend. "You look like you're in a good mood!"

Sophia smiled, a little out of breath from her quick pace. "I'm just really excited for tomorrow night."

Sylvia raised a playful eyebrow, curiosity gleaming in her eyes. "So, who's this mystery man you're having dinner with?"

Sophia laughed, shaking her head. "I told you, it's someone you don't know. Let's just focus on finding me something amazing to wear!"

Sylvia pouted but didn't press further, though her playful interrogation was far from over. As they began walking through the bustling streets, they chatted about everything from work to weekend plans, weaving through the crowd of late-night shoppers. The town was unusually lively for a Thursday, with shop windows glowing under the streetlights and couples strolling hand in hand.

Sophia and Sylvia popped into a few stores they usually frequented—M&S, Peacocks, Ted Baker, Next—but nothing felt right. Sylvia, ever the optimist, was ready to try a new tactic.

"Why don't we head over to the Lanes?" Sylvia suggested, her eyes sparkling. "There are some hidden gems over there. You know, those cute little boutiques?"

Sophia hesitated, glancing at her watch. It was getting late, and they had already walked a lot. But Sylvia's excitement was infectious. "Alright, let's do it."

The two hopped onto the number 9 bus, settling into seats near the back. The ride was short, but they were grateful for the break after hours of window shopping. As they watched the town pass by in a blur of streetlights and moving crowds, Sophia felt the tension from the week slowly melting away.

"So, what's this Oliver guy like? At least give me that much!" Sylvia teased, leaning in.

Sophia blushed but still kept her lips sealed. "He's… different. You'll meet him eventually."

"Eventually?" Sylvia groaned dramatically. "You're killing me, Soph!"

When the bus finally pulled into their stop at the Lanes, they hopped off and were greeted by the charming maze of cobblestone streets, lined with quirky, independent shops and cafes. The vibe here was different—more intimate, more relaxed. As they wandered through the narrow alleys, Sophia's eyes suddenly landed on a quaint boutique with a soft glow coming from the inside. In the window, there it was—a stunning blue dress that made her heart skip a beat.

Without thinking, she grabbed Sylvia's arm. "That's it. That's the one."

Sylvia laughed as Sophia nearly dragged her into the boutique. The shop was quiet, almost serene, with soft music playing in the background. The shop assistant, a young woman who had been absorbed in a paperback novel behind the counter, looked up, slightly startled by the sudden burst of energy from Sophia.

"Can I help you?" the assistant asked, setting her book aside.

"Yes, please!" Sophia exclaimed, pointing to the dress in the window. "I'd love to try that on."

The assistant nodded and retrieved the dress, her movements calm and methodical as she handed it to Sophia. The anticipation was palpable as Sophia disappeared into the fitting room.

When she stepped out a few minutes later, Sylvia's reaction said it all. Her eyes lit up, and she clasped her hands together in awe. "Sophia! You look amazing! You *have* to get it."

Sophia stood in front of the mirror, her breath catching in her throat. The dress fit like it was made for her, hugging her body in all the right places. It was a deep, rich shade of blue, one that brought out the warmth in her eyes and made her feel effortlessly beautiful. She twirled slightly, the fabric swirling around her legs.

"I love it," she whispered, more to herself than anyone else. "I'll take it."

The assistant smiled as she wrapped the dress up carefully, clearly pleased with the sale.

As they stepped out of the boutique, Sylvia looped her arm through Sophia's, grinning. "You're going to knock him dead in that dress."

Sophia smiled, feeling a surge of confidence she hadn't felt in a long time. Friday night couldn't come soon enough. She could already picture the look on Oliver's face when he saw her walk into the restaurant, wearing the perfect blue dress.

Chapter Forty Nine

It was the morning of Sophia's much-anticipated date with Oliver, a day she had been looking forward to for some time. Knowing how important the evening was, she had requested both days off from her job at the shop to make the most of it. She didn't want to feel rushed or stressed and hoped to be fully present for any surprises the night might hold. Today was all about relaxation and getting into the perfect mindset for the date.

Sophia decided to treat herself to a day at a local spa, a place she had passed by many times but never found the time to indulge in. As soon as she stepped inside, the calming scent of lavender and the soft sound of instrumental music welcomed her. She let herself unwind completely, with a deep tissue massage that seemed to knead away every ounce of tension in her body. Afterward, she got her hair styled into soft waves and her nails done in a delicate shade of pink that complimented her natural elegance. By the time the afternoon rolled around, she felt completely rejuvenated, her skin glowing, and her confidence at its peak.

When she returned to her small flat above the shop, reality struck as she was greeted by the familiar sight of clothes strewn across the floor, books piled on her desk, and shoes cluttering the hallway. Between her studies and shifts at the shop, cleaning was the last thing on her mind, and it showed. With her hands on her hips, she gave the mess a resigned smile—this was no time to get lost in tidying up. A glance at the clock showed it was already 6:30 PM, and panic flickered in her chest. She was running late!

Instead of rushing to walk, she called a taxi. This night was too important for any mishaps, and she was determined to make a flawless impression. As she quickly dressed, she slipped into the blue dress that she and her best friend Sylvia had picked out together, a purchase they had debated over for hours. The dress fit her like a glove, accentuating her curves in all the right places while still feeling elegant and understated. She took a moment to apply makeup, just enough to highlight her bright eyes and natural features, and with one last spritz of her favourite perfume, she was ready. When the taxi pulled up outside, she grabbed her purse, gave herself a final glance in the mirror, and stepped out into the cool evening air.

While Sophia was preparing for the night, Oliver had spent his day in a whirlwind of activity as well, though his was more professional than pampered. The morning had been filled with back-to-back calls with clients, managing the final details of a few deals he was closing, and organising potential new contacts. However, as the afternoon approached, his focus shifted completely. Tonight was important, and he wanted to make sure everything was just right for Sophia.

After weeks of flirting and meaningful conversations in the shop where she worked, he had decided to impress her with his culinary skills. Cooking was something he enjoyed, and he hoped it would be a way to show her that he cared. His apartment was spacious and modern, with clean lines and minimalist décor, but he wanted to create a warmer, more intimate atmosphere for their date. Candles were carefully placed around the dining area, casting a soft golden glow, and a bouquet of fresh flowers sat in the centre of the table.

He had spent the afternoon in the kitchen, preparing a vegetarian feast. Playing it safe, Oliver had assumed that Sophia, like many young women in their late twenties, might be a vegetarian, and he didn't want to take any chances. The meal began with a portobello mushroom stuffed with a creamy white cheese, followed by individual veggie lasagnas he had painstakingly handcrafted. For dessert, he planned to serve his famous apple pie, made with a secret blend of spices that never failed to impress. The finishing touch would be the wine selection—handpicked by Sophia herself during his frequent visits to her shop.

As the smell of the cooking filled his apartment, Oliver glanced at his watch and felt a slight flutter of nerves. It wasn't often that he felt this way before a date, but there was something about Sophia that made him want everything to be perfect.

Sophia's taxi pulled up in front of Oliver's sleek building, and she stepped out, smoothing her dress and taking a deep breath. Her heart pounded in her chest as she approached his door, wondering if the night would live up to the hopes she had for it. She rang the bell, and within seconds, the door swung open to reveal Oliver, looking effortlessly handsome in a crisp white shirt and tailored trousers. His warm smile and the way his eyes lit up at the sight of her instantly eased the tension she had felt moments before.

"Sophia, you look absolutely stunning," he said, his voice filled with genuine admiration.

Her cheeks flushed slightly as she smiled back. "Thank you, Oliver. You look great too," she replied, stepping inside his home and feeling the warm atmosphere, he had worked so hard to create. The scent of delicious food wafted through the air, and the sight of the beautifully set table took her by surprise. It was clear he had gone to great lengths to make the evening special.

They exchanged a few more pleasantries as Oliver guided her toward the dining area, and as Sophia took her seat, she couldn't help but feel a little spoiled. "I hope you're hungry," he said, grinning as he brought the first course to the table. "I've prepared a few things I hope you'll enjoy."

Sophia beamed at him, already feeling incredibly cared for. "Everything looks amazing, Oliver. Thank you for doing all this. It's really thoughtful."

Pouring them both glasses of wine, Oliver smiled. "It's my pleasure. I wanted tonight to be perfect for us."

As they raised their glasses, toasting to a night filled with potential, both Sophia and Oliver felt the unmistakable spark between them growing stronger. The evening was just beginning, but they already sensed it would be one to remember—a night where something beautiful might just take root.

Chapter Fifty

Oliver set the table with two tall, slender candles, their golden flames dancing softly in the dimmed light of room, which overlooked the serene river. The gentle flicker reflected off the glass windows, casting an amber glow that bathed the room in warmth, creating an atmosphere both intimate and inviting. The air outside was still, the occasional ripple on the river barely perceptible, making the scene inside feel like a quiet oasis.

"Something smells amazing," Sophia remarked, her curiosity piqued by the delightful aroma drifting from the kitchen. Her voice had a lilting quality, soft and appreciative, which made Oliver smile as he moved to help her out of her coat. He hung it up with care, taking a moment to appreciate her shy, almost hesitant demeanour. "Thank you. And you look amazing too, by the way. That dress... it's perfect," he said, his compliment heartfelt, his eyes lingering on her for a moment longer than necessary.

Sophia's cheeks flushed a delicate pink, and she tucked a loose strand of hair behind her ear, smiling softly. "Thank you," she replied, her voice modest but pleased. There was something comforting in Oliver's warmth, and it put her more at ease in the unfamiliar surroundings.

Oliver led her down the hallway, which was bathed in soft light and decorated with modern artwork and photographs of distant places—evidence of a life well-travelled. As they entered the dining room, Sophia's breath caught for a moment. The table was a work of understated elegance, with crisp linen, gleaming silverware, and the two candles at the centre, their light reflecting off polished wine glasses. The room itself was luxurious, with dark wooden furniture that contrasted beautifully against the light walls, and the windows offered a stunning view of the river below, now dark and tranquil.

Oliver poured two glasses of wine, the rich burgundy liquid swirling in the glasses as he handed one to Sophia, their fingers briefly brushing as she accepted it. They exchanged a smile, both feeling the subtle spark of connection. As he took his seat across from her, Oliver caught her gaze, and for a moment, time seemed to slow. He raised his glass slightly. "To a wonderful evening," he said softly, his eyes reflecting the warmth of the candlelight.

"To a wonderful evening," Sophia echoed, her voice a little steadier now, a soft smile playing on her lips as they clinked their glasses together. With that, the night began, the gentle hum of conversation filling the room, as outside, the river flowed quietly beneath the starlit sky.

⟡

Chapter Fifty One

The evening stretched far beyond what either of them had anticipated, morphing into an intimate affair that blurred the lines between night and dawn. As the soft glow of the city lights filtered through the windows of Oliver's penthouse, both Sophia and Oliver remained entirely absorbed in one another's presence.

Sophia, with her sparkling eyes and infectious energy, spoke animatedly about her journey through university, detailing the intricacies of Biochemistry, her chosen field of study. Now in her third year at 26, she had taken a slightly unconventional path, taking a few gap years to explore her interests before diving fully into academia. Her ambition was evident as she explained the research she was working on—focused on developing new ways to treat chronic diseases. Her passion shone through every word, and Oliver was mesmerised. It wasn't just her beauty that captivated him, but her intellect, ambition, and the subtle vulnerability she exuded when she talked about her future.

For Sophia, Oliver was unlike anyone she had ever met. He seemed to have everything: the sharp looks of a man in his prime, the confidence that comes with success, and the kind of wealth that spoke of years of hard work and smart decisions. Yet, despite the luxurious apartment, the expensive art on the walls, and the panoramic views of the city skyline, what truly drew her in was his down-to-earth nature. He listened to her with genuine interest, asking thoughtful questions about her work, laughing at her anecdotes, and sharing stories of his own stories about the world of business, investments, and travel that seemed a world apart from her university life.

Dinner had been a delightful surprise. Though they hadn't discussed it beforehand, Oliver had prepared a vegetarian feast—a fact that both impressed and relieved Sophia, given her own dietary preferences. As he cleared the table, she watched him with a sense of admiration. There was something so different about him—something mature, patient, and generous. He wasn't like the men her age who seemed to lack direction, focus, or a real understanding of how to connect with someone. Oliver made her feel seen, understood, and cared for in a way that felt new and exhilarating.

As the night wore on, the conversation grew deeper, more personal. They laughed, flirted, and exchanged subtle glances that held promises of things yet unsaid. When Sophia finally glanced at her phone, she was startled by how late it had become—well past midnight, and yet, she felt no desire to leave.

Emerging from the kitchen with two large glasses of XO brandy, Oliver smiled warmly. "I hope you don't mind," he said, offering one of the glasses to her. "I thought we could toast to an incredible evening."

Sophia took the glass with a soft smile, her heart fluttering. She wasn't much of a drinker, but the rich, amber liquid felt like an indulgence, a fitting end to a night that had already been full of surprises. "Shall we sit in the front room?" Oliver suggested, his voice low and inviting. She nodded, following him to the plush velvet sofa that sat beneath a grand window overlooking the twinkling lights of the town below.

As they settled in, Sophia kicked off her pumps, curling her legs beneath her as she got comfortable. There was an ease between them now, a quiet understanding that they had crossed a threshold. The tension that had buzzed between them all evening was now palpable, but it was softened by the warmth of the brandy and the softness of Oliver's gaze.

He sat beside her, their knees brushing gently, and lifted his glass in a toast. "To new friends," he said, his voice a gentle rumble.

Sophia smiled and clinked her glass against his. "To new friends," she echoed, taking a sip and feeling the warmth spread through her chest.

As the conversation wound down, Oliver turned to her with a gentle smile. "It's getting late," he murmured, his voice hushed. "I can call you a taxi, if you'd like."

Sophia met his gaze, her heart pounding in her chest. There was a softness in his eyes, a question hanging in the air between them. She set her glass down on the coffee table and leaned toward him, her lips curving into a slow, knowing smile. "Maybe in the morning," she whispered, her voice low and full of meaning.

With a boldness that surprised even her, Sophia closed the distance between them, her lips brushing against his in a kiss that was slow, deep, and filled with the promise of everything yet to come. Oliver responded in kind, his hands gently resting on her waist as the world outside faded away, leaving just the two of them, lost in the moment and in each other.

Chapter Fifty Two

Sophia was stunned that she had kissed Oliver, yet it felt like an inevitable release of a tension that had been building for far too long. She had been lonely, longing for connection, and now, as Oliver held her gently, his fingers tracing her jawline, she felt a sense of desire she had almost forgotten existed. Her breath hitched as he leaned in closer, the warmth of his skin against hers setting off sparks she couldn't contain. It was as though her body was awakening from a long, dormant slumber.

Her heart pounded in her chest, each beat resonating with the electricity of the moment. As Oliver's hands found the zipper of her dress, sliding it down her back with unhurried precision, Sophia shivered—not from cold, but from the flood of emotions rushing through her. When the fabric fell from her shoulders, exposing the smooth expanse of her skin, she felt both vulnerable and alive, her nerves tingling as his lips brushed over her collarbone.

His touch was delicate but charged with intent, and when his lips met her skin, her breath caught in her throat. A soft moan escaped her lips, and she closed her eyes, surrendering to the cascade of sensations flooding her senses. She hadn't allowed herself to feel this way in years, and the sheer intensity of it overwhelmed her, making her feel both exhilarated and exposed.

"Sophia," Oliver murmured into her ear, his voice low and thick with desire. "We can stop at any time. I want you to be sure."

His words brought a momentary flicker of hesitation. She bit her lip, her vulnerability laid bare in her whispered response, "It's just been so long... I'm a little scared."

Oliver paused, his gaze steady, offering her the reassurance she needed. "It's okay. We can stop whenever you want. There's no pressure." His tenderness melted away her apprehension, and the fear that had gripped her chest loosened its hold.

But the last thing Sophia wanted was to stop. Her body was responding in ways she hadn't anticipated, her desire growing stronger with each passing second. She knew she wanted this, wanted him. The warmth of his skin, the strength in his arms, the way he looked at her like she was the only woman in the world—she was consumed by it all. With newfound resolve, she reached up, her hands sliding over the smooth, hard planes of his chest as she unbuttoned his shirt. Her fingers explored his tanned skin, her lips soon following, pressing urgent, passionate kisses to his body.

They moved together, seamlessly, as though they had done this a thousand times before. Clothes fell to the floor, forgotten, as their bare skin met in a heated embrace. The hunger between them was palpable, and soon, their bodies were entwined, moving in perfect sync, each motion fuelling the fire that burned between them.

Sophia felt her earlier nervousness dissolve, replaced by pure, unfiltered passion. Each of Oliver's touches ignited a new wave of desire, and her body responded eagerly, arching towards him, craving more. His lips found her breasts, his mouth teasing and tasting, drawing soft gasps from her as her fingers tangled in his hair. Her body thrummed with pleasure, every sensation heightened as the world outside their shared bubble ceased to matter.

They were wrapped in the intensity of the moment, their connection more than just physical. It was raw, emotional, and all-consuming, leaving no room for doubts or fears. Every thrust, every kiss, every whispered word brought them closer, their movements a perfect harmony of longing and release. Time seemed to blur, and in that space, nothing existed but the heat of their passion and the undeniable bond growing between them.

⚜

Chapter Fifty Three

Oliver was taken aback by Sophia's boldness, but it excited him as much as it surprised him. He could sense the same yearning in her, their desires mirroring one another in a wordless exchange. He pulled her closer with a fierce intensity, their bodies fitting together like pieces of a puzzle, as if they'd been meant to find each other. Sophia's breath came in short, quick bursts, her heart pounding against her chest, each beat louder than the last. When Oliver lifted her effortlessly in his strong arms, her pulse quickened, but not just from excitement—doubt lingered beneath the surface.

As he cradled her, Sophia's mind spun with worry. Could she truly be enough for someone like Oliver? He was older, had more scars, more baggage. She'd been burned before, left behind by younger men who wanted someone else. Her thoughts swirled into a storm, the old insecurities rising up like a tide threatening to drown her confidence. But Oliver seemed to sense it all in an instant. His lips found the sensitive curve of her neck, his kisses slow and deliberate, as if he were writing a promise into her skin.

"I've wanted you since the moment I saw you," he whispered, his voice low, the words brushing against her like a caress.

His confession was a balm to her worries. Sophia's body relaxed in his arms, the tension in her shoulders releasing. She surrendered to the moment, letting go of the fears that had plagued her for years. There was a gentleness in Oliver's touch that melted her walls, a quiet strength in the way he held her that reassured her she was safe. She had known heartbreak, felt the sting of rejection, but none of that seemed to matter now. In Oliver's embrace, she was exactly where she was meant to be.

He carried her with a deliberate slowness toward the bedroom, as if savouring every second of being close to her. His steps were soft on the hardwood floor, the only sound in the quiet room the steady beat of their breathing, in sync as they moved. When they reached the bed, its plush silk sheets cool against Sophia's skin, she felt her body sink into the softness. The room was bathed in the soft glow of warm, ambient light from the lamps, casting shadows that danced gently around them.

Oliver's fingers traced paths along her skin with reverence, as though memorising every curve and line. His touch was confident yet tender, sparking a heat that spread through her, awakening sensations she had buried long ago. She hadn't realised how much she had missed this—being touched, being desired—not just for her body but for all that she was. Every kiss, every caress felt like a silent conversation between them, words unspoken but understood.

As he gazed into her eyes, Sophia felt the ghosts of past relationships fade. The empty nights, the unanswered questions of whether she would ever find someone who truly saw her, were banished. With Oliver, there was no hesitation, no doubt. She felt cherished. The age gap between them, once a source of anxiety, now seemed insignificant. It wasn't her years that defined her—it was the woman she had become because of them.

Oliver's lips moved to her collarbone, and he paused to whisper into her skin, "You are everything to me." His voice was thick with emotion, his vulnerability a mirror of her own.

Sophia's breath caught in her throat, and for a moment, her heart swelled beyond what she thought it could. In Oliver's arms, she wasn't just a woman trying to hold onto youth or outshine her past. She was simply Sophia—wise, beautiful, whole. She met his gaze, her eyes soft but brimming with passion.

"And you, Oliver," she replied, her voice quiet but firm, "are more than I ever thought I could have."

Together, they moved in harmony, their bodies intertwined in a rhythm as ancient as time itself. The room seemed to fall away, the outside world dimming until it was just the two of them, connected in a way that transcended the physical. Their souls seemed to touch, merging into something neither had expected but both had desperately longed for.

As the night deepened, Sophia realised that for the first time in years, she wasn't afraid of what came next. She wasn't searching for validation or trying to prove herself. Oliver didn't need her to be anything other than who she was. The silk sheets beneath them, the dim lighting, the warmth of their closeness—it all felt like a new beginning. With Oliver, she wasn't just living in the moment; she was stepping into a future where she could be loved fully, unapologetically, for everything she was.

Chapter Fifty Four

Sunlight streamed through the floor-to-ceiling windows of Oliver's penthouse apartment, bathing the sleek, minimalist space in a golden glow. The gleaming surfaces of polished marble and chrome seemed to sparkle under the sun's embrace, while plush, designer furnishings added a touch of warmth to the otherwise modern decor. The room felt impossibly still, save for the occasional flicker of shadows as the morning light shifted across the space.

Sophia lay quietly against Oliver, the lingering intimacy of their lovemaking still fresh on her skin. Her head rested on his shoulder, her fingers absently tracing the outline of his chest, savouring the feel of his skin. She still found it difficult to grasp the reality of the moment. This world, this apartment, this man — it all seemed so distant from her own life. Oliver was everything she wasn't: worldly, accomplished, dripping with the kind of effortless charm that comes with wealth and confidence. He had shared stories of exotic places she could only dream of, from the golden dunes of Morocco to the shimmering beaches of Bali. In contrast, the farthest she had travelled was from Shoreham to London, her university days spent studying and watching others embark on exciting adventures.

Oliver stirred beside her, his body shifting slightly as his eyes fluttered open. His lips curled into a soft, sleepy smile when he saw her watching him. There was something disarming about his gaze, the way it held hers as if she were the only thing in the world that mattered in that moment.

"Morning," he whispered, his voice thick with sleep.

"Morning," she whispered back, her heart fluttering in response to his warmth. She pressed her head against his chest, letting the sound of his heartbeat lull her into a peaceful reverie. For a few moments, they stayed like that, wrapped in the quiet intimacy of the morning, the outside world forgotten.

But eventually, Oliver slid out of bed, stretching his toned body before heading toward the kitchen. Sophia lay there for a moment longer, listening to the soft sounds of him moving around the apartment. The click of cabinets, the sizzle of something on the stove. Finally, she rose and padded barefoot to the en suite bathroom, one of three in the apartment, each more luxurious than the last. The bathroom was a sanctuary of marble and glass, the rainfall shower cascading over her as she allowed the steam and warmth to envelop her.

When she emerged, her skin glowing and wrapped in a plush white towel, the enticing aroma of breakfast greeted her. Oliver had laid out an impressive spread: fluffy scrambled eggs, toast perfectly golden, homemade pancakes stacked high, and fresh fruit arranged artfully on a serving tray. A rich, dark mug of freshly brewed coffee sat at her place at the table, its scent heady and comforting.

She took a seat, her eyes scanning the table before settling on Oliver, who had already taken a seat opposite her, his expression casual but content.

"Do you have any plans for today?" Oliver asked, slicing into his pancakes as though it was the most natural thing in the world to have a lazy morning together like this.

Sophia shook her head, suppressing the grin that threatened to take over her face. "No, I've got the whole day off. Why?"

"I have an appointment in London," Oliver explained, his eyes bright with unspoken plans, "but it won't take long. I was thinking, if you're free, maybe we could spend the rest of the day together. I could show you around the city—my version of London."

The idea of spending more time with him, of being pulled deeper into his orbit, thrilled her. "That sounds amazing, but I'd need to go home and change first."

Oliver leaned back in his chair, a playful smile tugging at the corner of his lips. "I'll give you an hour."

Sophia hesitated, feeling a flush of shyness as she replied, "Can we make it two?"

Oliver laughed, a rich, genuine sound that made her heart skip. "Two it is. I'll pick you up later."

As they finished their, breakfast easy conversation flowed between them, punctuated by shared smiles and lingering glances. The anticipation of the day ahead—exploring London with Oliver, deepening their connection—made Sophia's pulse quicken with excitement. For the first time in a long while, the future felt wide open, filled with promise and adventure, and she couldn't wait to see what would unfold next.

Chapter Fifty Five

Oliver pulled up in his sleek Aston Martin DB9, the metallic black paint gleaming in the sunlight. The purr of the engine softened as he parked just outside Sophia's flat. The air was warm, the kind of late summer afternoon that made everything feel a little more alive. There was a peaceful hum in the distance as traffic buzzed along the nearby streets, lighter than usual. Oliver glanced at his phone, shooting a quick message to Sophia: *"I'm here."*

Upstairs, Sophia's phone buzzed as she applied the finishing touches to her makeup, a hint of excitement bubbling up inside her. She peeked out of the window, spotting the stunning car below, its sleek lines and unmistakable presence making it stand out against the quiet street. With a final glance at her reflection in the hallway mirror, she smiled. Her outfit—a flowing navy sundress and a pair of chic sandals—was the perfect balance between casual and elegant.

As Oliver waited, he made good use of the time, pulling out his phone to confirm a reservation at The Bluebird, his favourite Chelsea restaurant. He liked to plan things with precision, especially when it came to time with Sophia. The Bluebird was ideal—sophisticated yet relaxed, just the vibe he wanted for their late lunch.

Sophia stepped out of her building moments later, her eyes widening at the sight of the Aston Martin. She wasn't particularly a car enthusiast, but even she had to admit, this one was impressive. Its design was sleek, almost predatory, with a deep growl under the hood that spoke of power and luxury.

She raised an eyebrow as Oliver stepped out, swiftly circling the car to open the door for her. "Your chariot awaits, madam," he said with a cheeky grin.

"Well, thank you, young man," she quipped back, a playful smile tugging at her lips. As she slid into the plush leather seat, she could feel the eyes of curious neighbours watching from nearby windows, their interest piqued by the car and the sense of occasion.

The drive northward along the M23 was effortless, the car slicing through the air as Oliver steered them toward London. They chatted lightly, the conversation easy as always. But once they merged onto the M25, the traffic started to thicken. The smooth flow of their journey soon slowed to a crawl, and Oliver's relaxed demeanour began to shift. He shot frequent glances at his watch, the faintest edge of frustration creeping into his otherwise calm exterior. His fingers tapped rhythmically on the steering wheel, a subtle indication of his impatience. Meanwhile, Sophia seemed unbothered, absorbed in her book, oblivious to the building tension beside her.

Two hours later, they finally pulled into the underground parking garage beneath Oliver's sleek modern high-rise in Canary Wharf. He eased the Aston Martin into his private parking space with practised precision. As they made their way to the elevator, the cool, polished floors reflected the building's understated luxury.

When the elevator doors slid open, revealing the entrance to Oliver's penthouse, Sophia was momentarily stunned by the sheer opulence of it all. It wasn't just wealth—it was a statement. The entrance hall was swathed in rich, earthy tones, the deep brown carpet underfoot so thick it felt like walking on clouds. The walls were lined with a striking Chinese mural depicting an ancient battle scene, vibrant with red and gold accents, intricate details that seemed to leap off the wall.

"Wow," Sophia said, almost breathless as she took in the grandeur. "This is…something else."

Oliver, running a hand through his hair as he glanced around. "Yeah, I might've gotten a bit carried away. Thought the mural would add some character."

"It's definitely got that," she replied, still soaking it all in.

They moved into the main living area, an expansive open space bathed in natural light, thanks to the floor-to-ceiling windows that offered an uninterrupted view of the London skyline. The city stretched out below them like a living, breathing tapestry of glass, steel, and history. It was a sight that took Sophia's breath away.

She walked toward the window, her eyes wide with awe as she gazed out at the panoramic view. The iconic skyline—the Shard, the Gherkin, the Thames weaving through the heart of the city— it was all there, laid out before her like a postcard come to life. "This view…" she whispered, shaking her head in amazement. "It's incredible."

"I never get tired of it," Oliver said softly, stepping up beside her. His eyes scanned the cityscape, but there was a warmth in his voice that suggested he was more focused on her reaction than the view itself. "It's one of the reasons I bought this place."

Sophia turned to face him, her eyes sparkling with excitement. "Thank you for bringing me here, Oliver. This day already feels special."

Oliver's smile softened as he looked at her, appreciating the way the city lights reflected in her eyes. "It's just the beginning, Sophia. How about we head to The Bluebird for that lunch I promised?"

"Sounds perfect," she said, linking her arm with his. Together, they stepped back into the elevator, ready to continue what promised to be an unforgettable day in London.

Chapter Fifty Six

Oliver and Sophia took a taxi to the Blue Bird restaurant, the city's finest, nestled on a picturesque street lined with chic boutiques and galleries. As they arrived, the sky was awash in hues of pink and lavender, casting a romantic glow over the restaurant's grand facade. The entrance was adorned with flowering vines and twinkling fairy lights, giving it an air of understated elegance.

Inside, the ambience was intimate yet lively. The soft murmur of conversations, clinking glasses, and the gentle hum of background jazz created a sophisticated atmosphere. Oliver, a regular patron, was greeted warmly by the head waiter, a tall gentleman with a distinguished demeanour, who knew him by name. "Good evening, Mr. Wright. It's a pleasure to see you again," the head waiter said with a broad smile, before leading them to a corner table.

The table, perfectly positioned by a large window, offered an excellent view of the restaurant's elegant interior and the bustling street outside. Oliver loved this spot for its blend of privacy and visibility. He enjoyed people-watching, finding it fascinating to observe the ebb and flow of the restaurant's guests.

Sophia, on the other hand, was slightly overwhelmed by the grandeur. The soft light, crisp white linens, and waitstaff in their impeccable uniforms gave the place an air of opulence that she wasn't used to. She shifted uncomfortably in her seat, her fingers brushing the edge of the fine porcelain menu, unsure of what to order. Sensing her discomfort, Oliver gently placed his hand on her arm and leaned in with a reassuring smile. "Relax, you're going to love it here," he said warmly. His touch and tone immediately put her at ease, and she smiled back, grateful for his steady presence.

As they settled in, Oliver confidently took charge, scanning the wine list with the ease of someone who knew it by heart. He offered Sophia a few suggestions, describing each dish in vivid detail as though he had tried everything on the menu. "The Piri Piri prawns are a must-try here," he said. "Spicy, but perfectly balanced. And the lobster...well, it's the best I've had anywhere."

Sophia nodded, still feeling a bit out of her depth, but she trusted his choices. When the waiter came to take their order, Oliver spoke with the assuredness of someone entirely in his element. "I'll start with the Piri Piri prawns and follow with the lobster," he said, his voice smooth and decisive.

Sophia hesitated for a moment, glancing down at the menu. "I'll have the Caesar salad to start, and then the mushroom risotto, please," she said softly, looking to Oliver for approval.

"Excellent choices," Oliver said with a warm smile, as though her selections were as perfect as his own. "And a bottle of your finest Chardonnay," he added, turning to the waiter with a nod of appreciation.

The waiter returned promptly with the wine, pouring a small taste for Oliver, who swirled it in his glass, inhaled deeply, and took a sip. His eyes brightened with satisfaction. "Perfect," he said, giving the waiter the go-ahead to fill their glasses. As they toasted, Sophia felt herself relax further. The wine was crisp and refreshing, and the conversation flowed easily between them.

Over the course of the meal, they shared stories about their lives. Oliver spoke of his early years in business, his voice animated as he recounted the challenges and triumphs of building his career. "London was a tough place to start out," he said, "but it taught me resilience." Sophia, in turn, spoke of her love for literature and how it had taken her on adventures around the world, her eyes lighting up as she described the places she'd visited.

As lunch turned into early afternoon, the sun streamed in through the restaurant's windows, casting a golden glow over their table. They lingered over dessert—Oliver had ordered a rich chocolate torte for them to share—savouring the sweetness and the lingering taste of wine.

After the meal, they decided to walk back to Oliver's apartment, the conversation still flowing easily between them as they strolled through the streets. The city was alive with the sounds of late afternoon: street performers playing music, couples walking hand-in-hand, and the distant hum of traffic.

Once back at the apartment, Oliver excused himself to take a few business calls, slipping seamlessly into work mode. Sophia, left to her own devices, wandered around the spacious living room, admiring the sleek, modern design. She eventually settled on the large, plush sofa, pulling out the book she had been reading.

Time passed quietly, the afternoon sun casting long shadows across the room. Sophia lost herself in the pages of her book, feeling more at home than she had expected. When Oliver finally finished his calls, he found her curled up on the sofa, absorbed in her reading.

"Sorry about that," he said, sitting down next to her with a tired sigh. "Business never really stops, does it?"

Sophia looked up, smiling gently. "It's alright, Oliver. I know how busy you are." She reached out and gave his hand a reassuring squeeze. "It gave me some time to catch up on my reading."

Oliver relaxed, feeling grateful for her understanding. "I'm glad you're comfortable here," he said softly. After a moment, he asked, "Would you like to go for a walk later, maybe grab a drink?"

"That sounds lovely," Sophia replied, setting her book aside. "I'd love that."

For a few minutes, they sat there in companionable silence, the city's soft buzz filling the space around them, content in each other's company. Outside, the sky had deepened into a rich twilight, promising a beautiful evening ahead.

Chapter Fifty Seven

After their leisurely walk along the riverbank, Oliver turned to Sophia with a suggestion. "How about I cook a light supper for tonight?" he offered, his eyes twinkling mischievously. Sophia smiled, already familiar with his culinary skills. "I'd love that," she replied warmly, recalling the many delicious meals he'd prepared for her in the past.

They wandered hand in hand through the streets of the bustling town, the aromas from various restaurants and cafes mingling in the air. Lively chatter and the clink of glasses filled the evening as they passed outdoor terraces, bathed in the glow of streetlamps. Soon, they reached a charming row of small shops. The grocery store on the corner, a quaint establishment brimming with character, beckoned them inside. The shelves were stacked with an impressive array of gourmet ingredients—everything from artisanal cheeses and freshly baked breads to exotic fruits and vegetables.

Oliver took charge, carefully selecting items for their dinner. He added a bottle of fine Chardonnay to the basket, along with freshly cut herbs and a selection of organic produce. "You've got quite the haul there," Sophia teased as he deliberated over which kind of cheese to choose. "Only the best for tonight," he said with a wink.

Once they returned to Oliver's sleek, minimalist apartment, the warmth and cosiness of the space instantly put Sophia at ease. She excused herself to freshen up while Oliver uncorked the wine. When she returned, the air was thick with the scent of garlic, herbs, and sizzling butter. Her stomach growled at the intoxicating mix of aromas. She tiptoed behind him, leaning over his shoulder.

"Something smells absolutely divine," she murmured.

Oliver, now without his apron, turned to her with a playful grin. "Well, I hope it tastes as good as you look tonight."

Sophia laughed and playfully raised an eyebrow. "If you're a good boy, I might have something special planned for dessert," she teased, leaning closer.

Without missing a beat, Oliver pulled her in for a tender kiss. "Then let's not waste any time," he said softly. They sat down at the dining table set simply but elegantly, candles flickering as soft music played in the background. The meal Oliver prepared was nothing short of perfection—a light but flavourful dish of pan-seared fish with a lemon-herb sauce, accompanied by roasted vegetables she had pasta with a deep rich tomato sauce and a crisp salad. Sophia couldn't help but marvel at how effortlessly he cooked.

After dinner, Sophia sank into the large, plush sofa, her legs curled beneath her as she sipped the last of her wine. The atmosphere in the room was serene, with only the faint hum of the dishwasher in the background as Oliver tidied up. His attention to detail, even in cleaning, was something Sophia admired; it was one of the many small things about him that made their time together feel special. She exhaled deeply, contentment spreading through her.

"You always make the best meals," she called out to him.

Oliver, finishing up in the kitchen, joined her on the sofa, a soft smile playing on his lips. "Well, I hope you've left some room for dessert," he said with a teasing glint in his eye.

Sophia, her curiosity piqued. "I always have room for dessert, especially when it's one of your creations."

Oliver disappeared briefly into the kitchen, then returned with two small plates. On each was a perfectly risen chocolate soufflé, crowned with a swirl of whipped cream. "Ta-da! Homemade chocolate soufflé," he declared with pride.

Sophia's eyes lit up. "Oliver, you've outdone yourself. This looks amazing!"

They savoured each bite slowly, the rich chocolate melting on their tongues, the sweetness lingering as they sat in comfortable silence. After they finished, Sophia leaned back, resting her head on the sofa, a blissful smile on her face.

"That was absolutely heavenly," she sighed.

Oliver reached for her hand, his expression softening. "I'm glad you enjoyed it."

Sophia's gaze met his, her voice tender. "You know, it's moments like these that I cherish the most. Just the two of us, no rush, no distractions. I feel... so at peace."

Oliver's thumb traced small circles on her hand as he smiled, his heart full. "Me too, Sophia. These evenings with you—they're everything to me."

Chapter Fifty Eight

Oliver led her gently by the hand to the master bedroom. With a press of a button on a sleek remote, the curtains gracefully glided shut, cocooning them in a private world. Another click dimmed the lights to a warm, inviting glow that cast soft shadows around the room.

Sophia, glancing around at the technology that surrounded them, whispered teasingly, "You have a gadget for everything."

Oliver's smile was full of mischief as he met her gaze, "Not everything," he murmured, closing the distance between them with a deep, lingering kiss. His lips were warm, igniting a fire inside her that she had been waiting to unleash.

With slow, deliberate movements, he slid the straps of her dress off her shoulders, the garment falling to the floor in a pool of fabric. Revealed beneath was the black silk teddy she had carefully selected for this moment, its delicate lace framing her curves. She felt a surge of confidence under his gaze as his eyes roamed appreciatively over her body. At 5'5", with her full breasts, narrow waist, and smooth skin that glowed in the soft light, Sophia was a vision. Her hair cascaded in soft waves down her shoulders, and her eyes sparkled with anticipation.

As her fingers deftly unbuttoned his shirt, exposing the firm lines of his chest and stomach, she admired the body he had clearly worked hard to maintain. He was older, but his muscles were still well-defined, his skin taut and smooth. The chemistry between them had always been undeniable, and tonight, it reached its peak.

Oliver's kisses grew more insistent, full of need, and Sophia matched his intensity, her hands exploring his body. They tumbled onto the bed in a tangle of limbs, their passion driving them forward. Oliver lay back as Sophia, with a confident smile, straddled him, pressing her body against his. Her lips travelled from his mouth down to his neck and across his chest, each kiss eliciting a soft groan of pleasure from him. His hands roamed her body, caressing her thighs and waist, pulling her closer as their breaths quickened.

Sophia's fingers teased the waistband of his trousers before sliding them off, revealing his arousal. She moved with purpose, her body aligning with his as she guided him inside her. Their eyes locked, and for a moment, time seemed to stand still as their connection deepened. She set a slow, steady rhythm, her body undulating against his, each movement sending waves of pleasure rippling through them both. Oliver's grip tightened on her hips as she rode him, her power and control intoxicating.

Sophia revelled in the sensation of dominance, feeling the heat of his submission beneath her. The longer she moved, the more Oliver surrendered, giving in to the exquisite pleasure she provided. His moans filled the air, and she felt a surge of satisfaction knowing she had him completely under her spell. Her body moved with precision, each motion deliberate, designed to draw out the intensity of the moment.

When Oliver could no longer contain himself, he flipped her onto her back with a growl of desire. His strength and passion ignited something deeper within her. The weight of his body pressed against hers, and the heat between them seemed to rise, filling the room as he kissed her again, his lips trailing down her neck. His hands found her breasts, his fingers teasing her nipples until they stood erect, sensitive to his every touch.

Sophia's breath hitched as his mouth moved lower, leaving a trail of hot kisses down her abdomen. Her back arched, her body responding to him instinctively, her fingers clutching the sheets as his hands ran down her thighs. His touch was electric, and with each thrust, she could feel herself slipping further into the sensation, her mind overwhelmed with pleasure. Their bodies moved together as one, their rhythm perfectly synchronised.

She gasped as he pushed her to the edge, the tension in her body building until she could no longer contain it. With a loud, desperate moan, she came undone, the waves of ecstasy crashing over her as Oliver continued, drawing out every ounce of pleasure.

Finally, spent and breathless, Oliver collapsed beside her, their bodies slick with sweat, still connected by the shared heat of their passion. Sophia could feel his heart racing beneath her as she laid her head on his chest, their breathing slowly returning to normal. The silence between them was comfortable, their connection now deeper than ever before.

"That was incredible," Sophia whispered softly, her voice still shaky from the intensity of their lovemaking.

Oliver turned his head and smiled, brushing a stray lock of hair from her face. "You make everything incredible," he said tenderly, pressing a kiss to her forehead.

They lay there, intertwined, the soft glow from the city lights slipping through a crack in the curtains. Sophia traced idle patterns on his chest with her fingertips, feeling his heartbeat slowly settle into a calm, steady rhythm.

After a few minutes, Oliver spoke, breaking the tranquil silence. "Do you want to stay here tonight?" His voice was low and gentle, full of affection.

Sophia lifted her head to meet his gaze, her lips curving into a soft smile. "I'd love that," she whispered.

Oliver pulled her closer, wrapping his arms around her protectively. "Then let's make tonight last," he murmured, his voice thick with emotion.

With that, they let sleep take them, their bodies still entwined, the warmth of their connection lingering long after the lights of the city faded into the night.

Chapter Fifty Nine

Sophia had spent the last few months diligently preparing for her finals, and her determination had turned into a routine. Every day was filled with hours of studying, surrounded by stacks of textbooks, highlighters, and notes filled with intricate diagrams. Her mind was entirely focused on mastering the material, as she tried to absorb every detail. The pressure was immense, but Sophia was resolute; she knew how important these exams were for her future.

On the day of her crucial exam, the weight of her anxiety mixed with a flicker of hope. She had envisioned Oliver by her side, offering support with a reassuring hug or a smile that could calm her racing heart. Instead, when she opened her front door, she found a bouquet of vibrant flowers and colourful balloons, all tied with a cheerful "Good Luck" message. It was a kind gesture, a reminder that he cared, but it also stung, emphasising the distance that had grown between them since those blissful early weeks together. Oliver had become somewhat distant lately, and on such an important day, his absence felt like a heavy shadow looming over her.

After the exam, which had gone better than she expected, Sophia felt a wave of relief wash over her. It was as if a weight had been lifted from her shoulders, and she could finally breathe again. Her parents, who had been her unwavering pillars of support throughout her education, decided to celebrate her achievement with a lavish lunch at a renowned restaurant downtown. The place buzzed with life, filled with the lively chatter of students celebrating the end of their academic journey, laughter ringing out as friends clinked glasses and shared stories.

As they settled into their seats, Sophia's parents were brimming with pride. Her father, a gregarious man with a contagious enthusiasm, couldn't contain his excitement. He leapt from table to table, sharing stories of Sophia's hard work and dedication, declaring her achievements to anyone who would listen. His voice carried across the restaurant, resonating with a sense of triumph. Each story made Sophia blush, a mix of embarrassment and gratitude bubbling up inside her. She was keenly aware of the sacrifices her parents had made to ensure she received the best education possible, and their unwavering belief in her made her heart swell.

Her mother, a calming presence with a knowing smile, noticed Sophia's discomfort. She gently tapped her hand and leaned in, whispering, "I'll have a word with him." Sophia felt a wave of relief wash over her at her mother's supportive gesture. "Thanks, Mum," she replied, her smile growing more genuine, feeling a bit more at ease amid the excitement.

As they enjoyed their meal, the atmosphere was filled with joy and laughter. Sylvia, always the supportive friend, kept the conversation light and fun. She shared hilarious anecdotes from their university days, peppering in inside jokes that made everyone erupt in laughter. The group reminisced about late-night study sessions, spontaneous adventures, and the little victories that had defined their time together. Despite the earlier disappointment with Oliver, Sophia felt a profound sense of gratitude for the love and support surrounding her. This moment, encircled by people who genuinely cared for her, was the perfect way to mark the end of an intense period of study and the beginning of a new chapter in her life.

As dessert was served, a decadent chocolate cake adorned with fresh berries, Sophia felt an overwhelming sense of gratitude. Looking around the table at her smiling friends and proud parents, she realised that while her journey was evolving, the connections she cherished remained steadfast. With each bite of cake, she savoured the sweetness of the moment, allowing herself to bask in the warmth of friendship and family, a reminder that she was never truly alone.

⋯⋯◆⋯⋯

Chapter Sixty

Sylvia was worried about Sophia after receiving a late-night call informing her that Oliver had dumped her. They talked for hours; Sophia's voice choked with tears, each sob a raw reminder of her heartbreak. Sylvia tried her best to comfort her, but it was no use. The pain was too fresh, too overwhelming.

"I'm so sorry, Sophia," Sylvia whispered, her own heart aching for her friend. "He's a fool for letting you go. You deserve so much better."

"I just don't understand," Sophia sobbed, her words tumbling out between gasps. "Everything seemed fine, and then suddenly… this." She paused, the weight of confusion mingling with her sorrow. "One moment, we were making plans for the future, and the next, he just… disappeared."

"Sophia," Sylvia said gently, "you are incredible, and anyone would be lucky to have you. Someone who will see how amazing you are, who will cherish every part of you." She wished she could reach through the phone and pull Sophia into her arms, to shield her from this pain.

Eventually, exhaustion took over. "I need to sleep, Sylvia," Sophia murmured, her voice barely above a whisper, thick with fatigue. "I'll call you soon."

"Of course. Get some rest. I'm here whenever you need me," Sylvia replied softly, trying to mask the worry in her voice.

But sleep was elusive for Sophia. Her mind raced, replaying every moment with Oliver, analysing every word, every laugh, trying to understand where it had all gone wrong. Memories flooded her thoughts—his smile, the way he would lean in when he laughed, the evenings spent curled up together. Each recollection twisted the knife of loss deeper. Her body ached from the tension of it all; she could feel it settling in her shoulders, her chest, her stomach. It was three in the morning before she finally drifted into a restless sleep, her dreams haunted by the remnants of their love.

Days went by without any word from Sophia, and Sylvia's concern grew. She sent texts filled with encouragement and worry, but there was no response. Desperate, she reached out to Sophia's parents, hoping they might have heard from her. They, too, had been unable to contact her and shared Sylvia's worry. With mounting concern, they decided to visit Sophia's apartment.

When their knocks went unanswered, they persuaded the landlord to let them in. Initially reluctant, the landlord agreed to meet them first thing in the morning after they explained the situation, his brow furrowed with scepticism.

At 9 a.m. on Sunday morning, Sylvia and Sophia's parents waited anxiously outside the apartment building. A silver Volvo pulled up, and a tall woman with red hair and brightly coloured clothes stepped out. She looked like someone from a circus, with her vibrant attire and flamboyant demeanour, a stark contrast to the sombre mood hanging in the air.

"Hello!" she greeted them with a wide smile, her voice overly cheerful. "Terrible business this, but I'm sure she'll be fine. You know how young girls are—full of hormones. I remember that age well," she continued, rummaging through a large, equally bright handbag, pulling out various items as if looking for a lost treasure.

After what felt like an eternity, she pulled out a large bunch of keys on a big, hooped key ring. She fumbled with the front door lock, and with a creak, it swung open, revealing a dark hallway that seemed to echo their unease. At the end of the hall was a red door, its paint slightly chipped, a silent witness to the life within.

Sylvia entered first, having been given the key. "Thank you," she said to the landlord, who seemed a bit put out at being dismissed after all the trouble.

"If there's any damage, it will come out of the deposit," the landlord huffed before turning and leaving, his footsteps fading away as he walked down the hallway.

Taking a deep breath, Sylvia walked down the dim corridor, Sophia's parents close behind. They reached the red door and hesitated, the gravity of the situation weighing heavily on them. Sylvia inserted the key and turned it slowly. The door creaked open, revealing a small, dimly lit apartment, the curtains drawn tightly, filtering the sunlight into muted shades.

"Sophia?" Sylvia called softly, stepping inside. The living room was neat, but there was a palpable air of sadness, as if the walls themselves were holding their breath. Sophia's parents followed; their faces etched with worry and fear.

"Sophia, it's Mum and Dad," her mother called out gently, her voice laced with concern. "We're here, sweetheart."

There was no response. They moved through the apartment, their anxiety growing with each silent room. The kitchen was dirty, the dishes piled up everywhere, but no sign of life. Finally, they found her in her bedroom, lying on the bed, her eyes red and swollen from crying, her hair tangled around her face like a curtain shielding her from the world.

"Sophia," Sylvia said, rushing to her side. "We were so worried."

Sophia looked up, her face a mixture of relief and sorrow. "I'm sorry," she whispered, the words barely escaping her cracked lips. "I didn't mean to scare you."

Her parents enveloped her in a hug, tears streaming down their faces, the warmth of their love wrapping around her like a security blanket. "We love you so much, Sophia," her father said, his voice breaking. "You're not alone. We'll get through this together. You're stronger than you think."

Sylvia sat beside her, holding her hand tightly, trying to transmit all the support and love she felt through that simple gesture. "We're here for you, no matter what," she said firmly, her voice steady.

For the first time in days, Sophia felt a glimmer of hope. Surrounded by the people who loved her most, she knew she would find the strength to heal and move forward, even if the path seemed daunting. In that moment, it dawned on her she didn't have to face this alone; together, they would navigate the storm, hand in hand.

Chapter Sixty One

Jack was fuming, his face a stormy red, as he replayed the events in his mind. How could Oliver have destroyed Sophia's life in such a callous way? The sheer audacity of that Oliver filled him with rage. His anger was palpable, and he paced back and forth in the small flat, the sound of his footsteps echoing against the bare walls, fists clenched tightly at his sides. Jackie, his wife, tried to calm him down, though she herself was just as upset, her brows knitted in concern.

After leaving Sophia's small flat, they opted for coffee at a nearby café, hoping the change of scenery might help them clear their minds and focus on their daughter. Jack stirred his coffee aggressively, the clink of the spoon against the ceramic cup echoing his frustration. "That Oliver needs to pay for what he's done," he growled, eyes ablaze with determination. "No one messes with my family and gets away with it."

Jackie placed a comforting hand on his arm, trying to ground him. "I know, Jack. I feel the same way. But we need to think this through. We need to be there for Sophia, not just seek revenge." Her voice was calm, but Jack could hear the undercurrent of shared anger and heartbreak in her words.

Jack was not the kind of man to let things go. As a very successful businessman, he had built his empire through sheer grit and resilience, often wielding a ruthless edge when necessary. Jackie knew all too well how tough he could be, having witnessed the lengths he'd go to protect his loved ones. She could see the determination in his eyes, the gears turning in his head as he weighed his options, plotting a course of action.

Meanwhile, Sylvia, Sophia's close friend, looked around the flat, taking in the disarray. It had never been particularly neat, but now it was a chaotic reflection of Sophia's inner turmoil. Wine bottles, their labels crumpled and faded, and takeaway containers from various fast-food outlets littered the room, standing as evidence of Sophia's despair—all thanks to Oliver.

The bathroom door creaked open, and Sophia emerged, having had a refreshing shower. She felt and looked a lot better, her hair damp and curling gently around her shoulders. Sylvia handed her a mug of steaming coffee, and they sat at the small kitchen table, trying to focus on the comforting warmth of the drink rather than the pile of unwashed dishes that loomed like a mountain before them.

"How do you feel?" asked Sylvia gently, taking a sip of her coffee, her eyes searching Sophia's for a glimmer of hope.

"Foolish," replied Sophia with a rueful smile, her gaze drifting down to her hands wrapped around the mug.

They both laughed softly, a brief moment of levity breaking the heavy silence that had settled over them. Sylvia looked around the messy flat and then back at Sophia, a spark of mischief lighting up her eyes. "Well, that's a good start. How about you give me a hand with the dishes?"

Sophia laughed again, this time a bit more genuinely, the sound a balm to her frayed nerves. Picking up a dry towel, she said, "You wash, I'll dry."

As they worked together, the rhythmic clinking of plates and utensils began to drown out the echoes of the past few days. The act of cleaning the dishes, while simple, seemed to cleanse some of the heaviness from the air. It wasn't just about tidying up the flat; it was a small step toward restoring order and clarity in Sophia's life. With each soapy dish, the chaos began to recede, allowing space for hope and healing to take root amidst the lingering shadows of betrayal.

Chapter Sixty Two

Karen Phillips sat outside in the shadow of the morning sun, the soft warmth of the rays illuminating her thoughtful expression. She had settled onto a wrought-iron bench, surrounded by a tapestry of vibrant flowers swaying gently in the breeze. As she sipped her coffee, the hum of the town filled the air, momentarily blending with her thoughts. Just then, Oliver strolled by, his hands tucked casually in his pockets. Hearing her voice break through his reverie, he turned, a look of surprise transforming into delight as he recognised his old friend.

"Hello, Oliver," she said warmly, her voice brightening the space around them.

"Karen, how delightful to see you! What on earth are you doing in these parts?" Oliver asked, a broad smile spreading across his face as memories of their past flooded his mind.

"Oh, I have a meeting with a client," Karen replied, her tone casual but her eyes sparkling with the excitement of their encounter.

"Are you still working for Coutts Bank?" he inquired, genuinely interested.

"Only consulting now, but yes, that's why I am here," she explained, her expression shifting slightly as if to signal a deeper story behind her words.

Oliver's curiosity piqued. "We must catch up," he suggested eagerly, remembering the late-night brainstorming sessions they once shared over cups of coffee and piles of documents.

"Yes, my meeting will finish around noon," Karen said, glancing at her watch.

"Great! I'll text you. Are you still on your old number?" Oliver asked, pulling out his phone, his heart racing a little at the prospect of rekindling their friendship.

"Perfect," Karen confirmed, standing up to lean in and kiss him on the cheek, a gesture that felt both familiar and pleasantly nostalgic.

As she walked away, Oliver watched her for a moment, intrigued. It had been several years since he last saw Karen. The memory of her from their early days in London flickered vividly in his mind: a young, attractive woman holding her own in a male-dominated world, her fierce ambition evident even then.

Later that day, Karen strode into the Sussex Yacht Club, her trademark yellow stilettos clicking confidently against the polished wooden floor. She wore a figure-hugging light blue dress that accentuated her silhouette, and her long blonde hair was expertly tied back, showcasing her fresh-looking face that seemed untouched by time.

"Hello, may I help you?" Ruby, the receptionist from the back office, noticed Karen's entrance and greeted her with a friendly smile.

"Yes, I am looking for Oliver Wright. I am supposed to meet him here," Karen replied, her tone both professional and warm.

Ruby's smile widened. "Yes, of course. He's up in the members' lounge. I'll let you in. If you take the stairs, the door is straight ahead. Someone will open it for you."

"Many thanks," Karen said, her excitement bubbling beneath her composed exterior as she did as instructed. Ruby returned to her desk, glancing back with a knowing smile.

"Who was that?" asked Izzy, her curiosity piqued as she watched Ruby.

"Another one for Oliver," Ruby said with a playful smirk, both women laughing softly before diving back into their work.

Karen climbed the stairs, her heels echoing on the polished wood, the sound a rhythmic reminder of her determined stride. She paused briefly in front of the door, taking a moment to adjust her posture and smooth down her dress before it swung open almost immediately. There stood Oliver, his face lighting up at the sight of her.

"Karen, it's wonderful to see you again."

"It's good to see you too, Oliver. This place is charming," Karen remarked, her gaze sweeping around the lounge, taking in the elegant decor and the gentle hum of conversation.

Oliver led her to a small round table by the window, sunlight spilling in and casting a warm glow around them. "It's a favourite spot of mine. How have you been? It's been too long," he asked, genuinely interested in her life beyond work.

"Busy as always, but good. Consulting has its perks," Karen said with a smile that reached her eyes, revealing a depth of satisfaction. "And you? How's life treating you?"

"Can't complain. I've been enjoying the slower pace here compared to London," he replied, leaning back in his chair, feeling at ease in her presence.

Their conversation flowed naturally, picking up where they had left off years ago. They shared stories of professional triumphs and challenges, the laughter intertwining with moments of nostalgia as they reminisced about their early days. Oliver found himself utterly fascinated by Karen's stories of success, her resilience inspiring him as they navigated through the years that had passed since they last worked together.

⋯◈⋯

Chapter Sixty Three

As the afternoon wore on, their conversation flowed effortlessly, much like the champagne that sparkled in their glasses, casting a golden hue in the soft evening light. Karen always enjoyed Oliver's company; there was something about his infectious laughter and the way he listened intently that made her feel special. Despite their relationship being purely platonic, she often found herself pondering the idea of them as more than friends. The chemistry between them was palpable, sparking under the surface like a hidden flame. Yet, for reasons neither had ever articulated, they remained firmly in the realm of friendship.

"I don't know about you, but I am starving. Do you have any plans?" Oliver asked, his eyes twinkling with mischief, the playful glint making her heart flutter just a bit.

"Not now," Karen giggled as the bubbles from the champagne tickled her nose, a slight blush creeping onto her cheeks. "Well, I know of a lovely little place we could try." She felt a sense of adventure swell within her; she was always up for a spontaneous evening.

"Well, let's go," she said, draining the last golden drop from her glass, the crisp taste lingering pleasantly on her palate. Oliver held out his arm to steady her as they stood up, attracting amused glances from others in the club. Their close camaraderie had a way of drawing attention, and Oliver, with his boyish charm and effortless charisma, had a bit of a reputation when it came to his love life. Their departure seemed to spark curiosity among the crowd, but the two of them were blissfully unaware, wrapped up in their own world.

The walk to Oliver's new penthouse apartment was short, the cool evening air refreshing against Karen's flushed skin. "Wow, that champagne went straight to my head," she admitted, laughing lightly as the buzz of the alcohol settled in. "I'm not sure I can drive home tonight." A hint of worry flickered in her mind, but she quickly brushed it aside; she felt safe with Oliver.

"Don't worry, I have plenty of spare rooms for you to stay the night," Oliver replied, his voice reassuring and warm. There was a spark of something unspoken in his eyes, and she felt a thrill run through her, but she pushed it down, reminding herself of the boundaries they had set.

She squeezed his arm playfully and teased, "Are you hitting on me?"

"Me?" Oliver responded with a mock scandalised voice, his mouth curving into a grin that made her heart skip. "Never! I'm just a gentleman, ensuring you don't end up stranded after a champagne-fuelled afternoon!"

He led Karen into his apartment, taking her coat and hanging it neatly on the rack next to his own. The space was more than just a living area; it was a reflection of Oliver's personality—stylish yet inviting, with art adorning the walls and plush furnishings creating an atmosphere of relaxed elegance. "Whoa, what a place," she exclaimed, her eyes wide as she took in the luxurious décor, each detail a testament to his refined taste.

"Yes, it's not bad for a little seaside town. It's not London, but it's pretty good," Oliver said, a hint of pride lacing his voice as he gestured toward the expansive living room filled with natural light.

"It's very nice. I might think about getting a place like this," Karen mused, allowing her imagination to drift to the possibility of living near him, where their friendship could flourish even further.

Oliver smiled, his eyes glinting with mischief. "Well, if you do, let me know. I could use a good neighbour—one who can indulge in champagne and late-night conversations."

He poured them each another glass of champagne and led her to the spacious balcony overlooking the river, the soft light of the setting sun casting a warm glow over everything. The sound of the water lapping gently against the river's edge added a calming backdrop to their evening, and the distant lights reflecting on the surface created a magical ambience.

As they sat there, sipping their champagne and talking about everything from work to dreams of future adventures, Karen couldn't help but feel a sense of contentment. It was more than just the drink; it was the ease of their connection, the way their laughter mingled with the sounds of the evening, creating a perfect harmony. Each shared smile and playful jab felt like stepping closer to that line they had never crossed, and for the first time, she wondered if maybe, just maybe, tonight might be the night that everything changed.

Chapter Sixty Four

"Who is your decorator?" Karen asked with a curious tilt of her head, her voice light and inviting.

"Her name is Lisa, recommended by a friend," Oliver replied, leaning against the doorframe with a relaxed posture.

"Why are you interested in her services?" Karen inquired further, her eyes sparkling with interest.

Oliver shrugged, trying to maintain a casual demeanour. "I'm just looking to give this place a bit more personality, you know,"

Karen laughed, a rich sound that filled the room like music. "Can you tell me if she is any good?" she asked, her tone teasing yet genuine.

Oliver's expression turned serious, a hint of protectiveness in his voice. "It's strictly business, you know. You never ruin a good thing."

"Well, I love the Moroccan vibe she has given the living room," Karen said, glancing around appreciatively. The warm earth tones, intricate patterns, and soft textiles created an inviting atmosphere that enveloped them.

Oliver smiled warmly, pride swelling in his chest. "You should see the master bedroom. It's like a retreat."

Karen placed her hand on his arm, her eyes twinkling with mischief. "Play your cards right, and I might take you up on that," she flirted, leaning in slightly.

Oliver chuckled, a warmth spreading through him as he headed into the kitchen. He opened the American-style fridge, scanning the shelves for something to cook. "I wasn't joking about being famished," he called out over his shoulder, hoping to keep the playful banter going. "What would you like to eat?"

Karen lounged back on the couch, her smile radiant. "I'm easy," she replied, her voice casual but laced with a hint of intrigue.

Oliver grinned to himself, thinking, "I hope so." He returned to the living room, balancing two glasses of champagne in his hands. He handed one to Karen, their fingers brushing lightly. "I have some leftover chicken casserole I can heat up. It's quite delicious, even if I do say so myself."

"Sounds perfect. I'll set the table if you show me where everything is kept," Karen offered, rising from the couch with a determined grace.

Oliver led her to the sideboard in the dining room, gesturing grandly. "Everything you need is right here," he said, the warmth of their interaction making him feel at ease.

As he returned to the kitchen, the ping of the microwave signalled that dinner was ready. Oliver plated the chicken casserole, its savoury aroma filling the air, and paired it with a side of fluffy brown rice and a fresh salad drizzled with balsamic vinaigrette. He poured a glass of Chardonnay, its crispness a perfect complement to the meal.

They settled down at the dining table, the soft glow of warm light creating an intimate atmosphere that made the evening feel special. As they began to eat, the conversation flowed effortlessly, weaving between stories of their lives, aspirations, and dreams. Laughter punctuated their exchanges, and shared smiles danced between them, making the evening feel like the start of something new and exciting.

With each bite, Oliver felt the connection between them deepen, and he couldn't shake the feeling that this night was a beautiful turning point in their friendship. As the meal progressed, he found himself captivated not just by the delicious food, but by Karen's vibrant personality and the chemistry that crackled in the air around them.

⊷⊶⊰❈⊱⊷⊶

Chapter Sixty Five

After the meal, Oliver cleared the dishes with a practised ease, moving around the kitchen like a conductor leading a well-rehearsed orchestra. When Karen offered to help, he turned to her with a polite but firm smile, "No, thank you. I'm a modern man, and guests are not allowed to lift a finger in my home." His voice carried a playful charm, and Karen couldn't help but admire his old-fashioned sense of hospitality. It was both charming and slightly amusing, a refreshing reminder of manners that seemed rare in modern life.

She watched as he disappeared into the kitchen, the sound of clattering dishes fading away, leaving her in a moment of unexpected solitude. With a curious heart, Karen took the opportunity to explore the rest of his apartment, her senses heightened by the gentle hum of the night.

As she wandered into the living room, she was struck by the tasteful decor that blended contemporary design with hints of classic elegance. A plush sofa in deep blue was accented by throw pillows in varying textures, while a sleek coffee table displayed a carefully curated selection of art books. She paused by a towering bookshelf, running her fingers over the spines of volumes that ranged from classic literature to gripping modern thrillers. Each title whispered stories, and she found herself imagining Oliver engrossed in their pages during quiet evenings.

A large, framed photograph of a serene beach caught her eye, the soft sand and gentle waves evoking a sense of peace. Karen wondered where it was taken, her imagination painting scenes of sun-soaked afternoons spent lounging in the warmth of the sun. As she stood there, a sense of admiration for Oliver grew within her; he clearly had an eye for beauty, both in art and in life.

Her wandering led her to the balcony, where the view of the river was nothing short of breathtaking. The moon hung low in the sky, casting a silvery glow over the water. The town lights reflected on the surface, creating a shimmering, almost magical effect that made her breath catch in her throat. The cool night air wrapped around her, filling her lungs with a refreshing calm, a stark contrast to the warmth she had felt moments before in the dining room.

Just then, Oliver emerged from the kitchen, wiping his hands on a towel. "Dishes are done," he announced, stepping onto the balcony with two glasses of Chardonnay in hand. He handed one to Karen, his fingers brushing against hers in a way that sent a spark of electricity through her. "Quite a view, isn't it?"

Karen turned to him, ready to agree, but she realised he wasn't looking at the river. His gaze was fixed intently on her, his eyes reflecting the soft glow of the moonlight. She felt her cheeks warm under his intense stare, a flutter of nerves mixed with excitement. "You're an old tease," she said with a laugh, feeling both flattered and slightly embarrassed by the attention.

Oliver's smile widened, crinkling the corners of his eyes. "Guilty as charged," he said, stepping closer to her. The air between them thickened with an unspoken tension. He leaned in, their faces inches apart, and gently placed their glasses down on the glass-topped table. His hands cupped her face, his thumbs brushing lightly against her cheeks, sending shivers down her spine.

Karen's heart began to race, a mixture of excitement and nervous anticipation building within her as she felt the heat of his body close to hers. His presence enveloped her, creating a bubble where the outside world seemed to fade away.

He kissed her tenderly on the lips, soft yet firm, igniting a fire within her that she hadn't anticipated. "Oh, Oliver, should we?" Karen whispered, her voice shaky with a mix of desire and uncertainty. The question hung between them, fragile and full of promise.

"Yes," he murmured back, his voice low and reassuring, like a warm blanket on a cold night. "There's no reason why we shouldn't. We're both adults with no partners. We could be good together."

Karen wasn't sure if it was the wine or the intoxicating pull of the moment that made her breath catch in her throat. She looked into Oliver's eyes and saw sincerity and longing reflected back at her, a connection that felt both exhilarating and terrifying. The world outside their intimate cocoon blurred into insignificance.

Succumbing to his wishes, she leaned into him, their bodies pressing together, the warmth radiating between them. He held her tightly in his arms, the kiss deepening, growing more passionate, more insistent. The night wrapped around them like a velvet curtain, muffling the sounds of the streets below. Time seemed to stand still as they became lost in each other, the rest of the world slipping away. They were committed to a night of desire and exploration that neither would soon forget, the magic of the evening forever etched in their memories.

⸺◈⸺

Chapter Sixty Six

Driven by passion, their bodies merged as one. Having moved to the living room from the balcony, Karen's clothes were torn from her in the heat of the moment. Oliver lifted her naked body with ease, and she ruffled his hair, pulling it as he unbuttoned his trousers, letting them fall to the floor.

They fell laughing onto the floor, composing themselves. Taking a breath, they moved to the nearest chair—a large brown leather one sitting in the corner of the room. Karen sat on Oliver's lap, roughly pulling his head back by his hair, looking down as his hands explored her back, moving down her spine, caressing her with his gentle touch.

Their body heat and sweat glistened in the moonlight as Karen took charge of Oliver. He moaned as Karen's hips worked up and down on his erect manhood, the pleasure on his face giving Karen a sense of power.

Oliver started to wilt, feeling disappointed and a bit embarrassed. Karen kissed him, hoping to arouse him, but that didn't work. Not willing to give up, she had a twinkle in her eye. She unclasped her necklace and unscrewed the top of the amulet, tapping out white powder onto the small table.

Oliver, intrigued, asked, "What are you doing?"

"Well, it's been a while, and I don't usually do this anymore, but it's handy," she replied.

She dipped into her handbag and retrieved a five-pound note, then rolled it tightly into a tube. After chopping the white powder into neat lines, she put the rolled note to her nose and hoovered up the powder. Oliver took the fiver and enjoyed the sensation, and the energy renewed his prowess.

He took Karen up in his arms, bending her over the leather chair, spreading her hips. With the blood flowing through his manhood, he entered her. She gasped as he pushed his hips forward, pulling on her long hair. They moved as one, both enjoying the intensity of their actions.

He pinned her to the chair, moving into a position where he could dominate her. She abandoned herself to the frenzied action of Oliver's pleasure.

Without thought, their bodies crashed together, feeling unstoppable. Oliver threw Karen to the floor; he was now in charge. The drugs in their system took them to new highs. His body tightened as he strained against Karen's body, and then they both hit erotic highs.

Lying on the polished wooden floor, their hearts beating fast and their bodies still on fire, they were unable to speak. Their chests heaved, gasping for air. The cool night air drifted into the apartment, cooling their bodies.

Chapter Sixty Seven

At 5 AM, Karen stood in front of the bathroom mirror, applying her lipstick in the dim light. The vibrant red of the lipstick was a stark contrast against the soft shadows of the early morning, bringing a splash of colour to the otherwise muted hues of the room. Each careful stroke highlighted her full lips, transforming her appearance into one of bold confidence. She picked up her yellow stilettos, the sleek heels clutched in her hand to avoid making noise on the polished wooden floor, and quietly tiptoed around the room.

As she glanced back at the bed, her heart softened at the sight of Oliver, still asleep, his breathing deep and even. She left a neatly folded note on the bedside table, its presence barely disturbing the serene scene, as if it were a whisper left behind. Leaning down, she kissed Oliver gently on the cheek, her lips brushing against his skin like a feather. He lay naked, half-covered with luxurious Egyptian cotton sheets that softly draped over his body, blissfully unaware of her departure.

Karen slipped out of the room, her heart racing with a mix of excitement and regret. The hallway was dimly lit, and she navigated it with a practised ease, the remnants of their night together swirling in her mind. As she reached the elevator, she pressed the button for the car park level, the soft ding of the doors opening.

Once inside, the atmosphere shifted; the soft hum of the machinery filled her ears, and she took a deep breath, inhaling the scent of leather and faint perfume lingering in the air. She made her way to her sleek black BMW Z4, its polished exterior glinting in the low light. Sitting in the driver's seat, she paused for a moment, allowing herself to reflect on the night spent with Oliver. Memories of laughter, shared secrets, and intimate touches danced in her mind, a smile playing on her lips. The thrill of their connection was intoxicating, but she also felt a weight of reality settling in.

Turning the key in the ignition, the engine roared to life, a powerful sound echoing in the quiet of the garage. She shifted into gear and drove out of Shoreham, the town's silhouette gradually fading in her rearview mirror, leaving behind not just a physical place but a fleeting moment in time.

At 7 AM, Oliver woke up from the most restful sleep he had ever experienced. The world outside was just beginning to brighten, golden rays of sunlight filtering through the curtains. He stretched out his arm, expecting to find Karen beside him, but his hand met only the cool, empty space of the bed. Confused, he lifted his head, his eyes searching the room for any sign of her presence.

His gaze fell upon the note on the bedside table, its corners perfectly aligned. He picked it up, unfolding it with a mix of anticipation and dread. As he read her words, the sunlight caught the ink, illuminating the carefully crafted sentences:

"Hi lovely, thank you for such an unforgettable night. Sorry I had to leave so early, but work never sleeps, and I have another meeting to get to this morning. It was a blast, though I don't think we would be more than what we had last night."

Oliver smiled, a wave of warmth washing over him despite the pang of loss. He got out of bed, the coolness of the wooden floor beneath his feet grounding him in reality and walked to the kitchen to make himself a cup of coffee. As the rich aroma filled the air, he contemplated the note's message, its sincerity resonating within him.

He leaned against the counter, watching the steam swirl from the mug as he took a sip. With each taste, he couldn't help but admit that Karen was right. Their connection, though intense and electric, was fleeting, much like the night they shared. Perhaps that was all it was ever meant to be—an exhilarating adventure, a beautiful moment suspended in time.

Yet, as he savoured the warmth of the coffee, he realised that some moments, no matter how brief, leave an indelible mark on our hearts. They shape us, teach us, and ultimately become cherished memories. Oliver smiled softly to himself, accepting that while their paths may not intertwine further, the essence of that night would linger, a vibrant thread woven into the fabric of his life.

Chapter Sixty Eight

Oliver's parents were not wealthy in the traditional sense, but they could afford the finer things in life, prioritising quality over quantity. They had a keen appreciation for beauty and artistry, which was evident in their home filled with an eclectic mix of decor. Oliver grew up in a loving household, where both his parents worked hard, instilling in him the values of dedication and perseverance.

His father was a successful importer of fine art, a career that not only brought in a good income but also filled their home with beautiful and unique pieces from around the world. Their living room was adorned with a stunning collection of paintings and sculptures, each with its own story that sparked Oliver's imagination. From a young age, he learned to appreciate the nuances of colour, texture, and form, often accompanying his father to galleries and exhibitions where he would listen intently to discussions about artistry and craftsmanship.

His mother was equally successful in her profession as a solicitor, eventually making partner at a prestigious law firm. Her work ethic was unmatched, and she often brought home stories of complex cases that taught Oliver the importance of justice, integrity, and hard work. She would sit with him at the kitchen table, poring over his homework while offering insights into legal principles, helping him develop critical thinking skills that would serve him well in life.

Recognising Oliver's exceptional gift and thirst for learning, his parents were determined to provide him with the best education possible. As their only child, they focused all their resources and attention on nurturing his talents. They enrolled him in the most exclusive private schools, where the quality of education and the opportunities available were unparalleled. Here, he had access to a wide range of subjects, from advanced mathematics to the arts, and participated in extracurricular activities like debate club and the school orchestra.

Oliver thrived in this environment, consistently excelling in his studies and various extracurricular activities, making his parents immensely proud. He was not just a good student; he was a natural leader among his peers, often taking charge of group projects and motivating his classmates to perform their best. His achievements were celebrated at home, where his parents would organise small family gatherings to recognise his milestones, whether it was a top grade on a report card or a successful performance in the school play.

Every achievement was not only a testament to his abilities but also a reflection of the love and support that surrounded him at home. His parents created a nurturing atmosphere where curiosity was encouraged, and questions were welcomed. They fostered his love for learning, whether through family trips to museums, discussions over dinner about current events, or quiet evenings spent reading together.

Oliver's upbringing gave him a strong foundation of confidence and ambition, instilling a belief that he could achieve anything he set his mind to. It also developed in him a deep appreciation for the arts and law, shaping his aspirations for the future. Their unwavering support motivated him to pursue a career where he could make a significant impact, combining his love for business with the values his parents had instilled in him. He wanted to emulate their dedication and success, contributing not only to his own life but also to the legacy of hard work and passion that his family represented.

Chapter Sixty Nine

Mr. and Mrs. Wright were brimming with pride for their only son, Oliver. He had always shown promise, but now, standing on the threshold of Winston Hall, he was about to embark on a journey that would set him apart from his peers. Winston Hall, nestled deep within the rolling hills and ancient woodlands of Hampshire County, was no ordinary school. It was a bastion of tradition and excellence, a place where young men were moulded into leaders. The school's legacy stretched back generations, and Oliver was no stranger to this, as his father's father had once walked the very same corridors.

On Oliver's first day, he stood wide-eyed in the grand entrance hall, utterly captivated by the scene before him. The majestic oak-panelled walls glowed with a rich, honeyed sheen, their surface intricately carved with the emblems and histories of alumni long past. A sweeping staircase dominated the room, its polished banister gleaming in the golden light that streamed through the towering stained-glass windows. Every day, Oliver would ascend these stairs, each step taking him further into the life his parents had dreamed for him.

He clutched his mother's hand tightly, drawing comfort from her presence. In his other hand, he grasped his brown leather case—a gift from his father. The case, though small, contained everything he would need for the years ahead: a few neatly folded shirts, trousers, notebooks, and his most prized possession—a well-worn copy of his favourite book, 'Treasure Island'. Oliver had been told that the next five years would be filled with rigorous study, discipline, and growth. He would face challenges, make friendships that would last a lifetime, and ultimately live up to the expectations that came with bearing the Wright name.

His mother's eyes were misty, a mixture of pride and the bittersweet realisation that her little boy was growing up. She knelt beside him, straightening his tie for the third time that morning, her fingers lingering on his collar as if to hold on to the moment just a little longer.

"You're going to do brilliantly here, Oliver," she whispered, her voice soft but full of belief.

Oliver nodded, his heart thudding in his chest. He wasn't just entering a school; he was stepping into a legacy. Winston Hall had been a beacon of excellence for centuries, and now it was his turn to leave a mark. He squared his shoulders, ready to face the future, and together with his mother, they took that first step toward the staircase that would lead him to his dormitory—and to the start of his new life.

Oliver soon settled into the school's routine, though it was not without its challenges. The sleeping quarters were sparse, with narrow single beds lined up in neat rows, their thin mattresses offering little comfort against the chill of the stone-walled dormitory. The early mornings were punctuated by the sharp clang of the wake-up bell, and the boys were expected to be dressed and ready for breakfast within minutes.

Despite the rigid structure of boarding school life, Oliver quickly made both friends and enemies. Among the latter was Dominic Smyth-Waterstone, a boy of privilege whose father was one of the school's esteemed masters. Dominic carried himself with an air of entitlement, using his father's position to his advantage whenever possible. From the moment Oliver arrived, Dominic seemed to take an immediate dislike to him.

Every opportunity he had, Dominic sought to get Oliver into trouble, often with the head boy, Johnston, a strict enforcer of the school's rules. Whether it was for being late to breakfast because Oliver couldn't find his school tie, or for some other minor infraction, there was always a common thread—something had been misplaced or tampered with, and the real culprit was none other than Dominic himself. Yet, with his polished manners and ability to feign innocence, Dominic never seemed to be caught, leaving Oliver to face the brunt of the punishments.

It wasn't long before Oliver learned to be wary of Dominic's schemes, though outwitting him would prove to be another challenge altogether.

Johnston pulled Oliver to one side; his expression unreadable. Oliver had noticed the head boy watching him closely over the past few weeks, though he had no idea why. Now, as Johnston led him through the dimly lit corridors, Oliver's stomach churned with unease.

They arrived at Johnston's quarters, a stark contrast to the cold and unwelcoming dormitories. A warm fire crackled in the hearth, casting flickering shadows across the walls. A large wooden desk sat near the fire, its surface scattered with open books and neatly stacked papers. Shelves lined with worn leather-bound volumes gave the room an air of quiet authority, far more inviting than the sparse sleeping quarters Oliver shared with the other boys.

Oliver stood rigid; his hands clenched behind his back. He was a little nervous—he had been in trouble almost from his first day at school, and he doubted this meeting would bring good news.

Johnston turned to face him; arms crossed. "Mr. Wright," he said, addressing Oliver formally, as he did all the boys. "How are you settling in?"

Oliver straightened his posture. "Well, sir. It's been a challenge, but I think I have the gist of everything."

Johnston gave a small nod. "Yes, it's difficult at the start, but I'm sure you'll fit right in. However," he paused, studying Oliver carefully. "I see you've crossed swords with Smyth-Waterstone."

At the mention of Dominic's name, Oliver's jaw tightened. He forced himself to remain neutral. "Sir?"

Johnston exhaled through his nose, shaking his head slightly. "He's a tricky character. My advice is to steer clear of him. His father's influence affords him more protection than most, and he knows how to use it."

Oliver hesitated before answering. "Yes, sir. Thank you, sir."

A faint smile tugged at the corner of Johnston's mouth. "Good lad."

They spoke for some time, and as the minutes passed, Oliver gradually relaxed. Johnston was stern but fair, and by the end of their conversation, Oliver felt more confident—more assured that he could handle Dominic and whatever tricks he might throw his way.

The first year flew by in a whirlwind of new experiences, friendships, and challenges. Oliver eagerly immersed himself in School life, joining several clubs ranging from sailing to literature. He had a natural aptitude for most things he tried—his competitive streak driving him to excel in sports, debates, and even the odd chess match. Literature, however, was a different story. Despite his best efforts, he found himself struggling through dense novels and poetry that seemed to speak in riddles. Yet, he stubbornly refused to quit. The reason? Penny Charlton.

Penny was a year older, effortlessly sophisticated, and utterly out of his league. With her sharp wit, confidence and an air of quiet mystery, she had an almost magnetic presence. Oliver knew she barely noticed him, but that only made the challenge more enticing. If joining the literature club meant spending more time in her orbit, he would endure Shakespeare, Dickens, and whatever else was thrown at him.

His best friend, Duncan, found the entire thing hilarious. Each day, without fail, Duncan would rib him mercilessly about his hopeless infatuation.

"You? A date with Penny Charlton?" he scoffed over lunch one afternoon. "Mate, I have a better chance of becoming Prime Minister. She only dates guys who wear blazers unironically and have family names that sound like country estates."

Oliver refused to let the teasing deter him. "You'll see," he said with quiet determination. "One day, I'll take her out, and you'll eat your words."

Duncan grinned, shaking his head. "Alright, dreamer. But if you actually manage I will clean your football boots for a month."

With that wager in mind, Oliver threw himself even harder into his literary pursuits, determined to prove Duncan wrong.

It was the final of the interschool sailing challenge. Oliver, captain of the school sailing club, felt his stomach churn with nerves. This was the last relay, and they were in second place. Victory was within reach, but it would not come easily. Their school had not won the coveted cup in five years, and the pressure weighed heavily on his shoulders.

Oliver and his crew had worked tirelessly throughout the season, refining their technique, learning from their mistakes, and forging a camaraderie that had strengthened their resolve. But their journey to the final had not been without its challenges—broken equipment, unpredictable winds, and gruelling training sessions had tested them at every turn. Now, with everything on the line, they had to dig deep, summon every ounce of skill, and execute their best performance yet. Their rivals had won the cup five times in a row, a streak Oliver was determined to break.

Duncan stood beside Oliver, adjusting the sail ropes with meticulous precision. They had once clashed over strategies and leadership, but through the trials of competition, they had become close friends. Duncan's normally confident expression was tinged with concern as he asked, "Do you think we can beat them?"

Oliver, too, felt the weight of uncertainty, but his years of experience told him that doubt had no place in a sailor's mind. He straightened, took a deep breath, and gave Duncan a reassuring nod. "If we stick together and sail smart, we can."

The race was about to start, and both teams were keen to claim victory. The air was thick with tension as the final competitors took their places. The wind was brisk, and the water shimmered under the afternoon sun, promising a challenging contest ahead.

The sharp crack of the starting pistol shattered the silence. The race had begun.

The course was a tight figure-eight, a layout designed to test the sailors' ability to manoeuvre swiftly and tack efficiently. Precision was key—one wrong turn, one miscalculation, and their dreams of victory would slip away like water through their fingers.

Oliver and Duncan sprang into action, their movements fluid and in sync. They adjusted their sails expertly, catching the wind just right to propel them forward. The first turn approached rapidly. Oliver called out commands, and Duncan responded without hesitation. They rounded the marker smoothly, their time looking promising.

On the rival boat, Ken and his teammate watched intently. They were seasoned sailors, veterans of this challenge, and they knew Oliver's team had improved significantly. But they were not about to surrender their winning streak without a fight.

The boats sliced through the water, neck and neck. The crowd on the shore erupted into cheers, urging their teams forward. The final stretch loomed ahead. Oliver clenched his jaw—this was it.

Every decision, every adjustment of the sail, every movement had led to this moment.

Would they have what it takes to finally reclaim the cup?

The wind howled across the water, carrying the sharp bite of sea spray that struck Oliver's face, leaving a salty sting on his skin. His hands were numb from the cold, gripping the ropes tightly as their small sailing boat surged forward. Duncan, his ever-reliable teammate, sat beside him, eyes locked ahead, scanning the challenge course and keeping a wary eye on their fiercest rivals, Ken and Ian.

The two boats weaved in and out of the markers, each manoeuvre precise, each adjustment crucial. The competition was fierce—neither team willing to concede an inch. Every gust of wind, every shift of the tide, could mean the difference between victory and defeat. The crowd on the shoreline—friends, teachers, and parents—stood in tense anticipation, their cheers muffled by the roaring wind and the crashing waves.

Then disaster struck.

Ken, battling the elements, made a costly mistake. His wet hands lost their grip for just a fraction of a second, the ropes slipping between his fingers. The sails slackened momentarily—just long enough for Oliver and Duncan to seize their chance. With practised precision and unwavering nerves, Oliver adjusted their course, and Duncan responded instantly. Their boat cut through the water like a blade, taking the lead by the slimmest of margins.

The final stretch was heart-pounding. Every breath, every movement, was in perfect sync as they pushed their boat to its limits. The finish line loomed ahead, and with one last coordinated effort, Oliver and Duncan surged forward—crossing just inches ahead of Ken and Ian.

A triumphant cheer erupted from the shore. The long wait was over. After five years, the coveted sailing cup was theirs once again. Oliver and Duncan looked toward the crowd, spotting familiar faces—teachers waving, parents clapping, friends jumping up and down in celebration. They had done it.

Meanwhile, Ken sat in his boat, his expression tight with frustration. His jaw clenched as he realised the weight of his mistake. The bitter sting of disappointment settled in, but he swallowed it down. As soon as they had secured their boats at the dock, Ken and Ian approached their rivals. There was no need for words—they all knew this would not be the last time they would meet.

Ken extended his hand, and Oliver shook it firmly. "Next year," Ken vowed, a determined gleam in his eye.

Duncan smirked, "We'll be ready."

For now, though, the victory belonged to Oliver and Duncan. The cup was theirs, and the celebration had only just begun.

Oliver wove through the bustling crowd, his pulse still racing from the thrill of victory. The salty breeze from the ocean tousled his hair, and the hum of excited chatter filled the air. As he neared his parents, a familiar figure caught his eye—Penny. She stood near the dock, her bright smile unmistakable.

Oliver hesitated for a split second before turning toward her, suddenly feeling a different kind of nervousness bubbling up inside him.

"Congratulations!" Penny beamed, her eyes sparkling with excitement.

"Thank you," Oliver replied, feeling warmth rise to his cheeks. He took a steadying breath before continuing. "I was wondering... would you like to go out sometime?"

Penny's smile widened, and for a moment, Oliver felt as if time had slowed.

"Yes," she said without hesitation. "I would love to."

Relief and happiness flooded Oliver. "Great! Can I message you?"

"Of course," Penny said, pulling out a small notepad and scribbling down her number. She tore off the page and handed it to him, her fingers briefly brushing against his.

Oliver tucked the number safely into his pocket, feeling like he had just won more than just a race today. "I'll text you," he promised, grinning.

As he turned back toward his parents, he found them watching with amused smiles. His father clapped him on the back with a hearty chuckle.

"That's my boy!" his father said, ruffling Oliver's hair.

Oliver laughed, ducking away slightly, but his mother wasn't about to let him off the hook so easily.

"First the big win, and now a date?" she teased, nudging him playfully. "You're on quite the streak today, aren't you?"

Oliver shook his head, unable to suppress his grin. "Guess it's just my lucky day."

His parents laughed as they walked together toward the celebration, the scent of grilled seafood and fresh ocean air mixing around them. Oliver glanced back once at Penny, who gave him a small wave before disappearing into the crowd.

The celebrations had finally come to an end, and Oliver sat with his parents, still basking in the warmth of the evening. His father, a keen sailor, beamed with pride as he looked at his son.

"You've done well, Oliver," he said, his voice filled with admiration. "How about we take the yacht out and sail the Mediterranean this summer? Just you, me, and the open sea—if you're interested."

Oliver's heart leaped. The idea of spending the summer sailing across the Mediterranean sounded like a dream. He could already picture the endless blue waters, the sun on his face, and the thrill of navigating through breathtaking coastal towns.

"That sounds amazing, Dad!" Oliver exclaimed, his excitement evident.

They spent the next hour talking about their upcoming adventure—where they would go, what they would see, and how it would feel to be out on the open sea. But soon, the evening had to come to an end. It was time for Oliver to say goodbye and head back to Winston Hall.

His mother fussed over him, hugging him tightly as if she didn't want to let go. "Take care of yourself, darling," she said, smoothing his hair as she always did. His father, in his usual composed manner, extended a firm handshake, though the warmth in his eyes spoke volumes.

Chapter Seventy

Penny opened her wardrobe, her fingers brushing against the fabrics of her dresses as she searched for the perfect outfit. Butterflies fluttered in her stomach—tonight was the school dance, and Oliver was taking her. It was surreal. For so long, she had watched him from afar, admiring the way he laughed with his friends, the easy confidence he carried. And now, he had asked her. It felt like a dream.

She finally settled on a deep blue dress that shimmered slightly under the light. Holding it against herself, she let out a deep breath. "It's just a dance," she whispered. "No big deal." But her heart hammered against her ribs, betraying her attempt at calm.

Meanwhile, Oliver stood in front of his mirror, adjusting his tie for the third time. His palms were slightly sweaty, and he exhaled sharply. He had won the bet with Duncan—he had managed to get a date with Penny—but that felt like the least important part now. Tonight, he just wanted to make it special.

"You ready, mate?" Duncan grinned at him from the doorway.

"As I'll ever be," Oliver muttered, giving himself one last look before grabbing his jacket and heading out.

The great hall was alive with colour and movement. Streamers hung from the ceiling, fairy lights twinkling like tiny stars. The music thumped through the room, filling the air with excitement. Groups of students laughed and danced, while others stood chatting near the refreshment table.

Penny and Oliver sat at one of the tables, both fidgeting—him with his tie, her with the hem of her dress. The silence between them stretched, wide and uncertain.

Oliver cleared his throat. "Would you like a drink?"

Penny looked up at him and smiled softly. "Yes, that would be nice."

Relieved to have something to do, Oliver quickly stood and made his way to the drinks table, where Miss Wilson, the ever-serious maths master, was dutifully pouring cups of fruit punch.

"Ah, Mr. Wright" she said, arching an eyebrow. "Behaving yourself, I hope?"

"Yes, Miss Wilson," Oliver replied quickly, grabbing two cups and making his way back to Penny. He handed her a cup and sat down, sneaking a glance at her as she took a sip. She looked radiant under the soft glow of the fairy lights, and Oliver knew he couldn't sit here all night doing nothing.

Summoning his courage, he set his drink down and turned to her. "Would you like to dance?"

Penny's face lit up, her nerves momentarily forgotten. "I would love to."

As they stepped onto the dance floor, the music slowed to a gentle melody. Oliver hesitated for a moment before placing his hands lightly on Penny's waist. She rested her hands on his shoulders, the warmth of the moment settling between them.

They swayed to the music, the world around them fading into the background. Oliver, emboldened by the rhythm and her closeness, leaned in slightly. "You look beautiful tonight," he murmured.

Penny's cheeks warmed, but she smiled. "Thank you. I was so nervous, but I'm glad I came."

"Me too," Oliver admitted.

The night stretched on, but in that moment, as they danced, all that mattered was the music, the warmth of each other's company, and the quiet promise of something new beginning.

Chapter Seventy One

The days and weeks leading up to the trip seemed to stretch endlessly, but Oliver knew the wait would be worth it. Finally, summer arrived. The morning sun cast a golden glow over everything as he boarded the train home, anticipation bubbling inside him.

When he arrived, his mother was waiting at the station, waving enthusiastically. "Welcome home, sweetheart!" she said, pulling him into a quick hug.

After a hearty meal and some time to settle in, they finalised the last-minute preparations. Tomorrow at dawn, they would set off on their grand adventure.

The following day, as they landed in Italy, the heat wrapped around them like a warm embrace. The salty breeze carried the scent of the sea, and Oliver felt an immediate sense of freedom.

Then, he saw it—their yacht, a magnificent 40-foot catamaran, sleek and elegant against the shimmering water. His jaw dropped.

"Wow, Dad! She's a beauty!" he said, eyes wide with admiration.

His father grinned proudly. "Yes, she is. Come on, let's get aboard and see what she's like."

With hearts full of excitement, they stepped onto the deck, ready to begin the adventure of a lifetime.

The first morning of their long-awaited family holiday dawned bright and clear, with the gentle lapping of waves against the hull of their chartered yacht. Oliver stood at the helm, his hands firm on the wheel, his heart pounding with exhilaration. His father stood just behind him, arms crossed, a watchful but relaxed presence. The

40-foot yacht, sleek and elegant, was a world away from the smaller sailing boats Oliver had raced in school. Yet, the fundamentals remained the same—the wind in his sails, the rhythmic rise and fall of the sea, the quiet power beneath him.

The salty breeze rushed through his hair as the yacht glided over the water, and he couldn't suppress the grin that stretched across his face. He was born for this. The sea had always called to him, but today, with the open horizon stretching before them, he felt it more deeply than ever. This was freedom—pure, unshackled, and exhilarating. His father, standing behind him, knew that feeling well. He recognised the fire in his son's eyes, the quiet joy that came with commanding a vessel across the waves. A surge of pride swelled in his chest.

"You're handling her well," his father remarked, his voice steady and approving.

Oliver nodded, his fingers flexing on the wheel. "She moves beautifully. Much more responsive than I expected."

They kept close to the shore, the coastline unfurling beside them like a ribbon of golden sand and lush greenery. They had no intention of venturing too far today; the plan was to enjoy a leisurely sail, pick up a few supplies, and then find a local seafood restaurant for dinner. The harbour town ahead was bustling with life—fishing boats bobbing in their moorings, sun-soaked tourists strolling along the waterfront, the scent of salt and grilled fish hanging in the warm air.

Meanwhile, Oliver's mother sat on the deck, her sunglasses shielding her eyes as she turned the pages of her novel. She let the sun warm her skin, the sound of the waves and the distant call of gulls lulling her into a state of peaceful contentment. Every so often, she glanced up from her book, watching her husband at the helm with their son, a soft smile touching her lips.

She had worried about him. The long hours, the mounting stress, the way he had pushed himself too hard for too long. His last doctor's appointment had been a wake-up call. The strain was taking its toll. He needed this break—time away from the relentless pace of his job, time to breathe, to rediscover the things that brought him joy.

And here he was, bathed in sunlight, his face alight with happiness. She exhaled, feeling some of her own worries lift away.

As the yacht glided toward the marina, Oliver felt an unmistakable sense of belonging. Tonight, they'd share a meal by the water, laughter and the taste of fresh seafood filling the evening. And tomorrow? Tomorrow, the sea would call again.

Chapter Seventy Two

It had been a tense few hours. The doctors worked tirelessly to save Gordon Wright's life. His condition was grave, and the atmosphere in the hospital room was heavy with the uncertainty of whether he would make it through. There was a moment of collective relief when they managed to restart his heart, but the battle was far from over. Gordon was now under constant supervision, his life hanging by a thread. A young nurse quietly moved about the room, checking his vitals with precision. Her expression was one of practised calm as she recorded the numbers on his chart, readying it for the doctor's rounds. The faint beeping of the heart monitor was the only sound in the room, steady but fragile.

In the corner, Valarie Wright sat in a chair, her head resting on the side of her husband's bed. She had fallen asleep, exhaustion etched into her features. The strain of the ordeal had drained her, but she refused to leave his side. From the moment they'd rushed Gordon to the hospital, she had been there, holding his hand through every minute of it. Even when the doctors told her there was nothing more she could do, that Gordon would likely sleep for hours, she couldn't bear to go home. The idea of leaving him, even for a few hours, felt impossible. Her mind was consumed with worry, replaying the terrifying moment when she found him collapsed on the floor, her heart pounding as she tried to revive him before the paramedics arrived.

Oliver, had reluctantly gone home to gather a few things his father would need if—and when—he woke up. The house was eerily quiet as he climbed the stairs to his parents' bedroom, each step heavy with the memories of the frantic hours that had passed.

Just earlier that day, he had raced up these same stairs, his heart in his throat, finding his father unconscious on the floor, his mother kneeling beside him in tears, desperately calling out his name. The scene haunted him.

Now, standing at the door of their room, he felt a wave of nostalgia hit him with full force. Memories of his childhood flooded his mind—nights when his father was working late, and he would curl up beside his mother on this very bed. She'd read him stories, her voice soft and comforting, and he'd drift off to sleep, feeling safe in her presence. When he woke up the next morning, he'd always find himself tucked into his own bed, his mother's kiss still lingering on his forehead.

But now, the roles had shifted. His father lay in a hospital bed, his fate uncertain. The weight of responsibility settled heavily on Oliver's shoulders. He realised that, from this point forward, it would be up to him to take care of both his parents. Whether his father recovered or not, things would never be the same. Even if Gordon pulled through, he would be weakened, changed. Oliver knew that the family would look to him to step up, and though he was willing to do whatever it took, the thought of losing the man who had always been his rock filled him with a deep sense of dread.

Chapter Seventy Three

Oliver stood at the foot of the hospital bed in the dimly lit private room, his hands trembling slightly as he watched his father's laboured breathing. The rhythmic beeping of the heart monitor filled the room, a constant reminder of the precariousness of the situation. It had been twelve long hours since his father was rushed in, and the frantic call from his mother still echoed in his mind. Her voice had been trembling, barely holding it together as she tried to explain what had happened.

His father, once strong and full of life, now lay frail and vulnerable beneath the sterile white sheets. This was his second heart attack, more severe than the first, and his mother had been terrified that it would be the one to take him. Oliver could see the fear in her eyes, the way she clutched her hands tightly in her lap, her knuckles white as she sat beside the bed, praying for a miracle.

The doctors had done everything they could, but now it was a waiting game. Oliver's thoughts were a swirling mix of fear, helplessness, and regret. He hadn't visited his parents as often as he should have lately, always caught up in the whirlwind of work and life. And now, standing in the stillness of the hospital room, he realised just how fragile time was, how quickly everything could change.

His father's chest rose and fell with painful effort, each breath sounding like it could be his last. Oliver's eyes stung, but he blinked back the tears, forcing himself to stay strong, for his mother's sake. He looked at her again, sitting by the bedside, her face etched with worry and exhaustion. She had barely left his father's side, her love for him palpable in the air, as if her presence alone could keep him tethered to life.

Oliver shifted his weight, the cold tiles beneath his feet grounding him as he took a deep breath, trying to steady himself. This wasn't how things were supposed to be. His father had always been his rock, the one who seemed indestructible. Now, everything felt uncertain, and the fear of losing him gnawed at Oliver's insides like a slow, relentless ache.

Chapter Seventy Four

The day Gordon was discharged from the hospital, Oliver received a call from an old family friend, Sir Ian, asking after his father. At the end of the conversation, Sir Ian invited him to London to discuss his future.

After the call, Valarie looked at her son, curiosity on her face. "Who was that, dear?"

Oliver smiled, tucking the phone into his pocket. "It was Sir Ian."

"Oh, how is he?" Valarie asked, her tone brightening with interest. "It's been such a long time since we've seen him."

"He's doing well," Oliver replied, leaning against the kitchen counter. "He was asking after you and Dad."

"Always such a good friend," Valarie said with a fond smile. "How nice of him to check in. And what did he want?"

"Actually, he's invited me to London for a chat."

Valarie raised her eyebrows. "That sounds promising! Sir Ian's a big name in the financial district. You might learn a thing or two from him."

Oliver nodded. "He hinted at something more than just a chat. He's looking into the possibility of me getting involved with his business."

Valarie's eyes widened, a glimmer of pride and excitement in her gaze. "Really? Your dad will be thrilled to hear that. Sir Ian's always been someone we've respected so much. This could be a huge opportunity."

Oliver glanced towards the living room, where his father was resting. "How's Dad doing now?"

Valarie sighed softly, her face softening with both love and weariness. "He's sleeping for now, thank goodness. He had a rough morning, but the doctors say he's on the mend."

"Good," Oliver replied, his voice lowering with concern. "And how are you, Mum? You've been running yourself ragged, looking after him and everything else."

"Oh, you know me, love," Valarie said with a wave of her hand, trying to sound reassuring. "I'm fine."

Oliver frowned slightly, walking over and gently putting his arm around her shoulders. "Don't overdo it, Mum. I don't want to see you in the hospital, too. Dad's going to need you, and so will I."

Valarie smiled up at him, though her eyes were tired. "You always were the thoughtful one. But don't worry about me. I'll be alright." She patted his hand affectionately. "I'm just glad Sir Ian's offering you something. He's always been like a second father to you."

Oliver smiled, thinking back on all the times Sir Ian had guided him, both as a mentor and a family friend. "Yeah. It feels like it could be a fresh start, doesn't it?"

"It certainly does," Valarie said, her voice filled with hope. "And after everything we've been through, we could use one."

Chapter Seventy Five

The conversation over breakfast started with small talk about Oliver's family and his personal life outside work. The aroma of freshly brewed coffee mingled with the sound of clinking cutlery as they settled into their discussion. Oliver filled Sir Ian in on the details about his father's illness and how his mother was coping. He described the emotional toll it had taken on their family, how his father's recent diagnosis had brought them closer together, but also how it had cast a shadow over their usual daily routine. As for a personal life, he admitted he had none, chuckling softly as he mentioned his long hours at work that left little room for anything outside the office.

Sir Ian listened intently, his expression shifting from curiosity to sympathy as Oliver spoke. "I'm really sorry to hear about your father," he said sincerely, his voice softening. "I wish him a speedy recovery. I promise I'll visit him and your mother this weekend if that's convenient."

Oliver smiled appreciatively, a weight lifting from his shoulders at the kindness. "They would both be delighted to see you. I can't thank you enough for that, Sir Ian. It would mean a lot to them."

"Of course, Oliver. Family is everything," Sir Ian replied warmly, his gaze steady and reassuring. "Now, let's talk about your future with the company."

Oliver straightened in his chair; his interest piqued. "Yes, sir."

"You're still green behind the ears," Sir Ian began, a hint of a smile playing on his lips, "but I've always believed in not letting the grass grow under our feet. Moving forward is the only way in business. So, tell me, Oliver, where do you see yourself in five years with us?"

Oliver paused, considering his response carefully. He took a moment to visualise his aspirations, the paths he might take. "I want to learn as much as I can and take on more responsibility. I see myself in a leadership role, driving the company towards new innovations and markets. I envision spearheading projects that could make a real difference in our industry."

Sir Ian nodded thoughtfully, his expression shifting to one of approval. "Ambitious, I like that. However, ambition without a plan is just a wish. Have you thought about the steps you need to take to get there?"

"I have," Oliver replied confidently, the enthusiasm bubbling in his chest. "I want to focus on our international expansion strategies. There's a lot of potential in emerging markets that I think we can tap into. I've done some preliminary research, and I believe our products could really resonate with our clients."

Sir Ian smiled, clearly impressed. "You've done your homework. That's exactly the kind of proactive thinking we need. I'll arrange for you to join the team handling our expansion in Asia. It will be challenging, but I think it will be a good fit for you."

"Thank you, Sir Ian. I won't let you down," Oliver said, feeling a mix of excitement and nerves coursing through him.

"I'm sure you won't, Oliver," Sir Ian assured him, glancing at his watch. "Unfortunately, I have to leave for an important meeting now. But let's continue this discussion next week. In the meantime, start preparing a proposal for our expansion strategy."

"Will do, Sir Ian. Thank you again," Oliver said, standing up as Sir Ian rose from the table.

As Sir Ian walked away, Oliver sat back down, his mind racing with possibilities. He gazed out the window, watching as the city bustled to life. He wondered what this new opportunity would bring and how it would shape his future with the company. Would he rise to the occasion? Could he really make a difference? Each question swirled in his thoughts like the steam from his coffee. With a renewed sense of purpose, he picked up his notebook and began jotting down ideas for his proposal, feeling a spark of determination igniting within him.

Chapter Seventy Six

Sir Ian's work ethic was second to none; he often worked more hours than his younger employees, showing up early and leaving late. He never seemed to need sleep or food, for that matter. His relentless dedication to the company was a source of both admiration and intimidation for Oliver. He tried to keep pace with him, staying late at the office and arriving early, but soon found out that it was quite impossible to match the older man's stamina.

One early morning, after a restless night filled with thoughts swirling in his mind, Oliver walked into his office, bleary-eyed and still half-asleep. The first light of dawn filtered through the blinds, casting a soft glow on his cluttered desk. The ping of the elevator just outside his office caught his attention, breaking the silence. Curious, Oliver rose from his desk to see who was in so early.

He wasn't surprised, Sir Ian stepped out of the elevator, briefcase in one hand and the Financial Times in the other. His tailored suit looked impeccable, and the faint aroma of a fresh cologne lingered in the air around him. Oliver greeted him with a smile, rubbing his eyes to shake off the fatigue.

"Oliver, have you been here all night? Did you sleep in your office?" Sir Ian asked, raising an eyebrow, clearly surprised to see anyone else at this hour.

Oliver chuckled and shook his head. "No, Sir Ian, though I might as well have. It's against company policy to sleep here. I've only just arrived. I was waiting for some important documents from a courier. I needed to sign for them and make sure they were returned promptly."

Sir Ian nodded approvingly, a glimmer of respect in his eyes. "Ah, dedication. That's what I like to see. Once you've finished with the documents, join me for a light breakfast in the executive dining room."

Oliver's eyes widened in surprise and excitement. He had never been to the executive dining room before, always hearing stories from colleagues about its exclusivity. "Of course, Sir Ian. I'll be right up as soon as I'm done."

As Sir Ian walked away, Oliver couldn't help but admire the older man's energy and commitment. Despite his years, Sir Ian moved with the vigour of someone half his age, his purposeful strides exuding confidence and authority. Oliver hurried back to his desk, determined to finish his task quickly, the anticipation of breakfast in the executive dining room spurring him on.

Moments later, having completed his task, Oliver straightened his tie and made his way to the executive dining room. He felt a rush of nerves mixed with excitement. As he stepped inside, he was struck by the elegance of the room. Polished mahogany tables gleamed under the soft, ambient lighting, and plush chairs surrounded the tables, inviting guests to sit and linger. Fine China was set for breakfast, complete with gleaming silverware and crystal glasses, making the room look like a scene from a high-end restaurant.

Sir Ian was already seated, pouring over his newspaper, the crisp pages making a soft rustling sound. He looked up as Oliver entered and gestured for him to sit. "Come, Oliver, take a seat. I hope you like your eggs scrambled. I've taken the liberty of ordering for us."

Oliver nodded, still taking in the surroundings, feeling both honoured and slightly overwhelmed. "This is quite something, Sir Ian. I appreciate the invitation."

Sir Ian smiled warmly, his demeanour instantly putting Oliver at ease. "Hard work should be rewarded, Oliver. It's important to take a moment to relax and refuel. Tell me, how are you finding the new project?"

As they talked over breakfast, with the delightful aroma of freshly brewed coffee wafting through the air, Oliver found himself more inspired than ever. Sir Ian's wisdom and experience were invaluable, and his willingness to share them over a simple meal made Oliver feel more connected to the company and its mission. They discussed strategies for the upcoming project, delving into the intricacies of market research and potential hurdles. Sir Ian shared anecdotes from his own experiences, each story imbued with lessons learned and insights gained.

It was in moments like these that Oliver realised why Sir Ian was so revered and respected by everyone around him. He wasn't just a figurehead; he was a mentor, a leader who genuinely cared about nurturing the potential of those around him. The breakfast felt like a turning point for Oliver, an affirmation that he was on the right path. With each bite of the perfectly scrambled eggs and each piece of advice from Sir Ian, he felt a surge of motivation, eager to rise to the challenges ahead and prove himself in the competitive world of business.

Chapter Seventy Seven

Oliver, young and ambitious, his hunger for success knowing no bounds. He had left school with the highest exam results over others at the exclusive private school, a feat that set him apart and served as a harbinger of his future triumphs. The accolades had poured in during his final year, with teachers lauding his commitment and peers looking up to him as a model of achievement. His parents beamed with pride at every awards ceremony, their admiration fuelling his ambition further.

At university, he continued to excel, surpassing even his own lofty expectations. He immersed himself in studies that piqued his interest—finance, economics, and political theory. He found himself particularly drawn to the dynamics of market trends and the intricate weave of investments. With a fierce determination, he engaged in numerous projects and initiatives, even founding a student investment club that gained traction among his peers. By the time he graduated, he had not only earned top honours but had also made invaluable connections with industry professionals, preparing him for the next step in his career.

One crisp morning, Oliver sat in the top-floor executive suite, overlooking London's famous skyline. The panoramic view of the city, with its iconic landmarks bathed in the soft hues of early light, filled him with a profound sense of belonging. He felt as though he were standing on the brink of something great. His confidence, tinged with a bit of cockiness, was evident. Sir Ian had been impressed with Oliver from the start; he saw in him a sharp mind and the potential to generate immense wealth for the firm—more money than Oliver had ever imagined.

"Some view," Oliver remarked as Sir Ian joined him at the large windows, the glass reflecting both their silhouettes against the vibrant cityscape.

"Yes," Sir Ian responded, his eyes scanning the horizon, taking in the blend of modern skyscrapers and historic buildings. "I never get tired of it. I love the city, particularly at this time of the morning. It's like a sleeping giant waking to start the day. Once the city is fully awake, the possibilities for making lots of money are endless. It's like a drug, really."

Oliver nodded, absorbing Sir Ian's words, feeling invigorated by the energy of the bustling metropolis below them. The city buzzed with a potential that mirrored his own drive. He could sense the energy of the day beginning to stir, each car honking, each pedestrian rushing, a reflection of his own ambition. This was where he belonged—in the heart of the financial world, poised to make his mark.

Sir Ian continued, "Oliver, you have a unique talent. I've seen many come and go, but you have something special. It's not just about making money; it's about understanding the game, the strategies, and knowing how to wield power."

"Thank you, Sir Ian," Oliver replied, his voice steady, a firm belief in himself growing with every word. "I intend to learn everything I can from you."

"And you will," Sir Ian said with a nod, his expression serious. "Remember, power is more than wealth. It's influence, connections, and the ability to shape the world around you. Never forget that."

The two stood in silence for a moment, the weight of Sir Ian's words settling over them like a cloak of responsibility. Oliver felt a surge of determination welling up inside him.

"Shall we get started?" Sir Ian asked, breaking the silence, a spark of enthusiasm evident in his voice.

"Absolutely," Oliver responded, a confident smile playing on his lips. "Let's make today count."

As they moved away from the window and into the heart of the office, Oliver felt a renewed sense of purpose. With every step he took alongside Sir Ian, he felt the thrill of potential unfolding before him, eager to learn and grow in a world where ambition and influence intertwined.

Chapter Seventy Eight

That night, Oliver was reading through the paperwork late into the night, the glow of his desk lamp illuminating a sea of charts and graphs. He wanted to impress Sir Ian, so he put in a lot of effort to ensure his presentation was impeccable. His determination kept him glued to his desk, and he meticulously reviewed every detail, making notes and adjustments until he was finally satisfied with the outcome. The silence of the night was punctuated only by the sound of turning pages and the occasional sip of cold coffee, but Oliver welcomed the solitude, relishing the opportunity to immerse himself in his work.

Finally, with his notes neatly organised and printed out, he collapsed into bed, feeling a mix of exhaustion and excitement. His mind, however, refused to quiet down. He tossed and turned, mentally rehearsing his presentation, replaying potential questions from his colleagues, and envisioning their reactions. Eventually, sleep overtook him, but it was fitful and restless, filled with fleeting dreams of success mixed with anxiety.

The shrill sound of his alarm clock broke the tranquility of dawn, jolting Oliver from a light slumber. He groaned softly, rubbing his eyes, still reeling from the lack of sleep. His mind was not fully rested, still buzzing with all the information he had to get through. He took a long, hot shower, letting the steam envelop him as he focused on the day ahead, hoping the warmth would help clear his head. He stood under the cascading water, allowing the droplets to wash away his lingering fatigue. Afterward, he made sure to have a good breakfast, opting for a hearty meal of scrambled eggs, toast, and fresh fruit to fuel his mind and body.

Arriving at the office, he found that Sir Ian, as usual, was already sitting in his office well before anyone else arrived, reading the Financial Times as he had done for many years. The soft rustle of the newspaper echoed in the stillness of the early morning. For Sir Ian, staying abreast of the latest news was crucial; his business, like most things in life, thrived on information. He believed that knowledge was power, and the need to evolve was the cornerstone of his belief in sustainable business practices. Oliver couldn't help but admire his dedication, even as the pressure of the day ahead weighed heavily on him.

With a deep breath, Oliver made his way to the conference room, the scent of fresh coffee wafting through the air as he set up. He meticulously arranged the seating, ensuring everyone would have a clear view of the screen. This was his big chance, and maybe his only one, so he couldn't afford to blow it. He checked the projector, ensuring it was functioning perfectly, and arranged the chairs to create a welcoming yet professional atmosphere. Rehearsing his opening lines in front of the large whiteboard, he felt a surge of adrenaline.

As the others started to arrive, Oliver's nerves began to take hold. He paced the room, trying to steady his breathing and keep his thoughts focused. Each time the door opened, he felt a rush of anticipation mixed with anxiety. He glanced at the clock, feeling the seconds tick away as he tried to calm himself. Finally, as the last person sat down, he stood up, straightened his tie, and welcomed them to his presentation.

"Good morning, everyone," he began, his voice trembling slightly at first, but quickly finding strength in the sincerity of his words. The room felt charged with energy, and he could sense their attention on him. He had prepared extensively, pouring over every detail, and now he was driven by that thorough preparation and the desire to succeed.

As he launched into his presentation, the initial jitters faded. He spoke confidently, articulating his vision for the company's expansion strategy with clarity and passion. He used visuals to highlight key points, ensuring that the audience remained engaged. Questions began to arise, but instead of feeling overwhelmed, he welcomed them, seeing each inquiry as an opportunity to showcase his knowledge and commitment. The room filled with an atmosphere of collaboration and excitement, and with each passing moment, Oliver felt a growing sense of accomplishment. This was his moment to shine, and he was determined to make the most of it.

Chapter Seventy Nine

Halfway through his presentation, Oliver's confidence grew as he noticed he had the full attention of everyone in the room. He scanned the faces of his colleagues and superiors, feeling the weight of their gazes. More importantly, Sir Ian was listening to every word with interest, smiling and nodding throughout. His approving expressions felt like fuel, igniting Oliver's enthusiasm as he moved through the key points of his proposal. The PowerPoint slides, meticulously crafted, flowed seamlessly alongside his narrative, showcasing his insights into emerging markets and strategic growth opportunities.

As the room began to empty, Sir Ian lingered, waiting for the right moment to approach Oliver. When he finally did, he congratulated Oliver on a well-thought-out and informative presentation. The firm handshake and Sir Ian's genuine smile made Oliver feel as if the months of hard work had finally paid off. "Well done! Let's have dinner tonight," Sir Ian said, his voice filled with warmth and encouragement.

Relieved that all had gone well, Oliver sat down and took a sharp breath, the adrenaline of the presentation slowly wearing off. He had worked so hard to make this moment happen, and now he felt the weight of expectation settling on his shoulders. He understood that this was only the beginning of a much larger journey. The excitement of success mingled with the pressure to continue excelling in a fast-paced environment.

However, the day was far from over. Before joining Sir Ian for dinner, Oliver had many meetings to attend. He moved swiftly from one room to another, discussing budgets, strategies, and team performance. The hours flew by, and it was almost 7 PM by the time the final meeting wrapped up. Glancing at the clock, he cursed under his breath—he had no time to go home to freshen up. But fortunately, Sir Ian had advised him to keep a spare shirt at the office—one of many pieces of good advice that Oliver had learned to appreciate over time.

With renewed urgency, he quickly changed into his fresh shirt, adjusting the collar and tucking it neatly into his trousers. He looked in the mirror, smoothing his hair back and straightening his posture. Feeling a rush of gratitude for Sir Ian's foresight, he grabbed his blazer and headed out the door. As he made his way to the restaurant, Oliver reflected on the day's events. The praise from Sir Ian had boosted his morale, but he knew that tonight's dinner was just as important as the presentation. It was an opportunity to solidify his relationship with one of the most influential figures in the industry, a chance to discuss ambitions, aspirations, and the path ahead.

At the restaurant, an upscale venue with dim lighting and elegant décor, Sir Ian was already waiting. He sat at a table adorned with crisp white linens and flickering candlelight, scanning the menu with a glass of red wine in hand. As Oliver approached the table, Sir Ian looked up and greeted him warmly. "You did exceptionally well today, Oliver. I'm looking forward to seeing what you'll accomplish next."

"Thank you, Sir Ian. I appreciate your support and guidance," Oliver replied, feeling a sense of accomplishment wash over him, mixed with anticipation for the challenges ahead. He knew that this dinner was not just a celebration of his successful presentation; it was an opportunity to deepen their mentor-mentee relationship and glean insights from Sir Ian's extensive experience.

Over dinner, they discussed various topics, ranging from current market trends and economic forecasts to personal anecdotes that revealed Sir Ian's early days in the industry. Oliver listened intently, absorbing every lesson embedded in Sir Ian's stories. He learned about the failures and triumphs that shaped his mentor's career, and how resilience played a crucial role in achieving long-term success.

As the evening wore on and the plates were cleared away, Oliver felt even more determined to succeed. The laughter and camaraderie shared over the meal felt like a partnership forming—a collaboration that could lead to remarkable opportunities. He knew that with mentors like Sir Ian guiding him, his future in the financial world looked not only promising but also full of potential.

As they wrapped up the evening and prepared to leave the restaurant, Oliver felt a renewed sense of purpose. The connection he had built with Sir Ian was invaluable, and he was eager to take on the challenges ahead, knowing that he had someone in his corner who believed in him and his ambitions. This was more than just a dinner; it was the forging of a bond that would shape his career for years to come.

Chapter Eighty

The party was in full swing, the music pulsing through the dimly lit room, and the clinking of glasses mixed with laughter as the night wore on. As usual, Oliver was in fine form, exuding charm and confidence with a beautiful woman on each arm. His tailored suit was immaculate, his smile easy, and his demeanour suggested he was the life of every gathering. His magnetic presence commanded attention wherever he went, and tonight was no exception.

Simon and Jonny, fresh-faced and in their early twenties, were still new to the firm and wide-eyed at the grandeur of the event. They had heard about Oliver's legendary parties but hadn't imagined they'd be part of one so soon. The two had worked tirelessly in recent months, pouring late nights and weekends into securing a massive client that would bolster the firm's reputation and ensure their future success. Tonight, they stood in awe, not just of the celebration itself, but of Oliver's seemingly effortless ability to move through the room like he owned it. In many ways, he did.

Oliver had taken it upon himself to school the younger associates on how to properly celebrate a win. After all, they had earned it. As the head of the team, Oliver knew the blood, sweat, and sleepless nights that had gone into securing the client. And now that the deal was sealed, he saw no harm in letting them enjoy the fruits of their labour. He flashed Simon and Jonny a grin as they stood next to him, still nursing their drinks, looking slightly out of place in the glamorous, high-energy environment.

"Boys," Oliver said, his voice smooth and confident, "you've worked hard, and now it's time to enjoy yourselves. What's the point of all this if we don't take a moment to celebrate our victories, right?"

Simon chuckled nervously, glancing at Jonny, who nodded in agreement, still trying to process the surreal experience of being in Oliver's orbit.

"We really put in the hours," Jonny said, his voice betraying a mix of pride and exhaustion. "But I never thought it would be like this."

Oliver smirked, swirling the whisky in his glass. "This is just the beginning, lads. You think this is big? Wait until the bonuses hit. You've earned every penny, and you'll see what I mean soon enough."

Simon looked around the room at the flowing champagne, the lavish decor, and the crowd of well-dressed socialites mingling as if they had no cares in the world. It felt a million miles away from the cubicles and conference rooms they had spent the last few months toiling in.

Oliver clapped them both on the shoulders. "But remember," he said with a wink, "it's not just about the money. It's about the lifestyle. Work hard, play harder. That's the secret."

Simon and Jonny exchanged glances. They were beginning to realise that this night wasn't just about celebrating the win—it was about being welcomed into a new world, one where success wasn't measured only in deals closed and clients won, but in moments like this, where the rewards were felt in the buzz of the party, the luxury of the surroundings, and the thrill of being part of something bigger than themselves.

As the night wore on, the two young associates slowly began to relax, letting the festive atmosphere pull them in. They weren't just on the sidelines anymore—they were part of the inner circle now. And under Oliver's guidance, they would soon learn that in this business, knowing how to celebrate was almost as important as knowing how to win.

⸺⸺◆⸺⸺

Chapter Eighty One

The atmosphere in the club was electric, pulsing with energy and anticipation. As usual, Oliver sat in the middle of the plush leather couch, exuding confidence. Beautiful women flanked him, their eyes gleaming with excitement, hanging on his every word as if he were the centre of their universe. He was in a fantastic mood—life was good. Money was flowing like water, and Oliver loved to indulge in every aspect of it.

London was his playground. A city that, much like Oliver, never seemed to sleep—a place where fortunes were made, where you could party every night of the week and still have room for more. The flashing lights of the club mirrored the city's frenetic energy, and the beat of the music thudded in his chest like a second heartbeat. Glasses of champagne sparkled in the low light, held by manicured hands, while laughter and chatter filled the air. The place was packed, as though all of London had come out to revel in the good times. The economy was thriving, and Oliver felt like the king of it all. With money, power, and influence at his fingertips, the world was his to command. In his early thirties, he felt invincible, with no limits to what he could achieve or take.

He had a big appetite—sex, drugs, drink—nothing was off the table. The pleasures of life consumed him, and he welcomed the indulgence, thrilled by the rush. His eyes sparkled as a tall blonde leaned over and whispered something suggestive in his ear. Her breath was warm against his skin, and his heart rate quickened at her words. Without a second thought, he grabbed her hand, a mischievous grin playing on his lips. She giggled as they manoeuvred through the throng of dancers, bodies pressed together in the dimly lit, smoke-filled air.

The private members' club came with its perks, and Oliver intended to make full use of them. As they ascended the discreet, spiral staircase towards the upper rooms, the energy shifted—more exclusive, more secretive. These rooms were reserved for the club's elite, where power moves were made, deals were struck, and illicit pleasures were indulged far from prying eyes. The soft hum of luxury surrounded them as they reached the top, the door closing behind them with a satisfying click, sealing them in a world where anything could happen. Here, in this private enclave, life was about to get even more intoxicating.

Chapter Eighty Two

Sunday morning was the one-day Oliver allowed himself the luxury of sleeping in. The usual rush of his weekdays felt distant as he stirred, his gaze resting on the young, beautiful woman lying next to him. They had met at the club the night before, a blur of laughter, drinks, and conversation under the pulsing lights. Now, in the calm morning light filtering through the curtains, his head throbbed, a reminder of the night's indulgence. Carefully, not wanting to wake her, he slipped out of bed.

Barefoot, he padded across the cool wooden floor to the bathroom. He opened the mirrored cabinet, rummaging through for an aspirin, his fingers clumsy from the dull ache in his head. The bottle rattled, and he quickly downed a couple of pills with a sip of water, feeling a small relief already in the act.

Returning to the bedroom, he reached for his blue silk robe, the fabric sliding smoothly over his bare skin, a familiar comfort. He slipped into his luxurious red slippers, the deep crimson a striking contrast to the muted tones of the morning. Glancing at the still-sleeping woman, he left the room, moving quietly so as not to disturb her.

As he made his way down the hallway, the quiet hum of the house surrounded him. Entering the kitchen, his mood lifted instantly. The sleek, modern design of the units, the polished countertops, the state-of-the-art appliances—it was his sanctuary. Every detail had been carefully chosen, and every corner reflected his love for precision and beauty. It was here, amidst stainless steel and marble, that he could unwind. After a week filled with business meetings, deadlines, and city noise, this was where he recharged. An accomplished cook, Oliver found solace in the ritual of preparing a meal. Cooking was his therapy, the onetime where he felt fully in control, where creativity and skill met in perfect harmony.

He opened the fridge, scanning the contents as ideas for breakfast began forming in his mind. This moment, quiet and unrushed, was his favourite part of Sunday—just him, his kitchen, and the promise of something delicious to start the day.

Chapter Eighty Three

Another day began for Oliver at the crack of dawn—6 a.m. sharp. The rain from the night before had ceased, leaving behind a crisp, invigorating scent that filled the air as he opened his window. It was the smell of renewal, almost as if the world had been washed clean overnight, and it mirrored the fresh opportunity that lay before him. Today was no ordinary day. For weeks, he had been working tirelessly on closing a monumental deal, and today was the culmination of all his efforts. If he could pull it off, it wouldn't just be a victory for his company—it would be the defining moment of his career. Riches beyond his wildest dreams were within reach, the kind of wealth that would put him in an entirely different league of business elites. Success today would mean everything.

Yet, Oliver's rise in the business world had been far from smooth. More than one deal had slipped through his fingers, leaving his company in dire straits, costing him more than just money—it cost him sleepless nights, his reputation on the line. Some failures still haunted him. But today felt different. Today, he would reclaim his status, rise above the setbacks, and put himself back on top.

The shrill buzz of his phone snapped him out of his thoughts. It was his calendar reminder, a prompt to leave for the office. Oliver always preferred to arrive early, often the first in the building. This gave him time to meticulously go over every detail of the contract, double-check the numbers, and ensure nothing was overlooked. He thrived on being prepared, leaving no room for error. It gave him a sense of control in a world where so much could go wrong.

Stepping out into the cool morning, he was pleased to find the streets almost empty. One of the perks of his early start was the lack of traffic—something of a rare luxury in London. On most days, the city's traffic was a nightmare, a sluggish wave of cars and buses crawling through its narrow, congested streets. Oliver had often joked that soon it wouldn't matter how early he left; the gridlock would become so bad that everyone, no matter their schedule, would be stuck in their cars for hours. But for now, the roads were open, and he zipped toward the office, his mind racing with plans, strategies, and what the day would bring. Today, he thought, *could change everything.*

Chapter Eighty Four

Sir Ian sat alone in his dimly lit office, the soft glow of his desk lamp casting long shadows across the room. The sleek, large flat-screen TV mounted on the wall was tuned to the news, though the sound was muted. His sharp blue eyes followed the scrolling headlines about the tragic mining disaster. He sighed heavily, shaking his head in silent empathy. **"Those poor people,"** he muttered under his breath, his voice barely more than a whisper in the quiet room. He was no stranger to the harsh realities of life—family and the fragility of human existence were things he understood all too well.

As he reclined in his leather chair, his attention drifted toward another pressing matter: the stock market. The premarket trading numbers danced on the screen of his tablet. His fingers tapped rhythmically on the smooth surface of his desk, a sign of his inner calculations. Mining stocks were in freefall, plummeting faster than he had anticipated. **"Many investors will lose their shirts over this,"** he mused. **"But at least not their lives."** He glanced at the news story again—images of rescue teams and desperate families at the mining site filled the screen. The disaster was a reminder of how precarious life could be.

Sir Ian's gaze shifted back to his financial screens, more intense now. The market was minutes away from officially opening, and he could already feel the tension in the air. The weight of responsibility hung heavy on his shoulders. Over the years, he had cultivated a reputation as a careful and prudent investor. Others had rushed headlong into the frenzy when the new CEO, Michael Donavan, had been appointed. Donavan was a seasoned leader, well-respected in the mining industry for his innovations and vision. Many hailed him as the one to steer the company toward a brighter future, a future that promised streamlined operations and higher profits. Investors had piled in, confident that Donavan's leadership would propel the stock to new heights.

But Sir Ian had seen this pattern before. Decades of experience had taught him to wait, to observe the hype from the sidelines before making his move. This was not a game for the foolish or those looking to make a quick buck. It required patience, strategy, and a deep understanding of market psychology. He had held back, resisting the allure of instant gains, and now, as the stock teetered on the edge of collapse, that caution was proving to be a wise decision.

The clock struck 8 AM, and the London Stock Exchange roared to life. Sir Ian's heart quickened, but his face remained a mask of calm. As expected, mining stock took an immediate and sharp hit. The sell-off was brutal. Investors panicked, hitting the sell button as the price plummeted. The trading floor, though distant, felt close enough to touch as he watched the numbers nosedive in real time.

Sir Ian leaned forward, his fingers steepled under his chin as he analysed the data flowing across his screen. **"Not yet,"** he thought, watching the stock drop even further. Timing was everything in moments like this. He could sense the fear in the market, the desperation of small-time investors who couldn't afford to hold on as the value of their portfolios evaporated. He felt a pang of sympathy for them—many would lose everything. But sympathy did not sway his decisions. He knew the game too well. Those who rushed in without understanding the risks were destined to be swept away in moments of crisis like this.

As the stock continued to fall, Sir Ian remained still, a predator waiting for the perfect moment to strike. When it reached the point where he believed the freefall would soon slow, he would make his move—buying at a rock-bottom price, knowing full well that in time, the market would rebound. It always did. He could afford to wait, to be patient. Others might not be so lucky.

His mind wandered briefly to the future. Once the dust settled, Donavan would undoubtedly stabilise the company. The innovations and restructuring he had promised would take root. Sir Ian had no doubt the stock would rise again—stronger, more resilient. And when it did, he would be positioned to reap the rewards. But for now, all that mattered was timing the fall.

He reached for his cup of coffee, taking a slow sip as he continued to watch the unfolding drama. The morning was still young, and there was much yet to happen. **"Soon,"** he whispered to himself, his eyes narrowing as the stock ticked ever closer to the level he had been waiting for. **"Soon."**

Chapter Eighty Five

Oliver was desperate to avoid the many calls. He had poured a significant amount of his own money into this companies shares, and he wasn't the only one. A handful of smaller investors had followed his lead, trusting his reputation and expertise. If the share price collapsed, they would lose everything. While Oliver would survive financially, it would come at a heavy cost—not just to his portfolio, but to his reputation, which could take years to rebuild. The weight of their expectations weighed heavily on him; their livelihoods were intertwined with his decision-making, and failure would devastate more than just his own bottom line.

His phone buzzed relentlessly throughout the night, vibrating on the nightstand like a persistent alarm he couldn't shut off. Each notification was another anxious message from someone waiting for reassurance, another voicemail pleading for answers. The constant stream had overwhelmed his inbox, leaving it full, and though he hadn't dared check his email, he knew it would be flooded as well. Investors, colleagues, analysts—they all wanted answers that he didn't have yet.

He tried to remain confident, telling himself that the company was solid. His research had been thorough, and the numbers had all added up. But in the volatile world of finance, where markets could turn on a dime, confidence was a fragile thing. And lately, the news had been dominated by the mining disaster in Chile. Reports of the human toll were heart-wrenching, but it was the financial fallout that had Oliver's stomach in knots. The disaster was expected to cripple the mining company, and billions of dollars would likely be wiped off the value of the stock he had invested in so heavily.

As the news poured in, it became clearer by the hour that the ripple effects of the catastrophe would devastate the sector, and by extension, his shares. He sold them as quickly as he could but there were few willing to buy the stock until the price was at an all-time low. What had once seemed like a sure thing was now on the edge of collapse, and he knew that if the markets reacted the way they often did in the face of tragedy, there would be no saving it.

Chapter Eighty Six

Two men sat in silence, their eyes glued to the ticker on the screen, watching the mining stock plummet. Both Oliver and David were deeply invested—emotionally, as well as financially. Oliver was set to lose a significant portion of his wealth, but it was David who stood to lose everything. Each drop in the stock's value seemed to pull him further into despair. His face, pale and drawn, reflected the devastation of a man on the brink of financial ruin. In a matter of minutes, years of hard work and saving had vanished.

David's mind raced as he realised the full extent of the disaster. His home, the one he had worked so hard to pay for, would have to be sold to cover his debts. The thought of telling his wife and Jenny their daughter would have to leave the prestigious private school tore at his heart. How would he explain that the life they had built, brick by brick, was now crumbling before them?

The phone rang sharply on his desk, interrupting his thoughts. The call was brief, just a few minutes, but the aftermath would echo for much longer. As David hung up, he walked over to the window, staring blankly at the city skyline. His mind was frantic with thoughts of how to fix this catastrophe. Desperate, he dialled Oliver's number again—one more futile attempt. The phone rang, unanswered, just as it had all the other times he'd called. Oliver wasn't returning his calls, and the silence was deafening.

David tried to think of solutions, calling friends, contacting banks, seeking any possible way to borrow more money, but deep down, he knew it was hopeless. He considered selling assets, but he had nothing left of real value. He had gone too deep into the hole, and now there was no way out.

Meanwhile, Oliver took the loss in stride, though it wasn't without pain. Selling off the stock had cost him dearly, but Oliver was a seasoned player in the world of high-stakes investments. Losing money was part of the game; it stung, but it wasn't the end. The trick was to stay in long enough to recover. Oliver had seen it happen before—greater men than himself had faced similar defeats, only to claw their way back. He was determined to do the same. While David's world was collapsing, Oliver was already planning his next move, knowing that this wasn't the end, just another chapter in a volatile business.

Chapter Eighty Seven

The TV flickered with continuous coverage of the Chilean mining disaster. In the mining community, families had been keeping vigil for days, praying fervently for the safe return of their loved ones trapped underground. David watched as the harrowing story unfolded, feeling the weight of the situation. The miners' plight was heart-wrenching—the uncertainty, the fear, and the toll it was taking on their families. But as much as he sympathised with them, David was also consumed by his own impending disaster. He and his family were about to lose everything. Their life savings, the security they'd built over years, would be wiped out in a matter of days.

Oliver Wright, the charismatic man he had met just a few weeks ago, had assured him that the investment was foolproof. "It's 100 percent safe," Oliver had said with unwavering confidence. He had even claimed to have invested a large portion of his own wealth, a testament to how sure he was of its success. But now, as the grim news from Chile blared in the background, David couldn't help but feel the creeping dread. He had borrowed money—used every bit of their savings—on Oliver's word. And now, it was all hanging by a thread.

"Dad, I'm ready!" Jenny's voice came from the stairs, breaking through the fog of his thoughts. Lost in worry, David didn't hear her the first time. "Dad!" she repeated, louder this time.

"Sorry, dear. I'll be right there," he said, forcing a smile. Jenny came into the room, her schoolbag slung over one shoulder. She paused, glancing at the TV screen where the news anchor was wrapping up another report on the miners. The image of the miners' families, huddled together with candles, praying for a miracle, flickered on the screen. It was a sombre, heart-wrenching sight, and Jenny's face softened with empathy.

"That's so sad, Dad," Jenny said quietly. "Those poor people."

David nodded as he switched off the TV, trying to shake off the heavy feeling in his chest. "Yes, it is, sweetheart. It's very sad," he replied, his voice tight with emotion. He couldn't help but think of the parallels between their situation and the families on the screen. He was about to lose everything, just like those people could lose their loved ones. The difference was, they had no control over their tragedy. He had made a choice—and it could cost him everything.

"Come on, let's get you to school," David said, grabbing his keys and trying to sound upbeat. But as he led Jenny out the door, the weight of his decisions hung heavy over him, casting a shadow over everything, including his relationship with his daughter.

Chapter Eighty Eight

The bills never stopped. Day after day, they piled up on David's desk, a cruel reminder of his financial collapse. Each envelope was a weight on his chest, and though he had done his best to keep up with the payments, his funds were quickly dwindling. It had been weeks since the mining stock crashed had obliterated not just his savings but his entire future. He had delayed telling his family for as long as possible, but the time had come—he could no longer put it off. His stomach twisted at the thought of facing them, of confessing the ruin he had brought upon their lives.

One afternoon, as the late autumn sun cast a pale light over his office, David rifled through the papers on his desk. He searched desperately, hoping against hope that he might have missed something—a forgotten account, a hidden savings plan, anything. But there was nothing. Only paperwork, bills, and more reminders of his debts. And then, buried beneath a stack of unpaid notices, he found it—his life insurance policy. The document felt heavy in his hands, as though it carried all the weight of his despair.

David sat down and read it over and over, scrutinising every clause, each line offering the faintest glimmer of hope. If he were gone, if he took that final step, the payout from this policy would be enough to give his family a chance. It was his last, desperate option— his only way to ensure they would be taken care of. They could keep the house, Jenny could stay in school, and his wife would have the financial cushion to weather the storm. But it meant making the ultimate sacrifice.

With trembling hands, David reached for the silver-framed photo that sat on his desk. The image of his wife and daughter smiled back at him, frozen in a moment of joy from a happier time. Tears welled up in his eyes and began to stream down his face as the reality of what he was contemplating sank in. They would be heartbroken, yes. But they would survive, and perhaps, in time, they would understand why he had done what he must. He wrote a note, each word a painful expression of his love and regret. He hoped that, in time, they would forgive him.

That morning, he rose earlier than usual, before the sun had even peeked over the horizon. The house was silent, the world still. David moved quietly, not wanting to wake his family. He crept to his daughter's room, just to look at her one last time. She was fast asleep, her peaceful face framed by the walls covered in posters of her favourite boy band. Her desk was littered with books, evidence of the bright, inquisitive mind that he had always been so proud of. His heart broke all over again as he realised he would never see her grow into the brilliant woman she was destined to become.

He walked back to his bedroom, where his wife slept soundly, her breathing steady and calm. David stood over her, his love for her filling his chest with an unbearable ache. Gently, he leaned down and kissed her forehead. She stirred slightly, murmuring in her sleep, and he took a step back, afraid of waking her. He paused at the doorway, casting one last look at the life he was leaving behind before slipping downstairs.

At the front door, he hesitated, taking in every detail of the home they had built together. With a heavy heart, he stepped outside, quietly closing the door behind him for the final time.

The streets were empty, the world still cloaked in darkness. The only sounds were the soft stirrings of people beginning their day, the clatter of breakfast dishes, the occasional distant voice. David imagined families kissing their loved one's goodbye before heading off to work, unaware of the burden he carried. He would never be one of them again. The number 9 bus arrived, and he boarded without a word, the short ride to the cliffside feeling like an eternity.

When he stepped off the bus, the cool morning air hit his face, crisp and biting. It was the kind of morning he would have loved on any other day, a morning full of promise and new beginnings. But for David, it marked the end. Up ahead, the crumbling path that led to the cliff's edge beckoned to him. The wind whispered softly, as if calling him forward.

He walked slowly, each step feeling heavier than the last. When he reached the top, he paused. The view was breathtaking—golden light spilled over the horizon as the sun began its slow ascent into the sky. For a moment, David stood in awe of the beauty, the serenity of the world around him. In that quiet, he allowed himself one last deep breath, closing his eyes as he whispered, "I love you both so much."

With the wind swirling around him, he took a step forward to the very edge. The ground beneath his feet gave way slightly, and he swayed in the breeze. For a moment, time seemed to stand still. Then, with one final, deliberate step, he crossed the threshold.

The wind howled as he fell, and as the sun rose higher in the sky, David was gone—swallowed by the vast, unforgiving world below.

The insurance company sent a formal letter explaining that they were unable to pay out the life insurance policy because, according to their investigation, David had taken his own life—a circumstance explicitly excluded from the policy's coverage. The letter expressed their deep regret, but nonetheless, they were bound by the terms of the contract. This news came as a devastating blow to David's family, who had been counting on the payout to provide financial security in the wake of his death. Despite David's well-intentioned plan to safeguard his family's future, the exclusion in the policy left them without the much-needed financial support, adding another layer of emotional and financial distress to their already overwhelming grief.

⋯⋯◁◇▷⋯⋯

Chapter Eighty Nine

Toby barked excitedly, his paws kicking up sand as he raced ahead of Sally and John, their two-year-old Springer Spaniel brimming with energy. The morning was crisp and clear, the sea breeze carrying the smell of saltwater as the couple strolled down the quiet beach. Both Sally and John, artists by profession, scanned the shoreline, searching for anything interesting that the tide might have washed up. Driftwood, shells, or any oddities could be turned into their next piece of living art.

Suddenly, Toby stopped barking and nosed around a heap near the waterline. "What is it, Toby? What have you found?" John called out, striding towards the dog. Sally, walking slower behind him, was still gazing at the ocean, lost in thought.

John froze mid-step, his face going pale. "Stop, Sally," he said, his voice tight.

Sally looked up, puzzled. "What is it?"

"Call the police... There's a body."

Sally's heart pounded in her chest as she hurried over to John, standing just close enough to see what had made him stop in his tracks. There, lying face down in the wet sand, was a man's lifeless body. Toby stood beside it, wagging his tail and barking excitedly, clearly unaware of the grim discovery.

"Oh no..." Sally whispered, her hands flying to her mouth in shock.

"Toby!" John shouted, his voice sharper now. "Come here, boy!" But Toby didn't listen at first, still circling the body.

Sally joined in, calling for their dog. "Toby, come back!"

At last, the dog bounded over to Sally, tail wagging, proud of what he'd found. "That's a good boy," she said softly, though her eyes were locked on the still figure on the shore.

John, already on his phone, was frantically talking to the authorities, his voice barely masking his anxiety. As they waited for help to arrive, a few other early morning walkers wandered over, drawn by the commotion. What began as curiosity quickly shifted to shock as they realised what had happened.

Within minutes, a small crowd gathered, murmuring among themselves, their gazes flickering between the body and the couple. The once serene morning had transformed into a scene of morbid fascination.

About half an hour later, the police arrived, quickly cordoning off the area. Officers moved with purpose, taking statements from John and Sally while others examined the body. One officer, carefully checking the man for identification, was startled by the sudden ringing of a phone. It came from inside the man's jacket.

The officer hesitated before reaching into the inside pocket. He pulled out a phone, and the screen lit up with a name—**Wife.**

Chapter Ninety

The constable stood in front of the ringing phone, his fingers hovering just above the receiver, uncertain if he should answer. His gut told him to pick it up, but something held him back. He glanced at his sergeant, a man with two decades of service under his belt, the weight of experience evident in his calm demeanour. Without a word, the constable handed the phone to him, relieved to be free from the responsibility. The sergeant, however, didn't even glance at the receiver. He let it ring out. "It's not our job to answer the call," he muttered. "We're professionals."

As the forensic team arrived on the scene, a ripple went through the crowd of onlookers that had gathered by the cliffside. People craned their necks, trying to catch a glimpse of the experts in their white suits as they meticulously combed through the area. The team set up a perimeter, securing the site. The crowd had grown, with curious locals mingling alongside tourists, their voices a quiet hum of speculation. An officer took down names, phone numbers, and statements, allowing the crowd to slowly disperse after their details were noted. "If we have any follow-up questions, we'll be in touch," the officer said, nodding in gratitude as he handed back identification. "Thanks for your cooperation."

The investigation stretched on for hours. The bright morning sun had given way to the dull light of late afternoon as the forensic team scoured both the cliff top and the beach below. Every inch was examined for clues. Bits of debris, scattered footprints, and the disturbed earth near the edge of the cliff were documented and photographed. Down on the beach, the tide was beginning to creep up, threatening to erase any remaining evidence in the sand. The body, discovered earlier that morning, had been carefully removed and was now on its way to the pathologist's lab, where the post-mortem would determine whether the fall was a tragic accident—or something more sinister.

Detective Matthew Thomas, the lead investigator, stood a few paces back from the scene, deep in conversation with the two officers who had been first to arrive. Their initial impression leaned toward an accidental fall—perhaps the victim had gotten too close to the edge, slipped, and tumbled down the jagged rocks. But there was something that didn't sit right. The officers voiced their concerns, acknowledging that while it could have been an accident, there was a slim possibility it wasn't. Suicide hadn't been ruled out yet, and Detective Thomas knew they needed to keep an open mind. They couldn't afford to overlook any detail.

Jenny sat in the kitchen, idly stirring her cereal as she took slow bites of her breakfast. The morning light filtered through the window, casting a soft glow on the worn wooden table. The air smelled faintly of toast and coffee, remnants of her mother's early morning routine.

Her mother entered the kitchen, dressed in her usual work attire, her hair hastily pinned up. Jenny looked up and asked, "Where's Dad?"

Her mother sighed, pouring herself a cup of coffee. "He must have gone to work early," she replied, taking a quick sip.

Jenny frowned. "How will I get to school?"

Her mother glanced at the clock and rubbed her forehead. "I'm busy this morning. I can ask Sally if she could take you."

Jenny wrinkled her nose. She didn't like Sally, one of her mother's friends. There was an odd smell about her—something stale and sickly sweet that made Jenny uncomfortable. She had complained about it before, but her mother insisted she was imagining things. "It's only for today," she added dismissively.

Sighing in reluctant acceptance, Jenny pushed back her chair and trudged upstairs to get ready for school. Meanwhile, her mother lingered in the kitchen for a moment, staring at the empty space where David usually sat. He had been acting strange lately; distant, distracted. When she had asked him what was wrong, he simply said it was work stress. But this morning, leaving so early and without a word, didn't sit right with her.

As she made her way upstairs to prepare for her own busy day, she passed by David's study and noticed the door was slightly ajar. That was unusual—he always kept it shut. A strange feeling settled in her stomach as she pushed the door open wider.

Her breath caught in her throat. The room was in complete disarray—papers strewn across the floor; desk drawers left open as if someone had rifled through them in a hurry. It looked like a tornado had torn through the space.

Amidst the chaos, her eyes landed on a blue envelope, placed carefully on the desk. Her name was written on the front in David's handwriting.

Her heart pounded as she reached for it, her fingers trembling slightly. She tore it open and unfolded the letter inside. At first, the words didn't make sense. She read them again, slower this time, the weight of their meaning settling over her like a thick fog.

Before she could process it fully, Jenny's voice rang from downstairs. "Mum! I'm ready to go!"

Shaken, she quickly folded the note and tucked it away. There wasn't time to dwell on it now. But something was wrong. Very wrong.

Once Jenny was on her way to school, Margaret sat back down at the kitchen table, her hands trembling as she unfolded the note once more. The morning sunlight slanted through the window, casting long shadows over the wooden surface. She read the words again, slowly this time, hoping for some hidden meaning she had missed in her panic.

But no—there it was, in David's familiar scrawl: a mention of an Oliver she had never heard of, and a large sum of money tied up in some mining stock. Her pulse quickened. Why had David invested so much without telling her? Was this a mistake? Or worse—had he lost everything?

A cold wave of fear settled in her chest. This wasn't like David. He was cautious, responsible. He wouldn't throw their savings into a risky investment without discussing it first. Unless... he was desperate.

Margaret snatched her phone off the counter, her fingers fumbling as she pressed to call David. She pressed the phone to her ear, listening intently. It rang. And rang. And then—his voicemail.

She tried again. Straight to voicemail.

Her stomach twisted. Where was he?

Determined to get answers, she stood up, grabbed her coat, and cancelled all her appointments for the day. Whatever was happening, it was bigger than her schedule.

Next, she called David's office, gripping the phone so tightly her knuckles turned white. A young-sounding receptionist answered, her tone polite but uncertain.

"I'm sorry, but he hasn't been in today. He actually missed an important meeting earlier this morning."

Margaret swallowed hard. "Did he say where he was going? Did anyone hear from him?"

"No, ma'am. We've tried calling too, but he hasn't picked up. We're starting to get a little worried ourselves."

Margaret murmured a thank-you and hung up. Her heart pounded as she stared at the note again, willing it to make sense. Oliver. Who was Oliver? And what had David done?

She sank onto the sofa, clutching the crumpled paper in her hands. Tears burned at the corners of her eyes. Her husband was missing, their money was tangled up in something she didn't understand, and she had no idea where to turn.

She whispered into the silence, "Where are you, David?"

Rereading the note from her husband for the third time, Margret felt her hands tremble, the paper crinkling slightly under her tightening grip. Her breath came in shallow, uneven gasps as her eyes darted over the hastily scrawled words once more, as if by sheer willpower she could change them.

David had done the unthinkable. He had gambled away their entire future—their home, their savings, and everything they had spent years building together—without so much as a word to her. Anger flared hot and sharp in her chest, battling with the icy grip of betrayal that threatened to consume her. How could he? How could he be so reckless, so blind, so utterly foolish? And worst of all—how could he keep this from her until it was too late?

Her gaze fell to the closing lines of his note, and a new, more terrifying emotion took hold: fear. The finality of his words sent a chill down her spine. What did he mean by "only one thing I can do to make amends"? Her stomach twisted as a sickening realisation settled over her. She needed to find him. Now.

She read the letter once more, her eyes scanning his confession with a mixture of disbelief and horror:

My dearest darling,

I don't know where to start. I have been foolish and believed that I was doing the right thing, that this would secure our future—Jenny's future—but I have lost everything.

Oliver Wright, a man I was introduced to, gave me his assurance that the Chilean mining stock was a sure thing. He was so convincing, putting his own money into it, making it seem like there was no way to lose. I trusted him, and I convinced myself that this was the answer to all our worries.

I remortgaged the house and borrowed heavily, believing that in a matter of months, we would be set for life. But it's all gone. Every penny. Our savings, our home—everything we worked so hard for. I am so sorry. I have failed you and Jenny in the worst way possible.

Please forgive me. There is only one thing I can do to make amends.

Forever your loving husband,

Kiss Jenny goodbye.

David

Margaret's heart pounded. The note slipped from her fingers as she leaped into action. Panic surged through her as she grabbed her phone and dialled his number with trembling hands. It went straight to voicemail. She tried again. Nothing.

Her mind raced, every worst-case scenario flashing through her thoughts. He was blaming himself—suffocating under the weight of his mistakes. She had to find him before it was too late.

Fighting back tears, she grabbed her coat and rushed out the door, praying she wasn't already too late.

A loud knock at the front door pulled Margaret out of her thoughts, her mind still racing with all the dreadful possibilities of what might have happened to her husband. She had spent the last few hours pacing restlessly, jumping at every sound, her heart pounding with uncertainty.

She hesitated before stepping towards the window, peering through the lace curtains, her breath catching in her throat. Outside, two uniformed constables stood solemnly, their faces unreadable. Between them stood a man in a shabby, ill-fitted suit, his hat crumpled in his hands. Margaret's stomach lurched. She feared the worst.

The knock came again, louder this time, more insistent. She stood frozen, unwilling to move. Every fibre of her being resisted opening that door, knowing that whatever lay on the other side would bring no good news. But the knocking persisted, echoing through the quiet house. Trembling, she forced herself forward, each step heavy with dread. Her hand hovered over the door handle, her fingers shaking as she heard muffled voices on the other side.

Summoning every ounce of courage, she pulled the door open. The night air rushed in, cool and indifferent to the turmoil within her. The constables shifted uncomfortably, exchanging brief glances before the man in the suit cleared his throat.

"Mrs. Moore," he began, his voice laced with an unsettling gentleness. "May we come in?"

Margaret stepped aside wordlessly, her body moving on its own, detached from the reality unravelling around her. She led them into the front room, where the clock on the mantelpiece ticked steadily, oblivious to the impending storm.

The detective, as he introduced himself, spoke in low, measured tones, but his words blurred together in Margaret's mind. She caught fragments—her husband's name, an accident, something terrible. Her breath came in shallow gasps as the room seemed to close in around her.

The female constable moved silently, retreating to the kitchen, and returned moments later with a tray bearing strong tea. The cups sat untouched on the coffee table, the steam curling in the dim light. Margaret barely noticed. Her hands clenched tightly in her lap, her nails digging into her palms as tears welled up and spilled over, streaking silently down her face.

"Mrs. Moore," the detective said softly, "is there anyone we can contact? Family, close friends?"

Margaret swallowed hard; her throat raw from holding back sobs. She opened her mouth, but at first, no words came. Finally, in a hoarse whisper, she said, "Our neighbours... Jasmine. She's a friend."

One of the constables nodded and slipped away to fetch her. The silence that followed was unbearable. Margaret sat stiffly, her ears ringing, her mind a whirlwind of thoughts too terrifying to voice.

Minutes later, the door opened, and Jasmine rushed in, her face stricken with concern. The moment Margaret saw her, something inside her cracked. She stood abruptly, and Jasmine wrapped her in a tight embrace.

"Oh, my dear," Jasmine whispered, her voice thick with sorrow. "I am so, so sorry."

Margaret clung to her, her body shaking as silent sobs wracked her frame. She could hear the detective shifting uncomfortably, giving them a moment, before clearing his throat.

Jasmine pulled back slightly, brushing a stray tear from Margaret's cheek. "What about Jenny?" she asked gently.

Margaret stiffened. A fresh wave of dread crashed over her. Jenny—her daughter.

She hadn't even begun to think about how she would tell her.

How could she? How could she possibly find the words to shatter her little girl's world?

Margaret, with the help of Jasmin, got ready to go to Jenny's school. The detective had offered to escort her, but she declined. She would tell her daughter herself; it was for the best.

Jasmin drove while Margaret sat in silence, her mind struggling to absorb what had happened. Their lives, once full of promise and stability, were now on the brink of upheaval. The unknown frightened her. What would become of them? How would Jenny cope with the changes? Her school, her friends—everything she knew was about to change, and Margaret had no answers.

As they pulled up to the main entrance of the impressive school building, Margaret hesitated, feeling a wave of nausea rise. Her hands trembled, and Jasmin, noticing her distress, gently took her arm in support. The grand facade of the school, with its towering columns and pristine brickwork, stood in stark contrast to the turmoil within Margaret's heart.

Inside, the school receptionist greeted them warmly, her smile faltering when she took in Margaret's pale complexion and anxious expression. Without hesitation, she led them down a long, polished corridor to the headmaster's study. The air smelled faintly of polished wood and old books, a familiar scent that should have been comforting but now felt suffocating.

The headmaster, a dignified man in his sixties, sat behind an imposing mahogany desk. The large study, bathed in soft natural light filtering through tall windows, was lined with portraits of past headmasters, their stern gazes watching over the room. The warmth of the space contrasted sharply with the cold dread gripping Margaret.

"Mrs Moore, please take a seat," the headmaster said gently, gesturing toward a chair. Margaret sat down stiffly; her hands clutched together in her lap.

A moment later, a knock at the door signalled Jenny's arrival. The headmaster nodded to the receptionist, who ushered the young girl inside. Jenny hesitated, her bright eyes flickering between her mother and the headmaster, confusion etched on her face.

"Mum?" she said tentatively, sensing something was wrong.

Margaret swallowed hard, trying to steady her voice, but the weight of the moment was too much. Tears welled up in her eyes and spilled down her cheeks.

Jenny stopped mid-step, alarmed. "Mum, what's wrong?"

The headmaster rose from his seat. "I'll give you both some privacy," he said kindly, stepping out and closing the heavy door behind him.

As he walked away, the muffled sound of Jenny's cries reached his ears. With a heavy sigh, he paused for a moment before continuing down the corridor, knowing that behind that door, a mother and daughter were facing a heartbreaking reality.

Chapter Ninety One

On the day of the inquest, Jenny and her mother steeled themselves for what lay ahead. The past few weeks had been gruelling; sleepless nights and relentless questions from the police and media had drained them both emotionally and physically. They longed for answers, though part of Jenny feared that today might only deepen their anguish. Yet her mother, pale and frail, was resolute. She believed that confronting the inquest would help them begin to make sense of the confusion and despair that had consumed their lives since that terrible day.

A knock on the door interrupted Jenny's thoughts. She glanced at her mother, who struggled to rise from the couch. Jenny moved quickly to help her up, wrapping a supportive arm around her. Her mother's insistence on attending weighed heavily on Jenny; she wasn't sure how much more her mother could endure. But there was a quiet determination in her mother's eyes that Jenny couldn't argue with. This was her mother's way of coping, of trying to find strength in the face of unbearable loss.

When Jenny opened the front door, the harsh reality hit her like a cold wind. The front lawn, once a space of peaceful retreat, had become a battleground of flashing cameras and probing questions. Reporters, clustered with microphones in hand, stood ready to bombard them the moment they stepped outside. The intrusion was suffocating, but Jenny had come to expect it; privacy had long been stripped away. Among the chaos, a small glimmer of relief arrived in the form of a family friend, who had graciously offered to drive them to the courthouse. His calm, steady presence was a lifeline amidst the sea of turmoil.

With heads down and coats pulled tight, Jenny and her mother hurried through the crowd. Their friend guided them, shielding them as best he could from the flashing lights and shouted inquiries. The reporters' voices blurred together, a cacophony of sensational questions that felt miles away, even as they chased them to the car. Once inside the vehicle, a tense silence settled over them, the quiet only broken by the hum of the engine as they left the spectacle behind.

The drive to the inquest felt endless. Jenny stared out the window, watching the familiar streets pass by as her mind wandered. The world outside seemed unchanged, oblivious to the gravity of their situation. Her mother sat beside her, staring straight ahead, her face unreadable. Every mile brought them closer to the answers they both craved and dreaded. Jenny wanted to speak, to offer some comfort, but the weight of the day pressed down on her chest, leaving her silent.

When they finally arrived at the courthouse, the sight that greeted them was no less daunting. The inquest room, large and imposing, was already full. Lawyers, journalists, and officials filled the space, their conversations a low hum beneath the formal air. The media sat in a row, pens poised to scribble down every word, every detail, every emotion that would feed tomorrow's headlines. Jenny could feel their gazes as she and her mother entered, their presence yet another reminder that their pain was now public property.

The room itself seemed almost too bright, sunlight streaming through large windows, casting long, golden rays across the polished floors. The contrast between the warm light and the cold, sterile atmosphere inside felt jarring. Jenny kept a firm grip on her mother's hand, offering support, though she knew her own strength was wavering. Together, they found their seats at the front, where they could hear everything, see everything. The weight of the moment settled heavily on them both.

As they waited for the proceedings to begin, Jenny's heart raced. She was bracing herself for the testimony, for the facts that would be laid bare today, no matter how painful. She glanced at her mother, whose gaze remained steady on the front of the room. The soft wrinkles in her face, now etched deeper with grief, told the story of sleepless nights and endless heartache. But there was something else in her expression too—a quiet resolve, as if she were gathering her strength for whatever lay ahead.

The room's murmur quieted as the coroner entered, signaling the beginning of the inquest. Jenny inhaled deeply, her hand tightening around her mother's fragile fingers. She knew that today would be brutal—each word, each revelation a potential trigger for fresh waves of grief. But she also knew that they couldn't keep living in the shadows of unanswered questions. This was a step, albeit a painful one, toward finding closure, toward rebuilding some semblance of life after tragedy.

As the first words were spoken, Jenny leaned closer to her mother, whispering quietly, "We'll get through this. Together."

Chapter Ninety Two

Jenny and her mother sat in an uncomfortable silence in the unbearably stuffy room, where even the air seemed to press down on them, suffocating in its stillness. The small, dimly lit room was crowded with faces they didn't recognise, yet every eye seemed to settle on them, as though they were the centrepiece of this grim display. The weight of their attention only added to the oppressive atmosphere as the inquest began.

The coroner, a tall, thin man with a receding hairline, stood behind his desk, his posture rigid. He pushed his wire-rimmed glasses higher up on his hawk-like nose, a habitual gesture that did little to conceal his discomfort. He coughed lightly, his voice low and scratchy, like a man weary of repeating such grim tasks. The cough, however, commanded the attention of everyone present, including Jenny, whose body tensed as if bracing for an impact she knew was coming but still dreaded.

Jenny listened intently, her chest tightening with each word, the coroner's nasal voice droning in the hot air. His tone was clinical, detached—almost devoid of humanity. Yet, in its monotony, it brought an unbearable gravity, making each word a sharp reminder of the nightmare they had lived through since her father's death. He meticulously outlined the facts, each sentence a scalpel cutting into the raw wound of their grief. Her father, dead from a fall off the clifftop that might have been accidental or might not. The ambiguity gnawed at Jenny, as the coroner explained he could not determine with certainty whether it had been an intentional act or a tragic miscalculation.

The open verdict, cold and indifferent, hung in the air like a question no one had the courage to answer.

The room seemed to hold its collective breath as the coroner continued speaking, the faint murmur of whispered speculation echoing from the front row. A few people exchanged furtive glances, their voices a low hum of gossip as they watched Jenny and her mother, their stares almost accusatory. Jenny fought to steady her breathing, trying to shut out the background noise and focus solely on the coroner's words, but the tension in the room was palpable, the pressure almost unbearable.

Her mother's hand tightened around hers, a lifeline in the middle of the storm. The skin of her mother's hand felt cold, clammy even, as though the life had been drained from it, but her grip was strong, determined. It was the only thing keeping Jenny grounded as the coroner's detached voice rattled on, dissecting the facts with little regard for the emotion they carried. Jenny could feel her mother's quiet resolve in that grip, though there was a tremor in her hand that betrayed her inner turmoil. Jenny glanced at her mother's face—eyes hollow, focused intently on the coroner, but clouded with a mixture of anger, sadness, and something that resembled resignation.

The room's harsh fluorescent lights reflected off the coroner's papers, illuminating the stark contrast between the sterile environment of the inquest and the turmoil churning inside Jenny. The white walls were unforgiving, making everything feel cold and clinical, far removed from the warm home her father had once inhabited.

And yet, the unanswered questions—why, how—refused to dissipate, hovering like a cloud above Jenny's head. The room felt smaller, as if the air was being sucked out of it, the tension squeezing tighter with every passing moment. Every word spoken, every detail revealed, seemed to loom over her, an inescapable reminder of the unanswered mystery that was her father's death.

The proceedings dragged on, but Jenny couldn't shake the overwhelming feeling of being watched—judged even. She could almost hear the silent questions being posed by the onlookers: **Was it suicide? Could it have been avoided? Was it really an accident?** Each unspoken thought added to the suffocating weight pressing down on her chest.

When the coroner finally concluded, his last words hanging in the still air, the silence that followed was heavy, thicker than before. It was as though the room itself had stopped breathing. Jenny's heart clenched painfully in her chest, aching with the hollowness the open verdict left behind. She glanced at her mother once more, hoping for some sign of solace, but found only a stony expression, eyes still fixed on the coroner. Pain, exhaustion, and resignation all swirled in her mother's gaze, as if she had been worn down to the core.

The silence deepened, not just in the room but in Jenny's mind, as the weight of the uncertainty pressed harder against her. No closure, no answers, just a void left in the wake of the coroner's indifferent declaration.

As the proceedings came to a formal end, the shuffle of feet and soft murmur of conversation filled the room once more, but Jenny remained seated, unable to move. The weight of it all—the verdict, the whispers, the stares—crushed her in place. The room might have emptied out, but the echoes of the inquest, the haunting finality of it, lingered around her like a shroud. There were no answers here, only more questions, and the certainty that nothing would ever feel resolved.

For Jenny, the worst part wasn't the verdict, but the gaping hole it left in her heart. She had lost her father, and now, in a way, she had lost the hope of understanding why.

⚜

Chapter Ninety Three

A furious Jenny and her mother fought their way out of the inquest, the ever-present media hounding them with a barrage of questions as they reached the heavy double doors that led to the street. The air was thick with tension, the cacophony of reporters' shouts blending with the relentless flashing of cameras, illuminating their every step like fireworks in a storm. Jenny's heart thundered in her chest, her frustration surging like a tidal wave. She could feel the weight of the eyes upon them, the sharpness of each question, each demand for answers they didn't have.

The din outside was nearly overwhelming. They were met with a sea of flashing lights, not just from the cameras, but the reflection off the metallic bodies of news vans, parked like vultures in wait. As they neared the car, Jenny's boiling anger erupted. She whirled around, fists clenched, eyes blazing, and hurled a vicious string of insults at the journalists closest to her, their faces illuminated by the harsh strobe of camera flashes. Her voice cut through the noise, harsh and unforgiving, a raw scream of defiance that echoed down the street. Even her mother, Margaret, who had been holding onto her own composure by a thread, recoiled in shock at the venom in Jenny's words.

"Jenny, please," Margaret's voice cracked, barely audible above the chaos, thick with a mixture of fear, surprise, and the unspoken pain that had brought them here. Jenny, realizing the extremity of her outburst, caught her breath and quickly turned to apologise, her face softening for just a moment as she reached for her mother's arm. She guided Margaret toward Malcom's waiting BMW, the silver paint gleaming under the pale autumn sun, its engine already rumbling, eager for escape.

The back door was flung open in anticipation, and Jenny bundled her mother inside with the urgency of someone trying to shield a precious, fragile thing from breaking. She cast a final, icy glare over her shoulder at the reporters, who had now resumed their relentless bombardment, then slid into the car and slammed the door shut with enough force to make the glass tremble.

Malcom, who had been watching the scene unfold with his jaw set in silent concern, wasted no time. His knuckles whitened around the steering wheel as he tore away from the curb, tires squealing in protest against the asphalt, leaving behind a plume of blue smoke and a trail of choking dust. The reporters, startled, scrambled to follow, but the BMW was already halfway down the street before they could react, their voices fading into the distance behind them.

As the car sped through the congested streets of the city, the frenzy of the media circus finally dissolving in the rearview mirror, a heavy silence settled inside. Jenny sat beside her mother, her arm draped protectively over Margaret's hunched shoulders. The anger that had once fuelled her now ebbed, replaced by a deep, aching sadness. Margaret, usually so strong and composed, had broken. Tears streamed silently down her cheeks, and Jenny tightened her hold, her own tears spilling over as she pressed her cheek to the top of her mother's head.

In the front seat, Malcom's face remained stoic, though his mind was racing. He knew they couldn't return to the flat—their once-private sanctuary had been invaded by the unrelenting press, their every movement watched, dissected, speculated upon. He couldn't bear the thought of them facing that again, especially not today. Without a word, he veered off the main road and drove them out of the city, into the quieter suburbs where the air was still and the world felt slower.

He pulled up to a small, unassuming pub nestled between rows of ivy-covered cottages. It was the kind of place few would think to look for them, a place of comfort and anonymity, far from the prying eyes they had just escaped. The pub's sign creaked gently in the soft breeze, a sound that seemed oddly welcoming after the chaos they'd endured.

Inside, the atmosphere was calm, the dim light casting long shadows across the polished wooden tables. It was nearly empty, save for a lone bartender polishing glasses behind the counter and a couple quietly talking in the far corner. Malcom led Jenny and Margaret to a secluded booth, hidden in the back, away from the windows and the world outside.

They sat in silence for a moment, the tension still clinging to them like a second skin. Malcom ordered drinks, his hands still trembling slightly from the adrenaline of the escape. He caught Jenny's eye and gave her a small, reassuring nod as if to say, "We're safe for now." But the safety felt fleeting, and Jenny could see the same apprehension in her mother's eyes.

The inquest had been a brutal ordeal, leaving them with more questions than answers, the coroner's findings offering no comfort, no closure—only a deepening mystery that seemed to twist tighter around them with every passing moment. Jenny ran her fingers absently over the rim of her glass, her mind far away, replaying the events of the morning. Margaret's voice, quiet and hoarse from exhaustion, finally broke the silence. "Where do we go from here?" she asked, though the question seemed directed more at herself than anyone else.

Jenny didn't know how to answer, and for a long time, no one did. They sat in the warmth of the pub, a temporary sanctuary from the storm that raged outside, but they all knew it wouldn't last. The media would find them again, the questions would return, and the answers they so desperately sought remained elusive, hovering just out of reach.

Malcom, glancing once more at the two women he cared so deeply for, clenched his jaw. The road ahead was uncertain, but he swore to himself, whatever it took, he would protect them from the storm.

In the calm of the pub, Jenny's mind drifted back to the day she learned of her father's death. The warm hum of casual conversation around her seemed worlds away from the icy shock that still gripped her heart whenever she thought about that day. It had been an ordinary school morning, with nothing to mark it as significant. She had been sitting at her usual desk in a stuffy classroom, half-listening to her history teacher drone on about the Industrial Revolution. The lesson was dull, filled with dates and names she had no interest in. Back then, she would have given anything to be anywhere else. Now, she'd give anything to be back in that monotonous hour, if it meant her father was still alive.

After the inquest, Margaret sat in the dimly lit kitchen, clutching the formal letter in her trembling hands. The letterhead bore the insignia of the insurance company, its crispness contrasting sharply with the weight of its contents. The neatly typed lines were cold and impersonal, delivering a verdict that shattered the fragile hope she had clung to in the weeks following David's passing.

The insurance company regretfully informed her that they were unable to honour the life insurance policy. According to their investigation, David's death had been ruled an open verdict—an ambiguous circumstance that fell within the exclusions outlined in the policy's fine print. The wording was clear and absolute, leaving no room for appeal. Margaret read the letter twice, then a third time, her mind struggling to grasp the full implications. It wasn't just a rejection; it was a cruel twist of fate that left her and Jenny vulnerable at the worst possible time.

The house was silent except for the rhythmic ticking of the clock above the sink, a reminder of how time moved forward, indifferent to her despair. The financial safety net David had meticulously planned for was now a mirage, a promise undone by bureaucracy and technicalities. She thought of the mortgage payments looming, the utility bills stacking on the counter, and the grocery expenses that would now stretch thin an already merger budget. The savings they had were modest, not nearly enough to sustain them for long.

She felt anger rising anger at the insurance company for their cold dismissal, at the system that allowed such loopholes, and at David for leaving them in this predicament, even though she knew it wasn't his fault. He had done everything he could to secure their future, never anticipating that the fine print of a contract would betray them in their darkest hour.

Her thoughts drifted to Jenny, who were still asleep upstairs, blissfully unaware of the storm that had just rolled in. How would she tell them that their lives would change even more? That their father's careful planning had come to nothing? The weight of responsibility pressed down on her, heavier than ever before.

With a deep, shaky breath, Margaret placed the letter on the table and buried her face in her hands. She could not afford the luxury of breaking down. There was no safety net, no financial reprieve, no one to swoop in and save them. If there was a way forward, she would have to find it herself.

Chapter Ninety Four

Jenny's mother knew her daughter was an intellectual girl, always devouring books far beyond her years, from the classics to complex biographies and scientific texts. Her insatiable curiosity reminded her mother of Jenny's late father, who had always believed in his daughter's potential. He often said, "Jenny's going to change the world one day, in business or whatever she chooses." His words echoed in Jenny's mind as she spent countless hours in the local library, a place that had become her refuge. After his sudden passing, Jenny's life had been upended. She had lost more than just her father; she had lost the stability and comforts that came with their old life. Now forced to attend a public school in a new town, she found solace only in the pages of her books, escaping into worlds where she didn't feel like an outsider.

At her new school, Jenny's intellect set her apart, but not in the way she might have hoped. Her academic prowess and quiet demeanour made her a target. The other kids were quick to sense her vulnerability, especially a group of girls from her year who seemed to take pleasure in reminding her of how different she was.

One chilly autumn morning, on her way to school, Jenny's thoughts were interrupted by the sound of mocking voices behind her.

"Hi, Jenny! Looking good!" one of the girls called out with a saccharine tone.

"Yeah, if you're into losers," another snickered.

Jenny's heart sank. She tried to quicken her pace, clutching her worn coat around her as if it could shield her from their taunts.

"Where'd you get that coat? The bargain bin at Peacocks?" the third girl jeered, pulling a face of exaggerated disgust.

Jenny, used to this cruel routine by now, bit her lip and kept her gaze fixed on the ground. Her breath came faster, and though she fought to suppress them, tears welled in her eyes. She could feel the girls closing in, their voices dripping with cruel amusement.

"What's the matter, cry-baby? Can't handle a bit of fun?" one of them sneered.

The laughter echoed in her ears as they finally walked away, their giggles fading down the street. Jenny stood frozen for a moment, her body stiff with the effort of holding back her emotions. When she was sure they were gone, she pulled out a crumpled tissue from her coat pocket and wiped the tears from her cheeks. Straightening her coat, she prayed no one had seen what had just happened.

As she took a shaky step forward, a soft voice startled her. "Are you okay?"

Jenny turned quickly, her heart skipping a beat. Standing a few feet away was Mark, a boy from her class. He had a kind, concerned look on his face, and unlike the other kids at school, he wasn't smirking or laughing.

"I'm fine," Jenny muttered, her voice barely above a whisper. Her face burned with embarrassment. She wasn't used to anyone, especially someone her age, showing concern.

Mark seemed to hesitate for a moment, then took a step closer. "Those girls are awful," he said quietly. "You shouldn't listen to them."

Jenny shrugged, unsure of how to respond. She had heard that so many times, but it didn't make the taunts hurt any less. She was about to turn and keep walking when Mark surprised her by offering his hand.

For a moment, Jenny stared at it, unsure of what to do. But something in his expression—genuine kindness, perhaps—made her reach out. She grasped his hand.

"Thanks," she mumbled, feeling a warmth spread through her despite the cold morning air.

Mark smiled softly. "Do you want to walk with me to school? It's better than walking alone."

Jenny hesitated, the idea of walking with someone both unfamiliar and strangely comforting. She wasn't used to having company, especially not someone like Mark, who seemed to see beyond the labels and rumours that followed her. Finally, she nodded. "Okay."

As they walked, the awkward silence between them was broken when Mark started talking about a book he was reading. Jenny perked up at the mention of books, her favourite subject. Soon, she found herself responding, and before she knew it, they were exchanging recommendations, discussing characters and plots as if they had known each other for years.

For the first time in what felt like forever, Jenny smiled—a real smile. She hadn't expected to find a kindred spirit at this school, especially not after all the bullying she'd endured. But as they reached the school gates, something shifted in her heart. The pain from the girls' cruelty still lingered, but it no longer felt as heavy. She wasn't alone anymore.

As they parted ways to head to their classes, Mark turned back and gave her a reassuring smile. "See you at lunch?" he asked casually.

Jenny felt a lightness inside her that she hadn't felt in a long time. "Yeah, see you at lunch," she replied, her voice more confident than before.

For the first time since her father's death, Jenny felt like maybe, just maybe, things were going to get better.

Chapter Ninety Five

Mark sat in the school dining room, the clatter of trays and chatter of students blending into the background as he nervously tapped his fingers on the table. His thoughts were consumed by Jenny. Their brief but meaningful encounter outside the school gate earlier that day had left him hopeful that they might become friends. He replayed the moment in his mind, remembering how her eyes, wide with surprise, had met his as he stepped in to shield her from the taunts of a group of girls. He couldn't shake the feeling that they shared an unspoken connection.

His eyes scanned the room, searching for her. Eventually, they landed on the group of girls who had made Jenny cry. They were huddled in the far corner, laughing and joking, as if nothing had happened. The sight of their carefree expressions sent a surge of anger through Mark. He clenched his fists under the table, his body tensing as he considered marching over to confront them. How could they act so heartlessly?

Just as he was about to stand, the dining room door swung open. Sunlight streamed through the large windows, casting a golden glow on the figure entering. It was Jenny. The light caught her hair, making it shine like spun gold, and her presence seemed to brighten the entire room. She looked radiant, and when her eyes found Mark's, her face lit up with a big, warm smile.

Mark's heart skipped a beat. His anger dissipated in an instant, replaced by a nervous excitement. He stood up quickly, his earlier jitters forgotten. As he walked toward her, his smile mirrored hers, and the room seemed to shrink until there was only the two of them.

"Hey, Jenny," Mark greeted, trying to keep his voice steady despite the butterflies in his stomach. "Would you like to join me for a while?"

Jenny's smile widened, and she nodded. "I'd love to, Mark."

As they made their way back to his table, Mark couldn't help but notice the shift in the room's atmosphere. The girls in the corner had noticed them too. Their laughter faltered, and soon it was replaced by whispers and envious glances. Mark was the captain of the football team, known for his charm and good looks, and seeing him with Jenny—a girl they had bullied—left them unsettled.

One of the girls, Lisa, leaned closer to her friend, her voice dripping with disdain. "What does he see in her? She's nothing special."

Her friend shrugged, though her eyes remained fixed on Mark and Jenny as they sat down together. "I don't know, but they look pretty happy."

At the table, Mark pulled out a chair for Jenny, a gesture so simple yet filled with thoughtfulness. He sat across from her, his eyes full of warmth and concern. "How are you doing?" he asked, his voice gentle.

Jenny's gaze dropped to the table for a moment, her fingers nervously tracing invisible patterns on the surface. "I'm better," she said softly, glancing up at him. "Thanks to you." Her voice, though quiet, held sincerity. "I really appreciate you standing up for me earlier. I don't know what I would've done."

Mark smiled, his expression softening even more. "No one deserves to be treated like that," he said, shaking his head. "Those girls... they're not worth your time."

Jenny bit her lip, the weight of his words stirring something deep within her. "It's just... hard," she admitted, her voice barely above a whisper. "Sometimes I feel so alone."

Without hesitation, Mark reached across the table and gently placed his hand over hers. His touch was light but reassuring. "You're not alone anymore, Jenny. You've got me now, and I won't let anyone hurt you. Not ever."

Jenny's eyes shimmered, this time with tears of gratitude rather than sadness. Her heart swelled at his words, the walls she had built around herself beginning to crumble. "Thank you, Mark. That means more to me than you know."

As they sat there, talking and laughing, the room around them seemed to fade away. They shared stories, laughter, and moments of silence that spoke louder than words. The whispers and curious glances from the other students no longer mattered. In that moment, it was just them—two people who had found an unexpected connection in the most unlikely of circumstances.

In the corner, the girls exchanged uneasy glances. They had never seen Mark so engaged with anyone, let alone Jenny. It was clear now that there was something different about her—something they hadn't seen but that Mark clearly did. A quiet envy brewed among them, but they remained silent, their taunts stifled by the undeniable chemistry between the two.

As the lunch period came to an end, Mark and Jenny stood up together, still immersed in conversation. They walked out of the dining room side by side, leaving the girls in the corner to simmer in their confusion and jealousy. Mark's actions had made his choice clear, and Jenny's confidence blossomed with every step she took beside him.

The school day continued as usual for most, but for Mark and Jenny, everything felt different. They had found something in each other—something that neither had expected, but that both realised was exactly what they needed. It was the start of a friendship that, deep down, felt like it could grow into something even more special.

⋅•⋅⋖⟨⟩⋗⋅•⋅

Chapter Ninety Six

Over the next few weeks, Mark and Jenny's relationship flourished. Their connection deepened as they became each other's constant source of support. In the fast-paced, sometimes overwhelming atmosphere of their school, they found peace in one another's company, often retreating to quiet corners of the campus to talk, laugh, and simply enjoy the presence of someone who truly understood them.

Jenny, determined to ace her upcoming exams, adopted a rigorous study routine. Every day, she made her way to the library, her backpack filled with textbooks, notebooks, and flashcards. Her focus was unshakeable her eyes often glued to her materials for hours on end, determined to absorb every detail she could. Mark, fully understanding her dedication, often accompanied her when he wasn't caught up with football practice or another sporting commitment. He admired her focus, watching as she poured over complicated formulas or dissected literary texts. More than once, he found himself sitting across from her at the library table, quietly reading through his own notes or quizzing her on complex topics. Their conversations often turned into impromptu tutoring sessions, where Mark would encourage Jenny through her moments of frustration, offering praise and a steady presence.

In return, Jenny offered her unwavering support to Mark as he juggled his own set of pressures. Since he was five, Mark had nurtured a dream of becoming a professional footballer. Now, in his late teens, that dream was tantalisingly close to becoming reality. He had been offered a chance to join a prestigious football club, a dream come true for many aspiring athletes. However, there was a stipulation: his parents, though fully supportive of his football aspirations, made it clear that he needed to pass his exams as a condition for joining the club. They believed strongly in the value of education, wanting him to have a solid backup plan in case his football career didn't pan out as hoped.

Faced with this challenge, Mark threw himself into balancing the demands of football and school. His days were long and gruelling, filled with exhausting training sessions that left him physically drained. Yet, even after a tough day on the field, he would return home, textbooks in hand, staying up late into the night to review his coursework. His commitment to his studies matched his passion for football, and it was that dual determination that kept him going. Jenny noticed the bags under his eyes some mornings and the tired slouch of his shoulders, but she never doubted his drive. She admired his perseverance and never hesitated to lend a hand, whether it was offering her own study notes or providing gentle reminders to take a break when he seemed to be burning out.

Their relationship became a safe haven, where both could lean on each other during this challenging period. Mark and Jenny turned their study sessions into shared battles against their respective challenges, cheering each other on and celebrating the small victories. Late-night conversations often drifted into future dreams—Jenny's hopes of entering a prestigious university and Mark's visions of playing in stadiums packed with roaring fans. They knew that their current struggles were stepping stones toward those dreams, and the thought of achieving them together only strengthened their bond.

In quieter moments, when the pressure of their respective responsibilities felt overwhelming, they found solace in each other's presence. Sometimes they would just sit in silence, exchanging a reassuring smile or a brief touch, knowing that they were in this together. And despite the mounting stress, they cherished the laughter, the late-night coffee runs, and the stolen glances during study breaks. These small moments kept them grounded, reminding them that even in the midst of hard work and high expectations, they had each other to rely on.

As exams loomed closer and Mark's opportunity with the football club drew nearer, the pair remained resolute. Their shared journey of perseverance and commitment only deepened their relationship, and they knew that, regardless of the outcome, they had grown stronger—both as individuals and as partners. They trusted that their hard work would pave the way for brighter days, and whatever challenges lay ahead, they would face them together.

Chapter Ninety Seven

Jenny came home from school to find her mother crying at the kitchen table. Bills had been mounting up, and she was unable to keep up with the payments. She was behind on the rent too. The sight of her mother in distress sent a jolt of fear and sadness through Jenny's heart. She dropped her backpack and ran to her mother's side.

"What's wrong, Mum?" Jenny asked, her voice trembling.

Her mother, embarrassed, quickly swiped at her tears and forced a smile. "It's nothing, sweetheart. Everything is fine," she said, but Jenny could see through the facade—the quiver in her mother's voice and the redness of her eyes told a different story.

"Mum, please tell me the truth," Jenny pleaded, her voice breaking.

After a few moments of silence, her mother finally broke down, her shoulders shaking with sobs. The weight of the situation poured out of her in gasping breaths as she confessed the gravity of their predicament. With the bills piling up and her wages barely stretching beyond the basics, they were sinking. They were behind on rent, and the landlord had already issued a warning. Eviction wasn't far off.

Jenny listened in shock, her heart pounding in her chest. As the story unfolded, her mother revealed the deep-seated financial troubles they'd been hiding for so long—how the debts had quietly snowballed, suffocating them. Every month had become a battle to scrape by a constant worry that gnawed at her mother's health and spirit.

And at the centre of it all was one name: Oliver Wright.

Jenny's stomach churned as a slow, burning rage bubbled up inside her. She felt powerless and furious all at once. It wasn't fair. Oliver Wright wasn't some faceless figure anymore—he was the man who had taken her father from them and left them drowning in debt. Her mother had tried to hold onto her dignity through it all, but the weight of it had broken her.

That night, long after her mother had retreated to bed, Jenny sat at the family's old computer in the dim glow of the living room lamp. Her hands hovered over the keyboard, her heart pounding as she typed Oliver Wright's name into the search bar.

The results came flooding in—articles, interviews, pictures. She stared at his face, a polished smile looking back at her from the screen. He was a prominent figure in the business world, hailed as a genius by some and loathed by others for his ruthless business manoeuvres. He was wealthy beyond imagination, living in luxury while her family was at the brink of losing everything.

Chapter Ninety Eight

After Jenny left school, she was thrilled to receive a place at Leeds University, where she would study Business Finance. This achievement felt monumental—a significant milestone in her life that marked the culmination of years of relentless hard work and determination. Her mother, who had always been her staunchest supporter, was overwhelmed with pride at Jenny's accomplishments. From the moment she received her acceptance letter, Jenny knew this was the result of the high grades she had worked tirelessly to earn, grades that had opened the doors to this prestigious opportunity.

However, the journey leading to this point had been anything but easy. Life had dealt Jenny and her mother a difficult hand. Financial hardships often loomed large over them, and personal struggles added to the weight they carried. The relentless uncertainty had, at times, been discouraging, but both Jenny and her mother were resolute in their shared goal of improving their circumstances. Jenny had watched her mother work long hours and make countless sacrifices to ensure that she had access to the best education possible, and in return, Jenny had pushed herself academically, determined to make those sacrifices worthwhile.

It was during those challenging years that their bond deepened. Late-night study sessions were often coupled with heart-to-heart conversations where her mother would offer encouragement, reminding Jenny that their struggles were temporary, and that education was the key to a better future. Jenny's drive to succeed was fuelled by more than just personal ambition; she was motivated by a desire to ease the burden on her mother, to repay the love and sacrifice that had defined so much of her upbringing.

Jenny's acceptance into Leeds University was more than just a personal triumph; it was a symbol of overcoming adversity, the end of a long chapter filled with hardship, and the beginning of a brighter, more hopeful future. The joy her mother felt was indescribable—a mixture of relief, pride, and a sense of vindication that all their efforts had been worthwhile. Together, they had clawed their way out of a difficult situation, rising above circumstances that would have defeated many. It was not luck that had brought them here, but grit, resilience, and an unshakeable belief in each other.

As Jenny prepared to embark on this new chapter at Leeds, both she and her mother were filled with a renewed sense of hope. University represented more than just academic growth—it was a gateway to new opportunities, new experiences, and the possibility of a better life. They looked forward with optimism, confident that the same determination and hard work that had carried them through their toughest moments would continue to guide them through the challenges ahead. The bond between mother and daughter, forged through years of shared struggles and triumphs, was stronger than ever. They knew that no matter what came next, they would face it together, just as they always had.

❖

Chapter Ninety Nine

Jenny's first day of university was a far cry from her earlier experience of moving from a private school to a public academy. Back then, the transition had been jarring. She had struggled with the culture change and found it challenging to adjust to the social divides. Having been accustomed to the insular and privileged environment of her private school, Jenny felt out of place among the diverse student body at the public academy.

Her private school had been a bubble of high society, where most of her peers came from affluent families, shared similar backgrounds, and adhered to a particular social etiquette. Extracurricular activities were polished and prestigious, often leaning toward classical music, fencing, or equestrian clubs—activities that further reinforced a sense of exclusivity. Conversations in the hallways revolved around summer trips to Europe or ski vacations in the Alps, and everyone seemed to know each other through their parents' social circles. Jenny's world had been predictable and comfortable, shielded from the broader realities of life.

The public academy, on the other hand, was a melting pot of different cultures, economic backgrounds, and perspectives. The contrast was overwhelming. She faced cliques that were not only divided by interests but also by socioeconomic status, something she had never encountered so blatantly before. The school environment was more rough-and-tumble; students were outspoken, less concerned with polished appearances, and more focused on survival. Conversations here revolved around part-time jobs, family responsibilities, and the struggles of balancing schoolwork with real life. Jenny had to quickly learn that fitting in required more than just wearing the right clothes or saying the right things—it demanded authenticity, something she hadn't had to develop before.

Navigating these uncharted social waters was difficult for Jenny. She had to learn to blend in and build connections from scratch, something that had once come effortlessly in her old world. The cafeteria was a battlefield of different social groups, each with their own unspoken rules, and the academic expectations were also far less rigid than she had been used to. At first, it felt as though no one was interested in her stories of private school life; her experiences seemed alien and irrelevant to her new peers.

Now, stepping onto the university campus, Jenny felt a renewed sense of hope and excitement. The diversity that had once intimidated her now seemed like an opportunity for growth and learning. The university promised a fresh start, a place where she could redefine herself and move beyond the confines of her past experiences. The campus buzzed with energy and possibility, offering a myriad of clubs, activities, and academic pursuits. Students from all walks of life mingled freely, their conversations reflecting a rich tapestry of experiences and ideas.

Jenny was determined to embrace this new chapter with an open mind. Unlike high school, where people seemed to fit neatly into predefined boxes, university life was dynamic and open-ended. There were no preset social hierarchies or cliques she needed to navigate; everyone was just trying to figure things out, and that made her feel like she had room to explore without the pressure of conforming.

As she walked through the sprawling campus, past groups of students lounging on the grass, professors hurrying to their lectures, and posters advertising everything from cultural festivals to political debates, Jenny felt a thrill of excitement. The possibilities seemed endless. The university library, with its towering shelves and vast resources, felt like a treasure trove waiting to be explored. The campus cafes buzzed with conversations that ranged from politics to art to philosophy, offering Jenny a glimpse of the intellectual environment she had always craved.

More than anything, she was ready to shed the skin of her high school persona—the girl who had been out of place at the academy and the one who had always felt the weight of privilege at her private school. University was a place where she could be whoever she wanted to be. The courses promised intellectual challenge, the clubs offered opportunities for personal growth, and the new friendships waiting to be made filled her with anticipation.

With a deep breath and a sense of wonder, Jenny stepped forward, ready to immerse herself in the vibrant, dynamic world of university life. She knew there would be challenges ahead, but unlike before, she felt equipped to handle them. This time, the diversity of experiences felt like an invitation rather than a barrier—a chance to become not just a student, but a more complete version of herself.

Chapter Hundred

Three years flowed by before Jenny knew it. They had been years of growth, challenge, and discovery. Now, standing in her cap and gown, holding her diploma tightly in her hands, Jenny could scarcely believe how much had changed. The university grounds, once so vast and intimidating, now felt like a second home—a place where she had found herself and forged lasting memories. Beside her, her mother was beaming with pride, her eyes sparkling as she looked at her daughter, a testament to resilience, strength, and hard work.

University had been a whirlwind of experiences for Jenny. Balancing the demands of her studies with moments of fun and friendship had been no small feat, but she had managed it all with grace and determination. Countless lectures, group projects, and late-night study sessions filled her days, but there had also been laughter, spontaneity, and joy. She had found a close-knit group of friends with whom she had shared it all—the stress of exams, the thrill of accomplishments, and the carefree moments of escape from it all.

There were the impromptu gatherings at the campus café, where they discussed everything from philosophy to the latest trends, and the nights spent at the student union's events, where they danced, laughed, and forgot the world for a while. Each friendship had carved a special place in Jenny's heart, making the graduation day bittersweet. As the ceremony concluded, the reality of it all began to settle in.

Tears welled in the eyes of her friends as they embraced tightly, knowing that this chapter of their lives was ending. They exchanged promises to stay in touch, though deep down, Jenny knew that life's unpredictable currents would likely take them in different directions. Some were heading abroad for jobs or further studies, others returning to their hometowns to begin new ventures, and some, like Jenny, were diving headfirst into the fast-paced corporate world. Despite the uncertainty, the bonds they had formed during these formative years would always remain, etched into their hearts forever.

Later that evening, Jenny and her mother found themselves in a cosy corner of a charming restaurant. The soft hum of conversation and the clink of silverware against plates filled the air, but all Jenny could focus on was the overwhelming sense of pride and accomplishment that surrounded them. It was more than just a meal; it was a celebration of everything they had overcome and everything they had achieved together.

For years, her mother had worked tirelessly to support Jenny through university, scrimping and saving every penny while ensuring that Jenny never felt deprived. And now, here they were, celebrating not only Jenny's hard work but also the sacrifices that had made it possible. Jenny had secured a highly sought-after position in a prestigious financial company in London's city centre—an opportunity that marked the beginning of a promising career. As they spoke about the challenges and opportunities that lay ahead, the excitement was palpable.

"I still can't believe it," her mother said with a soft laugh, sipping from her glass of wine. "My little girl is all grown up, starting her career in London. Your father would be so proud."

At the mention of her father, a wave of emotion washed over Jenny. She had been thinking about him all day—how much he had meant to her, and how different things would have been if he were still here to see her standing at this momentous crossroad in her life. The memories of him were bittersweet now, a mixture of fondness and longing. She glanced across the table at her mother, her heart swelling with love and gratitude.

Jenny raised her glass, her voice thick with emotion. "To Dad," she said quietly, her eyes shimmering with unshed tears. "To Dad, who I know is watching over us and who would be so proud of today."

Her mother's hand trembled slightly as she raised her own glass to meet Jenny's. Tears glistened in her eyes, and she leaned in to hug her daughter, her embrace filled with warmth and tenderness. "He would be so proud, Jenny. So, so proud," she whispered, her voice choked with love.

For a moment, the world seemed to pause. There, in that quiet restaurant, surrounded by the echoes of laughter and conversation, mother and daughter shared a deeply personal and emotional moment, bound by their love for the man who was no longer with them but whose presence they still felt every day.

The rest of the evening passed in a blur of stories, laughter, and dreams of the future. They reminisced about the past—the joys, the struggles, the moments that had shaped them. Together, they imagined the possibilities of what lay ahead. Jenny's future felt bright and full of promise, and her mother's pride was a constant source of strength and encouragement.

As they finished their meal, Jenny looked out the window at the city lights twinkling in the distance. This was more than the end of her university journey. It was the beginning of something new—a chapter filled with challenges, ambition, and the opportunity to make her mark on the world. She knew it wouldn't be easy, but with her mother by her side and her father's memory to guide her, she felt ready for whatever lay ahead.

Tonight marked the start of that journey, a celebration not just of her academic accomplishments but of the life she was about to step into. With hope, determination, and a deep sense of purpose, Jenny knew she was prepared for the road ahead, wherever it might lead.

Chapter Hundred and One

At the start of the day on Jenny's new job, she was introduced to Charles Whitman, the stern but well-respected compliance officer of Mason and Mason Stockbrokers in London. The meeting, held in a sleek conference room overlooking the bustling city streets below, was more than just a formality. Whitman meticulously went over the detailed regulatory protocols that governed the company's operations, from the latest financial regulations to stringent anti-money laundering policies. He spoke in measured tones, emphasising the consequences of non-compliance, and Jenny could sense that he had seen more than a few careers derailed by a careless mistake.

The session consumed most of her morning. Despite the overwhelming amount of information thrown her way, Jenny remained fully engaged, taking diligent notes. She knew how critical this knowledge was in her new role, especially in an industry as tightly regulated as stockbroking. Her past experience of overcoming adversity, especially after her father's death, had made her resilient. If anyone in that room could handle the complexities and pressures of such a demanding job, it was her.

After the meeting, she barely had time to process everything before the pace picked up again. She hurriedly grabbed a pre-packed sandwich from the company cafeteria and ate it at her desk, scarcely registering the taste as her mind swirled with the morning's discussions. Just as she was finishing her last bite, her supervisor, Stan Lawson, appeared at her side with a thick file in hand.

Stan was a tall, imposing figure with a no-nonsense attitude. He had the air of someone who had seen countless employees come and go, and though not unkind, he wasn't one for small talk. "This is for you," he said, handing over the file, which contained client portfolios, market analyses, and a series of detailed reports on the company's recent trading activities.

"This will give you a good overview of where we stand," Stan continued. "I'll need you to go through it thoroughly and be ready for a briefing tomorrow morning."

Jenny nodded, taking the file with a sense of determination. Her desk, already neatly organised, now became a sea of papers and charts as she dove into the work. The afternoon blurred into evening as she pored over the dense material. The terminology and data were familiar, but Mason and Mason's specific approach to stockbroking and their client strategies added new layers to what she already knew. She tried to absorb as much as possible, aware that in a fast-moving environment like this, there was little room for mistakes.

By the time she finally looked up from her work, the office was nearly deserted, with only a few stray desks still lit. Realising it was well into the evening, Jenny gathered her things and made her way to the Tube station. Her journey back to her small flat in Croydon was a blur, the clatter of the train and the murmur of other commuters blending into the background as her thoughts remained on the day's events. She was exhausted by the time she reached home, her mind still buzzing with everything she had learned. The day had been mentally draining, but there was a deep sense of accomplishment beneath the fatigue. She was where she wanted to be, in the heart of the financial world, and she was determined to succeed.

Over the next few days, Jenny quickly began to find her rhythm. The office culture at Mason and Mason was far from warm, but it was alive with ambition and energy. It didn't take long for her to recognise the subtle office politics at play. Some colleagues were helpful, offering advice and insights into the company's inner workings, while others seemed more guarded, eyeing her as potential competition. Jenny kept her interactions professional, careful to navigate these dynamics without becoming embroiled in unnecessary conflicts.

Stan, though demanding, began to offer more responsibility her way, testing her abilities with smaller client accounts and more complex tasks. Each challenge Jenny faced only fuelled her drive to succeed. She quickly learned who could be trusted and who was more likely to undermine her or step over her to get ahead. People like Lydia, the senior broker two desks over, who never hesitated to take credit for others' ideas, and Greg, the eager new hire, who was already aligning himself with the more powerful figures in the office.

The competitive atmosphere was almost cutthroat, but Jenny found herself thriving in it. The sharp edges of the workplace didn't scare her; they sharpened her own instincts. Each morning as she took her seat at her desk, she felt the familiar rush of adrenaline. She pored over market trends, monitored financial news, and worked late into the evening, keen to stay ahead. Every client report and market analysis became a puzzle for her to solve, a challenge she relished.

In between the busy workdays, she also started to make connections, forming alliances with those who could help her climb the ladder. There was Martin, an older broker who had been with the firm for years, known for his calm demeanour and sage advice. He took a liking to Jenny, offering her valuable insights on how to navigate the highs and lows of the stock market—and the office politics. And then there was Sarah, an ambitious associate who shared Jenny's drive and offered a valuable camaraderie in an otherwise isolating environment.

With each passing day, Jenny became more adept at spotting opportunities to advance her career. She knew the stakes were high, but she also knew that her success would depend on more than just hard work. She had to be strategic, seizing the right moments to showcase her talents. Slowly but surely, she was making a name for herself at Mason and Mason, and she could feel her confidence growing as she embraced the fast-paced, high-stakes world of stockbroking. The road ahead would be long and challenging, but Jenny was ready to tackle it head-on, just as she had done with every other obstacle life had thrown her way.

Chapter Hundred and Two

Jenny fell asleep on the sofa, exhausted from a long day at work. Papers were strewn across the floor, the remnants of her attempt to catch up on the endless paperwork. The TV was still on, casting a dim, flickering glow across the room, with soft shadows dancing against the walls. She stirred awake, her neck stiff from the awkward angle, and rubbed the sleep from her eyes, trying to shake off the heavy fog of exhaustion. The low hum of the television finally caught her attention, drawing her focus to the screen.

At first, it was just background noise—voices blending with the murmur of the day slipping away—but then she caught a familiar voice. Her heart skipped a beat as her eyes locked onto the screen. There, being interviewed live, was a figure from her past: Mark, from her old school, someone she hadn't thought about in a long time but whose presence was unmistakable.

She fumbled for the remote, her fingers shaky with a mixture of surprise and curiosity and turned up the volume. Mark was mid-sentence, discussing Manchester United's recent triumph, his voice filled with excitement and pride. The camera moved in closer, showing his sharp features, the same boyish charm but with an air of maturity and confidence that hadn't been there before.

Jenny's breath caught in her throat as a wave of memories hit her like a tidal surge. Mark had always been exceptional, especially on the football field. His raw talent and undeniable passion for the game had set him apart. It was one of the many things that had drawn her to him all those years ago. Back then, their connection had been magnetic—intense, immediate, almost too much at times.

They had shared everything—hopes, dreams, secrets—but life, as it often does, had pulled them in separate directions.

Their relationship had been brief but impactful, a whirlwind of emotions and youthful intensity. They had ended things because their paths were too divergent—Jenny, focused on her demanding studies and ambitions, and Mark, consumed by his relentless drive to succeed in football. It was a decision made with logic rather than their hearts, though the ache of parting had lingered for far longer than either of them had admitted.

She sighed softly, leaning back into the sofa, papers forgotten, as her thoughts spun back to those days. Mark had always had something in his eyes—a fire, an unyielding determination that hinted he was destined for something bigger. Jenny had always known it. They had tried to keep in touch after the breakup, but life had a way of getting in the way. A message here, a phone call there, but eventually, the distance grew too great, and they had drifted apart. It wasn't anyone's fault; it just… happened.

Now, seeing him again, looking so content and in his element, Jenny felt a twinge of bittersweet nostalgia. She was genuinely happy for him—happy that he had pursued his dream and succeeded. He looked good, like a man who had found his place in the world, a world where she no longer fit. Yet, there was an undeniable sadness, a quiet whisper of "what if?" that lingered in her mind. What if things had been different? What if their paths hadn't diverged so drastically? Would they have found a way to make it work?

The interviewer asked Mark a question, making him laugh—a sound that Jenny hadn't heard in years but remembered vividly. It was infectious, that laugh. She found herself smiling despite the lump in her throat. It felt surreal, watching him like this, so distant yet familiar, a ghost of her past who had somehow found his way into her present.

As the interview came to an end, the screen shifted to a commercial break, and the room fell quiet once more, except for the low hum of the TV. Jenny exhaled slowly, sinking deeper into the cushions. She felt a strange sense of peace wash over her. Life had a funny way of weaving old threads into new patterns, she mused. While their love had been real, maybe letting go had been the right choice after all. Both of them had grown, had followed their separate dreams, and maybe that was exactly how it was meant to be.

She glanced at the papers around her, reminders of her own life, her own ambitions. With a small smile, she picked them up and began sorting through them again.

Chapter Hundred and Three

It was a few weeks into her new role when Jenny's supervisor called her into his office. A knot tightened in her stomach as she approached his door. Had she made a mistake so early on?

"Please, take a seat," her supervisor said, motioning to the chair across from his desk.

Jenny perched on the edge, her hands clasped in her lap, trying to keep her composure. The office was modern but stark, with sleek furniture and large windows that offered a view of the cityscape, yet somehow, it felt confining at that moment.

Sensing her unease, her supervisor offered her a reassuring smile. "Relax, Jenny. There's nothing to worry about." His tone was warm, yet professional. "In fact, we've been really impressed with your work so far."

Jenny felt her shoulders loosen, though she still kept her hands tightly folded.

"I know you've only been with us for a few months," he continued, leaning forward slightly, "but you've shown such attention to detail and initiative. If you're up for it, we'd like to see how you handle a bit more responsibility."

"More responsibility?" Jenny echoed, her brow furrowing in curiosity. She had worked hard, but this was faster than she'd expected.

"Yes," her supervisor confirmed, his expression encouraging. "We believe you have great potential, and if you can thrive under more pressure, there's room for you to grow quickly here."

Jenny's heart raced, a blend of excitement and nerves swirling inside her. As she left the office, her mind buzzed with the possibility. This was it—a sign that she was on the right track. She felt light, as though her feet barely touched the ground on her way back to her desk. Could this be happening so soon? Just weeks ago, she was worried about making a good first impression, and now they were talking about growth and potential.

At the end of another long but exhilarating day, Jenny gathered a large stack of files to take home with her. She had always been ambitious, and if this opportunity was on the table, she knew she needed to push herself even harder. But first, she had to share the news with someone who would be as thrilled as she was.

As soon as she walked through the door of her apartment, she dropped her keys on the counter and immediately dialled her mum. Her hands trembled a little as she waited for her mother to pick up.

"Hi, honey!" her mum answered brightly. "How was your day?"

"Mum, you'll never believe it," Jenny burst out. "My supervisor just offered me more responsibility. He said they think I have great potential!"

Her mother's voice radiated pride, even through the phone. "Oh, sweetheart, that's incredible! I'm so proud of you, but I always knew you could do it. You've worked so hard for this!"

As her mother's words wrapped around her like a warm hug, Jenny couldn't help but smile, the excitement returning in full force. She chatted for a few more minutes, listening to her mom's encouraging advice, but her mind was already racing with thoughts of what lay ahead.

The ping of the microwave snapped her back to reality, announcing her dinner—a homemade vegetarian green curry. She took her meal to the sofa, balancing the plate on one knee while the files she brought home were spread out before her on the coffee table. The room was quiet except for the hum of the city outside her window, and with one hand, she spooned her dinner into her mouth, savouring the subtle heat of the curry.

With the other hand, she flipped through the first of many files, her thoughts still lingering on the conversation she'd had with her supervisor. His words played over in her mind, fuelling her determination.

If they saw potential in her, she had to prove them right. And maybe, just maybe, this was the beginning of something bigger than she had ever imagined.

Chapter Hundred and Four

Over the next few months, Jenny's workload ballooned, each new responsibility piling onto the last. She took it all in stride, never once complaining, and to her supervisor's delight, she seemed to thrive under the pressure. The more tasks she was given, the more determined she became to prove herself. It was as if the weight of the work only fuelled her. Her colleagues noticed her relentless drive—Jenny was the first to arrive in the morning and often the last to leave, the glow of her computer screen casting a lone light in the dimming office late into the night.

Weekends, once reserved for relaxation or time with friends, were now dominated by work. She became a regular fixture in the office on Saturdays and Sundays, her workspace cluttered with files, reports, and coffee cups. The quiet hum of the empty office and the tap of her fingers on the keyboard were the only sounds that accompanied her. Even at home, she would sit at her dining table, papers spread out around her, working long into the early hours of the morning. Her appetite for work seemed insatiable, and her ambition burned brightly, but the signs of strain were starting to show.

Early one Saturday morning, after a particularly late night of poring over spreadsheets and reports, Jenny was jolted awake by the persistent ringing of her phone. She fumbled for it on her nightstand, squinting at the screen to see her mother's name flashing. She answered with a groggy, "Hello, Mother."

Her voice, heavy with exhaustion, didn't go unnoticed. Her mother's concern was immediate. "Jenny, you sound so tired. Are you okay?"

Jenny sat up in bed, running a hand through her messy hair, trying to shake off the fatigue that clung to her. "Yes, Mum," she said, though her voice betrayed her. "Just been working a bit too much lately."

There was a pause on the other end of the line. "Well, dear, you need to take it easy. You can't burn yourself out like this." Her mother's tone was gentle but firm, laced with worry. "How about I take you out to lunch today? You could use a break."

Jenny hesitated, glancing at the stack of papers on her desk that had yet to be read. "Okay," she relented, "but can we make it a late lunch? I have some things to finish up."

Her mother sighed, a touch of concern still in her voice. "If you must but promise me you'll take a real break. I'll meet you at Alberto's at 2 p.m."

"Deal," Jenny said, trying to sound more enthusiastic than she felt. "See you then, Mum. Love you."

"Love you too, dear."

As soon as the call ended, Jenny sat on the edge of her bed, feeling a twinge of guilt for worrying her mother. She knew she had been pushing herself hard, perhaps too hard, but there was so much to do. Her career was on the rise, and she couldn't afford to slow down now.

She stood up, stretching her stiff muscles before heading to the bathroom. The hot water from the shower helped ease the tension in her shoulders, but as she washed her face, she caught a glimpse of herself in the mirror. Her eyes were puffy and lined with dark circles, a clear sign of her sleepless nights. Her once vibrant complexion now looked pale and drawn, and her usually neat hair was a mess of unruly strands. It struck her how much she had changed in these few months of intense work.

After the shower, she slipped into comfortable clothes and sat down at her desk, determined to finish the work she had left the night before. She shuffled through the stack of papers, her mind racing with deadlines and to-do lists. The apartment was eerily quiet, save for the occasional rustle of paper and the soft whir of her laptop. As she worked, her thoughts kept drifting to the lunch with her mother later that day. She felt guilty for not giving her more time, and for letting her work dominate every aspect of her life.

By noon, she had made a decent dent in the paperwork but was far from finished. She glanced at the clock, realising it was time to start getting ready. With a sigh, she closed the laptop, stacked the papers neatly on the desk, and got up to dress for lunch.

As she tied her hair back and grabbed her coat, Jenny couldn't shake the nagging feeling that maybe her mother was right—maybe she was pushing herself too hard. But then, the thought of all she had accomplished so far silenced her doubts. She could handle it. She had to. This was the price of success, wasn't it?

Chapter Hundred and Five

Jenny arrived at Alberto's just after 2 PM, the familiar chime of the doorbell sounding as she stepped inside. The café was softly lit, with warm hues of afternoon sunlight streaming through the large windows. The gentle hum of conversations and the clinking of cutlery filled the air. Her mother sat at a table by the window, absentmindedly staring out into the street, her fingers tracing the rim of her water glass. There was a crease of worry on her face that deepened when she spotted Jenny.

As Jenny approached, her mother immediately stood, a mixture of relief and concern flashing across her features. They embraced, Jenny pressing a kiss to her mother's cheek, the familiar scent of her perfume offering comfort.

"You look so tired," her mother said softly, her voice threaded with concern, her eyes searching Jenny's face for signs of exhaustion.

"I'm OK, Mother. Please don't worry," Jenny reassured her, though her voice was tired, carrying the weight of long, stressful days at work.

"It's my job to worry," her mother countered, her tone gentle but firm, as if it was a simple fact of life.

Jenny forced a smile, trying to ease the tension in her mother's eyes. "It's fine, really. Work has just been crazy."

Her mother sighed softly, shaking her head. "Well, you need to look after yourself."

"Please, let's not do this," Jenny said, her patience slipping for a moment, her tone edged with a hint of exasperation. She had hoped for a light, carefree lunch, away from reminders of her stress.

Her mother held her hands up in surrender, a soft smile tugging at her lips. "OK, I get it." She paused and then added, "I have ordered us a light lunch and a glass of Chardonnay."

Jenny's expression softened, and a grateful smile appeared. "Sounds good. I could do with a drink."

When the food arrived—delicate plates of salads and warm bread—the tension between them began to melt away. The Chardonnay was crisp and refreshing, and as they ate, they settled into an easy rhythm of conversation. They talked about the little things—her mother's recent gardening adventures, the neighbour's new dog, and Jenny's brief updates about work, careful not to dwell too much on the overwhelming parts. It was comforting, the familiar ebb and flow of their chatter, a balm to Jenny's tired soul.

For a little while, the burdens Jenny had carried with her—emails left unanswered, reports still pending—faded into the background. She felt present, anchored in the moment with her mother, grateful for the small reprieve.

As the lunch wound down, the plates cleared and their glasses nearly empty, Jenny reached for the bill before her mother could.

"I said I would treat you," her mother protested, frowning slightly.

"It's OK, Mum," Jenny insisted, pulling out her wallet. "I am making good money now, and it's about time I treated you."

Her mother relented with a soft sigh but a proud smile. "Alright. But next time, it's my treat."

Outside Alberto's, the autumn breeze greeted them, crisp but not unpleasant. They hugged once more, tighter this time, lingering for a moment longer.

"Promise me you'll slow down a bit," her mother said, her voice quiet but full of maternal concern.

"I will, Mum. I promise," Jenny replied, her words a gentle reassurance, though she knew it might be difficult.

They parted with the promise to meet again soon, and as Jenny walked home, the familiar thoughts of work started to creep back in. But for the moment, as the sun filtered through the trees lining the street, she felt a little lighter, the warmth of her mother's concern still lingering in the air around her.

Chapter Hundred and Six

Jenny enjoyed working at Mason & Mason; the work was fulfilling, and every day presented new challenges that tested her skills and adaptability. She thrived under pressure, relishing the problem-solving aspects of her role and the satisfaction of a job well done. Yet, despite her appreciation for the company and the experiences it had given her, she knew it was time to move on. She had ambitions beyond her current role, and when she came across the job listing for Oliver Wright's new assistant, she saw an opportunity she couldn't ignore.

Oliver Wright was a well-respected name in the industry—sharp, innovative, and known for his relentless drive. Working for him would mean stepping into a fast-paced environment, one that demanded excellence but also promised immense growth. Jenny felt a surge of determination. She knew she had what it took.

Smiling to herself, she opened her laptop and updated her C.V., carefully refining each section to highlight her accomplishments. She then turned her attention to the cover letter, outlining her ambitions and skills with precision. She wrote, rewrote, and tweaked every sentence until it perfectly conveyed her enthusiasm and qualifications.

Once satisfied, Jenny printed the documents on high-quality paper, the kind that had a crisp, professional feel. While most applicants would simply email their C.V.s, she believed in the power of a personal touch. A physical letter carried weight, showed effort, and demonstrated her attention to detail—qualities she was sure Oliver Wright would appreciate.

With everything neatly assembled in an elegant envelope, she made her way to Oliver's office. As she handed the letter to the receptionist, she felt a mixture of excitement and nervous anticipation. This was her next step forward, and she was ready for it.

Oliver started his day like most days—his alarm set for 5:30 AM, jolting him awake with its familiar chime. He stretched, exhaled deeply, and rose to begin his morning routine. A hot shower washed away the last remnants of sleep, the steam curling around the mirror as he stepped out and dressed in a crisp, tailored suit. Breakfast was simple but deliberate: a fluffy omelette with just the right amount of seasoning and a steaming cup of black coffee, strong and unyielding, much like the city he gazed upon from his penthouse apartment.

London sprawled beneath him, bathed in the muted glow of early morning. Light rain speckled the towering glass structures, hinting at the heavier downpour forecasted for later in the day. He sighed and turned from the window; his mood as overcast as the sky. Today was not just another day—it was Sally's last. His trusted assistant, efficient and sharp, was leaving him. She had fallen in love, as people sometimes did, and was getting married, as people often did. And just like that, he was left to find her replacement at the most pivotal moment in his business.

His company, a rising titan in its field, was on the brink of becoming one of the wealthiest in the country. The IPO was imminent, the culmination of years of relentless work and precise strategy. There was no room for distractions, no margin for error. Sally's departure, though understandable, was an untimely complication.

By the time Oliver reached his office, the city had begun to hum with its usual energy. The receptionist handed him his post as he strode in, and he took it without a second glance, placing it on his desk for later review. There were far more pressing matters at hand. Sally, ever diligent, briefed him on the candidates she had shortlisted for her replacement. The interviews stretched long into the day, one unimpressive applicant after another. None had the sharp intuition, the unspoken understanding, or the efficiency that Sally possessed. The frustration gnawed at him as the last candidate left his office, another wasted hour.

Pouring himself a glass of whiskey, Oliver sank into his chair, rubbing his temples. His gaze drifted to the pile of letters on his desk—mundane correspondence he had neglected all day. He shuffled through them half-heartedly until his fingers paused on something different: a handwritten envelope. The texture of the paper was thick and elegant, the weight of it intriguing. Curious, he opened it and scanned the contents.

The covering letter was from a Jenny Moore. She had taken the time to handwrite and personally deliver her application—an effort that was almost unheard of in this digital age. He read on, impressed by the confidence in her words, the clarity of her intent. A rare smile ghosted his lips.

"Sally," he called out, holding up the letter. "Arrange for Jenny Moore to come in."

Perhaps, just perhaps, the day hadn't been a complete waste after all.

Jenny Moore sat in the plush offices of Oliver Wright, her heart pounding as she took in the opulence around her. The walls were lined with bookshelves filled with financial tomes and framed accolades, while a large glass window overlooked the city skyline. This was the heart of Oliver Wright's empire, and she was moments away from stepping into it.

She glanced at the older woman sitting at the desk outside the imposing oak doors. Her silver hair was neatly pinned back, her glasses resting low on her nose as she tapped away at her keyboard. The nameplate on the desk read "Mrs. Miller." She had the air of a gatekeeper, the kind of woman who had seen countless hopefuls come and go.

The phone on Mrs. Miller's desk buzzed. She picked up, exchanged a few quiet words, and then turned to Jenny with a slight nod.

"Mr. Wright will see you now."

Jenny swallowed, straightened her skirt, and took a deep breath before knocking. A strong, confident voice called from within.

"Come in."

She pushed open the doors and stepped inside. Oliver Wright stood up from behind an impressive mahogany desk and walked toward her, extending his hand. He was a tall man in his early forties with neatly combed silver hair and a crisp navy-blue suit. His handshake was firm, his expression warm yet assessing.

"Miss Moore, pleasure to meet you," he said. "Please, have a seat."

"Thank you, Mr. Wright," Jenny replied, feeling some of her nerves dissipate. His voice was smooth, reassuring, and somehow made her feel like she belonged in the room.

He took his seat and opened a folder on his desk. "I've read your cover letter and your CV, and I must say, I'm very impressed. For someone so young, your time with Mason and Mason. has been remarkably productive. You've made quite a mark in a short amount of time."

Jenny smiled, relieved that he had noticed her efforts. "I was fortunate to work with a great team, but I also pushed myself to learn quickly. I thrive in fast-paced environments."

Oliver leaned back, steepling his fingers. "That's exactly the kind of attitude I appreciate. Now, let's talk specifics. How would you handle scheduling when my calendar is packed with international meetings, last-minute changes, and urgent calls?"

Jenny didn't hesitate. "I would prioritise tasks based on urgency and importance. I'm adept at managing time zones, so I would ensure seamless coordination. Additionally, I'd anticipate potential conflicts and provide alternative options before you even have to ask. My goal would be to keep your schedule smooth and efficient."

Oliver raised an eyebrow, a flicker of approval in his eyes. "Impressive. But let's say I'm in a meeting, and a call comes through from an important client. They insist on speaking with me immediately. What do you do?"

Jenny considered her answer. "I would assess the urgency. If it's truly critical, I would discreetly signal you and provide a brief summary. Otherwise, I would assure them that you'd return the call at your earliest convenience and offer assistance in the meantime. I understand that balance is key in maintaining strong professional relationships."

Oliver chuckled. "Very diplomatic. I like that."

The interview stretched on for nearly three hours, covering everything from crisis management to discretion, adaptability, and even hypothetical challenges she might face in the role. By the end of it, Jenny felt drained but exhilarated. She had held her own, and Oliver had seemed genuinely interested in her responses.

As she gathered her things, Oliver stood once more. "I have a few more candidates to interview, but I want you to know you're a strong contender. I'll be in touch soon."

Jenny extended her hand again, meeting his gaze. "Thank you, Mr. Wright. I appreciate the opportunity."

She walked out of the office, barely able to contain her emotions. Mrs. Miller gave her a brief nod as she exited. Once outside the building, Jenny pulled out her phone and dialled her mother.

"Mum, it was intense," she said, trying to catch her breath. "But I think it went well. He said he'd let me know soon."

Her mother's warm voice came through the line. "Oh, sweetheart, I'm so proud of you! I had no doubt you'd impress him."

Jenny smiled, watching the city bustle around her. "Now, I just have to wait."

A week after her interview with Oliver, Jenny received a letter from his office. Her heart pounded as she sat down, the envelope resting lightly on her lap. This was it—the moment of truth. Had she secured the job?

Her fingers trembled as she tore open the envelope, barely aware of the sound of paper ripping. She unfolded the letter with bated breath, her eyes scanning the words in a rush. And then— there it was. A smile flickered across her lips, growing wider as the words sank in.

Jenny reread the letter, this time more slowly, savouring every word. Oliver had been very impressed with her—especially with how quickly she had risen through the ranks at Mason & Mason. That alone, he noted, was no easy feat. The letter confirmed that she had been offered the position. She would start in four weeks, and from the very first day, she was expected to hit the ground running. Long, demanding days lay ahead, but she welcomed the challenge.

Without hesitation, she reached for her phone and dialled her mother's number. The moment she heard her mother's familiar voice, Jenny's excitement bubbled over.

"I got it, Mum!" she exclaimed, barely able to contain her joy.

Her mother's delighted laughter filled the line, warm and proud. They quickly arranged to meet over the weekend to celebrate.

As she ended the call, Jenny sat back, clutching the letter to her chest. The reality of it all began to settle in. This was the beginning of something new—something big. And she was ready.

The early morning sun streamed through the kitchen window, casting a golden glow across the countertops. Jenny took a final sip of her coffee, savouring the warmth before setting the empty mug into the dishwasher with a quiet clink. Today was the day she had been waiting for—the first day of her new job working for Oliver Wright, one of the most influential figures in the financial sector. The weight of the opportunity settled on her shoulders, but it was a burden she welcomed. She had worked tirelessly for this moment, pushing through late nights of studying, long shifts, and endless applications.

As she stepped out of her small flat in Croydon, a sense of pride swelled in her chest. Her mother had sacrificed so much to help her get here, and now, it had all paid off. The struggles, the self-doubt, the relentless pursuit of something better—it had been worth it. She smoothed the fabric of her neatly pressed blazer and took a deep breath, inhaling the crisp morning air.

Things would only get better from here.

Chapter Hundred and Seven

It was Jenny's last day working for Mason & Mason. Her colleagues, though sad to see her go, were thrilled that she was moving on to bigger and better things. Some couldn't help but feel a twinge of jealousy at the exciting opportunity ahead of her, but overall, the mood was one of celebration rather than sorrow. Jenny had been a well-liked and respected member of the team, and they wanted to give her a proper send-off.

To mark the occasion, they had arranged a farewell dinner at Luigi's, a cosy Italian restaurant they often frequented for office gatherings. The long wooden table was adorned with flickering candles, and the air was filled with the warm aroma of garlic and freshly baked bread. Laughter and conversation buzzed through the group as they reminisced about past office mishaps and inside jokes.

As the meal drew to a close, Louise, one of Jenny's closest colleagues, stood at the head of the table, raising a glass of bubbly— its label obscured by condensation. With a warm smile, she tapped the side of her glass with a fork, quieting the chatter.

"We wish you all the very best in your new job," she said, her voice filled with genuine emotion. "You deserve it, and you will be missed."

"Cheers!" the others echoed, raising their glasses in unison. Applause and cheers rippled through the group, some calling out their own well-wishes.

"Speech!" Gary shouted, grinning as the rest of the table erupted in agreement, urging Jenny to say a few words.

Jenny stood, holding up a hand to quiet the playful demands. "Okay, okay," she said with a small laugh, though emotion was already creeping into her voice. She took a steadying breath before continuing. "I'm not one for speeches, but I just want to say how much I've enjoyed working with all of you. It's not the company I'll miss the most—it's the people."

Her voice wavered slightly as she raised her glass, her eyes glistening. "To all of you—thank you."

The group responded with another round of cheers and clinking glasses. As Jenny took a sip, she glanced around at the familiar faces, knowing that while she was stepping into a new chapter, she would always cherish the memories and friendships she had made at Mason & Mason.

Another 5:30 AM alarm blared, piercing the silence of Jenny's small London flat. Groggy but determined, she rolled out of bed, already mentally reviewing the tasks that lay ahead. It was only her first week working for Oliver, and the learning curve was steep. His financial firm, recently floated on the London Stock Exchange, demanded absolute precision and tireless dedication. Early mornings bled into late nights, leaving little time for sleep, let alone a proper meal. But Jenny was determined to prove herself.

By 7:30 AM on Monday, she arrived at the sleek glass-fronted office, the streets outside still cloaked in the remnants of dawn. Having worked through the weekend, she felt confident she had all the necessary reports, projections, and briefings meticulously prepared for Oliver. The fast-paced world of high finance required her to anticipate his needs before he even voiced them.

Stepping inside, she spotted Oliver already at his desk, phone pressed to his ear, his brow furrowed in concentration. His desk, an organised chaos of reports and screens flashing live market updates, bore the marks of a man who never truly stopped working. Seizing the rare moment before he would inevitably turn his attention to her, Jenny slipped off her coat and made a beeline for the kitchen.

A strong, black coffee for herself and Oliver's usual—an oat milk flat white, no sugar. As she waited for the machine to whirr to life, she took a deep breath, steadying herself. Another long, high-pressure day awaited, but she was ready.

Oliver finished his call just as Jenny walked in, balancing his coffee in one hand and a thick file in the other—the one she had been meticulously working on over the weekend. She moved with her usual efficiency, her heels clicking softly against the polished floor.

"Good morning, Oliver," she said, offering him both the coffee and the file in one smooth motion.

"Good morning, Jenny. How are you this morning?" he asked, accepting them with a nod of appreciation.

"Good, thanks. And you?"

"Better now that we've completed the IPO and the stock has finally settled after a rocky start," he said, taking a sip of his coffee. "I just got off the phone with Josh at the Exchange—before opening, he was confident the price would hold at 34.80 per share, just as we predicted. Not bad, but we still have plenty of work ahead of us."

Jenny gave a satisfied nod. "That's good news for you. I had a chance to go over the company's position this weekend and put together some notes for you to review," she said, gesturing toward the file.

Oliver raised an eyebrow, half amused, half impressed. "Do you ever stop, Jenny? You've been working incredibly hard. You've only been with me a short time, but I already don't think I could manage without you."

Jenny smiled, the corners of her lips curving upward in a rare moment of appreciation. "Thank you, Oliver. That means a great deal."

She turned toward the door but hesitated. "Oh—Mick Cummings is outside. He said he needs a quick word."

Oliver exhaled, already anticipating the conversation ahead. "Alright, send him in," he said, setting the file on his desk. "Let's see what crisis we're tackling next."

Jenny gave him a knowing look before stepping out to fetch Mick.

The week had passed in a relentless blur of meetings, international calls, and last-minute changes. Jenny had been rushed off her feet, trying to keep up with the endless demands of her job. Oliver, on the other hand, seemed impervious to exhaustion, surviving on nothing but black coffee and sheer determination. He barely stopped to eat or rest, moving from one task to the next with unwavering focus.

By the time Saturday morning arrived, Jenny was grateful for the rare luxury of a sleep-in. Her alarm went off at 9 a.m., a welcome change from her usual pre-dawn starts. Oliver had insisted she take the full weekend off—he would be away, and she had earned a break. Despite the exhaustion that had accumulated over the week, she wasn't quite sure how to fill her free time.

She started the morning by making herself a leisurely breakfast, something she hadn't had the chance to do in ages. The aroma of fresh coffee filled her apartment as she sat by the window, savouring a plate of scrambled eggs on toast. Afterward, she indulged in a long, hot shower, letting the steam and warmth ease the tension from her muscles.

Feeling refreshed, she changed into her running gear. It had been far too long since she'd gone for a proper run, one of the few things that truly cleared her mind. As soon as her feet hit the pavement, a familiar sense of freedom washed over her. The rhythmic sound of her trainers against the ground, the crisp morning air filling her lungs—it was exactly what she needed. Though she didn't go as far as she would have liked, the short run was invigorating, leaving her feeling lighter and more energized.

Back home, she took another quick shower before heading out again, this time for a late lunch with her friend Louise from Mason & Mason. They had agreed to meet at the charming Greek tavern on the corner, a favourite spot of theirs. The weather was pleasant enough for them to sit outside, enjoying the gentle warmth of the sun as they watched the world go by.

Louise arrived just after 1:30, her blonde hair tied up in a loose bun, sunglasses perched atop her head. Jenny spotted her from a distance and waved, smiling as her friend approached.

"Hi, deary! How are you?" Louise greeted, pulling Jenny into a warm hug before taking a seat across from her.

"I'm good, actually. Enjoying a rare day off," Jenny admitted, setting her menu aside.

"Well, that's a miracle! And how's the new job? We're all dying to know what it's like working for Oliver. He's supposed to be quite the taskmaster," Louise said, raising an eyebrow as she flagged down the waiter.

Jenny laughed, shaking her head. "He is demanding, no doubt about that. The days are long, the nights even longer, and the workload is intense. But honestly? It's been incredible. I've learned so much in just a short time. He pushes you, but in a way that makes you better."

Louise smirked knowingly. "Sounds like he's made quite an impression on you."

They ordered a light lunch and a glass of crisp white wine, settling into an easy rhythm of conversation. Jenny found herself unwinding, recounting her experiences of the past few weeks—some exhausting, some exhilarating. It felt good to talk about it, to share the highs and lows with someone who understood. As they sipped their wine and enjoyed the relaxed afternoon, she realised just how much she had needed this break.

For the first time in a while, she wasn't just keeping up—she was catching her breath.

Chapter Hundred and Eight

Margaret sat at the kitchen table, the dim light casting long shadows across the small, cluttered space. In her trembling hands, she held the last letter her husband would ever write. Tears welled in her eyes as she traced the familiar handwriting, the ink slightly smudged from years of careful handling. It was the letter he had written on the day of his death, a letter only she had read, a letter that carried a truth too painful to share—until now.

For years, Margaret had carried the burden alone, shielding her daughter, Jenny, from the terrible reality of that fateful day. But the weight had grown too heavy, and the time had come to reveal what truly happened. She only hoped Jenny would understand why she had kept the secret for so long.

The door creaked open, and Jenny stepped inside, brushing the damp chill of the outside world from her coat. Her face, always a reflection of her father's, bore a mixture of concern and exasperation.

"Hello, Mum," she said, setting her handbag down. She glanced around the cramped flat, the one they had shared for so many years until she left for university and then work in London. "I do wish you'd move out of this dreadful place. It's too small, too cold. You deserve better."

Margaret managed a weak smile as she rose to embrace her daughter, holding on a second longer than usual.

"What is it that was so mysterious you couldn't tell me over the phone?" Jenny asked, stepping back and eyeing her mother with curiosity.

Margaret gestured toward the worn wooden chair across from her. "Please, sit. I have something to tell you. Or rather, something to show you. It's about your father's death."

Jenny's breath hitched. It had been years since her mother had spoken about him. The mention of his name alone was like an echo from a past too painful to revisit. She lowered herself into the chair, confusion flickering across her features.

Margaret reached into her bag and carefully pulled out a weathered envelope, its edges frayed with time. She placed it on the table between them. "Here. This was from your father. The day he died."

Jenny's eyes widened. She hesitated, glancing from the letter to her mother and back again. "What?" she whispered, her voice barely audible over the ticking clock on the wall.

"Please read it," Margaret urged, her voice thick with emotion. "We have much to discuss."

Jenny's fingers trembled as she picked up the envelope and carefully slid out the letter within. Her eyes scanned the words, her face shifting from confusion to shock to something deeper—something resembling grief and anger intertwining. She read it again, slower this time, as if trying to absorb every syllable.

Her hand came up to cover her mouth as the full weight of the letter sank in. She looked at her mother, her voice breaking. "Why did you keep this from me?"

"It has been very difficult to keep the truth from you," Margaret said, her voice heavy with emotion. "But I didn't want to burden you at such a crucial time in your life. You had school, and the shock of your father's death was already too much. To put this on you too—it would have been too cruel."

Her daughter's hands balled into fists at her sides, her body trembling with restrained emotion. The anger in her eyes was unmistakable. "But you should have told me," she said, her voice sharp, accusing.

Margaret reached out, pulling her daughter close despite the tension between them. "But you had so much to deal with," she murmured, smoothing a hand over her daughter's hair, though she knew it would do little to soothe her. "You were taken away from your private school, your friends—you lost so much. And then adjusting to a new environment… You didn't need the added stress."

"But—" She started to protest, her voice faltering as reality settled in. As much as she wanted to argue, deep down, she knew her mother was right.

A thick silence filled the space between them before she finally asked, her voice barely above a whisper, "Who is this Oliver Wright?"

Margaret's grip on her tightened for a moment, then loosened as she exhaled a slow, measured breath. When she spoke, her voice was laced with bitterness.

"He was the man your father trusted. The man who cost us everything."

Jenny and her mother sat together on the worn-out couch, the dim glow of the lamp casting a soft light over the modest living room. The aroma of freshly brewed tea lingered in the air, mingling with the faint scent of lavender from the diffuser on the small wooden table. The room was warm, filled with framed photographs of moments long past—Jenny's childhood birthdays, family vacations, and one particular picture of David, smiling warmly with his arms wrapped protectively around both Jenny and her mother.

As they sipped their tea, their conversation drifted to memories of David—father and husband, lost too soon. They spoke of what could have been, the life they should have had if not for that tragic day. Jenny's mother wiped away a tear as she reminisced about the way David would scoop Jenny up in his arms after work, spinning her around as she giggled uncontrollably. Jenny swallowed past the lump in her throat, her mind filled with thoughts of all the moments he had missed—her first school play, her graduation, her first big promotion. He had missed watching her grow into the woman she had become, and it wasn't fair.

"I think he would be so proud of you," her mother said softly, reaching over to squeeze Jenny's hand. "You've accomplished so much. You're strong, just like him."

Jenny forced a smile, though her heart ached with sorrow and resentment. She nodded, but the words felt hollow.

It was getting late, and Jenny knew she had a demanding day ahead. She set her teacup down with a gentle clink and pulled her mother into a tight embrace. "I'll call you over the weekend," she promised, her voice firm despite the emotions swirling inside her.

Her mother sighed and nodded. "Please do, sweetheart. And take care of yourself."

As Jenny stepped out into the cool night air, she wrapped her coat tighter around herself, the crisp breeze sending a shiver down her spine. But it wasn't the cold that made her shudder. Her thoughts were consumed by one name—Oliver Wright. The man responsible for stealing her father from them. The man who had left an empty chair at every holiday dinner, every milestone, every moment that should have been shared.

He had to pay.

As she arrived at her apartment, she was too wired to sleep. The surge of anger and purpose coursing through her veins refused to let her rest. Instead, she booted up her laptop, the blue glow illuminating her determined expression. Her fingers flew over the keyboard as she began her search, her breath shallow with anticipation.

Oliver Wright.

She scrolled through pages of information, scanning every article, every mention of his name, piecing together whatever she could find. His business ventures, his past scandals, his connections—she needed to know everything. If there was a way to make him answer for what he had done, she would find it.

Tonight was just the beginning.

Jenny had been planning this day ever since her mother showed her the letter from her late father. A single, yellowed sheet of paper had changed everything. The words, scrawled in her father's careful handwriting, had shattered the carefully constructed reality she and her mother had lived in for years. It was not a farewell letter. It was a warning. A confession. A desperate plea for justice from beyond the grave.

That day, standing in the dim light of their old living room, Jenny had vowed that she would set things right. It had taken years of meticulous planning years of suppressing her anger, of gathering the right information, of placing herself in the right position. She had worn a mask every day, perfecting the role of dutiful Jenny, the efficient and unassuming assistant to Oliver Wright, the man responsible for tearing her family apart.

Now, this was it. The final act to rebalance her and her mother's life—a life without her father and without the man who had stolen him from them.

She stood before the mirror in her modest apartment, adjusting the collar of her blouse, smoothing the creases in her pencil skirt. Every detail of her appearance had been chosen with care—practical, professional, and non-threatening. It was the same attire she had worn every day in Wright's office, blending into the background like an obedient shadow. Today, however, she was anything but invisible. Today, she was the reckoning.

Her fingers curled into fists at the mere thought of Oliver Wright. The name alone sent a slow burn of rage through her chest. He had no idea what was coming.

She exhaled, steeling herself. Just one more time. One final meeting. One last performance.

Jenny picked up her leather-bound notebook—the same one in which she had recorded every secret, every inconsistency, every betrayal Wright had ever uttered in her presence. She tucked it under her arm and turned toward the door.

Showtime.

Chapter Hundred and Nine

Oliver waited for Jenny, his long-serving and loyal assistant. They had some paperwork to finalise, and after his heart problems, he had leaned on her more than ever. She had proven her ability not just to run his office, but to oversee much of his business interests. The truth was, he couldn't have taken the time to fully recover without her expertise and trust.

His phone buzzed. He glanced at the screen—it was Jenny.

"I'm on my way up," she said.

He smiled. It had been several weeks since their last meeting, and he found himself genuinely looking forward to seeing her.

When the elevator doors opened, she stepped in with her usual confident grace. "Hello, Oliver. You look good."

"Hello, Jenny. You look lovely as ever," he replied, gesturing for her to come in.

She set her bag down and glanced around the penthouse. "I always forget how impressive this place is. But I hear you've been spending more time in Shoreham?"

Oliver nodded, pouring them both a drink. "Yes, it's been a great change of pace. The sea air agrees with me. And my health has improved considerably."

Jenny took a seat across from him, smiling. "That's wonderful to hear. You deserved a break after everything. But I bet you haven't slowed down much."

He chuckled. "You know me too well. But, honestly, the yacht has given me a new sense of purpose. Sailing clears my mind. I finally feel like I'm enjoying life, not just chasing the next deal."

"Filthy Rich, right?" she teased. "Quite the name."

Oliver grinned. "It suits her. Maybe I'll have you aboard one of these days. You'd love it."

She tilted her head, amused. "I might take you up on that. Though I doubt you'd let me just relax—I'd probably end up organising your crew."

He laughed. "You're not wrong. But let's get through this paperwork first. Then we can talk about sailing."

Jenny nodded, taking out the documents. As they began working through the details, there was an easy familiarity between them—one built over years of trust and loyalty. Oliver knew that with Jenny around, his business was in safe hands, allowing him to finally embrace the life he had once been too busy to enjoy.

Oliver spoke with an ease that made her stomach tighten. He had adapted. He had moved on. But she couldn't. Her grief twisted into something sharper, something stronger. It burned away the last lingering traces of doubt. She had made her choice, and there was no turning back. Whatever she was about to do, it was no longer just a plan—it was a necessity.

"That's all the paperwork done," said Oliver, setting his pen down with a satisfied sigh.

"No work is complete until the paperwork is finished," Jenny replied, her voice carrying the faintest hint of amusement.

Oliver leaned back in his chair, stretching his arms. "I think we've earned a small celebration. Shall I pour us a glass of champagne?"

Jenny's eyes gleamed as she rose from her chair. "Yes, that would be in order," Oliver agreed with a smile.

He moved out from behind his large oak desk, the polished wood reflecting the warm glow of the evening lights. Jenny turned towards the kitchen, a space she had been in countless times, yet tonight it felt different. The anticipation curled in her stomach, making her fingers tingle as she reached for the bottle of chilled champagne.

The pop of the cork resonated through the room, sharp and exhilarating, like the overture to a new beginning. She set down two crystal flutes and, in one swift movement, retrieved a small vial from her pocket. Her breath hitched as she carefully tipped the clear liquid into Oliver's glass, watching it dissolve seamlessly into the golden effervescence. She exhaled slowly, steadying herself before carrying the drinks back to the front room.

Oliver stood by the large windows, gazing out over London—his city, his empire. The evening lights twinkled against the darkening sky, casting reflections that danced along the glass. He looked at ease, unaware of the turmoil that brewed beneath Jenny's calm exterior.

Her hand trembled slightly as she offered him the flute.

"Are you all right?" Oliver asked, his sharp eyes catching the hesitation in her movement.

"Yes, sorry," Jenny murmured, forcing a reassuring smile. "It's just… it's been a long time coming."

Puzzled, Oliver took the glass from her, his fingers brushing lightly against hers. The moment stretched between them; a silent beat charged with unspoken words.

Jenny lifted her glass. "Cheers, Oliver."

Oliver returned the smile, raising his flute. "Cheers to you. Thank you for all your help today—and over the many years you've stood by my side."

Jenny's heart pounded against her ribs as he lifted the glass to his lips. She held her breath, watching every movement, every flicker of expression. The golden liquid disappeared in a single, effortless sip. Oliver lowered the glass, his eyes locking onto hers, and for a brief moment, something changed in his gaze—an awareness, a shift, as if he suddenly saw her in a different light.

Jenny smiled, but inside, she was counting the seconds.

Jenny stepped back, still watching Oliver, her eyes locked onto his as she waited for the inevitable moment when realisation would dawn upon him—when he would understand that his life was about to end and that there was nothing he could do to stop it. His chest tightened, fear flickering across his aging features, his breath coming in shallow, rapid bursts.

Oliver's gaze snapped to Jenny, confusion warring with terror. What had she done?

Jenny, emboldened by the sight of his panic, allowed a slow smile to creep across her lips. The power she held over him at this moment was intoxicating, years of suffering and meticulous planning culminating into this one final act of justice.

Oliver tried to speak, but his mouth was dry, his throat constricted. The words wouldn't come. A heavy fog of disbelief clouded his mind—why was this happening? Jenny was speaking, but her voice sounded distant, as if she were submerged beneath water, muffled and distorted. His vision blurred at the edges, the room seemed to tilt, and then suddenly, his knees buckled beneath him. He collapsed onto the polished wooden floor, gasping for air, a cruel echo of a memory clawing its way to the surface of his mind. The last time he had felt this helpless, he had been in this very room, grasping at his chest, his heart betraying him. Only then, Jenny had saved his life.

Now, she watched him suffer.

"What's the matter, Oliver?" Her voice was taunting, but laced with an eerie calm as she took slow, deliberate steps towards him. Her silhouette loomed over him as he clutched at his chest, wheezing, struggling to force oxygen into his lungs.

She knelt beside him, leaning in close so that only he could hear her whispered words. "Do you remember the Chilean mining stock, Oliver? The one you so confidently encouraged my father to invest in?"

His brow furrowed, his eyes dull with pain and the first creeping hints of recognition. He tried to shake his head, but Jenny continued, her voice like silk laced with venom.

"You told him it was a golden opportunity. A future secured. A way to provide for his family." She paused, watching as the weight of her words settled over him. "You lied."

Oliver gasped again, his body betraying him as his heart struggled against its impending failure.

"My father lost everything, and when the debts closed in, when the shame became unbearable, he took the only escape he could see." Her voice faltered slightly, but she steadied herself. "He took his own life, Oliver. And my mother? She was left to pick up the broken pieces, to drown in a sorrow she never recovered from."

Jenny exhaled slowly, then leaned in even closer, her lips mere inches from his ear. "I spent years planning for this moment, enduring my own pain and suffering, waiting for the day I could look into your eyes as you felt the same helplessness my father did."

Oliver's body convulsed slightly. His breaths came in shallow gasps, his pulse weak. His eyes searched hers for mercy, for a sliver of humanity that might call off his execution. But Jenny merely smiled again, tilting her head slightly as she whispered her final words to him.

"Tonight, Oliver, you pay for what you've done."

She straightened, stepping back as his body gave one final shudder. And then, silence.

Jenny let out a slow, measured breath, then turned away, walking towards the door. She didn't look back.

Chapter Hundred and Ten

The rain was relentless, pounding against the roof of St. James Church with a steady, rhythmic force, as if the sky itself was mourning the passing of Oliver. The church was dimly lit, its grand stained-glass windows muted by the storm outside. Inside, the atmosphere was thick with grief, though not all of it sincere. The scent of incense hung in the air, mingling with the musty dampness brought in by the umbrellas and rain-soaked coats of the mourners. Jenny sat motionless in the front row, dressed in a sombre black dress, a veil covering her face. Beneath the veil, her eyes were dry, her expression unreadable. She dabbed at her eyes occasionally with a lace handkerchief—a gesture for appearances more than anything else. Today, she had to play the part.

It was Oliver's funeral, and Jenny, like everyone else, had come to pay her final respects. She had spent years as his loyal assistant, and it was only natural she should be here, grieving for a man whose presence had loomed so large in her life. Hidden behind the veil, Jenny observed the gathering crowd. The church was filling quickly now, with family members, old friends, business associates, and those who simply wanted to be seen mourning the man who had once been such a towering figure in their community. Whispers passed among the pews, fragmented words of sympathy and speculation. Oliver's sudden death had shocked many, but few knew the truth. Few understood just how carefully planned it had been.

As Jenny sat, her hands clasped in her lap, she took in the familiar faces. There were people here who had adored Oliver—his family, his business partners—but there were others, too, who, like her, had been tormented by him in various ways. She could see it in their eyes, the hidden satisfaction, the veiled relief. They may have worn masks of grief, but their true feelings were just beneath the surface. Oliver had not been a kind man, and his legacy of cruelty had left scars that no eulogy could erase.

The vicar, a tall, stern-looking man in his late sixties, stood at the altar, his voice commanding yet respectful as he began his sermon. His words echoed through the stone arches, recounting Oliver's life—a life marked by power, wealth, and influence. Yet beneath the polished veneer, Jenny knew, lurked the darker truths: his manipulation, his cruelty, and his ability to crush those who stood in his way. The vicar spoke of Oliver's achievements, his 'successes', and how he had been a pillar of the community, but to Jenny, each praise sounded hollow, a distorted reflection of the man he had truly been.

She forced herself to listen, nodding along with the solemn hymns, but her mind kept drifting. Oliver hadn't been religious, and she doubted he would have cared for this grand show of faith. But appearances mattered. The press had gathered outside, cameras flashing beneath black umbrellas, capturing every moment for tomorrow's headlines. The funeral of a man like Oliver was an event. His death was news, and Jenny had known that. She had planned for it.

The vicar's speech seemed to drag on forever, a steady drone in the background as Jenny fought to control the swirling thoughts in her mind. She hadn't anticipated the emotions she would feel sitting here, facing the man who had once dominated her life.

Finally, the vicar concluded with a prayer, his deep voice reverberating off the stone walls. The organist began to play, filling the church with a haunting melody—one of Oliver's favourite songs, a piece that now felt unnervingly fitting. The mourners began to stand, shuffling out of their pews, filing past the casket one by one. Jenny remained seated, her body still, her breathing steady, as she watched the others. They moved slowly, offering quiet words of sympathy to the family, dropping roses onto the casket as they passed.

It wasn't long before the pews began to empty, the steady stream of mourners thinning until Jenny was alone. She stayed seated for a moment longer, listening to the soft echoes of footsteps fading away, letting the stillness settle over her. Then, with a deep breath, she rose from her seat and made her way to the front of the church. Her footsteps were slow and deliberate, each one echoing in the quiet space. She stood before the casket, looking down at the polished wood, knowing that inside lay the man who had caused so much pain, so much destruction. His face was hidden from view now, but she could picture it perfectly, the arrogant smirk he often wore, the coldness in his eyes.

"Goodbye, Oliver," she whispered, her voice barely more than a breath. The words were simple, but they carried the weight of years. Years of anger, fear, and humiliation, all culminating in this one final moment. She had thought she would feel triumphant, vindicated, but there was only a strange kind of release. She was free now, and yet, the enormity of what she had done left her feeling numb.

With one final glance at the casket, Jenny turned and walked toward the heavy wooden doors. Outside, the rain was still falling, a constant downpour that blurred the world beyond the church. As she stepped into the rain, the cold drops splashed against her face, soaking through her clothes, but she didn't care. The rain felt cleansing, as though it were washing away the remnants of the past, washing away everything that Oliver had been. She stood for a moment, letting it fall over her, and then, without looking back, she walked away, disappearing into the grey, wet streets of the city, ready to reclaim the life that had been taken from her.

⊷⊶◈⊷⊶

Chapter Hundred and Eleven

Jenny stood at the edge of the terrace, gazing out at the breathtaking view of the bay from the villa. The sun hung low in the sky, casting a warm, golden glow over the water, its surface shimmering like liquid gold. The gentle lapping of the waves against the shore blended with the soft rustling of palm leaves in the breeze, and the air was fragrant with the scent of salt, hibiscus, and jasmine. It was a scene of perfect tranquility—a far cry from the chaos and darkness that had consumed her life for years.

This villa, a secluded haven tucked away in a remote corner of the coast, was the perfect place for this moment of reflection. Everything here had been meticulously planned, just like everything else Jenny had orchestrated over the past several years. It was no coincidence that she had chosen this spot for the meeting with her accomplice. She wanted this place, this view, to be a marker of their victory, a symbol of the new life they were about to embark on, free from the shadows of the past.

As she stood there, her mind wandered back to the years of careful planning that had led to this moment. The murder of Oliver Wright hadn't been an impulsive act; it had been the result of years of strategy, manipulation, and patience. Jenny had been biding her time, playing her role perfectly. She had earned his trust, infiltrated his life, and slowly taken control of his businesses and financial affairs—all while appearing to be nothing more than a devoted assistant. The execution of the plan had been flawless, each move calculated to ensure that no one would ever suspect her. Now, with Oliver dead and the fortune within her grasp, the weight of her dark secret seemed to lift, if only for a moment, allowing her to enjoy the view with a sense of hard-won triumph.

The sound of the villa door opening behind her pulled Jenny from her thoughts. She turned slowly, her face bathed in the warm, fading light of the setting sun. The faint clink of glassware from the kitchen and the soft footsteps approaching signalled the arrival of the one person who had been with her through it all.

"I'm out here!" she called, her voice calm and composed, though the undertones of relief and quiet exhilaration were unmistakable. It was over. They had done it.

A moment later, her mother stepped onto the terrace, a smile already forming on her lips. Jenny smiled warmly in return, feeling a flood of emotions she hadn't allowed herself to feel until now. She stepped forward and hugged her mother tightly, both of them momentarily silent, letting the reality of their success sink in. For years, they had been bound together by their shared hatred for Oliver, a man who had destroyed their lives in different ways. Now, finally, they were free.

It had been a long time since they had shared a moment like this, free from the constant tension and fear that had plagued them since Oliver entered their lives. Their relationship, once strained by circumstance, had evolved into an unbreakable bond as they plotted their way to freedom. The burden of their dark secret, the murder that had consumed their every thought, had been lifted. There was no guilt in this embrace, no lingering doubt—only the pure satisfaction of knowing that the nightmare was behind them. They had won.

Jenny pulled back slightly, looking into her mother's eyes, her smile widening. "We did it," she said softly. The words hung in the air between them, a quiet declaration of their victory.

Her mother nodded, her eyes gleaming with pride and relief. "We did," she agreed, her voice barely more than a whisper. "And no one suspects a thing."

The plan had been foolproof, years in the making. Jenny had played her role with meticulous care, earning Oliver's trust, gradually insinuating herself into his personal and professional life until she had full control over his finances. Every decision had been calculated, every action precise. It hadn't been easy, but Jenny's patience and cunning had paid off. She had manipulated Oliver's affairs so expertly that when the time finally came to end his life, no one had thought to look in her direction. The authorities had concluded he had a fatal heart attack, and now, with Oliver out of the way, the future was wide open.

They stood together on the terrace, the sun dipping lower behind the horizon, casting long shadows across the bay. Jenny could feel the sense of finality in the air. They had crossed the threshold and emerged victorious on the other side. The years of deceit and manipulation had come to a close, and now, they could finally look forward to the rest of their lives—lives of financial freedom, unburdened by the man who had taken so much from them.

Jenny's mind flickered to the intricate web of deceit she had spun over the years. It had started slowly, with small manipulations here and there, little things to make Oliver trust her completely. She had skilfully managed his accounts, steering him into signing over control of his company while securing her own financial safety net in secret. As Oliver became more dependent on her, she took greater control, feeding his ego, making him believe she was indispensable. By the time the final blow came, Oliver was completely in her hands, unaware of the trap closing around him.

Now, standing on the terrace of the villa, she felt the full weight of her accomplishment. With Oliver's fortune now securely transferred, they could live in luxury for the rest of their lives. And the best part? No one would ever know. Oliver had been a powerful man, but his arrogance had blinded him to the betrayal lurking in plain sight.

The sun finally dipped below the horizon, casting the bay in hues of deep orange and purple. Jenny took a deep breath, savouring the sweet, salty air of their newfound freedom. The turmoil that had defined her life for so long was over. She turned to her mother, their eyes meeting in silent understanding. There was nothing left to say. They had achieved their goal, and now, they could finally enjoy the fruits of their labour.

As the night fell, Jenny knew that this moment, this villa, this view, would forever be etched in her memory as the beginning of her new life—a life she had fought for, and won.

www.ingramcontent.com/pod-product-compliance
Lightning Source LLC
Chambersburg PA
CBHW070423170726
48291CB00002B/335